Praise for Jonathan Garfinkel and
*In a Land without Dogs the Cats Learn to Bark*

"A clear-eyed, elucidating novel of the aftermath of the Soviet Union and the era's devastating effects on lost, wandering lives. A great read."

— Rawi Hage, author of *Stray Dogs*

"*In a Land without Dogs the Cats Learn to Bark* is a gripping, often hilarious, thrill-a-minute romp. This is the kind of novel that will have you forgo sleep to find out what happens next, as decades of secrets and lies are revealed in hypnotic prose. A stunning debut."

— Zoe Whittall, author of *The Fake*

"A wild, page-turner of a novel from the singular, seductive mind of Jonathan Garfinkel. *In a Land without Dogs the Cats Learn to Bark* is bold and otherworldly, a serenade for a lost nation, a love song to revolution. Reminiscent of Jennifer Egan's literary sleight of hand, and Rachel Kushner's structural and intellectual daring, Garfinkel takes on the legacy of the Soviet Union via a multigenerational mystery, deftly leading us from Moscow to Tbilisi, Charlie Parker to Noam Chomsky, performance art to political theatre — his humour cutting deeply and darkly through everything and everyone. A wholly electrifying debut from an exhilarating, rebel talent."

— Claudia Dey, author of *Heartbreaker*

# IN A LAND WITHOUT DOGS THE CATS LEARN TO BARK

## JONATHAN GARFINKEL

ANANSI

Published in Canada in 2023 and the U.S.A. in 2023
by House of Anansi Press Inc.
houseofanansi.com

House of Anansi Press is committed to protecting our natural environment.
This book is made of material from well-managed FSC®-certified forests,
recycled materials, and other controlled sources.

House of Anansi Press is a Global Certified Accessible™ (GCA by Benetech)
publisher. The ebook version of this book meets stringent accessibility
standards and is available to readers with print disabilities.

27  26  25  24  23    1  2  3  4  5

Library and Archives Canada Cataloguing in Publication

Title: In a land without dogs the cats learn to bark / Jonathan Garfinkel.
Names: Garfinkel, Jonathan, author.
Identifiers: Canadiana (print) 20220235457 | Canadiana (ebook) 20220235562 |
ISBN 9781487004163 (softcover) | ISBN 9781487004170 (EPUB)
Classification: LCC PS8563.A646 I5 2023 | DDC C813/.6—dc23

Cover and text design: Alysia Shewchuk

*House of Anansi Press respectfully acknowledges that the land on which we operate is
the Traditional Territory of many Nations, including the Anishinabeg, the Wendat,
and the Haudenosaunee. It is also the Treaty Lands of the Mississaugas of the
Credit.*

 Canada Council  Conseil des Arts
for the Arts  du Canada

With the participation of the Government of Canada
Avec la participation du gouvernement du Canada | Canada

*We acknowledge for their financial support of our publishing program the Canada
Council for the Arts, the Ontario Arts Council, and the Government of Canada.*

Printed and bound in Canada

To Paul Thompson — for bringing me there.

To Anastasia Aphkhazava — for taking me to the river.

And to the spirits of the Basement Theatre.

"You will hear thunder and remember me,
And think: she wanted storms."
—ANNA AKHMATOVA, "You Will Hear Thunder"

"Unfortunately, the past is still with us.
The problem of dictatorships is deep."
—GENE SHARP, *From Dictatorship to Democracy*

"Know that a rose without thorns
has never been plucked."
—SHOTA RUSTAVELI,
*The Knight in the Panther's Skin*

# ACT I

*

# AN AMERICAN IN MOSCOW

## September 1974 – January 1975

*

"Gaiety is the most outstanding
feature of the Soviet Union."
—JOSEPH STALIN

# 1

*Moscow, U.S.S.R.*
*September 3–5, 1974*

It all began with a Wrangler jean jacket.

"Hello and my name is Aslan. I am very happy to meet you, brand-new shiny American. May I inspect the contents of your room?"

Aslan had already crossed the threshold before I could answer.

"Uh, hi Aslan. I'm Gary."

Aslan inspected our surroundings like he was a sommelier appraising a rare vintage. He picked up my lead pencil, a notebook, a pair of sunglasses. Then he examined the amenities. My room was from the era of polyester curtains; a Formica desk and a sagging single bed that would be the ruin of my back were the only pieces of furniture.

"Very fancy," he declared. I couldn't tell if he was being serious or making fun of me. He made a beeline for my two suitcases and dumped their contents on the floor.

"We are almost neighbours. I live on the other side, Soviet dorm. This is very international and deluxe. A gentle, bourgeois domestics," Aslan said as he rifled through my clothes. Then he stood up and pointed at my jean jacket. "I see you wear Wrangler, greatest denim known to man."

"My mother gave it to me before I left America."

"They call me the Midnight Wrangler."

"Okay."

"I love your mother and I love Wrangler though I have never worn its studded jeans. Please, may I try?"

Before I could answer, Aslan pulled the jacket off my shoulders. When he put it on, it was two sizes too big. His wiry frame, coupled with his thin black moustache and Led Zeppelin *Houses of the Holy* t-shirt, made the jean jacket look absurd.

"It is perfection," he proclaimed.

"It looks good on you," I said.

"May I keep it, kind American friend? I pay good money, don't worry. There is a price for all things, I know."

I was reluctant to give it up — my mother had bought it for me as a parting gift, after all — but I felt I could not say no. In a strange and perhaps superstitious sense, I thought if I agreed to Aslan's request, he would teach me how to become a better writer. Like he claimed: there is a price for everything.

Aslan handed me a stack of rubles: "Please, I would like to see all of your merchandise for my black-market student operation."

Back home, I had been warned I would stand out. I was told people would want things from me. I had thought this sentiment ridiculous considering how little effort I put into my appearance. But on my first afternoon in Moscow, my life was being appraised, from a materialist perspective, by this strange yet likeable man. As I considered his request, he began sorting my clothes into two piles: "yes" and "no." Aslan announced the value of each item, punctuating his comments with an index finger pointed in the air:

2 x Wrangler jeans = 150 rubles!
1 green wool Woolworth sweater = 125 rubles!
6 pairs white Jockey underwear = 180 rubles!
4 white Jockey t-shirts = 80 rubles!
12 blue Bic pens = 120 rubles!
5 Hilroy notebooks = 40 rubles!

"I would like to buy these items," he said, piling them onto the bed.

"These are all the clothes I have."

"Fine. You make very hard bargains." He grabbed the jeans and two pairs of underwear. "How much?"

"They're not for sale."

"I give you two hundred rubles."

"What am I going to do with two hundred rubles?"

"Buy stuffs. Many stuffs."

"Can we do this later? After I've unpacked?"

Aslan made a sour face. Suddenly his attention was drawn to a box on the floor, its lid slightly open.

"Holy shit. You have original vinyls."

To stave off homesickness, I had brought my jazz LP collection, carefully boxed in alphabetical order. Coupled with my Yamaha YP-800 turntable, and a few beloved books, I believed it was everything I would need.

"I live for jazz," I said. "I mean, I love it."

"Me too, my new American friend. Charlie Parker is my number one daddy-o. He is ornithologist of the human soul. Are you also a Betty Crocker of melodies?"

"I've been known to noodle. But I didn't bring my trumpet. Do you play?"

"All the time. I am the greatest noodle chef in Moscow." He slung his arm around me. "I like you very much, Gary." He kissed me on both cheeks. "I will return so we can listen to jazz LPs in the dormitories of prestigious American diplomats. We will drink vodka and play music and pretend we are happy. We still be students of Charlie Parker, deep soul of American pain."

WHILE I HAD brought plenty of American jazz LPs to Moscow (much to the delight of Aslan), I had come here to follow in the footsteps of my literary idol, Mikhail Lermontov, author of *A Hero of Our Time*. A novel ahead of its time, a book whose passages consumed me. Lermontov had gone to Moscow State University 150 years ago. But what is a century and a half in the eternal halls of literature? Poetry exists in a space outside of time. (I wrote this in my application.)

After a rigorous interview process in New York City, where my political views were deemed safe and my love of books genuine, I was accepted as part of the first American contingent of Fulbright students in the U.S.S.R. The Iron Curtain would be pulled aside for American youth to see Russia in all its Brezhnevian glory.

Earlier that day I had arrived at Sheremetyevo International Airport, frazzled and disoriented. Due to a clerical error, I had been booked on an earlier flight than the rest of the Fulbright group. I was greeted by a bedraggled American in a rumpled linen suit and white tennis socks, who looked like he'd just stepped out of the shower. His wet blond hair was slicked back in a way that made me think of my mother; he was what she would call "a real tennis club goy." The American introduced himself to me as Jim and said he was to be our government liaison in Moscow.

"Sorry for the lack of ceremony," Jim said, loading my boxes and suitcases into the back seat of his Zhiguli. "They didn't tell me you were coming until an hour ago. The others will be arriving tomorrow."

As we drove into the city, vitality broke through the black-and-white images I'd held in my mind since I was a boy. Thanks to a Leningrad-born housekeeper, Stasya, I was brought up with a vivid if slightly mythologized vision of Russia. But here, the brightness of September's soft light reflected off tall buildings, and I felt overwhelmed by the liveliness of strangers going about their lives, the familiar rendered strange. Jim talked constantly, pointing out familiar landmarks as they came into view: the Ostankino Tower; the Beriozka hard currency shop; the GUM shopping mall; that wedding cake of a palace, the Kremlin.

"I know you're here to study literature, but you should still try to play the tourist if you can," Jim said, guiding the vehicle into the left lane. "Immersion is the best way to learn the nuances of a language. I encourage you to meet the locals. Study the culture — which is its own language, really." He paused, changing lanes again. "By the way, I was impressed with your application."

"Thanks."

"There is no better place for literature than Moscow. The city is steeped in it. But remember, you're representing America. You need to be careful. Everyone is watching you, everything listens."

He said this last part in the manner of a corny dime-store thriller. My mother, who had raised me on Raymond Chandler and Dashiell Hammett, would've loved this guy. Jim could be her soulmate.

"So, you're what, some kind of spy?" I joked.

"Isn't everyone?"

I smirked. "Sure."

"Heck, even literature is a kind of espionage. Peering into that one thing nobody can ever know: the mind of another. Surveillance disguised as art."

I liked Jim.

"You enjoy living in Moscow?" I asked.

"Moscow is an addiction."

The statement struck me as odd. How could a place become a habit, something you're not able to live without? Later, I would come to understand Jim's meaning.

He pulled up beside an enormous beast of a building. The thirty-six-storey red-and-grey concrete structure known as Moscow State University made me gasp. While this display of the Soviet grandiose, the crude egotism of Stalinist Gothic crowned by a blinking red star, had not existed in the time of Lermontov — it was built by German pows in the 1950s — it warmed me to know he had been in these same hills, overlooking the same Moscow River. This was to be my new home, the place in which I was destined to become a writer. Perhaps even a great one.

Jim helped me carry in my belongings, then left me in the hands of a grumpy babushka. She had me sign a million documents, handed me a key, and led me silently to the sixth floor.

AFTER ASLAN LEFT, I put away my clothes and organized the books on my desk. Lermontov, Tolstoy, Turgenev, Chekhov, and my well-worn Langenscheidt's English-Russian dictionary. I put on some John Coltrane, poured myself a glass of warm vodka, and began to read Lermontov in the original Russian, carefully marking the passages. A letter from 1837: "As I careered up and down the mountains in Georgia, I abandoned the cart and took to horseback; I've climbed the snowy mountain of the Cross to the very top, which isn't altogether easy; from it, one can see half of Georgia as though it were on a saucer." And later: "For me the mountain air is balm; the blues go to the devil, the heart thumps, the breast breathes high." I fell asleep, Lermontov resting on my chest.

The next morning, I awoke to Radio Moscow, the only available station. The voice of a furious woman commanded me to raise my arms, bend over, and march. I tried my best to follow her instructions — I never stretched, but her voice suggested I ought to. Later, I descended to the immense peach-coloured cafeteria in the basement for a breakfast of kasha with butter, followed by a cup of bitter tea. I was greeted by Igor: fellow literature enthusiast, journalism student, and Perfect Young Communist.

"I have been assigned to guide you," he said in highly formal Russian. "Please. It is my duty and pleasure. Now tell me. Are you Dustin Hoffman or Robert Redford?"

"Excuse me?"

"In my research, American men can be divided into two categories: Robert Redford or Dustin Hoffman. I believe you are Dustin." He switched from Russian to a stilted English: "Would you like me to introduce you to Mrs. Robinson?" He cackled at his own joke.

After breakfast, Igor laid out my schedule for the next few days. Everything he said was in the manner of the laborious. The controlled nature of his speech aged him; he was twenty-five going on fifty. Unlike Aslan, he did not wear blue denim acquired on the black market or from the suitcases of jet-lagged Americans. Igor was stern, wore a dark turtleneck and dark jacket, and walked like a military man. He proudly told me that he was a member of the Komsomol, soon to be Party kandidat. By the time he was thirty, he'd be a member of the Party. He would make a fine Soviet journalist — allowed to travel anywhere, so long as he composed reports on whom-ever he met and wrote dull monotonous articles for *Pravda*. As a point of pride, he showed me his annotated version of the Party rule book. This was a man who lived for bureau-cracy. In Moscow, he would be king.

Igor took me on a tour of the building. I was living in a socialist-shopping-mall-cum-medieval-fortress. Everything one could possibly need in Soviet Moscow was there: a fruit-and-vegetable stand, bakery, post office, magazine kiosk, drug store, shoeshine, and watch repairman. Igor proudly showed off Soviet resourcefulness in dimly lit corridors. Outside, on the university athletics track, students trained as though their lives depended on it. Girls play-acted holding a pin in their teeth, tossing fake grenades over verdant fields. Boys ran and jabbed imaginary bayonets at the air, then leapt back, dodging invisible missiles. All of them wore ragged grey sweatsuits, loose on their limbs.

Igor and I ended up back in my room. To my surprise, he also liked jazz. I put on some Ornette Coleman and we sat on my bed to listen. While Ornette wailed, Igor asked me questions about America.

"Dustin, is it true all Americans are racists?"

"Uhm, no."

"But you kill many Blacks and Indians."

"Some people did, yes."

"If your government controls the *New York Times* and *Washington Post*, how do you know what is true?"

For a moment I thought he was joking. His aspiration, he explained, was to write for *Pravda*, a newspaper not exactly known for its objectivity—though Igor claimed it was second to none. Then he asked what I wanted to write about. I told him I intended to write a novel from multiple perspectives. I explained that it is only through a multiplicity of viewpoints that truth can be gleaned. He looked at me like I was some kind of idiot. Was I using the wrong Russian words? Then I told him I wanted to write about someone average who does something great.

"You mean a hero," he said. "Maybe it's you who wants to be the hero, eh, Dustin?"

There was a knock at the door. I opened it and Aslan hesitated when he saw Igor smoking on my bed.

"Come in," I said.

He entered timidly, looking over his shoulder as though someone were following him. Igor and I leaned against the wall. Ornette played on his sax.

"Gary was saying he is in love with the Caucasus," said Igor.

Aslan looked at me, puzzled. "You have been?"

"No," I said. "I've only read about it in books."

Igor muttered, "He's in love with another century. Lermontov. He came all the way to Moscow to study dead literature."

Aslan clocked the books on my desk.

Igor got up and said, "I am sorry to be rude, but I must lead the work brigade for the potato harvest festival."

"Seriously?"

Igor's firm handshake and steely gaze told me he was dead serious. When he left the room, Aslan immediately shifted into English.

"Igor is Major Asshole. Even his rectum follows Party rules." Aslan's eyes returned to my books. "You really like Lermontov?"

"Of course."

"But why?"

"Literature can be stuffy. Lermontov let it breathe. He lived what he wrote; I admire that."

"Lermontov is too rich and white and complains too much—and he dies like a moron! But Pechorin is most excellent. I admire his conjugation of reality. He is a nihilist, yet he cares about people. He is lonely, but wants love. Real human tragedy."

Aslan said this with an intensity that only a Russian can have for their literature. For Aslan, a 150-year-old novel was life and death, and Pechorin the protagonist more real than Lermontov the author. He wanted to know what else I was reading. I showed him copies of Turgenev and Tolstoy; Djuna Barnes and William Faulkner; George Eliot and T. S. Eliot; Robert Lowell and Elizabeth Bishop. I asked if he wanted to borrow any. Aslan shook his head.

"You do not have my favourite book: the Miriam Webberstein English dictionary! It is where I learn how to speak so vociferously. I have left my copy in the village with my son Akhmad so he can also obtain keys to the West like his father."

"Where does Akhmad live?"

"He is with his mother in Kazbegi, Georgia, in the mountains. Too far away."

The name of the village jolted me. "Isn't Kazbegi close to where Pechorin had his duel?"

"Of course. I am from the land of Pechorin – this is how I know he is real! It is also why I sell so many clothes at black-market prices. I send rubles to my wife. They can eat, and I am happy. Life is literature, my lonely American. But we must eat misfortune too."

"I've always wanted to visit Georgia."

"One day I will take you. It is different and not so different from your books."

THAT NIGHT I dreamt I was in the mountains of Georgia following Pechorin on his horse. It felt huge and expansive, a mythical land. Pechorin was dressed in the garb of a Russian soldier and complained incessantly, ruining the mood. I asked him to be quiet, but this only ramped him up. He complained about the terrain, the locals, how everyone and everything got in his way. I saw myself from the outside, a third-person perspective, the word in three dimensions: "Authenticity." But Pechorin made fun of this too, casting a shadow over meaning. So I pushed him off his horse and left him with his head stuck in the snow, arms and legs flailing. I saw a church on a mountain and instinctively moved toward it. I heard a voice telling me to climb — was it inside me, or out there? The climb was long, and I sweated a lot. At the end of the trail, I arrived at an ancient stone church. A young boy stood by the door. Akhmad, Aslan's son. He asked, "Where is my father?"

THE NEXT DAY, mired by my own imagination and dumb American fantasies of escape, I was certain that, as I walked to my first class, I was being watched. I whirled around, and there was Jim, drinking black tea, gabbing with an American student.

In the classroom, Igor sat at the front in the same black turtleneck and black blazer he'd worn the day before. The teacher, Dmitry, looked like Igor but thirty years older: the same black turtleneck, the same black blazer. Even his hair was cut in the same manner of the stiff and boring. I was introduced to the class as "the American." A slight murmur travelled through the room.

"I am an expert in the subject of the American Indian Wars," declared Dmitry. "My Ph.D. dissertation focused on the great battle: The All-You-Can-Eat-Buffet."

He then described a scene from the eighteenth century that I had never read about in any history book. He spoke of White men slaughtering the Indigenous peoples of America, of African slaves and their beaten bodies, and of the hamburgers cooked on open flames in the celebratory aftermath, a gluttony of grilled meat and ice cream.

"They burned the bodies of their enemies next to the burgers," he declared ominously. "And ate only vanilla ice cream. This event displays the true horror of America."

I flinched at the distorted image of an America these people had never seen; the monsters and myths we hold inside.

"So, Comrade Ruckler? What do you make of this grand and horrific battle?"

"I've never heard of The All-You-Can-Eat-Buffet. Though they have a good one at Denny's."

Dmitry was taken aback. "I am shocked, yet not surprised. Soviet historians are the best in the world. I will lend you my dissertation—which won many awards—so you can learn about your country." He smiled smugly. "Now. Leo Tolstoy. Who can tell us how his revolutionary politics were impaired?"

Igor raised his hand, then spoke in a dull monotone about Tolstoy's radical notions of equality, inhibited by a Christian conservatism stuck in the past—not aimed at the future, as a true revolutionary should be. This was then followed by a strange and hard-to-follow Marxist-Leninist critique of *Anna Karenina*. It was exceedingly boring until a student named Anna Litvak ripped into him.

"Have you ever been fucked, Igor?" asked Anna.

Igor fell silent.

"Have you ever been heartbroken? Have you ever had something you care about taken away?"

She said it tauntingly. Igor looked down at his notebook.

Dmitry interrupted. "What are you getting at, Comrade Litvak?"

Anna continued: "Dialectical materialism is fine if you want to understand the workings of a factory. But not literature. We are motivated by power and desire. As Miss Karenina shows us, you pay for who you fuck."

The class erupted into laughter. Igor turned beet red.

Dmitry said, "Maybe when you grow up, Comrade Litvak, you'll understand that there is more to life than who you sleep with."

Afterward, I ran into Anna in the hall. She welcomed me to Moscow and asked what I was studying. I told her about Lermontov. She smiled in what seemed to be a condescending way, though I couldn't be sure. There was something overly familiar in her sly look. Anna unnerved me. She had the uncanny ability to make me feel like I didn't know where or who I was. Searching for something to say, I asked what the consequences would be of expressing anti-Marxist opinions in a Moscow classroom.

"You don't believe in that dialectical materialism bullshit, do you?" she asked.

"No."

"So why do you care?"

"I'm curious."

"My opinions don't matter. But if you want my prediction, I believe this will all collapse." She gestured to the walls as though they were made of paper. "Flimsy foundations make for catastrophic ends." She said this in a way that felt equally prophetic and flirtatious. "Would you like to come to a poetry reading tonight? It'll be fun. I promise."

Before I could answer, she produced a mechanical pencil from her shirt pocket and jotted down a room number on a scrap of paper. She handed me the paper, then turned and walked away. I watched her disappear up the corridor, the contours of her calves rippling below her brown pleated skirt.

*ANNA LITVAK.* I said her name over and over again that afternoon, trying to conjure her close to me. I told myself I wanted to get to know her. Just talk. But I could feel it swell. A crush worthy of poetry. And while I am not one to trust in the immediacy of feelings (emotions, I knew even then, are an untrustworthy and fickle lot), I decided to go to the reading. What else was there to do? Hang out with my American classmates in Moscow cafés, pretending we were locals?

So, that evening, I ventured away from my Fulbright counterparts and toward the Soviet wing of the MSU dorms. It felt like another country. The rooms were smaller, the students crammed in, five or six in bunks much smaller than mine. Russian students played guitar with doors open, crooning old folk songs. Cuban students sang boleros, filling the halls with a gentle warmth and softness, a wind from elsewhere. The music instilled a longing I did not know I had.

The poetry reading, I was surprised to learn, was being held in my denim-obsessed friend Aslan's room, which he shared with another Georgian named Zaza. The room was a stuffed and chaotic space. On the wall were photographs of American icons: the Marlboro Man and Neil Armstrong,

John F. Kennedy and Marilyn Monroe. There were pictures of Wrangler blue jeans and Cadillacs, of Martin Luther King and Malcolm X, Bessie Smith and Charlie Parker. Aslan was pleased to see me, and immediately introduced me to Zaza, his childhood friend. They were both from the village of Kazbegi.

Aslan may have been thin and sinewy, but Zaza was a jovial beast of a man, mythical in his proportions. When he stood, he towered above me, six and a half feet tall. A faint scar ran from ear to mouth, quietly dividing his face. His presence attacked me. A booming laugh from the chest; eyes that sparkled devilishly when he spoke. Even though it was hot in the small dorm room, Zaza wore a thick wool coat, and beneath, a dark grey suit and a white button-down shirt with blue-and-gold cufflinks. A cigarette dangled from his mouth as he drank vodka straight from the bottle. He was dressed to go. At all times, at any moment, Zaza was ready.

"The American is here!" he yelled, slapping me on the back. "Let's be friends. Drink!"

Zaza doled out shots to everyone. Then he stood up and put his hand over his heart, reciting an epic poem in what I assumed was Georgian. The entire room was under the spell of this giant of a man's transformation into eloquence, the drunken guttural rendered romantic. We drank, Zaza sat down, and the performance was over.

Then all eyes turned to Zaza and Aslan as they became engaged in an intense chess match. Zaza moved his rook to take Aslan's bishop; Aslan's queen took Zaza's rook; and, in a move that surprised everyone, Zaza flung the board across the room. The pieces went flying.

"What the fuck?" yelled Aslan. "I was winning!"

"Says who?"

"Ask anyone. We have witnesses."

A debate ensued. While yes, the group admitted, Aslan was technically winning, there was the possibility that Zaza could have clawed his way back. For example, by getting his pawn to the other side and retrieving his queen. Aslan declared everyone to be full of shit: chess, best friends, the entire Soviet Union.

"It is very sad. We will never know who would win. And I know, Aslan, you cannot stand a draw."

Aslan looked like he wanted to pummel his opponent. Zaza bowed his head and said, "But I relinquish the match. You are the better player."

"Shit-pants. You know nothing about chess."

"In a land without dogs..." Zaza proclaimed in the voice of the know-it-all and provocateur. But instead of coming to blows, they embraced like brothers. Zaza poured vodka and said, "I have known you longer than anyone except for my mother. And I love you." He kissed Aslan on the cheek. Aslan stood on a chair and made a toast.

"You love me, but I love the DNA molecule," he proclaimed with a fluency and grace I had not heard from his mouth. He was a different person in Russian. "There is nothing more beautiful than the double helix. The mysteries of life inscribed on a braid. A miracle!"

Zaza toasted the mountains of Georgia; Aslan toasted Charlie Parker and the jazz clubs of America. I was caught between myths. By the third bottle, the room spun. For a moment I thought I saw Jim watching from the hall. Instead, in sauntered Anna Litvak. She wore a black cardigan and black jeans and the same pink mechanical pencil in her shirt pocket. She carried a book of Akhmatova's poems. I sat up to talk to her.

"So the American came."

"I'm drunk. This Zaza guy is a profound lunatic."

Zaza was now dancing on the Formica table, balancing a bottle of vodka on his palm. With each kick of his leg, he flipped the bottle into the air, then grabbed the glass tightly around the neck. Everyone applauded this odd display of the acrobatic, egging him on. Everyone except Anna.

"Have you read *One Day in the Life of Ivan Denisovich*?" she asked quite seriously, unimpressed by the macho antics.

"Of course. Have you?" I blushed like an idiot.

"We read it in gymnasium. One week it was on the syllabus, the next week it disappeared, poof, like smoke. But I remember. The book is seared into my brain: 'Can a man who's warm understand one who's freezing?'"

Anna spoke Solzhenitsyn's words as though she'd written them herself.

"Empathy," I said, trying to collect myself. "It's a challenge for any writer."

"*Radical* empathy," retorted Anna. "The true potential of literature. Memory in the face of forgetting."

Zaza flipped the bottle high into the air. This time it smacked the ceiling, and the room let out a collective "whoahhhh" as a spray of booze rained down on the people. Somehow Zaza caught the bottle, grasping its neck even tighter. Anna drew on her cigarette with the same intensity I'd witnessed earlier. This time I could smell her perfume; my mother wore a similar scent. The lead pencil in her shirt pocket, I believed, was from Czechoslovakia.

I said, "I had no idea what this place was like until I got here."

"We have to experience to understand. But literature is also experience. The writing just has to be good enough." Then she leaned toward me and whispered, "There are rumours Solzhenitsyn has written something devastating and big. Mark my words—I will get my hands on it."

She said this with such certainty that I believed her.

"But how?" I whispered back.

She shooed away my words with her hands. "Let's talk about something else."

"Like what?"

"The end of the world," she said, narrowing her eyes and pulling another cigarette from her pack.

"How will it end?" I did my best to play along.

"With a really big bang." Anna cackled. Her glasses reflected my striking match. The smoke from her mouth mixed with wine. Someone put on a record: Russian disco. People began to dance. Anna leapt to her feet. I got up to join her but Zaza—still wearing his draping beige coat— jumped down from the table and cut in. They shimmied across the cramped space. Anna, a good foot shorter than Zaza, fit well into his body. I sat back down on the bed next to Aslan.

"The thing about genetics," he said to me in Russian, waving his exclamatory finger, "is it's all written down. Everything that ever was and will ever be. It's inside us. We just don't know the end, nor what we're capable of. That's the mystery." Then he switched to English: "Master Gary, we are writing new bibles every day."

Then Aslan did something I hadn't expected: he reached beneath the bed and pulled out a trumpet. He started to play along with the music coming from the speakers. But his playing was such that he seemed to be leading, even if the music was already recorded. I threw back two more shots of vodka and watched Anna and Zaza. They danced in perfect harmony to this wild melding of sounds. It was a scene out of Truffaut. The voices, the smoke, the singing. The last thing I remember was Anna sitting on Zaza's lap. Then I passed out.

I AWOKE ON the floor, a hungover mess. Aslan was already up and dressed for the day. He brought me bitter black tea heaped with spoonfuls of white sugar and instructed me to drink it. Then he told me to wash my face; we were going shopping.

Aslan, I learned, was studying genetics — hence his ruminations on the double helix the night before. He told me this at the rynok, a peasant market in a pleasant suburb of the city. Aslan inspected fruits and vegetables with the meticulousness of a scientist, for a much-anticipated repast.

"I am older than you," Aslan declared in Russian, expressing dissatisfaction with both onions and beets. "I have lived to the plum age of thirty-five. My life has not been straight nor stupid. But I will be a great geneticist." He switched to English. "I want a Golden Delicious life."

I paid for some mealy-looking apples and went in search of mushrooms. An old woman with gnarled hands caught my eye. She yelled and laughed at Aslan; he called her a "cretin" in jest. I asked for two bags of chanterelles and a bag of boletus. The old babushka handed me my fungi as I placed kopeks in her wrinkled hands.

"In America, everything is new and shiny, yes?" Aslan asked.

"For the most part. Though shiny and new isn't always good."

"Sometimes I wish to live there so bad, Gary. I want supermarkets and baseball, hot dogs and Charlie Parker. And I want to take my son. This is why we study English. The gateway to golden lives. Other times I think, even if I could, I would never leave. Home is the worst and best conundrum. And besides, in this black market they call me the Midnight Wrangler. How can I abandon such notoriety and fame?"

As we left the stand, the old babushka yelled something indistinct at Aslan. He shouted back, words I couldn't make out. I didn't say that I liked it here because it wasn't America. That the gnarled hands of the old woman handling mushrooms picked from the Lenin Hills and the Forests of Moscow were more real to me than the glistening cans of Chef Boyardee I ate as a child in Chicago. I didn't say that I liked the perversions and paradoxes of this country, the way people spoke their hearts and minds as though their lives depended on it. That I believed this might teach me how to write, and more importantly, how to live.

"I will give it to you," Aslan said.

"Give me what?"

"Tell me, why do you like Lermontov? He fought in the Czar's army. Do you know what the Czar's army did? They killed us then conquered the Caucasus. From Tbilisi to Grozny. From Sukhumi to Circassia. The Russians are occupiers. Occupiers are never good. They never go away."

"I understand."

"Yet you ignore the politics," Aslan said, holding up a dusty cucumber. "You say the writing is beautiful. How is a lie beautiful?"

"But you like Lermontov too. Why?"

"I don't like Lermontov. I love Pechorin. He is my most favourite skeptic. An honest man in a dishonest world."

I felt movement and turned to see Igor at the stall behind us holding up a purple cabbage. He listened to it, as though it were telling him a deep secret. I motioned to Aslan, but he wasn't affected by the young Komsomol's presence. Aslan threw the cucumber back into the pile.

"I cannot stand these vile Bolshevik fruits. It is too depressing. Lermontov was a bad man, but a classic heavy-weight drinker," he declared. "Shall we drink at the altar of your number one daddy-o?"

It wasn't yet eleven in the morning. But, in the spirit of Lermontov and my budding friendship with Aslan, I followed him into the local ryumochnaya. At the edge of the market, we stood at a high table and drank vodka and ate pickled herring. Old babushkas screamed and shouted, haggling over onions, dill, and garlic. Life, it seemed, was full.

Aslan said in Russian, "When I stand behind my microscope and peer through the vacuous mirror, I see the beauty of the gene. I read it, like a book." Then he leaned toward me and said in English, "I have written a book, too. For my son. To preserve our legacies. To tell the real story of the Caucasus. Will you help me translate it?"

"I'd be happy to."

"Will you please call it *Jeans and Genes?*"

"That's the title?"

He nodded his head. I noticed Igor again, lurking across the way at a newsstand with a copy of *Pravda*. In the manner of spy movies, he pretended — rather poorly — to read. I caught him, several times, watching Aslan and me. Aslan didn't seem bothered.

"Maybe one day you could help me publish it in the West."

"Sure," I said, distracted by Igor. Then I asked a question that had been bothering me all morning: "Is Anna Litvak Zaza's girlfriend?"

Aslan said, "I do not know the arrangement of their wild copulations."

"So, they're sleeping together?"

"Oh no, Master Gary. They do everything but sleep. Unfortunately, I must listen to their not-sleeping like the horrible music on the turntable I do not possess."

When I looked up, my eyes met Igor's. He tucked his *Pravda* under his arm and exited the market.

*Jonathan Garfinkel*

### Jeans and Genes:
### The Legend of the Midnight Wrangler

**by Aslan Varayev**
**Translated by Gary Ruckler**

Dedicated to my son, Akhmad

You won't hear the name Trofim Lysenko mentioned in your classrooms. And you won't find it in your Soviet textbooks either. While researching my doctoral thesis on genetics, I came across only scattered references to Lysenko. I was curious about this heretic scientist, banished from collective memory. But I was quickly disappointed: his science was appalling. A Soviet biologist and agronomist in the '30s and '40s, he refuted the theory of DNA in favour of more politically convenient ideas. For example, regarding milking cows, he believed better production was a result of kindness and nurturing, rather than genetic predispositions to better milk ducts.

Similarly, Lysenko advanced a theory that plants are self-sacrificing. The sunflower does not die from lack of sunlight or moisture, he claimed, but for the greater good of sunflowers to live better and healthier lives. (Imagine, the bold tomato plant, a foot soldier in the field of vegetables, laying down its tired body at the foot of the potato. All praise the heroic Solanum lycopersicum!) Based on his "law of the life of species," Lysenko implored farmers to plant seeds close to each other, since vegetables always work together in collective harmony, Darwin be damned. By submerging crops in freezing water, he sought to educate grains to sprout during the colder seasons. Future generations of seedlings would remember these glorious Soviet lessons. Yes, the idea is as crazy as slicing off the tail of a cat and then hoping she'll give birth to tailless kittens. And this man ran our country's biology and genetics program.

All of this would be laughable if Lysenko's pseudo-science hadn't been deemed essential by Stalin. It advanced the politics of his time. Stalin used Lysenko to prove his Homo Sovieticus. Lysenko's insane agricultural theories—in conjunction with Stalin's collectivization plans—helped kill millions during the Ukrainian famine. (Lysenko has a murderous legacy. As director of the Institute of Genetics, he sent countless good scientists to the Gulag. Yet he was notoriously kind to his beloved cows, Mathilde, Lali, and Anastasia.)

Marx, ever the economist, wrote: "It is not the consciousness of men that determines their being, but, on the contrary, their social being that determines their consciousness." The New Socialist Man builds his own destiny, makes of himself what he believes. The past is irrelevant. Marx said: We are freeing ourselves from all that. What matters is the gleaming future, toward which we must march bravely. Together.

Stalin, the bloodthirsty maniac, took this logic to its extreme. He perverted it. He smashed ʻthe idea of culture, identity, and genealogy out of people's heads. Stalin destroyed the lives of so many ethnicities, dividing and mixing them up like so many spices. He moved Georgians into Abkhazia, Azeris into Nagorno-Karabakh, Russians into the Baltics, Jews from Moscow and Leningrad into Birobidzhan. And what did he do to us? Expelled us on the paranoid basis of some betrayal we did not commit. And while Stalin's monstrous regime has collapsed, his legacy lives on. We still pay the price for Stalin and Lysenko's lies.

Genealogy matters. Like any good Chechen, I can recite my lineage seven generations back. I carry the history of my people. The past is a phantom limb. Our bodies do not forget. Maybe the limb isn't there anymore, but the feeling is. The mutilated cat may not give birth to tailless kittens, but the pain, the trauma, persists.

I'm a geneticist. I believe in the principle

of the double helix. There is a ladder and chain that contains the story of a bird, a tree, you, and me. I believe our bodies are books—that if we study them long enough, we can understand who we are and where we come from. But to say we are only what we inherit is not true either. Who and what is Akhmad? You carry so much of us inside you. But you make your own choices, choose your own path. To do that, you need to know where you come from. The true dialectic.

I believe in freedom. We're from the Caucasus, the land of Prometheus, that great Titan who stole fire from the gods and gave it to humanity. A tragic hero. Yet perhaps Prometheus is the real Homo Sovieticus, and we his rebellious sons and daughters. The question — the problem — remains: what to do about the past?

I only remember fragments. I was a child when they came for us. Waking up in the middle of the night, my mother shaking, soldiers in long wool coats that billowed at their feet. I remember she told me we were going on vacation, which sounded pretty good, though I'd never actually gone on a holiday. I had no concept of leaving. What it means to say goodbye to your home, your neighbours, the garden in the back with the apple and plum trees.

Then: a train ride. Did it take hours,

or weeks? I have no memory. I love trains—
their speed and their sound. The doors sealed
shut. And even though it was dark and hard
to breathe, I believed things were going to
be okay. I fell asleep against my mother's
leg and dreamt it was a tree, the one in the
backyard with all those beautiful apples, red
and brown and green. I dreamt that tomorrow
is also today, that the past was better than
it really was. I dreamt numbers and equa-
tions, the diameter of my mother's leg, which
is the circumference of love.

When the train stopped, the doors swung
open. Everything was different. The air, the
light, the voices harsh and brutal. Bread
that tasted like ash. Soup that smelled like
another country. Faces tired and unrecognizable. And my mother, no longer beside me, whom
I would never see again.

I was raised in a land not my own. I have
felt a foreigner all my life. Even here in
Moscow, I am always in exile. Yes, the past
is a scar. It affects and shapes us. But like
the mark on my friend Zaza's face, our scars
won't determine who we are.

As punishment for stealing fire from the
gods and giving it to humanity, Zeus chained
Prometheus to Mount Kazbek in the Caucasus
Mountains. For all eternity, a great eagle
would come and devour his liver. Each day

his liver was eaten; each night it would grow back. An eternal cycle of violation, trauma, and healing. Followed by re-violation and re-traumatization. Hercules, another tragic hero, challenging his father Zeus, killed the eagle and broke Prometheus's chains. Zeus allowed it, on one condition: that Prometheus wear a ring containing a piece of rock from the mountain he'd been chained to.

So, we wear our rings, the mark of where we come from. Eventually we'll live freely. In a better world, in a freer society, we can do that. This is the world I wish for you, Akhmad. But how do we do that, and where is that place? For a long time, I thought we had to leave. Seek a better future in the West. In America. But I don't want to trade one exile for another, to cut the final roots that keep us. To do to you what Lysenko and Stalin did to me.

# 2

*Moscow, U.S.S.R.*
*January 10–11, 1975*

After his initial excitement in the market, Aslan had delayed
showing me his manuscript for several months. There was
always one reason or another: it wasn't ready, he had to
make changes, he believed I wasn't in the right "space
of heads." Sometimes I wondered if he had written anything at all. But when he finally handed me loose pages in
a brown envelope shortly before Thanksgiving, I found
myself drawn into a life I could not understand. Perhaps
that's why I agreed to translate it. I wanted to watch and to
listen. To decode an Otherness that compelled me. Maybe
Jim was right. Perhaps literature is a gazing at the forbidden
and vast interior of other people's lives. But this was not
*A Hero of Our Time.* It was intimate, private, and strangely
unsettled me.

Life took on a quiet and monotonous rhythm in those
months in Moscow: a ritual of reading and writing. I went

to class, explored the city with my fellow Americans. Aslan would drop by and we would drink vodka and listen to records. Sometimes he'd bring his trumpet and play for me. While I had momentarily regretted leaving behind my instrument, he had an assured deftness I could never achieve. He played the way he spoke: absurd, deep, provocative. We never talked about his manuscript. It sat in the envelope in my desk like a forgotten secret. Over the following weeks, I slowly plodded through, carefully translating his words and writing notes of my own in the margins: questions I intended to ask Aslan when I finished the draft.

During this time, I did my best to avoid Anna Litvak. I do not know why; perhaps I understood she would only disrupt things. After class, we often engaged in small talk, but I declined her invitations to further poetry readings and parties. Then, one afternoon in January, I ran into her. Beneath the glow of fluorescent lights and set against the peach-coloured walls of the cafeteria, her grey button-down and black pants took on a peculiar glow.

"You've been avoiding me," she said.

"I have?" I said, looking down at my feet.

"Did you meet a girl?" she asked tauntingly.

"No."

"That's too bad. You could use a girlfriend, Gary. You always seem so lonely."

"I've been writing," I said, which was actually true. I glanced at the pink mechanical pencil tucked into her front pocket. Indeed, it was from Czechoslovakia. She had confirmed this one day after class and shown me the ingenious sharpener tucked into the back like a good mystery. Then I added: "There's something I'd like to give you. Would you come by my room later?"

She looked at me, a mixture of suspicion and intrigue. "Okay."

I WENT BACK to my room to tidy up. The big question: how should I organize my books? Alphabetically, or by theme? Do I scatter them randomly, or do I keep them in a line, guarding the desk like so many soldiers? I ran down to buy vodka from the kiosk, and a few Zhigulevskoye beers to wash it down with. I purchased a loaf of rye bread and a can of Baltic smoked smelts. When I returned to my room, I changed my shirt, forgetting that Aslan had recently "acquired" my best button-down — a mint-coloured Pierre Cardin — so I opted for a casual yellow polo with only a hint of tomato stain. I held the first chapter of Aslan's manuscript loose in my hands.

At 20h05 Anna sauntered in wearing a black pleated skirt and a grey-and-white checkered shirt. She sat on my bed and immediately lit up a Kazbek cigarette, named for the famous mountain in Lermontov's opus. I opted for the desk chair — the only other place to sit — and lit up a joint.

"Hashish?"

I nodded. "Afghani." I passed it to her.

"Let me guess — Aslan?"

"Who else?"

Aslan had a reputation. His black-market American clothing emporium — and really, his reputation for getting his hands on anything you might want — were well known and much appreciated by the students of MSU. But he was much more than that. In the past few months, Aslan and I had become close. Yet the more time I spent with him, the less I believed I really knew him.

Lately he had been spending a lot of time worrying about his son. According to Aslan, Akmad was a sickly child, and he was concerned that he wasn't eating well. When he confessed his feelings of guilt for spending so much time away from his family, I reassured him: he was getting this degree so he could give his son a better future. This seemed to assuage him. I believe it helped him to see that he could trust me. For when Aslan gave me his manuscript of *Jeans and Genes*, I gained a window onto someone I didn't know. It both delighted and unnerved me. Why was this intimacy so deeply threatening? For whom did he want me to translate it? And why did I want to show it to Anna Litvak? I suppose I was trying to impress her. But I was also hoping she might help me make sense of it. To tell me if it was any good.

ANNA'S LIPS PRESSED on the joint and a sweetness permeated the room. I cracked open the window and a couple of beers. The Zhigulevskoye was warm. Anna swilled. I pulled out *Led Zeppelin II*. The falsetto of Robert Plant erupted from my speakers.

"Why does he sing like that? It's so weird."

Taken out of the normal context, Robert Plant did sound weird.

"He stole the lyrics from Willie Dixon," I replied.

"You see? I can smell the lie in his voice."

"So, you're a spy?"

"One of Moscow's best."

Anna inhaled on the joint.

"Where are you from originally?" I asked.

"Vilnius. I moved here five years ago. Fell in love with a hippie."

"You have hippies in the Soviet Union?"

She passed the joint back to me.

"We used to listen to the Beatles, but we had no idea what the words meant. Why is your Russian so good?"

I explained that, growing up, I had a Russian nanny who used to read to me. That I fell in love with literature at an early age and I attributed it to her voice. That something in the language clung to me, like music. I decided I needed to read my favourite authors in their original language, so I could learn to write like them. Because that's what I wanted to do.

She nodded. "So, is this book you want to show me something you wrote?"

I shook my head and passed her the stack of pages in Russian. Anna's eyes devoured sentences, gulped syllables, syntax, and grammar. I drank, smoked, watched her closely. Then she carefully put down the pages, grabbed hold of the *Zeppelin II* cover, and examined the song list. I cracked open the vodka and relit the joint. Jimmy Page's guitar wailed sheepishly in the background.

"Why do you have this manuscript?"

"Aslan asked me to translate it. I suppose he wants me to get it published in the West."

"That's not a good idea."

"It's no good?"

Anna shrugged. "He's right, what he says about DNA and history, I think."

"So the deportations were real?"

Anna told me how Stalin had claimed the Chechens and Ingush sided with Hitler during the war. There was no truth to it, of course, but Stalin was never one for banal things like evidence. He was determined to make an example of them, to punish them. So, on February 23, 1944, Stalin's NKVD henchman Lavrentiy Beria began Operation Lentil with the goal of expelling the entire Chechen and Ingush nations from the North Caucasus. More than five hundred thousand people were deported by rail car to Kazakhstan. I tried to imagine the multitudes of men, the cities of soldiers pushing women and children into boxcars. No one was left behind. Thousands died on the long trip east. Over a quarter of the Chechen and Ingush populations perished in exile. Mountain people put out to live on the plains.

When Khrushchev finally allowed them to return in 1957 — citing a gross error on the part of dear father Stalin — many found their homes in Chechnya occupied by Russians. Some wandered over the mountains to Georgia. And that's how Aslan's family ended up living in Kazbegi, where Aslan met Zaza as a young teenager.

Anna drew on the joint. "I guess if you look at it from the point of view of genetics, you could say it's another chromosome of historical trauma." She started to cough. "I don't know what I'm talking about. I'm stoned."

She put out the joint. The record came to an end and the needle lifted. I got up from my chair and went to sit next to Anna on the bed. I was stoned, confused, and didn't know what to do next: not about Anna, not about Aslan's book, not about anything. When I put my arm around her, she rested her head on my shoulder. We stayed like that for some time.

Later, when it was time for her to leave, I gave her Aslan's manuscript in its brown envelope, telling her she was welcome to read the whole thing. She immediately handed it back to me.

"Give this back to Aslan. Get rid of it as soon as possible."

THE NEXT MORNING, Anna was not in class, so I tried to take notes for her. *War and Peace*, Dmitry claimed, was the perfect antecedent to the Soviet project — from the demagoguery of the upper classes to the rise of the Bolshevik spirit. (He cited Prince Andrei's liberation of his serfs as a model for the Socialist example.) But my mind was elsewhere. I was trying to decode what people were saying versus what they meant to say. Why had Aslan really given me his book? I needed to speak to him.

That afternoon I went out for a walk by the athletics track. Girls launched each other into the air like projectile missiles, landing awkwardly on a thick mattress in the middle of the field. Boys wormed their way across the pitch on their stomachs, as though trying to disappear into the earth. I smoked, wondering if I'd made a mistake sitting next to Anna on the bed. When I turned around, Igor was standing next to me.

"It is good to see the students of the university training so vigorously."

"It makes one hopeful," I agreed.

"Why is that?"

"Because they're so perfectly capable of following orders."

Igor adjusted his collar. "Have you seen Aslan today? He was missing from the lab. His instructor notified me."

"I haven't."

"You gave him your Wrangler jean jacket."

"Is that a problem?"

"Of course not."

I did not want to antagonize Igor. But I also wanted to establish a clearer footing.

"Some months ago, I saw you at the Usachevskiy market," I said. "You were buying a newspaper."

"They were sold out near the university."

"A long way to go to buy a newspaper."

"A long way to go to buy mushrooms," he replied.

"Why were you following us?"

"Are you sure you don't know where Aslan is?" he asked, ignoring my question.

"Yeah. I'm sure."

"You should be more careful, Dustin. Moscow can be a dangerous place."

I PICKED UP Aslan's manuscript from my room and headed back to the Soviet wing. A group of Cubans danced around a bottle. Russian students laughed and wailed. Aslan and Zaza were nowhere to be found. Their neighbour, Marius from Vilnius, told me they had left earlier that afternoon for Kazbegi.

"Just like that?" I asked, having heard no mention of such a trip.

Marius spun his finger at his head and leaned in toward me: "These Caucasian men are crazy."

"Do you know why they went to Georgia?" I asked.

"To party, of course. Why else?"

When I got back to my room, Anna was smoking in the

hallway. I was happy to see her. I felt awkward about how the evening had ended and wanted to apologize. I opened the door and led her inside. She sat on my bed. I returned Aslan's manuscript to the drawer of my desk.

"About last night —"

"I talked with Zaza," Anna interrupted. "I told him."

"Told him what?"

"I'm pregnant."

"You're what?"

Anna grimaced. "Zaza is excited. He wants to get married right away. I told him I didn't want to keep the baby. Then we got into a fight. I am not cut out to be a mother, Gary."

I poured her a drink.

"He asked where I had been last night. I told him I was here with you, listening to records and getting high. He became jealous and demanded to know everything. I had to tell him."

"Okay…"

"It's not a problem. We worked it out."

I did not like the fact that Zaza — a man twice my size and ten times my strength — might be angry with me. Then I thought about Aslan's manuscript. Had Anna told him about it too? She got up from the bed and sat next to me, legs dangling off the edge of the desk, hands in her lap.

"Is it normal that Zaza and Aslan suddenly went off to Kazbegi?" I asked.

"They do it all the time," she said.

I started to feel sick. What had I got myself involved in? And what should I do now?

"Zaza promised he'd marry me when he came back."

"Do you want to?"

Anna pressed her hands hard into her thighs.

"I have aspirations that don't include marriage."

She got up and lit a cigarette, eyeing me through thick smoke.

"I love Zaza, he's wild and fun..." she said, trailing off.

"What about the baby?"

Anna's tight smile cut through me. I felt it in the centre of my gut. She put her hand on my knee.

"Let's be friends, Gary. Good friends."

She kissed me on the cheek and stood up from the desk. When she was gone, I found her empty cigarette pack. The black mountains, printed on blue packaging, seemed ominous.

THAT NIGHT I dreamt of Kazbegi. I saw the mountains and the stone church high in the hills. I hovered above it, looking down. With a bird's-eye view, I gazed at the monastery door. Light poured through, revealing altitude as illumination. I heard a call from below. I swooped in and landed by an altar, at the foot of Christ. Aslan shivered in the dark.

"Help," he said. "Gary, please."

# 3

I was eating my morning kasha in the cafeteria when Igor arrived at my table.

"Dustin," he said, sitting across from me. "Why don't you like me?"

"I never said I didn't like you."

"You're avoiding me."

I looked down at my plate. Igor glanced around the cafeteria. The room was crowded with students, eating and talking and reading books.

"I received a phone call in the middle of the night." He spoke in a flat, matter-of-fact tone, as though delivering the evening news. "It was Zaza. He was drunk and babbling something about a betrayal. He mentioned Anna Litvak, you, and something about Aslan that I couldn't make out. Zaza wouldn't answer my questions but said he planned to act." Igor smoothed his black blazer and primped up his turtleneck. "Is there something you want to tell me, Dustin?"

I focused on my kasha. I noticed a long black hair in the groats which I deftly pulled out.

Igor continued. "I'm not who you think I am." He swallowed a spoonful of kasha. "Tell me, Gary Ruckler, where is Aslan?"

He said this in perfect American English, with no hint of accent, while covering his lips with the brush of a napkin. For a moment I wondered if he'd said anything at all. My mind racing, I told him to come to my room that evening.

THE PROBLEM OF living in a foreign country is fundamentally a problem of language. You might speak it, read it, and even understand it, but the truth is, you really know nothing at all. The local dialect is always and essentially not your own. Hand gestures, innuendoes, assumptions; one is always several steps behind. It is a constant dance of interpretation and decoding.

When Jim entered my room alongside Igor, fear began coursing through me. So, I did what I always did. I put on a record. While Charlie Parker hurried melodiously on his sax, Jim flitted through my LPs.

"Great collection, Gary. Any of these for sale?"

"No."

"Wow, *Led Zeppelin II*. You could never find this here. Are you sure? I'll pay good money. And it won't be in rubles."

"They're not for sale."

Jim put down the record and turned to face me.

"We're glad you and Aslan have become friends. We like that. And while we don't care that you sold him a few items from back home, other people are less forgiving. Isn't that right, Igor?"

Igor leaned against the window ledge and lit a cigarette.

"What other people?" I asked.

Jim shooed away my words with his hand. "Is there something you want to tell us, Gary?" Jim looked right into my face. His blue eyes hardened. "Now's the time."

"I'm worried about him," I said.

"So are we. What do you know?"

"Not much, I'm afraid."

"Do you know where he is?"

"Yeah, he went home to Georgia."

"'He went home to Georgia.' See? Was that hard?" Jim looked at Igor. Igor looked at a spot on the floor. "Help us help him, Gary."

"How?"

"Go to Georgia. Find him. Tell him we'd like to speak to him. We can work this out together. We can do the right thing."

Then he patted me on the knee and got up to leave. Igor butted out his cigarette and followed. I looked at the books casually arranged on my desk and saw Lermontov's *A Hero of Our Time*. The cover showed Pechorin sitting astride a horse silhouetted by mountains. I wasn't sure I could find Aslan. But I needed to see for myself.

I began packing a bag while muttering to myself, "I am staying put." I said this out loud. If I were being watched and listened to, then I would say precisely what I was not doing. "I am staying right here," I said, grabbing a Hilroy notebook (value: eight rubles), three blue Bic pens (value: ten rubles each), and three pairs of Jockey underwear (thirty rubles each). I slipped Aslan's manuscript between the note-book and underwear, put on my green Woolworth's sweater and my blue Wrangler jeans. "I am staying put," I said, and grabbed my copy of Lermontov. This I slipped into the inside pocket of my warm coat. Against my better judgement, and defying shoulder shrugs, knee pats, and cold, uncomprehending American eyes, I left my dorm and took the Metro to Paveletsky station, where I bought a ticket to Kazbegi.

THE TRAIN LEFT Moscow through sprawling suburbs. The landscape gave way to cottages, cabins, vegetable patches, and outhouses. It was over a day's journey to Vladikavkaz, the southern edge of Russia. When we passed through the northern plain — dreaming, inquisitive — that enormous expanse of unending landscape opened something inside me. I felt I had split into two parts. There was an eye that marvelled at the endless space that is Russia. And there was another eye that looked elsewhere. It interrogated the babushka selling sausage on the street; it pried into the heart of the child practising her flute in an open window; and it turned on me, examining my thoughts, secrets and fears. Everything I had thought in the past four months fell under its gaze. Paranoia bloomed inside me. I wished Lysenko was a name I did not know.

Out of nowhere, mountains erupted from the verdant earth. Nothing can prepare you for the breathless beauty of the Caucasus Mountains. Snow clung to the rock, and the mountain lines cut through me. I remembered my Lermontov: "The dark-blue mountain tops, furrowed with wrinkles, covered with layers of snow, were silhouetted against the pale horizon." I could not have said it better.

When the train pulled into Vladikavkaz, I was filled with neurotic, slippery feelings of dread. I bought fresh bread from a vendor and made my way to a collective taxi stand next to a group of men in grey trench coats. In a van crammed with a dozen others, amidst the smell of urine, vomit, and booze, I tried to make out the landscape through a sliver of window. I caught glimpses of the terrifying Daryal Gorge, black rock sliding through ice, and felt claustrophobic at the sight of the cliffs.

Some hours later we arrived in the village square of Kazbegi. I was dropped off with an older gentleman, a local wearing a thick sweater. The village was surrounded by mountains. On one sat the ancient Gergeti Trinity Church. "All these snows burned with a ruddy glow," Lermontov wrote, "so merrily, so brightly, that it made one wonder why one should not stay here forever."

At a kiosk in the main square, I asked if anyone knew where Aslan Varayev lived. I was pointed to the other side of the river. By the graveyard, amidst the wandering pigs and cows, I asked a woman who pointed to a grey door falling off its hinges. I knocked, and was greeted by a young boy.

"Akhmad?" I asked.

He nodded shyly.

"Is your father here?"

He slammed the door shut, so I knocked again. This time a woman answered holding a baby. She had striking green eyes and wore her hair tied back in a blue scarf. I told her I was a friend of Aslan's from the university.

"He isn't here," she said.

"Do you know where he is?"

"In Moscow, studying."

"He never arrived in Kazbegi?"

She shrugged. "He was never supposed to."

The baby clawed at the air. I reached into my bag and handed her the brown envelope containing Aslan's manuscript.

"What is this?" she asked.

"It's for Akhmad. Please, keep it safe for him." I hesitated. "Have you seen Zaza?"

She laughed and shook her head. "No," she said, and slammed the door shut.

Back in the main square, I asked if anyone had seen Aslan. Nobody answered me. A toothless babushka turned away. I descended to a bridge by the river, found a restaurant, and ordered thick soup. While I waited for it to arrive, I raised my hand as a shield against the sun, which blinded me with its reflection off the mountains. A man with wild hair plunked a bottle down between us. He poured me a glass and gestured for me to drink. I took a sip and nearly fell over. It tasted like gasoline.

"I am Vano!" he declared in Russian.

"What the hell is this?" I sputtered.

"Chacha!" he exclaimed, smacking me on the back. "Drink!"

I took another tentative sip and told him I was looking for my friend Aslan.

"He arrived yesterday! With Zaza!"

With Vano, every statement ended with an exclamation mark.

"But his wife said he isn't here."

Vano howled maniacally. "Of course he isn't here. They are having a party!" He said this with a nod and a wink. I began to feel woozy.

"This is strong stuff," I said, gesturing to the bottle.

"Of course!" Vano exclaimed. "It's chacha!"

Vano ordered copious amounts of meat dumplings — giant softballs that quickly appeared before us on a white plastic tray. I bit into one, and its juice rolled down my chin. Vano laughed at my clumsy display. He showed me how to bite off the top then suck, suck, suck. We ate like this, a drunken rapture, the world reduced to a plate of dumplings.

"Do you know where they went?" I asked when we had finished eating.

Vano shrugged. "Why do you care?"

"Aslan is my friend. I came to visit him."

Vano eyed me in a way I could not decipher. Was it the look of the suspicious or the gaze of the endeared? Did he see the love I felt for Aslan, or the guilt that was driving me to help him?

"You're a good friend!" he declared. Standing up, he pointed to the church on the mountain. "Gergeti!! They went there!"

Vano explained that Aslan and Zaza had been seen carrying booze and food up to the church. The plan was to have some kind of picnic. Vano implied — with another nod and wink — that they might be joined by some women too.

An hour later I was submerged waist-deep in snow on my way up the mountain. It took another three hours before I passed the treeline and reached the summit. There I found a monastery, a church at the end of the world. It was only then that I realized this was the same church from my dream. Towering above was Mount Kazbek. I felt my own smallness in the face of things.

I entered the monastery courtyard. It was full of stone and light, hundreds of years old. I approached the door and pushed at fourteen feet of wrought iron. Inside, the floors were made of earth and the walls old rock. I found a candle and lit it and walked through a tunnel slick with moisture. The farther I descended, the more I felt I was falling through layers of consciousness, my fears turning this way and that.

I reached a stone sanctuary and lit more candles. Walls of musty prayer books stared back at me from ancient shelves. In the centre of the room stood two wooden chairs arranged to face each other. Beside one I could see a pile of coiled rope stained with what looked like blood. In the corner, I saw a mop and bucket. I heard a noise coming from behind the bucket and walked toward it. There I found a cage. Inside, a rat rattled against the sides. The cage had no bottom, so the rat's efforts pushed it forward and back, side to side, spinning, the animal seeking a way out. But the cage was too heavy to be turned over easily. I felt a sudden urge to grab one of the chairs, to bring its leg down and smash the vile creature's head. Then I saw my Wrangler jean jacket, folded neatly by the altar. On top of that was Aslan's *Houses of the Holy* t-shirt. And beside that, a pair of blue-and-gold cufflinks. I heard footsteps coming from the stone tunnel. Quickly I ducked out the back door and began my descent down the mountain toward the village. I did not look back.

# ACT II

## LOST AND FOUND

### April 1989 – November 2000

"People have so much pain inside them
that they're not even aware of."
—MARINA ABRAMOVIĆ

# 1

*Tbilisi, U.S.S.R.*
*April 9, 1989*

Tamar buttons up her old jean jacket as she leaves the Vake Swimming Pool. She makes her way across Cholokashvili Avenue, darting and weaving to avoid oncoming traffic. When a blue Lada accelerates toward her, she stops in her tracks. Stares into the driver's eyes. *There it is*, she thinks. *The scar that divides his face, running from ear to mouth.* The world slows down as the car speeds up. Now Tamar can see his face clearly. Tiny black eyes, dirty blond eyebrows. *No, it's not him.* Still, she doesn't move. She needs to be sure. At the last moment the car swerves right. Tamar jumps left then runs toward Davit. He paces by the newspaper stand.

"Jesus fuck, Tamar, you're going to give me a heart attack. Why can't you take the underpass like a normal person?"

"I prefer to see the world."

"What does that even mean? You're going to get yourself killed."

"Don't be so melodramatic. Where are we going to eat? I'm starving."

"Here." Davit hands her a piece of bread. Tamar bites greedily into the thick pastry stuffed with bean paste. Lobio, her favourite. "There's no time to stop. There are people gathered by the parliament. This is history, Tamar."

Davit is obsessed with being a part of "history." As though participating in the mess of politics is synonymous with being truly alive. Tamar finds it both endearing and annoying.

"Davit?" she says with her mouth full. "What do people *do* at a protest?"

He strokes his fourteen-year-old chin to lend himself an air of wisdom.

"I guess we're going to find out."

TAMAR CARES ABOUT history, but she feels most alive when she smells chlorine on her skin. The dryness and itching she feels from swimming — the history she makes. Six days a week, before school and after. For Tamar, swimming is a kind of religion, a way of feeling her body in the world. She loves the swell in her shoulders after finishing four thousand metres, loves the tick-tock of *push harder, pull faster*, the bellow of her swim team coach racing through her brain. And she loves looking up at the banners of Brezhnev and Lenin while she glides and kicks through the water of the fifty-metre Vake Pool, the enormous barrel-vault temple to physical fitness for the *Homo Sovieticus*.

Tamar finishes the lobio but she is still hungry. On cue, Davit hands her a sandwich courtesy of the old bebia on Ritsa Street. Tamar bites into it. The bebia's eggplant and cheese sandwiches are delicious. Tamar is always hungry after swimming, a ravenousness unlike anything, and Davit knows to expect it. He is her oldest friend and soulmate. They've known each other since they were four.

Davit natters on about the crowds — he's seen them, he's seen them — and the soldiers on lookout. Davit is a scrawny teenager with journalistic aspirations. He wants to be the Georgian Joan Didion, committed to telling "the naked truth," as he's fond of saying. Tamar has no idea who Joan Didion is, but she thinks Davit's writing is the bravest she's read — though she is partial to dead poets like Tsvetaeva and Mandelstam.

While Tamar eats her sandwich, Davit stops to buy a newspaper. "History," he proclaims to the newspaper seller, and whoever else will listen, "will not wait." Davit speaks more with his hands than his voice, his black eyes darting back and forth. Despite Davit's urgent demands for "justice," "freedom," and "change," the newspaper man shrugs indifferently as he hands Davit his change.

A marshrutka screeches to a stop nearby, they get on and head downtown.

*Out of the swimming pool and into history*, Tamar thinks to herself. *To* make *history*.

She has never been to a political demonstration before. Never seen one on TV, even with all the new freedoms and the restrictions lifted since perestroika. As the van speeds up, she huddles against Davit for warmth. She imagines enormous thirty-foot letters assembled by the side of the avenue. Words like "Freedom" and "Independence" constructed to voice their deepest yearnings. She imagines the people climbing these letters, great jungle gyms of desire, their desperate attempts to mount and surmount, trying to make themselves heard.

"Why did you stop like that on the road?" asks Davit.

"The driver looked familiar."

Davit looks at her incredulously. "Seriously? That guy was going to hit you."

It happens in moments when she least expects it. A voice pulls her down into the murky waters of her past. "That's him," the voice says, and she has to stop what she's doing to see, to make sure. It never is, though. Not yet, at least.

"You make me crazy, Tamar. It's like you always need to live life right on the edge."

Maybe Davit is right. But maybe she needs to go past the edge. She isn't afraid of death. For her, death is like swimming. While Davit fantasizes about their escape to Berlin, to the underground cafés and nightclubs strewn with old rubble, where they'll stay up all night with artists, smoking and talking about whatever artists talk about, Tamar daydreams of a plane crash into the Black Sea. It's a fantasy of panic and plunge. Under the stars, waves push against her as she's surrounded by eternal darkness. The swim of her life.

"Gacheret," yells Davit.

The van pulls over next to the Tbilisi Concert Hall. Everyone gets off. From a verdigris fountain, water spills innocently into the air. Even the driver abandons the vehicle. They are blocks away from parliament and the street ahead is bottlenecked with foot traffic.

THE PROTESTS HAVE been building for days. Dissident hero Zviad Gamsakhurdia staged a hunger strike, while others gave passionate speeches to the thousands gathered. The Soviet foreign minister, Eduard Shevardnadze — himself Georgian — begged the protestors to back down. "There'll be bloodshed," he intoned. Nobody listened, of course.

"It'll be peaceful," Davit assured Tamar. "You'll see."

The Georgian Committee for Independence has called for a free Georgia for the first time since 1921, the year the Bolsheviks murderously conquered their country — yet another chapter in the long book of foreign occupations. In time they were ruled by another Georgian, a bloodthirsty and ruthless poet from Gori. But Iosef Djugashvili is a dark story for another dark time. For now, as Tamar follows Davit into the crowds, she feels lightness pulsing through her limbs. She didn't anticipate this river of humanity, this sea of goodwill and longing.

"Georgia for Georgians!" a voice proclaims.

The crowd cheers while young Soviet soldiers in long, grey coats stand watching, armed with bayonets and spades. They eye the spectators wearily from atop high buildings and grand monuments, pointing their AKs. But no one seems to be afraid. It's infectious. *When there is no fear*, Tamar thinks, *anything is possible*. A new confidence gilds the air.

Tamar is curious but doesn't know what any of it means. It is hard for her to conceive of a world other than the one she's grown up in. Her adoptive parents, Sasha and Nana, are theatre artists funded by the Soviet state. "What do I need to protest?" Sasha asked earlier that week at dinner. "I want to make Brecht! That's my political statement. It's yours too, Tamar."

Tamar was raised in the theatre. When she was a child, after her father Zaza left, she spent more time at the theatre than she did in school. It was a lifeline for her, and a second family. She loved the banter of actors, their mundane gossipy lives suddenly and mysteriously transformed on stage. She remembers Sasha smearing globs of makeup on his face, focusing his breathing in front of a mirror while he rubbed colour into his skin. On many an afternoon she sat with Nana in the back of the theatre, listening to the trace of her pencil on graph paper, illuminating designs for the stage. It was both soothing and affecting. Sometimes it felt as though her adoptive mother's HB pencil was tracing the outline of Tamar's body, her future, her self. Sometimes she imagined rubbing out the lines and reshaping the borders.

But it was the performances she loved most as a child — the colour and the light. When she was seven, she watched Brecht's *Caucasian Chalk Circle* directed by Robert Sturua at the Rustaveli. She loved the feeling of carnival, of magic and history woven into fable, 1,500 people crammed into 750 seats. The band struck up, the audience went silent, and the narrator — played by her adoptive father Sasha in a crumpled grey suit and black fedora — walked upstage and addressed not the audience, but Bertolt Brecht himself.

"You think you know the Caucasus? You understand nothing, Mr. Brecht. This is *our* story."

Seven-year-old Tamar was riveted to her seat. She wanted that: to be the narrator of an epic tale that told the story of both self and country. It is why she started attending theatre school. But now, walking through these crowds of protestors, she understands she doesn't need to learn how to act. As they pass the Rustaveli Theatre, the multitudes march, gesticulate, cry, and sing. They have all become actors on the stage of their country. It is the beginning of the end for the only world they've known. And it excites her.

"Georgia for Georgians!" more people chant and scream.

Tamar draws her hand around Davit's and gazes at the rivers of people. She finds the protest beautiful. People are crying and joyful. As though the very proclamation of nation-hood is love, and identity akin to freedom. Does it matter what country she belongs to? What does it mean to fight for a nation that doesn't yet exist? Tamar has never considered these questions before. Yet she is glad she is here.

Then she thinks she sees Zaza's beige wool coat. She tries to move toward him, but it is impossible: the crowds swell and there is nowhere to go. For a moment, she lets herself imagine it is his hand she holds, not Davit's. She wants to know what Zaza would think of this protest. She wants to know her father.

TAMAR WAS SIX years old when he left. She remembers Nana in a flower-print dress, drawing backstage at the Rustaveli Theatre. Suddenly the page grew wet, she wiped and smeared it. Tamar understood these were Nana's tears.

"Zaza's gone."

"Where did he go?" asked Tamar.

"Into the world," said Nana.

Tamar wasn't convinced. She took Nana's pencil and tried to draw him. The outlines of his enormous body were easy, but as soon as she attempted the details of his face the image of Zaza disappeared. She did not know what to do.

"It's you, me, Sasha, and Levan now," said Nana, grabbing another pencil from her bag. "I'll be your mother, Tamar. I promise."

Her adoptive parents were kind and generous; she was raised in the House of Love. Regarding Zaza, Nana was not angry nor vengeful if she spoke of him, which she rarely did. She never asked Tamar to forget him. And he often came back to Tamar: fragments of memories that never formed a coherent whole.

"Watch as though not watching," he had once intoned to her. "And listen to everything."

AN OLD GRANDMOTHER hands Tamar a piece of fresh bread. A group of men gather in a circle, passing around a plastic bottle of chacha and singing loudly. She feels light here, floating through the streets of her youth. The grand state theatres and elegant chestnut trees and the avenues crammed with people. It is amazing to see them transformed. She sees a yogurt seller scratching his head, looking for his son amidst the throng. She watches a woman rub her temple, thirsty and sad. She witnesses a man whisper in the ear of his beloved; hope in the eyes of an octogenarian; exhilaration in the eyes of an infant.

At first, she thinks they're firecrackers. Children in some back-road alley making mischief. But when she sees bodies falling, a swell of panic ripples through her.

"Get down," she hears someone say.

Tamar falls to the ground and a foot crushes her hand. A boot digs into the back of her neck and her elbows invert. She shoves her head toward the concrete as bullets spray through the crowd like rain. Her face is pushed farther into the pavement as a hand pulls her up.

"Come on," yells Davit.

They run up Rustaveli. Metal ruptures concrete and shatters windows. Near the parliament steps Tamar sees a young woman escape the melee only to have soldiers attack her with their spades — bak, bak, bak — as though trying to break earth. They mutilate her teenage body. An older woman sprints through the police lines to collapse at her daughter's feet. The soldiers beat her too. The bodies of the two women, mother and daughter, disappear as though never there.

Davit and Tamar turn on their feet and head toward Merab Kostava. The military has cordoned off the area and is funnelling the demonstrators. Tamar feels her stomach lurch as she fights the urge to vomit. The army continues to hit people with spades and shovels. Those who don't fall crush those who do. The nausea in Tamar's stomach won't let up. A young man sits atop a Soviet tank and beats it with a stick, an absurd image that somehow makes more sense than anything else she's seen during this afternoon of massacre.

Suddenly Tamar keels over and pukes.

"Come on, we have to get out of here," says Davit.

"I don't feel well. I can't see." She holds on to Davit for support.

"They're spraying the crowd with CS gas."

The darkness makes her afraid. Davit leads her by the hand. Near-blind, they begin to run again. She squints, rubs her eyes with her scarf. Now she's sure she sees him. Zaza, leaning against a fountain, smoking a cigarette in his beige wool coat. She pulls on Davit. "This way."

"What are you doing?"

The man falls, crumpling like paper. Shot by a sniper in the back. She cries out, but Davit pulls her, and they zigzag through the emptying streets. She isn't sure if it's the gas sprayed by the army or the pain of Zaza abandoning her that hurts most. Why does a father leave a child? How could he disappear without a word of goodbye? And why has he never come back?

WHEN TAMAR GETS HOME, Nana and Sasha are furious.

"Nineteen dead, Tamar. Seventeen of them women," says Sasha.

"I was sure you were one of them," says Nana, weeping.

"The army fired on us," yells Tamar. "Their own people."

"I told you to stay out of politics," says Sasha.

"They used gas on the crowd," Tamar says. "They poisoned us."

"You could've been killed," cries Nana.

"I don't care."

"Well, I do."

Tamar goes quiet. Her sixteen-year-old adoptive brother, Levan, forever a boy, enters the room and asks, "What's for dinner?"

Nana brings out the plates while Levan cracks jokes to ease the tension. Sasha downs a glass of wine. Then another.

As they sit down to eat, the images of the day won't go away. She listens as Sasha and Levan avoid politics, dips bread into Nana's fresh pkhali and badrijan, devouring everything.

"Watch as though not watching," Zaza said. "And listen to everything."

In the morning, Tamar will go to swim practice. But she will pay closer attention to the banners hanging above her. In her acting class, she will feel distant from the texts she memorizes. Tamar wants to feel what she felt that day in front of the parliament. The world is a stage and from it flows change. She doesn't want to act; she wants action.

# 2

"Life in Georgia," Davit likes to say to Tamar, "is an education in the world." She can't help but agree. In the five years since the April 9 Massacre, she has grown into adolescence. And her country has changed in extraordinary and devastating ways.

Life in the aftermath of April 1989 was anything but glorious—or banal, for that matter. Tamar dreamt of the banal like a child dreams of ice cream. The hope of an independent Georgia became reality in 1991, when the U.S.S.R. dissolved and Lenin's dream splintered into a chaos of nations. For a moment there was a glimmer of something that gripped the streets—freedom? A collective dream? Tamar and Davit were caught up in the hubris. They chatted non-stop while slurping tarhun, the industrial green tarragon drink that erupts from soda fountains in summertime. What kind of democracy would they have? Would they be more like the

Swedes or the Americans? (Tamar preferred the Swedes; Davit adored the Americans.) Would they be able to travel? What would their passports look like?

This growing excitement was quickly dispelled when Zviad Gamsakhurdia was elected president of the Republic of Georgia. While he had been a brave dissident back in the day, even surviving incarceration in a psychiatric hospital for his political views and for scrawling samizdat writings that threatened the Soviet elite, Gamsakhurdia proved not only inept in the job but a nationalist maniac. Tamar never trusted him; he made Davit cringe. The two watched as pious elderly women and brusque leather-jacketed men followed the humourless leader as though he were some kind of demigod.

Tamar watched and listened to everything. In speeches given on the parliament steps, Gamsakhurdia promised a paradise for Georgians. Tamar thought of summers in Sukhumi at Nana's family dacha. Tangerines and pomegranates hung thick on the trees, while the Black Sea shimmered in the distance. Their neighbours, the Papidoulas, were Greek. Their family had lived there for centuries. Next to them, the Abkhaz Iskanders had been there as long as anyone could remember. They had a penchant for chacha and eccentric storytelling and happened to be Muslim. Tamar never cared. Those summers in Abkhazia were happiness. The blueprint for bliss she could never return to. In part it was the richness of the diversity. They spent many a sweltering evening together, eating fresh barbequed fish, singing, and drinking.

Tamar watched and listened to everything. But what she really wanted to do was yell "Gacheret," like she did on the marshrutkas.

*Stop.*

The post-Soviet Georgian demise was both spectacular and one of a kind. For all the problems in the Baltics, Ukraine, Belarus, even Armenia, the Georgian unravelling was horrifyingly dramatic. In a manner of two years, it went from one of the richest countries in the Soviet Union to a totally failed state. Tamar watched as three wars erupted: one by the sea, one in the mountains, and one in the streets of Tbilisi. Stories of war crimes blossomed amongst neighbours like cancer. Hundreds of thousands were internally displaced. The Papidoulas fled to Greece — a country they had never been to before — on flotillas sent by the Greek government. The Abkhaz reclaimed their land and drove out the ethnic Georgians. Rivers of refugees flowed up mountains and into the cities. The Sukhumi Football Massacre, the Zugdidi Assault, rows of mines planted in fields like so many flowers. Nana's parents were amongst the internally displaced. Their beloved house, Tamar learned, had been occupied by a Muslim Abkhaz family. Apparently, the old matron loved the garden.

"At least someone's using it," said Nana, which drove Sasha nuts. Levan wanted to go there and kill the old woman and "take back what is ours." But Nana would have none of it. Tamar bristled at the violence.

It was an education in the world. In the absence of a stable government, Tbilisi street gangs assumed control over the various neighbourhoods. Like small-time mafias they controlled the local shops, construction, gas supplies, oil supplies, and farm production. Then public funds disappeared, replaced by that most insulting of euphemisms: a "secondary market."

Everyone bribed everyone: cops, professors, judges, doctors, politicians, even taxi drivers demanded a little extra on the sly. As for food, there was less on the shelves than during Soviet times. Days without electricity, heat, or running water. Then, to add a final insult to injury, former Soviet foreign minister Eduard Shevardnadze was made emergency president and tasked with leading them out of this mess.

(Though Tamar heaved a sigh of relief the day they learned Gamsakhurdia was found mysteriously dead in Samegrelo, a bullet in his head, accompanied by a suspicious suicide note.)

It was, as Davit said, an education in the world.

Nana and Sasha were clueless. Too mired in their own messed-up lives, they didn't know Tamar rarely went to class, and when she did, there was nothing to study — no books, no lessons, just a teacher who shared his cigarettes if you promised to make him laugh and handed him a few lari. They didn't know that when she went over to Mikheil's to play backgammon or chase the local street cats, his mother Manana was in the bedroom, a rubber tube around her arm and a needle in her vein. They didn't know that Manana paid for the heroin — or Subutex, or whatever she could get her hands on — by inviting UN and USAID workers over for sex at discounted rates. And though Tamar wasn't tempted by the dirt or the dope, it was an education in the world. She grew up in those years. Fast.

She watched and listened to everything, as Zaza had instructed her so many years ago. At a certain point one needs to do something. But what can a nineteen-year-old girl do?

IT IS A warm autumn day when Tamar grabs her bag, steps out onto Tabidze Street, closes her eyes, and lights a cigarette. There is something about smoking that feels honest to Tamar, a mirror of the world. Honesty calms her, though she cannot say her conversation with Nana last night made her feel at ease. What Nana told Tamar threatened to upset things in ways she is still only beginning to understand. She presses her hand against her jean jacket pocket. Still there. When she takes a back alley, a shadow leaps out of a trash bin; the noise startles her. A black cat darts past. Tamar runs into Vanushka and Irakli.

"Hey, Tamar."

She's known these two since they were all kids. They were best friends with Levan, but no matter how respectful they are — and they *always* are — it's disarming to be greeted by two twenty-one-year-old boys carrying Kalashnikovs and grenades.

"You going to school?"

"Yes," she says. "And I'm late."

They let her pass. In truth, she isn't going to school; she hasn't been to the art academy in weeks. She's going to meet Davit. They made a plan yesterday. And since the phone lines are down, she has to keep to it: 10 a.m. at Vake Park by the World War II Memorial. She turns on her heel and walks down the hill while drawing on her cigarette. She can feel Irakli and Vanushka's eyes locked on her, their male hunger unflagging. She stiffens her body, buttons up her jean jacket, and marches forward, never looking back.

IT WAS AN education in the world, and it touched all of their lives.

In 1991, following two years of anti-Soviet demonstrations and unrest, pro-independence rioters broke into the Committee for State Security building off Rustaveli Avenue. It was an emotional event, fuelled by a desire for truth and justice. (Tamar and Davit had the sense to skirt past these particular riots.) A few days after, Nana shared the news with Tamar that Zaza had been in the building when the rioters entered. Caught between the rushing crowds and KGB agents defending the last vestiges of Soviet power in Georgia, he was killed in the clash.

Tamar hadn't heard from her father in a decade. The news upset her. She wanted proof of his death, but Nana had none. There was no body. She wanted to know what Zaza was doing in that notorious building. Nana explained that the demonstrators had tried to seize classified KGB documents, that weapons had been drawn and in the melee dozens were killed.

"But what was *he* doing there?" she pleaded.

Nana shrugged. "How should I know? He's dead. Isn't that enough?"

Tamar had trouble with the story. There was no body, no grave for her to visit. Yet a month later, Nana received a death certificate in the mail. The name, Zaza Gogoladze, was written in both Georgian and Russian. He'd been given a small plot in the Vera cemetery. Sometimes Tamar would visit him. She would bring chacha and pour out several shots by his grave. She wanted to ask him questions, to learn what he had been doing at the KGB archives, to know where he'd been all those years. But the dead provide no answers. Instead, she found herself listening to the sound made by the wind as it skimmed through the parched grass.

Some months later, during the Tbilisi war, the KGB building caught fire, and hundreds of thousands of files were destroyed. Those that survived suffered significant water damage. What remained of the past was shuttled in the dead of night to a remote archive in Russia. Thousands of memory fragments disappeared.

AND THEN, LAST night, Nana presented Tamar a mysterious note and a set of blue-and-gold cufflinks. She holds both in her front jean jacket pocket, pats it every few seconds to make sure they haven't fallen out. Thanks to Nana, the cufflinks are one of the few items of her father's that she possesses. And though they are a beautiful, brightly polished gold, with deep blue lapis lazuli in the centre, they unsettle her. But it is the mysterious note accompanying them, written on a tiny scrap of paper, that rattles Tamar most of all. She committed the words to memory. Nana had presented these objects as though they held the answers to all her questions. Instead, they only created more anxiety in Tamar — the uncertainty of not knowing.

TAMAR STOMPS OUT her cigarette, her boot brushing against a crushed syringe on the road. When the marshrutka arrives, Tamar sits next to an old woman carrying a bag of apples. She bites hungrily into the hard, fleshy fruit. Tamar touches her left jean jacket pocket. They pass tanks sitting roadside, rows of people waiting. Everything looks ashen and tired. Soldiers watch over bread lines, gabbing lazily with the people waiting to be fed. When they hurtle past Vake Pool and its boarded-up doors, she feels a stab in her gut. Too expensive to maintain, the pool was emptied of its water and sits largely unused. For a time, her swim team met to practise, doing calisthenics and push-ups in the vast concrete basin. Now there are rumours some Russian oligarch has bought the place and plans to convert it into a dolphinarium. Soon it will be filled with salt water and exotic sea creatures. At least, as Nana likes to say, someone gets to use it.

DAVIT IS SEATED on a bench reading Mandelstam and drinking tea from a thermos. The world could be in flames, bombs could be falling, and Davit would still manage to drink his tea and read poetry.

"Tea?" he offers.

Tamar pulls out her pack of Viceroy Blues. "I'm good."

"You do know those things are made with genetically modified tobacco, right?" Davit says disapprovingly. "They're actually designed to make you more addicted."

Tamar joins Davit on the bench and inhales. "A perfect metaphor for capitalism."

"Give me one."

She tosses Davit the pack. The sun warms her skin, this grandmother's sun, the waning heat of autumn. Davit continues to read. Traces of eyeshadow from last night remain on his face. They were out dancing on the left bank. DJs played music on stolen stereos powered by diesel generators and battery packs. She strokes Davit's dark hair. They are inseparable. They read together, write together, dream and build worlds together. He is the only thing in her life she can count on.

"Anna Litvak."

"Who?"

"That's my biological mother's name."

"Says who?"

"Nana told me when I got home last night. She was sitting up waiting for me." Tamar hands Davit the slip of paper. It looks like it was torn from an old Soviet school notebook. Davit's eyes scan the lines: *This is not for me to give and not my story to tell. Maybe you decide to give this to her when you think the time is right.*

"Nana says it's from Anna."

"So what's the story Nana is supposed to tell you?"

Tamar shrugs. "She wouldn't say. But she gave me these, too." Tamar holds out the blue-and-gold cufflinks in her palm.

"Cufflinks?"

"They were Zaza's. I can sort of remember them, I think."

Davit grimaces. "But why now? And with no explanation? Does Nana mean to torture you?"

"No, of course not. She cried when she gave them to me. Said she didn't know what else to do." Tamar crushes one cigarette with her boot, then lights up another. "You know, it's such a cliché. Why do I even care?"

"Most people want to know where they came from."

"I'd rather know where I'm going." Tamar draws back smoke and closes her eyes. "The crazy thing is, after she drops this bomb on me, she tells me she wants me to get married. She says she even found a suitor. Maybe you're right; maybe she is trying to torture me. But don't worry, I've got a plan."

"Oh god. Not another one of your plans."

Tamar strokes Davit's nose. It's wide, and flattened near

the top where it joins his forehead. She finds comfort in his face.

"Will you marry me?" she asks.

"Excuse me?"

Tamar kneels beside the park bench. "Marry me, Davit Anoshvili. Please?"

"That's your plan?"

"We can live together, I can finish art school, you can write—"

"Why the hell would I do that?"

"Because I know you like boys, and you know if people knew this you'd probably be beaten up or killed. So really, it's the only option. Will you marry me?"

Davit groans. "Sure."


WHEN THEY WERE children, Tamar and Davit played an unusual game of house together. In the forest at the Young Pioneer camp outside the village of Bolnisi, they constructed their abode out of tree branches and bark. In those years— on Tamar's command—they built ever more elaborate versions of Amirani's forest castle, with Tamar playing the heroic Amirani and Davit taking on the role of half-goddess Qamari, who insisted on a domestic paradise of clean dishes and orderly cupboards. The year they turned eleven, how- ever, they embodied something new. In their minds, they built a forest palace made of glass: walls, roofs, floors. They invited the world to witness their transparent existence. The adults thought it endearing.

Sasha said, "Look at our young lovers. Aren't they the picture of innocence?"

It was anything but. The imagined glass house was political in its conception. Tamar and Davit played an intricate game: "The General Secretary and her First Minister." Tamar, as General Secretary, was an enlightened, female Gorbachev, with dyed pink hair. Davit was the Minister of Foreign Affairs...and Disco. They proclaimed to the world—at their imagined press conference, seated at a picnic table with a tin can microphone—that the people needed to *see* their leaders. Trust was essential for a healthy society.

"The New Communism will live in glass houses!" Tamar yelled to the bluebirds and the oak trees. "Long live Perestroika! Long live Glasnost!"

"Money, money, I want money," sang Davit.

Now, when Tamar announces to Nana and Sasha their plans for marriage, they are not surprised. After all, Davit is family.

TAMAR AND DAVIT are married at Gergeti Trinity Church by a priest named Shota who has a penchant for chacha. So their glass house becomes sanctioned by church and state. At the ceremony, Tamar is surprised by the air of solemnity that envelops the old monastery. Nana and Sasha weep. Levan claps ebulliently. Davit's parents beam proudly, and even Tamar lets herself believe in the sanctimony of their marriage. For a moment, she imagines her birth parents, Zaza and Anna, watching from the gallery. She knows nothing of their story, and it bothers her that she feels the need to render them a place in her life. Yet she lets the fantasy live. When Davit places the ring on her finger, she imagines Anna nodding approvingly, happy that her daughter has found a kind man. Everyone loves Davit.

The party is for twenty friends in a house in the Georgian countryside. It's the stuff of legend. The celebrations go on for three days. There's enough food and wine to feed half the Georgian army. Friends sing songs in spontaneous displays of love and affection. Sasha makes bold declarations to his new son over chacha and wine. A band plays and everyone dances with desperation and abandon.

At dawn, Tamar discovers Davit and Shota the priest in a corner of the country house, moving beneath bedsheets. Their ferocity astounds her. Tamar doesn't seek the love that is reckless abandon. She does not believe in its clouding and deception. But she loves Davit, and she loves that he loves the priest that married them, even if it is just for one night. In her mind she blesses them before returning to argue with her friends about art, the fate of Abkhazia, the death of capitalism, and the future of resistance in the former Soviet Empire.

# 3

*Tbilisi, Republic of Georgia*
*August 8, 1995*

A memory: When the train left the station, Tamar cried for her mother. Zaza did not know what to do, so he told his two-year-old daughter a story. "Once upon a time, there was a half-god named Amirani. He was a fire eater, a dragon slayer, and a worm swallower — a legend born in the dark forest, son of Dali, Georgian goddess of the hunt."

Tamar stopped wailing. She was lulled by Zaza's voice that seemed to merge with the rhythm of the train. A packet of white and blue Kazbek cigarettes rested on the table beside them; a silhouette of a man on a horse racing through the mountains.

Zaza continued: "Amirani had amazing strength. He could out-drink and out-eat three men. Once, when seeking treasure, he came upon a three-headed monster. Just before Amirani killed him, the monster asked the brave man not to slay the three worms that would emerge from his mouth when he died. Amirani consented, murdered the monster, and three worms came forth. But the worms turned into dragons, white, red, and black. Amirani knocked off the white and red dragons, but was gulped down by the black one. His brothers had to cut him out from the dragon's stomach to save him."

At first, the story of this mythical man who did impossible things excited her. But the more Tamar focused on the details of what Zaza said, the more she felt unnerved.

"After his rebirth, Amirani began his search for a wife," Zaza continued, leaning back in his seat and removing a cigarette from the pack. "He found Qamari, and she stunned Amirani with her beauty and intelligence. He begged her to run off with him, and she agreed, but only on the condition that he wait for her for seven days, until she had a proper wedding dress made. Then she would join him at his castle. Amirani — lovestruck — agreed. He returned to his castle in the dark forest and waited. But as skilled as he was at dragon slaying, Amirani wasn't gifted in the art of patience. Every day he was seen restlessly pacing the halls of his castle and riding along the borders of his kingdom to look for Qamari's approach. On the fourth day there was still no sign of her, so he sent armed riders to find her and bring her to him. The riders found her at the dressmaker's shop and drew their swords when she rejected their pleas for haste. Qamari grew terrified, and when Qamari's father saw this from his heavenly palace, he grew angry. He sent a storm that drowned the riders and whisked Qamari away to a foreign land."

"What happened to my mother?" Tamar finally asked.

"I couldn't wait," Zaza confessed as the train catapulted through the open Russian steppe. Then he started to sob. It scared her. "Your mother is far, far away. And she's never coming back."

FOR TAMAR, TBILISI is the most beautiful city in the world. She and Davit live at its pinnacle. Perched on a tiny cul-de-sac atop Ritsa Street, their apartment — on the second floor of an old courtyard — clings to the high cliffs of the ancient city. Coal heating, kerosene lighting, and an outhouse on a balcony shared amongst residents. A metal gate painted pastel green protects them. A lead pipe — dug into the city's natural springs — drips a constant flow of water into a large tin bucket. They chose the place because of the view, and because it was dirt cheap. It is also just up the street from the old bebia who makes Tamar's favourite food. From her tiny one-room apartment, the bebia constructs miracles of the kitchen on a single propane stove: kharcho and khajapouri, whatever she can muster up the ingredients for. She sells them for whatever you can afford.

Tamar's room is crammed with paintings and drawings made during her two years at the art academy. A series of black-and-white photographs taped to the walls — ghostly images of bodies and abandoned buildings blurring into each other, as though bodies could be abandoned, and buildings could be light. Davit has an Olivetti typewriter and a small card table he converted into a desk. A local newspaper hired him to write stories about cultural events and the budding alternative music scene. He also keeps a diary, his "practice pages," as he calls them, a weaving of political commentary with the daily struggles of the times.

They live in the harmonious zone of the creative. They

share a kitchen and a small table on the balcony where they drink coffee, smoke cigarettes, and listen to old records on an ancient phonograph Davit procured from a relative. Davit is a master collector of all things beautiful, especially music. He loves to visit the local record shop owned by a former Soviet musician named Daniel Daniel — a store famous for its jazz.

"*Jeans and Genes*," declares Davit, showing Tamar the album cover.

"What kind of name is that?"

"Riga, 1984. Recorded in one take. Totally brilliant and subversive. Want to listen?"

"Sure."

They drink cool wine, listen to Davit's cooler music. In this way they endure the summer heat. Ever since Abkhazia fell out of Georgian control, Tamar has refused to go to the sea; the war scared her away. Tensions are never far from spilling over into conflict. This means they have to endure the thick, oppressive heat of a city where temperatures often climb past forty degrees.

On sweltering August nights like these, Tamar and Davit take the steep concrete steps down to the main avenue, Rustaveli, to join the city in their evening walk. This evening Tamar has her Kyiv 88 medium format strapped around her neck. They wander past stray dogs lolling roadside; trees heavy with oranges, bent from heat.

Davit presses a wet towel to his head and complains, "Why can't we be like everyone else and go to Batumi?"

"I love the heat."

"Come on."

"Remember in *L'Étranger* when the narrator murders the

man on the beach, simply because it's too hot? That's exactly what this is like."

Davit groans and draws the wet towel over his face as they wander past mounds of stinking garbage.

"Tbilisi is not a Camus novel. And you're not a murderer, Tamar."

No, she isn't. But she understands the narrator's confusion. The boundaries that break down in heat. Overflowing thoughts and feelings we can't control. She likes to dwell in this place of unsanitary thinking. To play with our boxes marked "control" and "urge" and "this-is-who-I-am." Because it feels honest and human, and part of being human is the ability to kill.

They turn right onto Rustaveli toward the opera house and its opulent gardens. In the evenings, the people of Tbilisi come out of their houses and teem onto the wide avenue. After a day of being shuttered indoors, the night is for cooling. A sea of people eat ice cream and drink tarhun or beer. Men greet each other with a kiss on the cheek. Women hold hands and speak intimately to each other. Tamar loves the feeling of an August evening, the warm breeze through her thin linen shirt.

Though she captures it in black-and-white, Tbilisi is a city of colour. Pomegranate and fig, mandarin, alder and lime, dark men drinking thick wine, perched on footstools shouting at the sky. Women selling fruit from stalls tucked under sinking balconies: peaches and apricots, walnuts and almonds, churchkhela beaded by string, a rainbow of candied grape must. Enormous watermelons overflowing from the bins. It is so much abundance, and it is beautiful. Old men play cards, dominoes, or backgammon, fiercely throwing their pieces down on tree stumps. They smoke, yell, and gesture. Tbilisi isn't Moscow or Kyiv. Even the priests — smoking in parks, cracking jokes to those who'll listen — betray a yearning and a zest.

Tamar leads Davit past Kashueti Church and into the gardens. The city lights are out but it doesn't matter; these are concerns for winter. Fountains erupt in open spaces, lime trees heavy from summer rain. They cross Atoneli Street, slink through the underpass, and head toward the right bank. A man sits on the sidewalk, carving with a scalpel, focused on a tiny piece of wood. He is missing his left leg.

"What are you making?" asks Tamar.

"My mother's garden," says the man.

She can see it worked into the wood. Palm trees the size of matchsticks. Orange and pomegranate the length of a fingernail. A miniature wheelbarrow. A tiny toothpick of a night lamp with a swing made of string. An empty lawn chair. There is one thing missing.

"Where's your mother?" Tamar asks, noting the scene without any people.

"Sukhumi."

"Is that where you lost your leg?"

"What are you, a gossip columnist?"

"No, I go to the art academy. If I take your picture, will you let me get you something to eat?"

"I don't want your pity."

He stops to look up at her. His eyes are dark, and his hair is long, tied back in a ponytail. *He's handsome*, thinks Tamar, *and he knows it*. He resumes his work.

"I'm hungry; Davit's hungry too. We could all eat some-thing. What do you think? I like picnics. Don't you, Davit?"

"Love them."

"Then it's settled. Davit will get us the food and wine, and I'll take your picture."

"Whatever you want, kalbotono."

"My name is Tamar."

During Soviet times, everyone had a home and a job. Sure, the supermarket shelves were often bare, but this was Georgia: fresh fruit and vegetables were plentiful, as was the wine. They had never seen homeless people before the war with Abkhazia. Now they are everywhere, living beneath bridges, on main streets, and by the river. At first Tamar found it curious — she assumed it a temporary situation. But when weeks turned into months, and months into years, Tamar came to understand that homelessness is as much a conse-quence of the capitalist project as Coca-Cola or the dream vacation in Switzerland.

From the shop across the way, Davit grabs a couple loaves of bread, some salted cheese, and a plastic pop bottle filled with homemade wine. He breaks off a piece of bread and passes it to the man, who eats greedily. Tamar points her camera and asks questions. His name is Tamaz. He has a thick mous-tache and a large, hooked nose. She guesses he's around forty. Studying him through the frame of her Kyiv 88, she makes out the wooden stump where his left leg used to be. The skin is reddened and chafed at the edges. She wants to take his pic-ture because she's afraid she'll get used to it, the way she got used to the ads that now clutter every building, lamp post, and subway underpass. *Capitalism*, thinks Tamar, *is a noisy place.*

"Is this what they teach you at the academy? How to take a poor man's picture?" Tamaz asks, taking a big glug of wine before passing it to Tamar. He wipes his mouth with his sleeve.

"To be honest, they don't teach you much at all. In the life drawing class, the model has to wear underwear. Can you believe it?"

"This is Georgia. What do you expect?"

"I want to go to Berlin."

"Kalbotono, anyone can go to Berlin. Here it is actually interesting. Things are happening. Maybe not in the academy, but on the streets. These are unusual times."

"That's one way of putting it."

Tamaz sweeps back his long dark hair, silver at the edges. He continues to focus on the piece of wood. And she sees the scene emerge through his carving: a small table with a backgammon board. A tea set. It feels eerie and haunted, this miniature world without any people.

"I was at a gallery in St. Petersburg, and there was a naked man on his hands and knees, a sign hanging from his neck that said, 'Dangerous,'" Tamaz explains. "He barked at the patrons like a dog. They complained to the gallery about his behaviour. They found it 'disturbing' — especially when he ran howling out of the gallery into traffic. Only later did they learn that the barking man was the artist — and their reaction the art piece."

Tamar laughs. "Anyone can do that."

"But not everybody does. The art," says Tamaz, "is in waking people up. To make them see things."

"And what are we supposed to see?"

"An entire country in shock. Wouldn't you agree that we live in a state of trauma? Seventy years of occupation, brutality, and paranoia, followed by five years of civil war and the invasion of capitalism."

Tamar cannot disagree. "So, I should drop out of the academy and bark on the street like a dog?"

"Do what you want, kalbotono. Study art, move to Berlin, become an ecstasy addict. Personally, I'd rather try to match the outer world with what's going on inside. Become a truth teller. It's the only thing that will keep you sane."

Tamar wants to say, "But what you're making is much more beautiful and meaningful." The orange tree, the pomegranate, and the garden. His mother, dead and gone, her ghost living in these objects. Tamaz focuses on his work, carving fastidiously.

Later they stumble back to Ritsa Street, drunk.

"He liked you," says Davit.

"He liked *you*," says Tamar.

They laugh. Davit says, "Sometimes I worry that you'll never get a boyfriend if you're hanging out with me all the time."

"What do I need a boyfriend for? I've got a perfectly good husband." Tamar plants a kiss on his cheek.

Davit puts on a macho swagger. "Do you want to go for a drive, kalbotono?" he asks in the husky manner of Tamaz.

"How?"

"A little taste of freedom. Come on, I've got a surprise for you. Let's go look at some stars. It's too bright in this city."

Tamar laughs. There hasn't been electricity in days; everything is incredibly dark. But she likes the idea of leaving, even if just for a bit.

A MEMORY: It was summer, and Tamar was five years old. They were packing the family car. The plan was to go to Nana's family dacha in Sukhumi. Zaza was struggling to fit the luggage into the tiny Lada boot. As he strapped a few extra suitcases to the roof, one slipped and fell open.

"Kurva," he yelled.

Zaza was shirtless and sweating from the heat. Tamar watched rivers of black hair curve then narrow on his chest, a Kazbek cigarette dangling from his lips.

When he went to retrieve the suitcase, Tamar said, "Why don't we take the train like we did that other time?"

Zaza shot her a look that made her want to hide. "What other time?"

Her father had an uncanny ability to make her feel shame. Why didn't he want to talk about the train ride? Zaza turned his attention back to the car. Tamar kicked listlessly at a rock. When he paused for another cigarette, he would not look at her. She watched him, his right-hand clenching into a fist, open and shut.

DAVIT'S SURPRISE IS parked in an alley behind their house. An ancient green IMZ-Ural motorcycle draped in camouflage. It has to be thirty years old.

"Where the hell did you get this?" Tamar asks.

"I am a resourceful man."

Davit lights up a Viceroy Blue and dons a pair of old leather motorcycle goggles, playing the part. The engine revs. Davit looks both cool and ridiculous with his broad shoulders, lean legs, and mad eyes. She climbs onto the back and holds on tight. The motorcycle sputters and coughs. Davit guides them through the hot and stinking city. A truck hurtles toward them. She closes her eyes and buries her cheek into Davit's back. When she sits up again, they've left the city and travel under a curtain of stars. Davit rides the clutch and shifts the gears, smooth and effortless. She clings to his back as they glide through the dusty hills. Leaning into him, Tamar inhales his blue cotton shirt. She likes the smell of him, lavender and sweat. She has no idea where they are going, and she likes that too.

Later Davit cuts the engine, and they drift into tall grass where they disembark and lie watching stars falling from the sky. Her eyes sting, and her lips are coarse and sore. Davit tells her it's because of a dust storm coming from Azerbaijan. She likes that Davit knows things. There is a distance sand can travel; it moves on a curtain of wind. She wants that. To sail to parts of herself she doesn't know the names of.

"Do you see that?" Davit says, pointing to a military tower in the distance.

"South Ossetia, right?"

"Yes, Tskhinvali. It's in Russia now," he says. "After the war, Yeltsin gave the South Ossetians Russian passports. Did you know every year they move the border a few inches south?"

"No," says Tamar.

"The Russians," says Davit, "are never going away."

She can't help but agree. They share the same politics, though he retains the specifics.

"What did you think of that performance stuff Tamaz was talking about?" she asks.

"Man barking like dog? Interesting," he says, producing a

plastic bottle of wine from his bag. "But you could do better."

"You think?"

"Tamar, you're an actor. You were raised in a theatre. It's a no-brainer."

"They don't teach you that kind of stuff at the art academy."

"Who needs the art academy? Do it yourself."

Tamar looks toward South Ossetia. She believes, for a moment, she can see the border creeping toward them. *No line is permanent*, she thinks, *and no boundaries certain*.

"What am I thinking?" asks Davit as he passes her the wine.

"You're thinking, is Tamaz gay?"

"No."

"I give up then." Tamar takes a drink, then passes it back to Davit.

"I'm thinking, you're the most beautiful person I've ever met."

"You're drunk."

"You're my truth teller. And I'm yours."

"So what's the truth you feel compelled to tell me?"

Davit leans on his elbow and props his head up in the tall grass, a cigarette dangling from his lips. "Drop out of the academy. It's not like you're actually learning anything. You're always complaining: the teachers are corrupt, the school's closed half the time, and you don't have the freedom to work on what you want. Leave that place. Do something you want."

"Bark like a dog?"

"Howl at the fucking moon."

Davit barks. Tamar howls. Suddenly the lights of the border flash, on and off and on again, as though responding to their maniacal call.

"You see?" says Davit. "It's meant to be."

"Deigned by the lights of the shifting South Ossetia border."

"We can come up with something together, something amazing. You're my wife, Tamar. My truth teller."

# 4

One week after she drops out of the Tbilisi art academy, Tamar visits Nana and Sasha. When she arrives at the house, she finds Sasha standing beside a metal can that emits flames. Next to him is an enormous bag stuffed with coloured paper. He reaches inside and heaps handfuls onto the fire. It takes her a moment to realize the coloured paper is money.

"What are you doing?" she asks.

"Burning it," says Sasha.

"Are you nuts?"

"They call it 'inflation.' Three hundred percent, Tamar. In one night. This paper is worthless."

Smoke stings Tamar's eyes.

"They're saying I should have saved gold. Is a man paid in gold? What is this world? What is anything?" Sasha continues to heap his life savings onto the fire.

But instead of consoling him, Tamar grabs the bag and scoops up a handful. She watches the coloured paper disappear into the blaze. She can't quantify the calculus of sanity. For the first time she understands the story Tamaz told her about the performance artist in St. Petersburg. As she and her adoptive father dump rubles into the fire, their pace quickens, and the flames rise higher. She understands that her body, her life, embodies the politics that engulf her. And she needs to try to speak to that.

A WEEK LATER Tamar stands with Davit on the parliament steps dressed in hospital scrubs.

"This is not exactly what I had in mind when I told you to drop out of art school," says Davit.

"You don't have to be here."

"I'm not letting you do this alone."

Tamar explained her idea to Davit after her afternoon with Sasha, and he told her about a friend of his named Bruno who worked in the psychiatric ward at City Hospital Number One. Bruno, a lover of all things anarchist, was more than willing to help.

"Just remember," Bruno said, "you have to return it in one piece."

The electroconvulsive therapy machine looked like something out of a science fiction movie. The green and brown knobs, the eroded dials and corroded black tubing. It both delighted and frightened Tamar. Then Bruno wheeled out a hospital gurney, a small generator, and a plastic bag full of electrodes and a rubber bite block.

"Well," Tamar said. "I guess we're doing this."

Davit sets up the equipment at the bottom of the parliament steps. He smooths out the blue hospital sheets while Tamar connects the machine to the generator. She yanks the generator's brown frayed cord to let it warm up. Sasha, the consummate theatre performer, is their first volunteer. Tamar sets the machine at a low voltage while Davit straps electrodes to Sasha's temples. Then she shoves the rubber bite block into her adoptive father's mouth.

"What's going on?" asks an elderly man. He leans on his cane to inspect the scene.

"Shock therapy," says Tamar. "Would you like to try?"

"Is it free?" asks the old man.

"Of course."

The old man shrugs. "Why not?"

Tamar has written on a sign: "Are you depressed about the future? The past? Are you fucked up? Messed up? Maniacal? Then step right up for your free and only remedy to shock capitalism."

By noon the line is down the street. Tamar plays the psychiatric doctor; Davit the nurse. She asks the crowd, "Have you had enough of bread lines? How about shock therapy lines?"

The amount of electricity Tamar has chosen — on the advice of Bruno — is almost negligible, and an alarming number of participants ask Tamar to up the voltage.

"But why?" Tamar asks one.

"I want to feel *more*."

When the procedure is over, people laugh like they've just been on a rollercoaster.

"Why do you like doing this?" Davit asks a man wearing

an orange hat, who has come back for his third treatment of the afternoon.

"It just makes sense," says the man.

"It makes me feel less crazy," agrees the woman wearing a green peacoat who is behind him in line.

"Less crazy?" asks Tamar.

"We need this because . . . it's what we've been feeling on the inside," says the woman.

"We need it so we don't feel insane," says the man.

Someone brings over bottles of homemade wine, chacha, and fresh bread. Levan arrives with a cooler of raw meat. A fire is lit on the sidewalk and Levan makes an impromptu grill. Later, the police drop by. And while they decline the offer of free electroconvulsive therapy, they happily accept a few glasses of wine and snack on Levan's divine shashlik. The man in the orange hat purchases a dozen red roses and offers them to the woman in the green peacoat. She blushes when he proposes marriage. But the crowd won't let her say no. They erupt into applause when she agrees, and a priest appears to bind the newlyweds. People continue to line up.

That's when Tamar thinks she sees him. Standing near the back of the throng, wearing his thick beige coat. She can just make out his gold filling where the incisor used to be, and a faint scar that travels from ear to mouth.

Davit says, "Tamar?"

She comes back to herself, attaches the electrodes to the next volunteer, and flicks the switch. When she looks up, he's gone.

# 5

A memory: When she was four, Tamar wanted to know what happened to Amirani when things didn't work out with Qamari.

Zaza said, "Though Qamari gave up on him, Amirani did not stop his quest for greatness. He travelled the world, ridding it of dragons, monsters, and other wild animals. Amirani even stole fire from the gods and gave it to the people as a gift."

"But what kind of present is that?" asked Tamar.

Zaza stroked his chin thoughtfully. "It's the gift of heat and light," he said. "And knowledge."

Zaza told her that God was angered by Amirani's blind arrogance, but Amirani persisted. He wanted to challenge God, to become God himself. So, God drove a stick into the ground and challenged Amirani to pull it out. Amirani couldn't; the stick had secret roots and would not move an inch.

"You think you're so great, God?" Amirani cursed. "I don't. I think you're insecure and greedy. You're afraid to share the light."

As punishment for his arrogance, Amirani was bound to the peak of the indomitable Mount Kazbek. To taunt him, God sent a raven with a piece of bread and a glass of wine. The raven offered to feed him. This really pissed Amirani off. He threw stones at the bird. When he missed, his chains were driven more firmly into the mountain. This was a daily occurrence that lasted for eternity."

"Amirani seems to have an anger problem," said Tamar.

Zaza did not disagree.

THERE IS A line travelled by artists, by bus or old Soviet train, from Tbilisi to Moscow, Moscow to Kyiv, Kyiv to Warsaw, and Warsaw to Berlin. A three-to-four-day journey in total. Berlin is the dream: after the fall of the Wall, rent was dirt cheap and now the city crawls with artists from all over Europe. But even cheap rent in Berlin is more than a poor Georgian can afford. Besides, Tamar knows she can't leave her home. She feels connected to her city in ways difficult to explain.

It's late afternoon when she runs into Lali.

"Where are you headed?" Tamar asks.

"The Underground."

"Are you DJing tonight?"

"Yep." Lali points to the rack on her red Puch bicycle. An 8-track and a giant black battery pack are tied to the metal frame. "You coming?"

"Later. I've got to finish something first."

Tamar watches Lali cycle off. The battery pack on the bicycle's rack is ancient and corroded. Her 8-track was once state-of-the-art—in 1955. Enormous grey buttons are affixed with brown packing tape. There is a budding electronic-music scene in a city with no electricity. Everyone makes something out of what they can.

TAMAR SITS BY a window in Daniel Daniel's Record Emporium. Patiently, she waits for the drop-ins. Davit has put an ad in a local newspaper on her behalf: "Bring me your Tbilisi." It is an open invitation. A letter or a piece of clothing, a picture or a pen, a confession or an image: any personal object that contains a memory and reflects the place through time. Stories told through the things people use in their daily lives. She wants to create an archive of Tbilisi, a living library of the city. In this way, Tamar might make the present touch the past.

At noon, an old bebia brings in an envelope stuffed with photographs, a red Young Pioneer scarf, and a box full of Soviet pins. When she was a child, Tamar loved the pieces forged onto brass. Lenin, suspended on a red star, smiling at the future. Now, when she cups a space pin in her hand and looks at the blue-and-gold rocket ships and red atoms travelling in figure eights, she feels the horrible Soviet paradox: idealism cloaking murderousness.

The old bebia points to a postcard in the pile. "My grandmother was friends with him. He used to come over for tea."

On the postcard, Joseph Stalin appears in full colour standing in front of a black-and-white army. He wears a white suit with red epaulettes.

"He was a nice boy, my grandma said. He liked her soup. We're all family here in Georgia. How can you hate your family?"

Tamar knows people long for Stalin like a lost father. Who can blame them? When she stares at the postcard, Stalin's face is easily replaced with Zaza's. As the bread lines lengthen and the electricity situation worsens, people think longingly about the past. *Even the most brutal dictator glows in the light of nostalgia*, thinks Tamar.

Tamar thanks the old bebia, then puts the material away in a box, glimpsing the other contents: a watch with an image of Lake Baikal printed on the base; a menu from an old mountain restaurant; a recipe book crumbling at the edges; a hand-knitted sweater. This archive is the place where past greets present. She needs these remnants from strangers: surrogate histories to tell her who she might be. For Tamar knows so little of her own history. She collects them like beads on a string.

TAMAR DESCENDS A steep flight of stairs into a room full of bass and flashing lights. Music competes against thrumming diesel generators. Lali spins beats on a small, makeshift stage. The music thunders and swells. A film projector is set up beside her, broadcasting an image of President Shevardnadze saying "Fuck the future" in tandem with the music. Levan smokes and drinks by the bar.

Housed in a basement warehouse across the street from the grand Rustaveli state theatre, the Underground was Levan's idea. The first non-state-funded theatre in Georgia, it speaks to the '90s generation. The Underground embodies the conclusion to the Communist enterprise: for the first time in their lifetimes, artists can make what they want. And while the theatrical choices made by Levan veer toward the conservative, he welcomes a subversive scene. His theatre bar is often occupied by a wild mix of people, raucous gatherings going on all night. "Freedom" is a word Levan likes to use to describe his theatre. But Tamar understands that freedom is a complicated thing.

When Levan first opened the Underground, Tamar and Davit were immediately drawn to it. While the outside world spiralled from one disaster to another, the Underground was their sanctuary. She loved the motley crew, the debauchery, the I-don't-give-a-fuck attitude that permeated everything. *We have nothing*, Tamar thought, *so we have nothing to lose*.

In the West they call it "punk," though nobody here bothers with such labels. People make their own clothing, wild constructions of recycled Young Pioneer outfits with busted-up road tires and Turkish denim. A duo calling themselves Stalin's Daughter perform with an instrument that combines a guitar with cello — they dub the thrashing instrument a "gello." Actors make soup on a one-burner stove for strangers. And while the soup verges on the watery, and the homemade booze toward the blinding, it nourishes those gathered.

Actors and artists, musicians and dancers, drug dealers and drinkers, poets and gamblers, ex-pats and locals, academics in suits and mercenaries in army camouflage. Levan brings in people from all walks of life. He has his hands in everything. And while the Underground overhead is low — rent is next to nothing and nobody bothers paying the electricity bills — the theatre tickets are virtually free. Tamar often wonders where the money comes from, how the place survives. *Freedom*, she thinks, *is a complicated thing*.

TAMAR SIPS HER beer, leans against the wall, and watches a group of men with Kalashnikovs strapped to their shoulders. In the chaos of the post-Communist '90s, this is how business is often conducted in Tbilisi. It's how neighbourhoods are protected and rivalries negotiated. Every man has a gun.

One man stands out to her from the crowd. With his shock of white hair shooting up the centre of his head, flanked by sides of deep black, Tamar cannot take her eyes off him. She watches him grab two warm Argo beers from the bar, his hands thick around their necks. To her surprise, he saunters over and hands her one.

"Hi, Tamar. My name is Skunk. I knew your father, Zaza."

She swallows hard. Skunk sips his beer.

"He went to school with my father in Moscow. Aslan Varayev. They were good friends. I used to sit in your father's lap. He used to bring me candies. Mishka Kosolapy, Clumsy Bears. We're practically related, you and me."

Tamar feels her chest tighten as Skunk adjusts the gun on his shoulder and breaks into a warm smile. Then he reaches into his vest pocket and pulls out a photograph. She recognizes the moment immediately: it's her and Zaza packing up the Lada as they prepare to go on vacation.

"Where did you get this?" she asks.

"I can tell you some stories."

She hesitates.

"Keep the picture. It's a present." Skunk hands it to her. "It's a question for moral philosophers. A human question.

Are we born evil, or do we become that way because of circumstance?"

"What are you talking about?"

"Take Stalin. If he'd succeeded in the seminary and become a priest, would we have had the purges?"

"All men have the capacity for good and evil."

"Yes," says Skunk. "I agree. But can evil be averted?"

"Probably not."

"Have you ever seen the dead come back to life?"

"What does that mean?"

"Miracles, Tamar. I can show you," he says, and he hands her a business card. "Call me when you're ready to talk about Zaza."

He turns on his heel and saunters back toward his buddies. Tamar's heart races. As if sensing her need, Davit appears next to her.

"You look like you just saw a ghost," he says.

"That man..." Tamar says. But when she turns to point, Skunk is no longer there. She looks at the picture of her and Zaza and feels her face burn. Davit buys her one beer, then another. She drinks heavy and fast, needing to cool the heat.

IT IS WELL past midnight when Levan joins her. He hugs Tamar, and she can smell the sweat of too many drunken nights on his skin. He pours two drinks and raises a toast.

"We do not have the same parents, and yet you are my sister," announces Levan the sentimental drunk. "I love you, Tamar."

"Who was that Skunk guy? Do you do business together?" she asks.

Levan waves off the question. "Would you like to see my Shishiga?"

"What are you talking about, moron?"

"My Swamp Goddess. My power machine. I love you, Tamar." And he holds her cheeks in his hands. "Let's go for a drive."

Ten minutes later Levan is hoisting her up over wheels high above her head. It is a GAZ-66 4x4, green military-issued.

"Where did you get this?" she asks as Levan lets the heavy engine roar.

"Biz-nizz," he says in heavily accented Russian, then laughs.

He accelerates with the experience of a military man — even though he hasn't fought a day in his life. She's impressed by the way he handles the truck, taking corners with confidence. They disappear beyond the city limits. Yet there's something in his demeanour tonight that frightens her.

"Where are we going?" Tamar asks.

"You have to know everything," he slurs.

"You're not kidnapping me, are you?"

"That's right, Tamar. I'm going to sell you to Skunk for a thousand donkeys. Skunk-head! How many asses for my beautiful seeeee-ster?"

He cackles drunkenly. The truck handles the road, unaffected by sweeping winds. Tamar studies his face. There is a scar on his left cheek from a knife fight. She knows so little about him.

They are a good hundred kilometres west of Tbilisi when Tamar sees the airfield. It is bleak, cold, concrete. A row of MiG airplanes stand quiet and ominous, their green metallic bodies sharp against the night sky. Levan drives onto the base and up to the barracks, backing in so the rear of the truck faces the door. He turns off the vehicle and says, "We're here."

Two men in military fatigues greet him with a hug and an envelope stuffed full of cash. They laugh and a bottle comes out.

"Tamar," says Levan. "Come and meet my friends. The patrons of the Underground Theatre."

One of the men passes her the bottle, shifting from boisterous to chivalrous. He bows and offers her the moonshine as though it were champagne, not the homemade chacha that burns. She takes a sip and coughs. Levan opens the barracks door with a sweeping, theatrical gesture. It reveals a sea of gleaming electric light.

"Guns?" asks Tamar.

"Kalashnikovs," says Levan, grinning. He passes her one. Its weight surprises her. When she grabs the curved cartridge, it falls to the floor.

"Not like that, Tamar." He picks up the cartridge and shows her how to hold it, carefully, tenderly, the way you might handle a child.

"Am I supposed to be impressed?"

Levan shrugs.

Tamar passes the Kalashnikov between her hands while the men load the vehicle. Fifty feet back a black Volga idles. The back window slides down. She recognizes the ridiculous hair. Skunk nods at her. The loud revving of the truck filled with semi-automatics — dozens of them, pyramids of firepower — is unnerving. So is Skunk. He waves his hand and the tinted window rises slowly, ominously, like a warning.

# 6

HAPPINESS IS A WARM GUN

A film by TAMAR TUMANISHVILI
Directed by DAVIT ANOSHVILI

SCENE 1
EXT. GEORGIAN NATIONAL BANK—TBILISI—11:00 AM

[TAMAR addresses a video camera, handheld.]

TAMAR

Irakli and Vanushka had been best
friends since they were kids. They did
everything together. But when Irakli
found out Vanushka was sleeping with his
girlfriend, Irakli challenged Vanushka
to a duel. Irakli was thinking fists;
Vanushka showed up with a knife. Irakli
lost the girl — and took a knife gash

across the face. So one day Irakli
followed the young lovers to the Tbilisi
sea. He waited until they were asleep in
each other's arms, then he shot them in
the head and the heart. That's justice
in Georgia. The boys and their guns.

SCENE 2
INT. GEORGIAN NATIONAL BANK—11:05 AM

[The video is black and white, silent, and
somewhat out of focus. From time to time the
frame jumps. Time and date in the bottom
right-hand corner, camera frozen in place.]

[A long counter separates a bank teller from
her client. Customers wait patiently in a long
queue. Enter TAMAR wearing a blonde wig and
sunglasses. SHE walks to the security camera
and addresses it].

                    TAMAR
         Good morning, Tbilisi.

[It happens quickly. TAMAR approaches TELLER,
pulls out a gun from her purse, and shoots at
the ceiling. TELLER raises her hands. PATRONS
are scared. TAMAR points her gun.]

                    TAMAR
        Fill the bag. Please.


[TAMAR points the gun at the ceiling and
fires a second time. If you look closely you
will notice no evidence of a bullet entering
the ceiling—no sprinkling of dust, no gaping
hole, nothing. TAMAR smiles at TELLER and
grabs the bag of cash.]


                    TAMAR
        Uhm, have a really nice day.


[TAMAR walks toward the security camera.
TAMAR smiles, points, and shoots. The screen
cuts to black.]

*Tbilisi, Republic of Georgia*
*October 14–31, 1997*

When the video ends, the Underground crowd erupts. Raucous beats spin from the hands of an inspired Lali, a bass that thrums through everything. Everyone dances. Then the electricity cuts out, and with it comes darkness and a sudden silence. It is stunningly dramatic. Someone lights a candle. Then another. Soon the Underground glows with a soft light. Levan gathers several actors in a circle. They huddle, press their heads against each other and sing a song about two siblings defending their village against marauding invaders. It is a song about martyrdom, bravery, and loss. Soon everyone is in tears. Women hand out cups of chacha, pails of beer. Tamar realizes everyone is looking at her.

Davit says, "Say something."

"About what?"

"Your video, dumbass."

She made the video not long after the night she met Skunk. Their conversation had haunted her. His atmosphere of violence, and whatever secrets he harboured. She also felt anxiety about the weapons. It upset her that Levan dealt in them. In recent months, she'd seen the violence worsen in Tbilisi: friends getting shot, gangs turning on each other. Nobody seemed to communicate with words anymore. One morning she woke up and decided: enough is enough. She went to the Underground, borrowed a fake gun from the prop shop, and headed to the bank with Davit and a video camera. And while robbing a bank with a stage prop might seem ridiculous and futile, what else could she do?

"Sometimes you get tired of your own government ripping you off," Tamar says to the Underground crowd. "Sometimes you get tired of people who eat like kings while you freeze your ass off. You get tired of the politicians in their limousines with their fat bank accounts stuffed with money they took from you. What is the crime of robbing a bank compared to running one? When a government steals from its own people, you think maybe things could be different."

Tamar produces the bag of stolen cash from her knapsack.

"Who's hungry?" Tamar asks. "Who needs a sweater? Who would like to buy a generator? Please, help yourselves. Leave enough for the next person."

She passes the bag into the crowd. At first everyone thinks it's a joke. But when someone drunkenly pulls out a handful of bills, people gasp. Then someone laughs; the mood turns ebullient. People throw money into the air like confetti. Even Levan gets in on the action, planting a kiss on Tamar's cheek and promising free chacha for all. The electricity kicks back in, the lights come on, and the music resumes. An older woman with long grey hair, wearing a grey cardigan, approaches Tamar.

"My name is Rachel Grabinsky. I've been wanting to meet you for a long time, Tamar. Can I buy you a drink?"

RACHEL SPEAKS RUSSIAN with an accent and many English words mixed in. Though she can't be more than five foot three, Tamar immediately feels intimidated in her presence. In part it's her English. For Tamar, English is whatever she's learned from American pop songs. She might not be fluent, but she knows the words to "Like a Virgin" backward and forward.

Rachel hands her a beer and says, "I want to help you with your work."

"What work?"

"I work for an NGO called Freedom Ink. I want you to make more videos like this one today of the bank robbery. We'll fund you."

"You want to pay me to make performance video art?"

"Yes."

"Why? Nobody gives a shit about this."

"These people do," Rachel says, pointing at the crowd passing around the bag of money.

"That's because I'm giving away free money."

"You risked your life to get it."

"So?"

"Nothing is free, my dear. Everything has a price."

Tamar sips her beer. Rachel has a pen clipped to the pocket of her grey cotton shirt. Her hair is dishevelled, like she just woke up. Her cardigan is riddled with holes. Yet she wears the most stunning pair of jeans. Perfectly curved at the hip, a denim bright and blue.

She continues, "What you're doing is a precise enactment of my principles of non-violent resistance."

"What are you talking about?"

"Tamar, you and I are going to topple totalitarianism in the former Soviet Union and set up a real democracy. Together."

Tamar laughs. But Rachel is dead serious.

"With performance art videos?"

"Why not?"

IN THE WEEKS that follow, Tamar and Rachel spend all their time together. They wander through the Dezerter Bazaar, a former railway station converted into a covered market. Tamar likes to get spices here from an Egyptian merchant. It is chaotic and colourful, with giant watermelons sliced open with machetes.

In addition to working for Freedom Ink, Rachel is an academic and writer based in Toronto. She's here in Tbilisi doing scholarly research on post-Soviet countries. Rachel informs Tamar she intends to write about her performance art in a new book about social activism in the former Communist bloc. Tamar is flattered, though uncertain she is deserving of the attention. Nor is she a fan of the term "social activism." To her ears, it sounds clinical and removed, like a diagnosis at a doctor's office.

Yet she spends days on end with Rachel, whose ambition she finds seductive. When Rachel tells Tamar about her plans to set up an office in Tbilisi for Georgian political activists, she makes it sound like the most important thing in the world. Maybe it is. By the end of the conversation, Tamar wants to join her. Rachel's conviction is both infectious and alluring.

For all her talk of mobilization and work, Rachel is also interested in having a good time. Tonight, Davit, Rachel, and Tamar are at the ex-pat Beatles bar on Rustaveli. With black-and-white photographs of the Fab Four looking down at them, they gorge on vodka, pickles, and dumplings.

"Tamar tells me you're an investigative journalist," says Rachel, sucking the ice cubes in her drink.

"He's going to be the next Anna Politkovskaya," Tamar says on Davit's behalf.

"You like digging up the truth?" says Rachel.

Davit shrugs. "I have a knack for finding out things people don't want me to know."

"That's an excellent quality."

"Is it? Seems a lot of trouble for not much pay."

"You can't put a price on a vocation," says Rachel, clinking her glass against his.

"Well," says Tamar tauntingly, "I asked Davit if he could dig up some shit on my father. But he hasn't come up with anything interesting yet."

"Do you really want to know what he was like?" Rachel asks.

Tamar says, "Of course."

"I don't think she does." Davit whispers conspiratorially to Rachel. "The thing about digging is you only ever find out the worst about people. It's like the evening news. Nobody's interested in reporting on happiness. It's incredibly boring."

Tamar laughs, pleasantly drunk. Rachel silently downs her drink then orders another. "A Hard Day's Night" plays on the speakers and Rachel jumps up. She shimmies onto the dance floor, closes her eyes, and gets lost in the lights. When she shakes out her grey hair, Davit and Tamar join her. Paul and John scream, Rachel screams too. Tamar and Davit follow her lead, dancing and screaming together, three maniacal children having the time of their lives.

SOME DAYS LATER Tamar and Rachel are sitting on stacked wooden crates by the ground-floor window of the bebia's house on Ritsa Street. The bebia cooks on her single propane tank. While stray dogs eye them hungrily, Rachel and Tamar eat food passed through the sliding window on small plastic plates. Rachel devours fried eggplant, washing it down with chacha and a Viceroy cigarette. It isn't yet eleven in the morning and they are getting drunk.

Tamar asks questions about where Rachel comes from. Rachel says she was born to a Jewish family in Vilnius, Lithuania, her father a professor and her mother a teacher. She emigrated to Canada when she was in her twenties.

"I didn't know you were Jewish," says Tamar.

"I'm not a believer. But it clings to me, in spite of things. I'll cook for you some time. I make a kickass chicken soup and my matzo balls are to die for."

"Matzo balls?"

"Leaden gluten. Kosher-style constipation. It's hard to get rid of the past."

Tamar wants to know how she left the Soviet Union. But Rachel is vague about details, elusive with dates. She tells Tamar that, through a series of deft bureaucratic manoeuvres, including a long-lost aunt in Wiarton, Ontario, who volunteered to adopt her, she was able to move to Canada in the '70s.

Rachel prefers to tell stories of how she taught herself English when she first arrived in Toronto. "I learned it in public libraries, from fashion magazines, and pointing at items on restaurant menus," she says. She takes pride in how hard she worked to get into an English-speaking university, to be granted a Ph.D. in a language she'd only just learned. She won awards, accolades, and eventually a job: full professorship in the Department of Political Science at the University of Toronto. "It's not easy when you're a woman," says Rachel, "let alone a foreigner."

"So why are you here in Georgia?" Tamar asks. "Why not Lithuania? What does this country mean to you?"

"Something special is going on here with your generation. You're the hope for change."

"What are we changing?"

Rachel butts out her cigarette with a fierceness that scares Tamar.

"Here's the question: can you have a real democracy in the former Soviet Union? One without corruption, bribery, state violence, and secrets?"

Tamar laughs. "Sure, when cows fly."

"Democracy, religious freedom, gender equality, gay rights. One day, in countries like Georgia, Ukraine, Belarus, and Russia, there'll be real elections because of people like you."

Tamar says nothing. It's hard to believe such changes are possible.

Rachel unnerves her. It isn't just Rachel's confidence and vision, but the circumstances of her fate. What would Tamar's life have been like if she'd gone away? She tries to imagine a professorship at a prestigious university in North America, an arts residency in France or Germany. She daydreams a house, stained wood floors and rooms full of too many books, art openings and conversations without worrying about the lights going out. She wonders what a pair of American blue jeans might feel like, denim that doesn't fray after three washes, zippers that don't snap and break after a month.

THE NEXT TIME they meet, Rachel has her own questions for Tamar. They're at Daniel Daniel's Record Emporium, a favourite of Rachel and many an ex-pat's. As they drink coffee and listen to jazz, Lali — Basement DJ by night and record store barista by day — brings them a mixed plate of cakes.

"We didn't order these," says Tamar.

"They're on the house," says Lali, nodding over her shoulder. "The owner would like you to have them."

A funny bearded man waves at them and smiles. Of course they're on the house. Rachel seems to be friends with everybody. Tamar dips her fork into something that resembles baklava.

"Why don't you have a boyfriend?" Rachel asks.

"I have Davit."

Rachel shoos away her words. "What about love?"

"I love Davit. Just because we don't sleep together doesn't mean we aren't soulmates."

Rachel lights up a cigarette and grimaces. "You're just like me. You know what the problem with men is?"

"No."

"They're men."

Tamar laughs.

"I can't stand marriage. Or love for that matter. But I have a son," says Rachel. "His name is Joseph. He's a few years younger than you."

"Oh." Tamar puts down her fork then slurps black coffee.

"You're wondering why I never mentioned him," says Rachel, lighting up two cigarettes, one of which she hands to Tamar. "We're complete opposites. He wants to get an MBA. Finance, he believes, is his calling."

Tamar laughs. "He's rebelling against you."

Rachel frowns. "In Toronto, all anyone cares about is real estate and hedge funds. Joseph is no exception. He's a product of his environment."

"What are hedge funds?"

"Who cares? My point is Joseph's needy."

"What does he need?"

"Love. Attention. Affirmation."

"Sounds like a real monster."

Rachel draws on her cigarette and eyes Tamar through the smoke.

"Someone once gave me some sage advice: 'Life is messy.' Joseph has trouble with the mess. But you don't. I like that about you."

"Circumstance," says Tamar, "breeds self-reliance."

Rachel slides a brown paper bag across the table. She gestures for Tamar to look inside. Tamar opens the bag to find Rachel's blue Wrangler jeans.

"I have to go home tomorrow, but I wanted to say how nice it has been getting to know you, Tamar."

"Are you giving these to me?"

"Of course."

"I don't know what to say."

"Tell me you'll enjoy wearing them. I'll be back in a few months..." Rachel hesitates. "Do you want to come to Canada?"

"And do what?"

"I could get you a fellowship at the university. You could live with me."

Tamar laughs. But Rachel is dead serious.

"I'll think about it," she says.

"Leaving home is the most difficult thing. When I was a little older than you, I boarded a plane for Vienna. I felt like everything had been stolen from me. But there is so much ahead that we cannot see. It's okay to be afraid."

After coffee and cake, they go for a walk to the Dry Bridge Market. Rachel wants to get Joseph some tourist trinkets. She chooses wool slippers, a snow globe, and a postcard. Suddenly, Rachel's demeanour changes. Her face becomes haggard and pale, her legs lag. As they stand on Baratashvili Bridge, the Mtkvari River flows beneath them. Rachel puts her head on Tamar's shoulder. It surprises Tamar, but she settles into it, and lets herself feel the warmth of this stranger's body.

# 7

*Bolnisi, Republic of Georgia*
*October 19, 1999*

The chartered bus stops outside the Poladauri railway station on the edge of Bolnisi, a small town two hours southwest of Tbilisi. Tamar stares idly out the window. Rachel gets off the bus with Eugene from Minsk and Lena from Riga. Tamar watches Rachel haggle with the kiosk seller for Viceroys and other essentials — homemade booze in old plastic Pepsi bottles, and paprika-flavoured potato chips. Rachel is addicted to paprika-flavoured potato chips.

In this nothing village in the flatlands, on the edge of the grassy pastoral, Tamar watches the elderly loiter outside the station. Like slow animals rising from the dust, they sway in front of kiosks with their plastic bags filled with fresh dill and parsley, wild boletus mushrooms picked from the forest, and black hand-knitted socks. Everything is homemade, do-it-yourself, and for sale. Behind them stands a mammoth supermarket, its doors and windows boarded up.

"What do you think, Davit?" she asks. "Should we get a farm, grow our own vegetables and make wine?"

"Hazelnuts," says Davit, looking up from his notebook. "The future is in hazelnuts. We'll sell them to Nutella for a fortune."

"How do you grow a hazelnut?"

"I don't have a clue."

"I heard the craziest thing the other day. Americans are coming to Tbilisi to pay someone to knock on their hotel door in the middle of the night, arrest them, and lead them to a former KGB prison for interrogation."

"They call it 'dark tourism.'"

"Why would anyone want to do that?"

"These days the fucked-up is exotic and highly marketable, Tamar. You see? Our futures are bright after all."

Tamar grimaces as she lights a cigarette. Davit scribbles in his blue notebook. A year ago, *Der Spiegel* published a feature of his entitled "In a Land without Dogs the Cats Learn to Bark." Tamar never uses this old, well-worn phrase; for her, it reeks of the traditional and conservative. But, in taking a common Georgian proverb, Davit used it to make a scathing critique of the ineptitude of Georgian politicians' recent past. Tamar can't help but agree that it applies perfectly to the dramatic collapse of her country; the unqualified and corrupt leaders who stepped in after the fall of Communism and promised hope and freedom, and never delivered. Who spiralled an entire nation into chaos, violence, and poverty. Needless to say, no one local would dare publish the piece.

For Davit, the *Der Spiegel* article was the biggest success in his young journalistic career. In part, it was timing.

When he wrote it a year ago, Georgia was about to re-enter the Western news cycle thanks to a proposed oil pipeline that would run from Baku, Azerbaijan, through Tbilisi and on to Ceyhan, a port city in Turkey. It would be the longest pipeline in the world, funded by BP and the American government: oil, straight from the Caspian Sea, without Russia or Iran to contend with. Davit had anticipated the significance of this project of Western arrogance and greed. And he was right. Now, posters of James Baker and Bill Clinton are everywhere in Tbilisi — American heroes meant to save the Georgian people from financial ruin. In a land without dogs, indeed.

For the feature, Davit interviewed a group of Georgian farmers kicked off their land without compensation. While BP hired cheap Georgian and Armenian labourers, Russia threatened the pipeline by flying MiGs over South Ossetia, tempting the shifting borderline with pretty displays of the aerial. It was bad for business and frightened prospective investors, but now Davit's career is taking off because of it.

So is Tamar's. In the two years since she'd met Rachel, Tamar had been contacted by various Western European galleries. She's been offered residencies in Stuttgart and Berlin, grants from Bosch and Siemens, and financial assistance from Freedom Ink. And there are rumours she'll be asked to represent Georgia at the Venice Biennale. *Davit is right*, she thinks. *The fucked-up is exotic and marketable these days.*

But Tamar hesitates in the face of this newfound success. At an opening at the K20 in Düsseldorf six months ago, she felt out of place. As her bank robbery video played, projected on a twenty-foot space on a sterile white wall, patrons flitted through the files of her project, *This Is Your Tbilisi*. She cringed as they smiled smugly at photos of Stalin drinking tea as a youth in Gori, fingered pins displaying Soviet space propaganda. Taken out of context, the objects felt frivolous. The art world — the privileged rich in their colourful suits and thick-framed glasses drinking chilled dry Riesling — clapped at the speeches given by the gallery's curators. They explained the importance of Tamar's work, though the work itself was quickly forgotten. After some polite applause and even politer conversation, people's attention turned to the cheese trays. Most notable, Tamar learned, was a soft cheese from Strasbourg covered in the cinders of volcanic ash. Tamar couldn't blame them. The cheese was delicious.

THE DOORS CLOSE as they accelerate on broken streets. Within minutes they leave the village limits and begin travelling through the countryside. It's not a bad plan to move to the country with Davit. They could buy land for next to nothing in Mtskheta. He could write and she could tend to the garden and learn how to grow hazelnuts. It comforts her, this fantasy.

As they enter the forest, Tamar considers another, more audacious, plan. Rachel has secured a one-year visiting contract for her at the University of Toronto, to teach a course in performance art and political activism. But Tamar isn't sure it's the right move. The problem, she understands, is that she doesn't trust Rachel's generosity. She imagines arriving in Toronto and not finding her at home. She imagines a city of tall skyscrapers covered in snow. She imagines not understanding the language, the customs, or the people.

She imagines abandonment, disappointment, and failure. And she imagines returning to Tbilisi with her tail between her legs.

TAMAR WATCHES RACHEL argue with Goran, a long-haired, keffiyeh-wearing twentysomething from Belgrade. They are seated in the front row of the chartered bus, discussing the political situation in his hometown.

"Do you know what I really wish for?" Rachel asks.

"No," replies Goran.

"For someone to slice Milošević's balls off. Do you think you could manage that for me?"

Rachel eyes him through thick rings of smoke. She may be pushing fifty, but her energy is infectious — and flirtatious. In part, it is the way she follows through on an argument, punctuating her points, as though the air were paper and her finger a pen. Tamar loves the way Rachel lets down her thick grey hair without inhibition, though sometimes she wonders how much of it is for show. This idea she promotes — her "brand," as they say in America — where she purports never to cover up the truth.

The bus pulls into the former Young Pioneer camp. The sight of brown pointed roofs on yellowing houses with tin metal awnings brings back a flood of memories. Tamar remembers tying her red Young Pioneer scarf around her neck, loose at the ends, flaps assailing her cheeks. She remembers a blue skirt and white starched shirts, white socks she tried to pull up to her knees. *Communism*, she thinks, *is many things*. The strictness of the Young Pioneer outfit was an order she could believe in.

Tamar hadn't wanted to come on this chartered trip. But when Davit heard about a gathering for social activists from former Soviet countries, to share ideas and strategies for future social and political change, he insisted they attend.

"I'd love to write about it," he said.

And then Rachel told them about the pro-democracy workshops. "You won't want to miss the lessons in non-violent resistance, Tamar," she said with a wink.

TAMAR FEELS THE disconnect between past and present. She examines the familiar field with fading blue swings and metal slides where she and Davit first built their transparent palace. How the moss and grass that once clung to their feet is now parched dirt and rubble. The transparent palace — and the hope for a kinder, more honest Communism — is an architecture that no longer exists.

The bus stops outside the former Young Pioneer barracks. There are four houses in total. Rachel announces in English: "It is wonderful to see all of your beautiful faces. Over the next few days, we will work, eat, and sleep together. We will share our experiences, ideas, and strategies for the future. Find yourself a bed, get to know someone you haven't already met. Dinner's at six. We have an exciting few days ahead of us."

As she walks into Bunker #2, Tamar is greeted by a waft of old wood, wet cross beams, and mildew. Tamar flings her rucksack onto a top bunk, spilling out clothes and books. The Wrangler jeans, given to her by Rachel two years ago, remain unworn. She has not felt comfortable putting them on. They belong to a Tamar she wishes she could be. *Maybe that's why I'm hesitating about Toronto*, she thinks.

There are three books in her backpack, all written by Rachel. She's read them all. The first two are political memoirs from the '80s: *Lot's Wife: How I Learned to Hate Nostalgia* and *The Haunting: Stories from a Soviet Refusnik*. Turning the books over, Tamar scans the blurbs and reviews. Hailed by the *New York Times* as "the lost kin of Sontag" and "a child of Hannah Arendt and Ernesto Laclau," the memoirs hold the panache of the political and personal. She enjoyed reading them, but it is Rachel's books written since the fall of Communism that Tamar is most attracted to. These books veer away from literature toward the practical: political tricks and guidelines for social activists.

Her latest, *How to Get Rid of a Dictatorship: A Guide for Non-Violent Resistance*, published just last year, includes chapters on "How to Use the Media to Gain Attention and Convey Your Message"; "Love Your Irony: The Importance of Humor and Other Subversive Tactics of the Democracy Revolution"; "Turning David into Goliath: How to Exaggerate the Size of Your Small Movement (and Make Them Believe it)"; "Truncheon Luncheon: Why You Want the Police to Hit You and Why You Shouldn't Hit Back"; "Know Thy Law: Advice for Creating New Legal Defense Institutions"; and "Think Democratically, Act like a Fascist."

Tamar is struck by the central premise of the book: that without the consent of the people, the dictator holds no power. At first the argument offended her; it felt like blaming ordinary citizens for the crimes of the powerful. Yet the more she read, the more she understood that Rachel wasn't casting blame, but making a call for mobilization. It was a rule book for how to fight political apathy. In this sense,

Tamar was grateful for Rachel's lessons. She wanted to help people take control of their lives.

For Tamar, *How to Get Rid of a Dictatorship* is a book about belief in government, institutions, and the notion that democracy can create a more equitable civil society. It's a radical yet practical concept. Rachel writes that she hopes to help create "a kinder and more honest world." Tamar feels drawn to this idea, but she doesn't know what any of it looks like. How do you get rid of generations of corruption through humour? How do you teach a government to care for its citizens through graffiti art? And how do a nation's citizens learn to trust a government after decades of abuse?

TAMAR PUTS ON the Wranglers. The jeans cling to her waist and the zipper works effortlessly. She hides the books under her pillow and joins the group assembled by the firepit. A bonfire rages under the cool autumn sky. Tables laden with food are there for the picking. A dozen of the thirty-odd activists are Georgian. Some she knows from art school, like Lali and Mariam, but others she is meeting for the first time, like the two theatre directors from Belarus and the queer activist from Warsaw who edits a zine dedicated to the Soviet homoerotic. There are street activists from Belgrade, a poet from Vilnius, and an anarchist from Riga. A couple from Lviv, Galyna and Andriy, have studied Yiddish and converted to Judaism, arguing that any true Eastern European emergence means embracing the past.

Tamar feels shy in this company of mostly strangers. Everyone seems more certain, more virtuous, and more experienced than her. She doesn't have answers for how to overthrow a government. And she hasn't really participated in more than a couple of demonstrations. She feels out of place and over her head, so she watches and listens. What she hears is both hard to trust and something she wants to believe in: change.

Goran, the activist from Belgrade, strums a Bob Dylan song on a guitar while Rachel hands out bowls of soup. Fresh bread still hot from the bakery in Bolnisi warms Tamar's stomach. Davit sidles up next to her and they sit together by the fire.

"Having a good time?" he asks.

"Sort of. You?"

Davit leans in close to whisper, "Sometimes I wonder who Rachel really is."

"Just read her books. It's all there."

"Just because you tell a story doesn't mean it's true."

Tamar shrugs and takes a bite of the bread. "Who knows who anyone really is? I like her."

"We all love Rachel." Davit smiles. "Nice jeans by the way."

"Thanks."

"Will you go to Toronto with her?"

"I'm not sure." Tamar doesn't say that, when she leaves Georgia, she might not return. "I'd miss you."

"You'll always be my wife." He kisses her on the cheek. "So, remember how you once asked me to look into your father, Zaza?"

"Yes..." Tamar takes a deep breath. "What did you find out?"

"Nothing yet, but I might have a lead. I wanted to know if you still want me to pursue it."

"Of course."

"Good." Davit says, and they both relax. "Don't worry, Tamar. Everything is fine."

She wonders what Davit will discover. *Nothing good*, she thinks, *can come of the truth*. But she puts the thought out of her head. It's nice to be back at the Young Pioneer camp with him. The fire rages, and the cool October night turns festive. She lets herself get caught up in the spirit of the gathering. She drinks warm beer and traces the lines of the soft denim jeans Rachel gave her. Maybe Davit's right. Maybe Canada will be okay. Tamar falls asleep this way by the fire, only occasionally jolting to wakefulness.

# 8

*Tbilisi, Republic of Georgia*
*November 10–11, 2000*

In the months following the pro-democracy workshops, Tamar comes to understand that Rachel had access to even more money than she initially let on. She handed Tamar envelopes from Freedom Ink stuffed with American dollars, which Tamar used to buy better equipment for her videos. The money flowed freely. Rachel rented an office in the Tbilisi city centre, filling it with half a dozen computers, a photo-copier, a fax machine, office supplies, and a diesel generator. Some of the Georgians who had attended the workshops in Bolnisi gathered here to work. There were twice-weekly meetings where they went over strategies for mobilizing the Georgian public.

The pro-democracy workshops in Bolnisi proved to be an important catalyst for the movement. In Serbia, after another fixed election and the murder of political opponents, peace-ful protests began in Belgrade under the banner "Gotov je"

("He's finished"). Slobodan Milošević's days were numbered. Led by youth like Goran, the Serbian political group Otpor (Serbian for "Resistance") employed tactics outlined in Rachel's book. Throughout Belgrade, their graffiti appeared on walls: a black stencil of a fist. The demonstrations swelled, along with political actions and sardonic performances mocking the old men clinging to power. It was a non-violent revolution that won over the hearts of people — even the military and police put aside their weapons and joined the demonstrations. They called it the Bulldozer Revolution, after a worker named Joe fired up his wheel loader and charged the building that housed the state-run media company controlled by Milošević.

When the president was finally removed from office in October 2000, it was a moment of inspiration for the entire movement. Tamar cheered along with others from the Tbilisi Freedom Ink offices when she heard the news on the shortwave radio. More importantly, it was proof that Rachel's non-violent methods actually worked, and young people like Goran were shown to be capable leaders. Tamar kept a black-and-white photo of Rachel and Goran on the parliament steps, their fists clenched in the air, next to her bed.

After the success in Belgrade, Rachel returned to Tbilisi to lead a workshop. Inspired by Otpor, they began calling themselves Kmara (Georgian for "Enough"). Freedom Ink purchased a few thousand cans of spray paint, hundreds of video tapes, and several dozen large-screen TVs and projectors. Graffiti actions were carried out around the city: six people spray-painted the word "Kmara" ten thousand times, creating the illusion of a mass movement. Tamar, Lali, and

Mariam handed out pamphlets to students at Tbilisi State University and organized a march and student elections. Davit, now a reporter at the only independent news station in Georgia, Kartli 2, did a feature on the demonstrations. That October, thousands of students marched through the city streets demanding an end to bribery and corruption in the university system.

ONE DAY RACHEL and Tamar arrive at the Kmara offices to find the computers trashed, windows broken, and the photocopier demolished. Several of the hard drives are missing too. It throws Tamar into a state of panic. But Rachel just laughs.

"What's so funny?" asks Tamar.

"Isn't this exciting?"

"No. I'm scared, Rachel."

Rachel's face turns solemn. "I understand. But believe me, this is a good thing. It means they're afraid of us. It means we have *power*."

Tamar looks around the office. Everything is a mess.

"What if one of us were here?" Tamar asks. "What if they were hurt?"

Rachel puts her arms around Tamar, giving her one of her signature hugs. "They wouldn't have come if someone was here. Don't worry, Tamar. Nobody's going to get hurt."

But Tamar isn't reassured. On her way home, she is stopped by a man in a blue hoodie and black jeans.

"Hey, don't I know you?" he asks in Georgian.

Tamar keeps walking.

"You're the one who makes those videos, right?"

Tamar keeps her head down. When she turns the corner, he's there again. As she's about to cross the street, he grabs her arm.

"Tell Davit to back off," he says in Russian.

THAT NIGHT DAVIT asks Tamar to meet him at Ritsa Street. She hasn't seen him in weeks. He looks beautiful in his blue pinstripe suit, a purple flower in the lapel. In recent months he has become a hot commodity: the nation is riveted by this dashing and bold investigative journalist. For one hour a week on Friday night at 6 p.m., Davit broadcasts tales of corruption and lies from the highest echelons of power. Politicians hate him, but everyday Georgians adore his bold honesty. Occasionally, his work is syndicated in Germany and the U.K., and he's been called to speak by satellite phone with news anchors at CNN and the BBC. Things have been going so well that he invested in a condo on the fifteenth floor of a new building in the Saburtalo neighbourhood. Tamar now lives alone in the artistic palace of Ritsa Street, happy for her best friend's success. But even her days on Ritsa are numbered. She has firmed up plans to move to Toronto with Rachel. In a few months, she'll be in another world. She misses Davit already.

When she gets home, Tamar puts on a pot of coffee. Her heart swells when she sees Davit walk through the front door. He's excited about a story he's working on regarding compromising videos made of the Georgian political opposition. Filmed by the Russian FSB and Georgian secret police, young politicians were "caught" in illegal brothels with underage prostitutes. Really, it was all a set-up so the

Shevardnadze government could maintain their monopoly on legitimacy and power.

"Plus ça change," says Davit. "In a land without dogs..."

Tamar flinches, remembering the warning from the man in the blue hoodie earlier that day. In the Georgia she and Davit have grown up in, nobody is qualified to lead, and no one lives in the House of Honesty. Leaving only thieves, murderers, and the duplicitous. Cats, where there should be dogs. Davit wants to change that, and it scares her.

"Everyone knows Putin is in cahoots with Shevardnadze. But Shevy wants Western oil money too. The bastard is playing all sides: the Americans and the Russians. I'm going to prove it."

Tamar says, "Somebody told me to warn you to back off today."

He scoffs. "Tamar, I get death threats all the time."

"And Zaza? What have you found out?"

"That lead I told you about? It took a while, but I'm meeting someone."

"And?"

He shakes his head. "I won't know for sure until tomorrow, but..." Davit hesitates. "Tamar, I think Zaza is alive."

"What?"

"My source says he faked his death."

"Where the fuck is he then?"

"That's what I'm trying to find out."

"What else do you know?"

"The day he supposedly died, Zaza was at the KGB archives in Tbilisi. But he wasn't one of the protestors."

Davit rests his hand on her shoulder. Tamar clenches the

sides of the kitchen table so hard she thinks she might break it. She takes a deep breath and says, "Will you stay with me tonight?"

When Davit's in her bed, Tamar falls asleep in his arms, calm for the first time in weeks. But when she awakes, he's gone. Her phone rings.

"Come to Davit's condo," says Rachel. "Now."

Tamar's heart races as she pulls on her blue Wrangler jeans and jean jacket. She drapes herself in a grey acrylic scarf, coiling it around her neck. She feels the hand of something grab her, but when she turns to look, no one is there.

When she arrives at Davit's condo, it's cordoned off with police tape. Rachel holds her back as Tamar pushes to get inside.

They're told by a police officer to go to City Hospital Number One. Beneath the yellow stained wall tiles, on the broken stone floor, Davit's body lies on an ancient stretcher. Young and suave in his blue pinstripe suit, a purple coneflower in his lapel, and a dime-sized hole in his forehead.

# ACT III

# OMISSIONS AND LIES

## November 2003

"The heart is a magnet."

—JOHANN WILHELM RITTER,
*Fragments from the Estate of a Young Physicist*

# 1

Four times Joseph dials. Four times Joseph hangs up. Rabbis annoy him, while God scares him, even though Rachel always insisted that God doesn't exist. Joseph believes that certain people can see things he wishes they didn't. Like Rachel, like the rabbi. He feels this in his more pathetic moments: that God or something is watching him fail, over and over again.

He closes his eyes. He hates when he is not in control — of his body, of a situation. He rubs his palms into his temples. When the migraines come, he can see things — a chaotic, turbulent universe of swarming, unsettled colour. Joseph waits like this until the Vicodin does its work, its long tentacles enveloping him. It is both insulating and emboldening. He dials again and this time he doesn't hang up.

"Hello?"

"Rabbi Gurnisht? It's Joseph Grabinsky."

The rabbi sounds surprised. "To what do I owe the pleasure, Joseph?"

Joseph drops the phone base. For a moment he hopes he's lost the connection. He bends over and picks up the ancient contraption. No, the line hasn't died.

"She's dead."

"Excuse me?"

"Rachel. She died of heart failure, Friday night."

"Joseph, I'm so sorry."

He doesn't tell the rabbi that, four days ago, Rachel called him in the middle of the night and asked him to bring her medication, an unusual request even for her. She complained of a "strange headache." Two days later he found her dead in her living room. Now he is in his mother's kitchen trying to make arrangements for a funeral he isn't even sure she'd want.

"Don't worry, Joseph. We'll give her a good funeral," the rabbi says. "Will you speak?"

"I don't do public speaking," Joseph says. The words feel sheepish and lame. He adjusts the phone in his hand. "Noam Chomsky wants to say a few words." Chomsky called this morning. He'd seen the obit in the *New York Times*.

Rabbi Gurnisht makes a strange sucking noise.

"Chomsky," he says as though Chomsky were an exotic drink. "Really?"

"They were friends." Chomsky used to crash on their couch back in the day.

"How about we keep politics out of the funeral home?"

For a moment he regrets the phone call. He's calling the rabbi out of duty and respect. Rachel would probably have wanted something eccentric for her funeral, her ashes scattered in the Seychelles while a mariachi band played and everyone danced. She loved mariachi music and she loved a good time. But Joseph isn't one for grand gestures. And besides, Rachel didn't leave a will. Joseph is left to interpret what she wanted. He's been doing that his whole life.

"The problem with religion," Rachel used to say, "is a lack of humour. God is funny, Joseph."

"I thought you said God is dead."

She'd ignore him. "Hypocrisy. Stuffy rabbis rambling on about what is right one moment while they fuck the shiksa down the street on Yom Kippur the next. At least admit the contradiction. Embrace it. When I die, Joseph, I want you to write on my grave: 'Here lies a contradiction.'"

"Rabbi," says Joseph, "if we're going to give Rachel Grabinsky a proper burial, we have to be honest: keeping politics out of the funeral home isn't going to happen."

"Fine. But no Chomsky."

"Can you say something?"

"I'm a rabbi, Joseph. It's my job to say something at a funeral. But your mother was an important woman. Someone close to her ought to speak."

Joseph can hear the rabbi's kids running around in the background.

"Your mother and I didn't often see eye to eye. But I'm prepared to let go of the past. That's what death is. Letting go." The rabbi is referring to a public argument he had with Rachel two years ago. Rachel had written a scathing editorial for the *Globe and Mail*: "Dear Palestinians: It's Not Your Fault the Holocaust Happened." Rabbi Gurnisht's irate response was printed below hers. The newspaper went full hog: half-page photographs of both of them, snarling at each other like Vegas prizefighters. Rachel loved every minute of it.

"Your mother deserves a funeral. A Jewish funeral. It's what she would have wanted," says the rabbi. He makes a strange sucking noise. Joseph wonders if it's candy or false teeth. "You're her only child. You knew her better than anyone," the rabbi adds. "Consider it a mitzvah."

Joseph hangs up the phone. Of course Gurnisht believes it's what she would have wanted. Every Jew, no matter how far they stray, ought to be buried a Jew — so sayeth Gurnisht. His mother, according to the rabbi, is no exception. Joseph isn't so sure.

He feels the tension in his head build so he pops another Vicodin. Then he pours himself a glass of Johnnie Walker Red from a bottle he found in Rachel's liquor cabinet. The cheap whisky is warm on his throat, and he savours its comfort. He pours himself another. The rabbi is right: he should give a speech. Joseph unsheathes the Montblanc fountain pen given to him by his boss for Christmas last year. He starts to put pen to paper, but he doesn't know where to begin. So he pours himself another drink and passes out in his chair.

JOSEPH WAKES TO the sound of his phone ringing.

"Where the hell are you?" Tamar demands. "We're ready to begin."

Joseph is still wearing yesterday's suit. A slug of mouthwash, a spritz of Hermès, his black Tom Ford sunglasses, and two Ativan later, Joseph is racing across the city in a taxi. He arrives at the funeral home fifteen minutes late. It's packed with professors from Rachel's department, various political people from Rachel's days of doing policy work, and a wide assortment of other friends and acquaintances.

The Ativan starts to kick in. Joseph flows toward people he pretends to know. There are celebrity lefties like Judith Butler and Naomi Klein, and big name academics whose names were never important enough for Joseph to remember. Senile Aunt Gertie is here. She isn't actually his aunt, but an old neighbour from their High Park days. Gertie plays with her dentures until they leave her mouth and fall onto the lush blue carpet of the funeral home. Her husband, the ever-devoted Louis, bends down, brushes them off, and returns them to her mouth.

It is almost time for the speech and Joseph still has no idea what he's going to say.

"You knew her better than anyone," the rabbi said. On the one hand it's true. As an only child raised by a single mother, Joseph saw a version of Rachel that most people don't know existed. No one else had his access to her over the years — no one except Tamar. But what did his mother really reveal about herself? She could talk about post-Communist regime change, solidarity, and non-violent revolution until the cows came home. But herself? Her feelings? Just because a person constantly talks doesn't mean you know them.

The *New York Times* obit described Rachel as "the bastard lovechild of Mother Theresa and Slavoj Žižek." There was no lack of hubris surrounding Rachel Grabinsky. She was certainly prolific. She always had a pen in one hand and another clipped to the front pocket of her grey button-down shirt (she insisted on wearing monochrome, as though her life were a grainy art film). When she wasn't writing articles or preparing lectures, she was reading, always reading. The house was a museum of her books.

But it also housed her mystery. Joseph can still remember the first time he realized his mother wasn't who she said she was. He was eight. He was in her bedroom playing with some of her jewellery, a pair of silver filigree clip-on earrings he liked to run his fingers along — she had bought the earrings in an Istanbul market. Sometimes he'd put them on and pretend he was from another place, another time. In his childhood mind he was a pharaoh, a Mayan prince.

On this occasion, something compelled him to dig deeper. After he removed the jewellery, he noticed a small hole in the bottom of the box. Joseph pulled out the thin wooden slat. A man's watch with a Russian inscription; a rusted razor; a pair of blue cufflinks framed in gold.

"Joseph," says the rabbi, putting his hand on Joseph's elbow. "We're ready for you."

THREE HUNDRED PEOPLE are crammed into the wooden pews of the Benjamin's Park Memorial Chapel. The room smells like it was just cleaned. Joseph imagines a room full of dead bodies, sponged and washed by tired hands. Suddenly Tamar is next to him with a cup of coffee.

"You look like you could use this."

Joseph manages a half-smile. "Thanks."

The coffee is just what he needs. When he leans into the podium and takes a sip, he can see the stain on the carpet where Gertie's dentures landed earlier.

"I'm not a writer. I'm not the one with five books to my name, nor am I known for connecting the dots of the twentieth century. That's Rachel, my mother." Joseph clears his throat. He always wanted to call her "Mom," but she didn't like that. It was always "Rachel."

"Rachel would weave history, politics, and pop culture together over morning coffee. When I was five, she'd read me passages from Hannah Arendt's *The Origins of Totalitarianism* at breakfast." People nod their heads, a symphony of support. "Everyone admired Rachel. Students, peers, even a few rabbis." A light chuckle spreads through the audience.

Joseph eases into it. The coffee keeps him focused; the Ativan lets him flow. For a moment he feels like he's riding a wave. This is easier than he expected.

"I can't give you the whole picture. Like you, I only have bits and pieces. So, I'd like to share a memory."

He sees Tamar standing at the back. She nods, encouraging him to continue.

"I was six years old, and it was a Friday night. Rachel was an atheist, but she liked her Shabbat dinners, a leftover from her childhood in Vilnius." He sips his coffee. "As usual, the kitchen was full of intellectuals, academics, and journalists. These were gods with enormous egos and huge ideas, people capable of changing the world. Or at least people who thought they could." A few people laugh. "There was plenty of booze. I was serving hors d'oeuvres on a silver tray—I liked to play the waiter at her parties. Rachel turned down the music, gathered everyone into a semicircle in her living room, and started to give her lecture."

Joseph does his best Rachel impression: a thick Eastern European accent and the swallowing of all consonants. "'And now I'd like to present tonight's lesson in social justice: my son, Joseph Grabinsky.'"

The funeral crowd chuckles warmly. Joseph leans into the microphone. He likes when people listen to him.

"Rachel hoisted me onto the mantelpiece and whispered, 'Now Joseph, do it just like we practised.' My tiny legs dangled over the edge. I was supposed to push myself off so she could catch me. But in our rehearsal earlier that afternoon I hadn't imagined so many people watching. 'I don't want to,' I said. I felt like I was sitting atop Mount Everest. Rachel said, 'Joseph, darling, Rachel loves you. Don't you love Rachel?' Her eyes were hard. I didn't want to jump. But I wanted her love, her approval. So I pushed myself off the ledge. Rachel stepped back, letting me fall to the floor.

"'You see, my dear?' she announced triumphantly to the room. 'You see what the world is like? Assholes and liars. Cry your eyes out, Joseph Grabinsky. The world is kind to no one.'"

A few people clear their throats. Joseph wants to say something more — a real clincher to end the speech on a high note, the way a loving son should — but when he opens his mouth, nothing comes out. Then he does something he hasn't done in a very long time: Joseph starts to cry. Rabbi Gurnisht approaches the podium. But before he can offer comfort, Joseph pushes past him and sprints down the aisle, catching his foot on the thick blue rug. Everyone gasps. When he recovers, Joseph dashes out the back door and into the parking lot. The Vicodin, the Ativan, and the whisky: everything has bloated his head. It's all coming out. Every memory, every thought. The mother he thought he knew. The mother he longed to know.

# 2

Joseph sits on the steps feeling stunned, like he's been hit with a saucepan.

"That was some performance."

Tamar is dressed in faded blue jeans and a black jean jacket. Her neck is covered by a long grey scarf. She tosses him his coat.

"You forgot it when you did your hundred-metre dash." Her eyes look moist, though he can't tell if it's from crying. "You want a ride?"

"Where?"

The question comes out funny. The word has more weight than it should.

"The cemetery." Tamar grimaces when she says this. "You know, the burying part?"

Joseph says nothing, so she leads him down the stairs and into Rachel's beat-up old Buick. There's dirt smeared on the back of her left leg, and for a moment Joseph wonders where she's been. He has the strange thought that maybe she's already buried his mother, something he has no interest in. Tamar, he knows, is not one to avoid what needs to be done.

Tamar guides the Buick through the funeral home parking lot. It smells like Rachel — Dunhill cigarettes and Yves Saint Laurent Opium. Though Joseph has been in it plenty over the years, the car is suddenly unfamiliar. He turns on the radio and searches for a station. Tamar flicks on the left turn signal as the car jerks onto the road. A taxi careens toward them. At the last second Tamar calmly merges into the right lane. Joseph wipes sweat from his brow. He wants to ask her to slow down. Instead, he continues fiddling with the radio. Tamar's driving makes him nervous. If he's honest with himself, everything about Tamar makes him nervous. They couldn't be more different. It's almost a miracle they're friends. And yet, over the last few years, they've become close.

They met at a party at Rachel's house almost three years ago. He was drinking in the kitchen, close to the bar. Bottles of wine, whisky, and vodka crowded the oval table. Rachel liked when he came to her parties; though she was larger than life, she still wanted validation from her son. Joseph would drop by for an hour, make his requisite appearance, then leave.

That night there was the usual mix of people he'd grown up with. Their ideas served to inflate an inordinate sense of self. Joseph understood that it was because it's all they had. In lieu of money and fame, for academics there is only the reputation wrought of posturing. But even Joseph had to admit Rachel had something special that few others in her crowd possessed. He was reminded of it that night, but wasn't quite sure how to describe it — charisma? Presence? A flair for the dramatic? Rachel was an inconsistent and often distant mother, but he couldn't deny she had that ineffable quality great people possess.

Rachel turned down the music and stepped onto a kitchen chair. She may have been five foot three, but she commanded attention when she wanted to.

"We can hear it in the winds from Kyiv and Belgrade, Minsk and Moscow, Tbilisi and Almaty: a new generation wants democracy, justice, and change. But how do we get rid of the past and the habit of servility? The Soviet trauma has been passed down from one generation to the next. It takes enormous effort to change." Rachel paused for effect. You could hear a pin drop as everyone stood listening, waiting.

"As many of you know, I've been running political work-shops in Tbilisi for the last few years. Some of you have read my articles about the civic institutions Freedom Ink has helped the Georgians to build, and the small but burgeoning pro-democracy movement we've established. You've also heard me speak about a performance artist named Tamar Tumanishvili, one of the most important young artists work-ing in Europe today. Well, she's here with us now and it's time for you all to meet her. Tamar?"

A tall woman with cropped black hair waved and smiled shyly as people broke into polite applause. She wore blue jeans, a white t-shirt, and a brown hoodie, with a grey scarf coiled around her neck. She seemed cold, even though it was blazing hot in that kitchen.

"Tamar is here on a visiting scholarship at the university and will teach a class in political performance art. She's here because things are dangerous for a woman like her in Tbilisi. Because the forces of the past are still strong in her part of the world. But we have hope for people like Tamar. We have hope for Georgia and the former Soviet Union. There will be democracy. There will be a new and open society, thanks to people like her."

Joseph watched as the crowd surrounded Tamar. She seemed embarrassed by the attention, yet spoke animatedly. It was a strain to overhear her words, so he followed the rhythm of her body language. He liked the way her soft words were punctuated by firm hand gestures. His phone buzzed, a text message from his fiancée, Cindy.

Cindy: Home for dinner?
Joseph: Yep :)
Cindy: Chinese?
Joseph: Yep :)

He hadn't seen Cindy all week — she was an investment banker, and like him, she put in the hours. Lately she'd been away on business more than he'd have liked. Joseph grabbed his coat, but when he looked in Tamar's direction, he noticed her glass was empty. He took a bottle from the table and went to fill it.

"You must be Joseph." He nodded. "Can I ask you a question? Why is there no food here?"

"Rachel believes that humans can live on booze alone."

"I'm starving," Tamar said.

"Do you like greasy spoons?"

"You mean unwashed cutlery?"

Joseph laughed. Without thinking he said, "Meet me outside in two minutes."

"Why would I do that?"

"Because we both know you don't want to be here. And I'm hungry too."

Joseph was surprised by the boldness of his words. On his way out he ran into Rachel. She hugged him so hard his chest hurt.

"Thanks for coming," she said. "Did you meet Tamar?"

"Yeah, she's great." He didn't mention their getaway plans.

"I think you two will get along famously."

He kissed her on the cheek and walked to the car. As he sunk into the plush leather seats of the black Lexus (Cindy's company car), he debated between Bill Evans and John Coltrane. In the end he went with Cannonball Adderley's *Somethin' Else.* The leading bassline, coupled with the soft piano chords, spilled out of his stereo speakers. Joseph closed his eyes. He loved the way Miles Davis's trumpet sounded like a breath of fresh air. He wished his life could be this beautiful. He pulled out his phone and texted Cindy.

Joseph: Be home late. Brunch tomorrow? :)
Cindy: Needed in the office in the AM. Drinks in the eve?
Joseph: Yep :)
Cindy: Chinese in the fridge xoxoxo

A beam of yellow light poured onto the lawn as Tamar emerged from the house. He'd never done anything like this, though he wasn't entirely sure what he was doing. Joseph's life was predictable, a fact he was proud of. His time was laid out in weekly segments, broken down by the hour. He'd been with Cindy for two years, two months, and twenty-six days. They'd met when he was just starting business school; she was several years older, his mentor-turned-girlfriend. Their relationship was as solid as a GIC. So why was he about to have dinner with a performance artist he'd just met from the Republic of Georgia?

"Can I change the music?" Tamar asked as she settled into the front seat.

"Sure."

Tamar flicked off the CD and tuned the radio to some electronic dance station. The car thrummed, the bass shaking the seats. Tamar closed her eyes. For a moment, he wondered if this was a colossal mistake.

Joseph parked next to the Vesta Lunch on Dupont Street, a neon hot dog flickering against a large window.

"Voila. Le greasy spoon," he said.

"A diner! Just like in the movies," Tamar said with a squeal.

Joseph likes to replay that first conversation. Tamar was excited by every detail: the laminated menus, the tiled walls, the stainless-steel napkin dispensers, the vinyl stools bolted to the floor along the counter. Joseph quickly found himself at ease with her, like he could be himself, though he wasn't really sure who that was most of the time. It felt good to be with her. What he needed more than anything, he realized, was a friend. Growing up he hadn't had many. And now he didn't have time to make new friends. But he enjoyed talking to Tamar. There was something familiar in her, though they couldn't have been more different. To his surprise, that night at the Vesta Lunch he even liked when she told him about her performance art.

"Once I stood naked outside the Georgian parliament for two days, covered in oil."

"Why on earth would you do that?"

Tamar shrugged. "I was protesting the Baku-Tbilisi-Ceyhan pipeline."

"But aren't they creating jobs for Georgians?" He knew some of the facts thanks to a couple of Ukrainian clients he'd done some investment work for.

"Does British Petroleum care about jobs for unemployed villagers in Rustavi? Does George W. Bush? They're kicking farmers off their land to get their hands on cheap oil."

Joseph tried to imagine Tamar standing naked dripping oil in front of hundreds of people. For a moment, he felt embarrassed for her.

"Did they end up building the pipeline?"

"Of course."

"Then why do it?"

"Because you have to do *something*, Joseph. Now, what do you do again?"

"I'm finishing my MBA. When I'm done, I plan to get a job at a top firm on Bay Street and become a hedge fund manager."

"And what exactly is that?"

Joseph found himself explaining the basic principles of investing. He became animated when he discussed underrated securities, calculated risks, and outperforming his colleague's portfolio. Excited, even.

"For me, money is about security. It's about creating a future for yourself and your loved ones. It's about building a world for our children and grandchildren."

But Joseph knew it was not just about security. It was about the possibility of earning small luxuries that grew bigger over time. When he was nine, Joseph dressed in a navy blue double-breasted suit he'd saved up to buy from the Hudson's Bay department store on Queen Street. He'd had to fight hard to get Rachel to take him to buy it. She hated spending money on frivolous things like clothes. They fought all the way to the cash register. Later he brought a briefcase to their Shake 'n Bake dinner — a meal he proudly cooked himself and dubbed "poulet élégant." By candlelight, Joseph poured his mother a glass of Welch's grape juice in a crystal wine glass. Then he opened the briefcase, handing Rachel the file he'd put together for his social studies project on the virtues of Reaganomics and trickle-down capitalism. Inside the Duo-Tang, there was an 8.5-by-11-inch photocopy of the lunch menu from Scaramouche, the most expensive restaurant in Toronto. Forty bucks an entree, not including tax. The year was 1987.

Tamar shifted in her seat. "Are you married?"

"No, but I'm engaged. My fiancée's name is Cindy."

"I'd like to meet her."

"Okay. But first, have another grilled cheese. I insist."

Tamar giggled. "I love this place. The way the cook rubs his greasy hands on his apron is incredible."

"His name is Sid."

"Do you see that man in the corner? How many sugar cubes will he put in his coffee? I've seen six already."

Joseph glanced at the insomniac John Paul in the kitchen mirror, stirring on repeat.

"Maybe he's a spy," said Joseph.

"He's definitely watching us."

"Do you think he's with the Russians or the Americans?"

"The Russians, for sure," said Tamar. "If you checked his pockets, you'd find they're full of free sugar cubes."

Joseph laughed.

"Can I make a confession?" Tamar asked. "When you talk about hedge funds, I have this image of you going to work in the morning with a pair of gardening shears. I imagine you standing on a ladder in the courtyard of a big glass building, pruning a tree. But instead of leaves falling, it's money. Is this what a hedge fund manager does?"

Joseph laughed so hard he nearly fell off his chair.

"Yes, Tamar. That's exactly what I intend to do."

A WEEK LATER, Joseph picked up Tamar down the street from Rachel's house — best not to tell his mother just yet — to take her to the movies and then back to the Vesta. So began their weekly routine. One month turned into six, then six months turned into a year. They talked about everything: childhood, favourite books, best friends, first kisses. Tamar told him about Davit. He told her about Cindy.

There were vast discrepancies in their lives: geography, history, language, occupation. The differences were formed by the political worlds they'd grown up in. She was three years older and had seen things Joseph would never understand. But he loved her stories of the chaos of Tbilisi. He also liked the way she listened to him. She never seemed bored by what he regarded as a rather ordinary life. In this way, they bonded over their need for companionship. Which is another way of saying: they were lonely. And neither of them knew their fathers.

Usually, Joseph didn't like talking about Gary. His father had never been around much, treated his mother poorly when he was, and then disappeared when Joseph was still a kid, under mysterious circumstances. Yet he didn't mind talking to Tamar about Gary, in part because she didn't prod. One night, over coffee and cold cherry pie at the Vesta, he went on a rant: he told her how, as a kid, he would always beg Rachel for stories of his father. He wanted to know what Gary liked for breakfast, what side of the bed he preferred to sleep on, who his favourite baseball player was. She was evasive, so he pushed harder. Finally, one day, Rachel told him that Gary had jumped off the Bloor Viaduct, plummeting to his death. Joseph was six years old.

Tamar looked down at her plate. "It's terrible when someone kills themselves. The pain they must feel…"

Joseph wanted to tell her how the violence of his father's suicide had upset him; how after Rachel told him the story, he'd had nightmares of men falling from the sky for years. Instead, he shook his head and took another sip of coffee.

Tamar sensed his hesitation and said, "You can tell me anything, Joseph. You don't have to hold back." When he still didn't respond, she continued. "You remember me telling you about my best friend in Tbilisi — Davit?"

Joseph nodded.

"We used to call each other 'truth tellers.'"

Joseph could tell there was more to the story, but he didn't pry. "That's beautiful," he said.

"It's important to have someone in your life that you can be completely open and honest with. I don't have Davit anymore. Could we be truth tellers instead?"

Joseph nearly choked from the sentiment. "Of course," he said, raising his grilled cheese and clinking it against hers.

A FEW MONTHS later, only days after Joseph graduated from his MBA program cum laude, he came home to find Cindy's laptop open on her desk. He knew he shouldn't, but instinct told him to look at her emails. He found a world of surprises and lies. Cindy was having an affair with her boss at the firm, Menachem. They'd been working a lot of overtime lately, and they were doing it in shared hotel rooms and king-sized beds. They even had code words and burner phones. The discovery rocked Joseph.

"Blindsided," he kept saying, as he sunk his fork into a slice of Vesta Lunch apple pie. "Why do I never see what's right in front of me?"

Tamar said, "I'm going to get you out of this mess. But we have to act fast. It's like ripping off a Band-Aid. Don't think twice."

She helped him find a condo on King Street West. Then she helped him move out of Cindy's two-storey house in the Annex. She even wrote a note and left it on Cindy's desk: "Respect is a six-letter word." Joseph wasn't quite sure what that meant, but he appreciated Tamar helping him get through a difficult time. He was grateful for her friendship. Yet, after he moved into his new condo, he often felt confused. Sometimes the lines would blur, and a trip to the movies would start to feel like a date. He found himself lingering on a word, pausing between thoughts. He wanted to open up to Tamar, to tell her how he really felt. He looked forward to the Friday nights when he'd get a text from her: Codeword: Vesta. Fifteen minutes later, he'd be waiting for her by the elm on Sorauren, up the street from Rachel's house. The clandestine nature of their meetings was charged. They existed in a separate space. To Joseph, it felt like breathing.

JOSEPH LANDED HIS first job at a major firm several months after graduating. Tamar was proud of him, but also curious, so one night he invited her to his new Bay Street office. "How'd you like to see where the wheels of capitalism turn?" he asked.

It was near midnight when Tamar stepped off the elevator onto the seventy-second floor. She had never been so high in a building before. When she looked out at Lake Ontario, he could see she felt both scared and delighted. The city lurked beneath them. Joseph handed her a glass of whisky and they sat together on the edge of his desk, drinking it all in. Tamar removed her wool coat. She wore a t-shirt that said "Underwear is a Conspiracy of the Government to Control the Mind." Joseph felt she was being flirtatious but couldn't be sure. He liked her long, lean ears, and for a moment he felt the strange urge to protect her.

"The stock market is based on speculation," Joseph said, turning to show her the computer screen. The numbers focused him, and his confidence swelled. "I call them 'hopes and dreams.' What people believe will happen, what they hope will happen, and what they want to happen."

"And what do you hope will happen, Joseph?"

He turned to face her. "I mostly go for what feels right."

"Intuition," she said.

Joseph hesitated. He knew this was his cue, yet he didn't lean in and kiss her. Instead he turned his eyes back to the screen, preferring to show Tamar how he managed port-folios from the Hong Kong division. The next morning, he would replay this scene in his head: she wore a sexy t-shirt; he showed her his data.

THAT WAS OVER a year ago. Now Tamar pulls into the cemetery parking lot and turns off the car. Joseph checks his phone.

"The rabbi," he says. "Three missed calls. Probably wants to know where I am."

Tamar rolls down the window and lights a cigarette. Joseph fiddles with the radio. This time it works. A country song sounds tinny coming from the old speakers. The lyrics are both funny and sad.

"I'm going to miss Rachel," says Tamar.

"Me too."

Joseph means it. For all his griping — and in spite of the speech he just gave — he feels lost without her. He's an orphan now. And while he's a full-grown man, able to take care of himself, he decides there's nothing emptier than a life without a parent. No matter how difficult they were.

"My father had this cat named Ilya he really liked," says Tamar, smoking and watching the parking lot as though it were a movie screen. "When Ilya died, I couldn't accept it. How this perfect little creature was active one moment, and then still the next. Death is the greatest injustice."

Joseph agrees. When he found Rachel, he thought she was napping, passed out on the couch with a copy of *The New Republic* splayed on her chest. Yet the feeling of something different in the air clung to him. He moved to wake her, touched her cold arm, then jumped. He'd never felt so scared in his life.

"If you could talk to your father now, what would you say to him?"

Tamar hesitates. "I would want to have a normal conversation, to see if we have anything in common."

"The details wouldn't matter?"

"Why should they?"

Joseph agrees, somewhat. The truth is, he doesn't know what he would say to Gary, if there was a Gary to talk to. He knows he'd have a lot of questions. Hank Williams croons from the radio, a song about midnight trains and falling stars.

"Have you ever been to the Yukon?" Tamar asks.

"Nope."

"Me neither. But I love the novels of Jack London."

"He's one of my favourites."

Joseph hasn't read a page of Jack London in his life.

"*Call of the Wild* is my favourite. Want to go there with me? We could take your mother's car."

From her hoodie Tamar produces a metal flask. She takes a sip then passes it to Joseph. He feels something hover between them. She's right. Rachel is dead. Anything is possible. *The Yukon*, he thinks. *Why the hell not?* He takes a sip of whisky and looks at Tamar.

She says, "Oh no. That's a really bad idea."

But it's too late. He leans over and kisses her. To his surprise, she kisses him back. Without thinking he reaches for her waist, and she goes for his tie. He tries to yank off her jeans, but they get caught around her hips. She pulls his pants down to his ankles. Suddenly there's the sound of car doors slamming around them and he hears the voice of the rabbi.

"Joseph? Joseph, where are you?"

"He's by the grave!" someone yells.

The voices trickle away. Tamar and Joseph, half-naked, start to laugh. He climbs on top of her.

"I don't have a condom."

"It's okay."

Joseph imagines how they must look from outside, what the rabbi and his congregants deduce from this bouncing, shaking old Buick. He tries to look in Tamar's eyes, but he can't. So he stares at her neck. A short line of birthmarks form a constellation running from her neck to her jaw. Joseph wants this more than anything. He hopes she does too. The back of his head hits the rear-view mirror, and they laugh again before turning grim and serious, as if they are trying to get somewhere fast. And they do.

# 3

Joseph steps out of the car to find Noam Chomsky bent over, fixing the laces on his brogues. Joseph tries to slip past him but it's too late.

"Joseph," he says, straightening himself. "I found your speech quite moving."

"You don't have to say that."

"It's true. Your mother was very dear to me. I understand that family can be difficult. It's hard to speak honestly about a parent." Chomsky brushes his camel-haired trench coat, then examines the sky. "Your mother loved these crisp November days."

Chomsky makes him uneasy. When Joseph was ten, Chomsky taught him how to make a dry Bombay martini with olives. When he was twelve, Joseph caught him and Rachel on the couch drinking cheap plum wine, as Chomsky nattered on about the end of capitalism and Israel's unholy alliance with America.

Finally, Rachel said, "You know what I'd like?"

"No."

"A really good pearl necklace."

A car door slams behind him, and Joseph turns to look. Tamar fidgets with her belt. There's a streak of something wet on her blue jeans. When she looks up at him Joseph averts his gaze.

"Excuse me," he says to Chomsky. "The rabbi's waiting."

By the grave, Joseph tries to straighten his dishevelled suit. The stain on Tamar's jeans bothers him; he worries that what just happened in the car was a mistake. Tamar was his mother's protégée, and more than that, a close friend.

Rabbi Gurnisht shifts on his feet. He chats with three men in old jeans, lumberjack shirts, and kipahs. A forklift sits beside the wooden casket. The casket makes Joseph think of a tiny animal. He can feel the pressure in his head building again. Instinctively he slides his hand into his coat pocket. But instead of the bottle of Vicodin he was expecting, he feels a tiny cardboard box. He forgot he put it there.

"Joseph, why don't you come to the synagogue when all this is done? I can teach you the Kaddish. I know what it's like to lose a parent."

Joseph looks into the soft eyes of Rabbi Gurnisht. He feels the gentle reassurance of his faith.

"Your father liked to pray," the rabbi adds.

"He did?"

"When he visited Toronto, he came to shul on Saturday mornings. We used to talk."

Joseph has few memories of Gary. Once, his mother showed him a picture of his father asleep in a chair. It was an unflattering photograph, and it made Joseph feel embarrassed.

"I didn't realize you knew him."

"We spoke Russian together." Rabbi Gurnisht strokes his beard pensively.

"Gary spoke Russian?"

"Of course. He lived in Moscow for a time. That's where he met your mother." The Rabbi leans toward him. "I'm not supposed to know this, but sometimes Rachel came to shul, too. She would sit in the women's section and listen."

"My mother?"

The rabbi nods. "Come to the synagogue, Joseph. We can talk more about them."

There's no way his mother went to a synagogue to pray. Joseph is annoyed by Rabbi Gurnisht's fanciful thinking. He pulls out the small box, a Hershey's Cherry Blossom. He found it in his mother's kitchen the morning he found her dead body. He hasn't eaten one since he was a kid. He spots Tamar in the second row, chatting with senile Aunt Gertie. Gurnisht gives a signal and one of the kipah-wearing men climbs into the forklift to lower the casket into the grave. Joseph doesn't want to watch, so he looks at Tamar instead. Her face is open and bright. Maybe the rabbi's right. It can't hurt to pray. And besides, he'd like to know more about his father.

Joseph opens the small box and bites into the chocolate. Cherry syrup bursts into his mouth. It tastes like childhood. Rabbi Gurnisht gestures again, and Joseph bends down to scoop up a shovelful of earth. He's surprised by the weight of the soil. As he carries it toward his mother's grave, questions fire off in his brain. What was Rachel doing in Moscow?

Why was Gary there too? When he dumps the soil onto the coffin, it makes a loud thunk. Joseph peers into the grave, hoping for one last look at Rachel. For a moment, he wishes the dead could speak.

# 4

After the funeral, Joseph takes a taxi to the synagogue. But as soon as he sees the large curved doors and stained-glass windows, he changes his mind. He tells the taxi driver, "Rachel's house," which of course the driver doesn't understand. How can anyone understand where he needs to go?

Rachel's kitchen is a total mess. Empty wine bottles and plates caked with Friday night's dinner still cover the kitchen table. Normally, Tamar would've cleaned up, but she was up north at a meditation retreat until Joseph called her with news of Rachel's death. Joseph pours himself a glass of wine from an open bottle. Standing in the centre of the room, he feels the urge to recite a prayer, but he doesn't know any. His Judaism was Rachel's: the graveyard of Europe.

"If it wasn't Hitler, it was Stalin," Rachel would say to Joseph when he was a child. Those of her family who weren't slaughtered in the Holocaust perished under the

Soviets; Hitler and Stalin were the two devils of the house. If the dishes weren't done properly, it was Hitler's fault. If the counters were stained, it was Stalin's. In reality, Rachel simply hated cleaning.

Joseph came here to clean. Yet he freezes now when faced with the sheer magnitude of the task. A tube of Rachel's lipstick stands erect on the kitchen table, tall and slender. He imagines removing the cap and touching the grooves where Rachel's lips pressed. The wine is slightly off and makes his stomach churn. That Rachel died leaving a disastrous kitchen was inevitable. Life with Rachel was an exercise in constant disorder: pyramids of books, piles of papers, ubiquitous dust, a legacy of unwashed dishes. In high school the kids called their house "Poltergeist."

"Why Poltergeist?" Rachel once asked him.

"Because we are haunted by mess."

"My dear Joseph, life is a question of priorities. Of course we could live in a cleaner house. But how do you want to be remembered? For your sanitary bathtub, or for making a difference in the international fight against fascism?"

"Can't heroic fighters of fascism also have clean counters?"

Joseph drains his glass, refills it, and opens the top kitchen cupboard. To his surprise, there's an entire box of Cherry Blossoms, their red and blue lettering on a yellow box promising delicious sweetness. He grabs a couple then heads upstairs.

Crossing the threshold into Rachel's office is like entering another universe. As a child, Joseph would hover by the door, an invisible force keeping him at bay. He'd imagine his mother sitting at her desk with a map of the world. In his mind, little chess pieces were scattered across Russia and Brazil, India and America, Cameroon and Korea. She'd move the pieces and the next day's news would be made. For Joseph, Rachel wasn't an academic; she invented headlines.

He pries open a window to let in cool air. Her enormous wooden desk occupies half the third-floor office; not one part of its surface is left uncovered. There are piles of paper, drafts of articles, lectures-in-progress, books dog-eared or splayed open, bottles of ink, and empty tuna cans filled with crushed cigarettes. On the bookshelf Joseph finds the old jewellery box, the one he played with as a kid. He dumps its contents onto the desk. Out spill colourful earrings, beaded necklaces, and stone bracelets. He removes the wood slat hiding the false bottom, expecting to find a pair of blue cuff-links framed in gold and the watch with Russian lettering. Instead, he finds a postcard and a burgundy passport with gold embossed Cyrillic writing, a red star above a hammer and sickle. Joseph flips it open.

At first, he doesn't recognize her. She's young, twenty years old maybe, and beautiful. Her hair is deep brown, short, and parted at the side. Her right eyebrow is slightly higher than her left. She wears a collared shirt, with two buttons open at the neck. Tracing her high forehead and cleft chin, he realizes that Rachel had been young once too. He puts the passport into the pocket of his blazer.

The postcard is from another era: 1970s stock. A woman made of aluminum, twenty metres tall, stands on the edge of a cliff overlooking a city on a muddy river. Her face is strong and sculpted, her torso immense. She holds a sword in one hand and hoists a bowl in the other. Joseph recognizes the feel but not the place. He flips the postcard over. The stamps are familiar: brown and grey rockets swirling the planets, an homage to the miracles of science. A man dons an astronaut's helmet, ready for the stars. The writing is tiny, microscopic; he assumes it is in a foreign language. But when he looks closer, the writing is in English.

*September 1984*

*Dear Rachel,*

*Post offices are like train stations. That's why people collect stamps — they like to think they're going somewhere. I'm not. I'm writing [wobbly-wobbly] from the post office [wobbly-wobbly] because if I don't, I'll never send you anything. I'm a coward but you already knew that. You ask why I disappeared, and you're right . . . You lost something and I need to fix that. An old bar in Tbilisi, a candle, a bottle of something. God, I wish you could drink with me. Did you know if you look at the Caucasus long enough it starts to resemble a heart? Wendy took a bus to the mountains and got drunk with a local named Vano. Then she got snowed in. Vano offered his bed. He removed a sword from the wall, laid it between them, and said, "If I so much as pass this threshold, you must plunge my great-grandfather's sword into my heart!" They got married that spring. People do the right thing here. I'd like to do the right thing too. I've got a Georgian soul . . . and a wife. Well, there you have it. The cat's out of the bag, the worm's off the hook, and so on. I do still love you, Rachel. But I can't live with someone who doesn't love me. I'm sorry I can't help raise our son. You're going to have to tell him something.*

*Cheerio,*
*Gary*

Joseph reads the postcard several times. Each time, the words become smaller, the sentences more crooked, the meaning more obtuse. He feels he is travelling along the streets of an unmarked city. So he clings to numbers. But the numbers don't ground him; they pull him back in time. In October 1984, when he was six, he prodded Rachel:

"How did Gary die?"

"He killed himself."

"Was he sad?"

"He was lost."

"Can we visit his grave?"

"His grave is far, far away."

Under the jewellery box, Joseph finds a file folder with his name on it. It contains notes Joseph wrote then slipped under Rachel's door when he was a child.

*"When you smoke it kills me."*

*"It makes me sad when you don't say good night."*

*"You need to pay more attention to the policies of Reagan and Thatcher."*

*"Sometimes I think you love Perestroika more than you love me."*

*"Have you heard from Dad since he died?"*

THE CREVASSE WIDENS and sparks of pain shoot out. He knows he has to take something or he'll get another migraine. But he doesn't want Vicodin; he wants to drink. He pockets the postcard and runs downstairs. For a moment, he considers calling the rabbi. Instead he looks for a clean glass but can't find any, so he fills the sink with hot water and dumps in globs of soap. He feels a jab against his hand, broken glass. Blood drips from his palm into the water. The cut stings like hell.

He should run the wound clean under the tap then put on a bandage, but Joseph takes the blood as some kind of sign. He pours himself a whisky, drains it, then turns on the radio. The volume control is broken so it plays at one level — really loud. He told Rachel a million times to replace the stupid thing. He even offered his old Bose stereo, but she refused, insisting this worked just fine. She said that about a lot of things.

He yanks the cord from the wall and hurls the radio across the room. It nicks a vase on the kitchen table, and the vase teeters, falls, and explodes into a thousand pieces of blue. The radio's LED numbers blink on and off. Then his cell phone rings. Unknown caller.

"Hello?"

He hears something crash on the other end of the line.

"Tamar?"

The bleeding is getting worse. He grabs a tissue and presses it firmly against the wound.

"Who is this?" asks Joseph. "Hello?"

The line goes dead.

THE YEAR IS 1988. Joseph is ten years old. Rachel is headed out to buy cigarettes.

"What do you do if someone knocks at the door?"

"Don't answer it."

"And if they keep knocking?"

"Don't answer it."

"And if you do?"

"I'm in big shit."

"Good." Rachel pats him on the head. "Rachel will be home soon. I'll get you a treat, okay?"

It's a routine, mother and son. Saturday mornings, Rachel leaves the house for cigarettes. She always brings Joseph something. Usually it's a Cherry Blossom, his favourite chocolate in the whole world, though recently, according to Rachel, there's a shortage in their production. Left to his own devices, Joseph likes to play his favourite geopolitical game: "Reagan and Gorbachev: The Ultimate Summit." He runs his hand through tightly greased hair and gives his best cowboy Reagan look. Staring into the mirror, he makes Gorby an offer he can't refuse: in exchange for the promise of democratic elections in Russia, he promises a free trade deal, a decrease in mid-range nuclear weapons, and access to broadcast reruns of *Family Ties* starring Michael J. Fox.

A knock at the door. Joseph hesitates. A knock again. It feels insistent. In spite of his mother's orders, he opens it. A man stands on the threshold wearing a Chicago Cubs cap and carrying a brown paper bag.

"Would you like a Cherry Blossom?" he asks.

Without thinking Joseph reaches his hand inside the bag, rips open the yellow box, and shoves the candy into his mouth.

"Do you like baseball?"

Joseph nods.

"Would you like to go to a game?"

"My mom's going to be home any minute."

"Next Saturday. I'll get tickets, Jays-Yanks."

Rachel doesn't like baseball. Joseph does, though he's never been to a game. He listens on the radio in the quiet of his room.

"Meet me next Saturday by the elm tree on Sorauren. But don't tell anyone. Can you keep a secret?"

Joseph nods.

"Secrets," says the man, "are sweeter than Cherry Blossoms."

JOSEPH WAKES TO Tamar shaking him. He's by the stairs, an empty bottle of whisky at his feet. There's puke in his clothes and hair.

"Get in the shower," she commands. So he does.

The shower takes him back to that secret Saturday at the baseball game. The man smelled like stale tobacco and Old Spice deodorant. They sat in the CNE grounds and ate hot dogs and drank Classic Coke while the Yankees pounded the Jays. If it had ended there, he might've wondered if the afternoon had happened at all. But instead of taking him directly home, the man in the Chicago Cubs hat drove him to Sam the Record Man on Yonge Street, where he insisted on trudging all the way up to the third floor to flip through jazz records. Joseph was bored as hell.

"Do you know what jazz is?" the man asked.

Joseph shook his head.

"You know that feeling when you're in your room and you just want to be somewhere else? Somewhere totally amazing?"

Joseph nodded.

"That's jazz. And these are two of the greatest jazz albums of all time."

He held up two records: *Somethin' Else* by Cannonball Adderley and *Blue Train* by John Coltrane. Joseph felt there was something holy about the albums, and he concentrated on their covers to make sure he never forgot them.

That night, when he finally got home, Rachel was beside herself with worry.

"Where the hell have you been?"

"I was with dad."

"What do you mean?"

"Why didn't you tell me he's still alive? Why did you lie to me?"

"He's dead to me."

"I hate your secrets."

IT'S EVENING WHEN they finally clean the kitchen. Tamar and Joseph work in tandem, fastidious and quiet. When they finish, she puts on a pot of coffee then inhales in a way that makes the cigarette seem essential. Joseph hasn't smoked since he was sixteen, but he asks for one anyway. The cigarette tastes like wildness, deep and hidden. When he's finished, he asks for another. They don't discuss what happened in the car. He doesn't mention the passport, the postcard, the past, or Gary. He wouldn't know where to begin.

Instead, he asks, "Want to see a movie?"

Tamar nods. "Yes."

They drive Rachel's car to the theatre and watch a film neither knows the title of. They don't see themselves in it, so the movie is a kind of relief. Later they curl into the single bed in Joseph's old bedroom, the room Tamar now sleeps in. And they hold each other, fiercely, as though their lives depend on it.

# 5

When Joseph was fourteen, he worked a paper route. Over the autumn months he saved up and bought a record player. Then he travelled across the city to Sam the Record Man. He walked up to the third floor, knowing exactly what he was looking for: *Somethin' Else* by Cannonball Adderley and *Blue Train* by John Coltrane. Later, he lay down on his bed and listened. He couldn't say he loved the music; he had no context or feel for the notes and there were no lyrics to hold on to. But he liked trying to decode their meaning. Somewhere in those lines lived Gary's secret, which was his secret too.

Joseph didn't grow up with a father, but during his youth Rachel took in numerous families, sometimes for months at a time. They were a halfway house between East and West. Entire families newly emigrated from the U.S.S.R. would cram into the spare room across from Joseph, rendering the Grabinsky house as crowded as anything they'd left behind in Moscow, Leningrad, or Riga. It was hard to explain this arrangement to his friends in high school — the details embarrassed him. He found it difficult to live in such cramped conditions. Everyone was always shouting. Seven or eight strangers shared a kitchen, a shower, and a toilet with a jittery handle.

When Joseph tells Tamar this, they're lying in bed together. It's 4 a.m., the morning after the funeral. She snuggles into him and says, "So you know what it's like." And then she promptly falls back asleep.

She breathes deeply and without hesitation. Likely, there's nothing particularly special about the way Tamar breathes. What's special about any of us? And yet, listening to her, he feels he is listening to the music of the world. John Coltrane's incomparable saxophone solos. The warm basslines of *Somethin' Else*. He has the urge to put his hands over her slender ears. To cup and protect them.

Tamar's eyelids flutter, and he wonders if she's happy, if anyone's ever made her happy, if happiness is even what matters. Then he thinks, *What if I'm happy now, watching Tamar sleep?* Which he feels badly about because Rachel just died. So he thinks about Gary's postcard instead. The message guts him, in part because it offers a missing piece to the puzzle: Gary left because Rachel didn't love him. Yet Gary's behaviour also angers Joseph. Why couldn't Gary have kept in touch — if even just a little?

While she sleeps, Joseph doesn't tell Tamar that he hated sharing the house with the Soviet immigrants. When he retreated to his room to get away from them it was to listen to jazz, the music that dreams of elsewhere. Yet more than music or escape, he longed for love. Something he understood neither Rachel nor Gary was capable of. Cupping her slender ears, he watches Tamar sleep, holding the space in his hands. Then he whispers, "I love you."

JOSEPH WAKES LATER that morning unsure of where he is. It takes a moment to realize he's not in his condo on King Street, but naked in his childhood bedroom. The imprint in the bed where Tamar was sleeping is still warm from her body. He dresses and goes downstairs. There's a pot of coffee on, still warm. A copy of the day's *New York Times* has been placed on the kitchen table. It's Wednesday morning, and his boss has sent him no fewer than ten text messages. Apparently he's wanted at the office.

Joseph feels a draft and goes over to the back door, finding it slightly ajar. Stepping into the backyard he sees the metal gate swing open and shut.

"Tamar?" he calls out.

Sorauren is unusually silent. There's no sign of Tamar. She must have gone to get breakfast, he thinks. Joseph closes the gate and goes back inside to pour himself a coffee. He takes a sip, feels the inside of his blazer, and realizes his mother's old passport isn't there. He goes upstairs with his coffee to see if he left it in her office. When he enters, his heart drops. The room has been ransacked. Books everywhere, garbage bin emptied, files open and scattered, notebooks on the floor. The open window, and the swirling wind, echo Joseph's sense of fear and dread.

He calls Tamar's number, but her phone is off. He leaves a message, trying his best to sound calm. He thinks, *Someone was here looking for something and they took Rachel's Soviet passport. Did they take Tamar too?* Worry blooms and Joseph imagines the worst. On the floor, he finds an open folder with press clippings of Tamar's performances and photos of her with family, friends, and on stage. There's a series of pictures showing a woman dressed in combat fatigues. She wears a blonde wig and sunglasses and stares down the camera. In the last frame, she removes her wig and sunglasses to reveal Tamar. His phone rings.

"Joseph?"

"Tamar! Where the hell are you?"

"I'm at the airport."

"Is everything okay?"

"There's something I need to figure out. But I can't tell you about it now, okay? I'm going home."

The ensuing silence guts him.

"Were you in Rachel's office?" Joseph asks.

"Yeah. Sorry about the mess."

He breathes a sigh of relief. "I thought someone broke in. I thought you were in trouble—"

It takes Joseph a moment to realize that Tamar is sobbing.

"Tamar?"

The line goes dead.

# ACT IV

*

# JOURNEYS IN THE MANNER
# OF A DOUBLE HELIX

## November 2003

"We need to be ourselves.
And to be our not-selves too."
— Traditional Chechen saying
(as told by Peter Nasmyth)

# 1

*Toronto, Canada*
*November 12, 2003*

On the flight to Istanbul, a baby wails in the arms of her mother. The cry is piercing, but it's also a mirror. Tamar wants to cry too, so she hides in the bathroom and weeps. Streaks of mascara trail down her swollen face. She feels stuck in a black pit impossible to escape. That's what sadness is, she realizes: a cave of so much loss. When she returns to her seat, the baby has been lulled to sleep. But Tamar sits awake, not knowing what to do or think. She traces her finger along the cover of the Soviet passport. She opens it to the page with the photograph and name: Анна Литвак. She touches the woman's black-and-white face. What does a face reveal? What story does a photograph hold?

Tamar retraces the events of the past few hours. When she fell asleep in Joseph's arms, she felt the sadness of Rachel's passing, but she also felt comforted. She slept until he spoke. It felt like a dream. She likes the way Joseph talks, the soft undulations of his thinking. His rhythms slipped into her half-sleeping brain. When she got up, she washed her face with cold water and watched him curled beneath the duvet, his blue blazer sprawled on the ground like a small animal. She picked up the jacket to fold it across a chair and the passport fell out. Анна Литвак, said the name in Russian. Anna Litvak. When she looked at the picture, she saw Rachel, just twenty years old.

Her first thought was her eyes were living in error. Then her mind raced through a deluge of explanations: it was a coincidental resemblance or Rachel had an identical twin or Anna Litvak was a long-lost aunt. But the more she stared at the photograph, the more Tamar understood that Rachel Grabinsky was not who she'd claimed to be.

Tamar searched Rachel's office. Scoured files and notebooks and random bits of paper. There had to be an explanation. Maybe she had conjured the resemblance out of longing; surely, mourning could cause such mad inventions of the mind. But the birthdate in the passport was Rachel's, and her grey eyes identical. Even with the absence of wrinkles and with the glow of youth, Tamar knew without knowing. Rachel Grabinsky was Anna Litvak. And Anna Litvak was Tamar's birth mother, as Nana had told her so many years ago. Which meant that Rachel was Tamar's mother too.

She smoked and paced the office. She showered, scrubbed herself, and rubbed the skin raw. Nothing could obliterate the truth. *The maybe-truth*, she thought. She needed to be certain before she told Joseph. She got dressed, brought in the morning paper, and made a pot of coffee. She tried to stick to normal, everyday tasks, but what was normal about any of this? It was incomprehensible.

The world shifted into focus. Every moment, every conversation with Rachel, suddenly took on a different meaning. The pauses, the lingering silences, the tears. Coincidences where nothing was an accident at all. Their first meeting at the Underground; the funding from Freedom Ink; her position at the university; living here and meeting Rachel's son... Joseph, her half-brother.

Tamar's head swelled and her stomach became a violent sea. She fell to her knees and puked up the coffee she'd just consumed. It was too much, everything, and she needed it gone. She felt like she might pass out, so she placed her hand on the kitchen counter. She didn't want to think about Joseph. When the light-headedness dissipated, she wiped up the mess and dumped copious amounts of bleach onto the linoleum floor. She scrubbed with a violence she hadn't felt in ages. The smell of bleach calmed her; she needed to erase what had happened. Then she called Levan.

"Hi, Tamar. I was just about to call you." She listened to him light a cigarette. "I heard about Rachel. I'm really sorry. You must be devastated."

"Who the hell is Anna Litvak?" she said through gritted teeth.

Levan drew deeply on his cigarette, rendering his vocal cords musty. It made her think of a submarine sinking. But it was her that was falling.

"We can talk when you come to Tbilisi."

"And why am I coming to Tbilisi?"

"Skunk called. Zaza's alive and Skunk knows where he is."

"Excuse me?"

"Apparently, Zaza lives in the mountains. Skunk claims he's become some kind of monk. Says he's seeking penance. I tell you, your father's a lunatic, Tamar."

She wanted a cigarette but her hands wouldn't stop shaking.

"Tamar," said Levan, "you need to come home."

# 2

*Toronto, Canada*
*November 12, 2003*

Joseph stares at the pile of mail in Rachel's hallway. There
are dozens of new condolence cards every day. But he
doesn't have the stomach to read them. A crumpled tele-
gram: `slavoj zizek sends regrets won't make it
in time for funeral`. To Joseph's surprise, there's a
large manila envelope with his name on it: "Comrade Joseph
Grabinsky." Cautiously, he picks up the envelope to look
closer at the postmark. A dozen stamps line the right side
of the package. He tries to decipher their country of origin, but the writing is in a language he does not recognize.
He takes the envelope into the kitchen and opens it. Inside
he finds a letter and several documents in a file folder. He
puts the folder aside and reads the letter, typewritten on
yellowing paper.

Dear Comrade Joseph,

You do not know me, yet I am no great Franz
Kafka mystery. I am enabled by your very
lame story. I know the true melodies of your
father, Gary Ruckler. So I send this small
package to illuminate big truths. Do not
be afraid. I play history like the Charlie
Parker jazz solo: highly improvised and very
disturbed. I am forever fan of Charlie Parker,
virtuosic genius of our ancient ornithologies.

I write you from the greatest record store
in the world—my store. Maybe you prefer
the shining CD. Or perhaps you are diehard
Napster, sad music of the stolen MP3 and
destroyer of our souls. If this is the case, I
will learn to tolerate your idiocies. But you
must love the vinyl record, for, as Thelonious
Cat intones, what is the Lengthy Vinyl if not
beauty printed onto time? Thus I present to
you the old record to play anew: a double
box-set of your life.

This is not music, but papers from the
cupboard. Yes, you come from the Land of Dark
Secrets. Do you want to know the truth? When
the Great Common Socialist Diet dies, every-
one wants the facts—and nice Wrangler jeans.
"We need to know our past!" shout the people.
But do we? We are human, terribly. Therefore,
I give you an inconvenient opportunity. You

may say, "No thank you, homeboy," and this B-side is finished.

And yet the balladry of genes is unlike the prosody of Wrangler. What you inherit is already written inside. To read these pages is to learn what you already know. Look, and be careful. Read between the lines, beside the words, and inside your foolish genome project. The father leaves for reasons which are more than you think and less than you hope for. Later you may send me the grand postal defibrillation to inform me of your thoughts.

And please, if you read, listen to Charlie Parker at very high decibels. Only the Birdman can play the pain of our sad and pathetic lives.


Yours truly,
Daniel Daniel
Impresario and owner of Daniel Daniel's Record Emporium
Tbilisi, Republic of Georgia

**THE ANNA LITVAK PAPERS (1977–1978)**

CO-AUTHORS: Colonel A.M.; Comrade O.V;
Junior Lieutenant Z.G., Committee for
State Security (KGB)

TRANSLATED BY: Gary Ruckler,
Central Intelligence Agency,
Langley, Virginia, U.S.A.

RANKING: Classified

WARNING: UNAUTHORIZED DISCLOSURE OF ANY
CLASSIFIED MATERIAL IS A CRIMINAL OFFENCE
AND MAY BE PROSECUTED UNDER U.S.
FEDERAL LAW

Dossier #4123

File 82104 (formerly files 44833 and 18932)

Name: Litvak, Anna

Age: 27

Date of Birth: 12 August 1951

Place of Birth: Vilnius University Hospital
(Lithuania, S.S.R.)

Father: David Litvak

Mother: Devorah Litvak

Height: 162 cm

Weight: 58 kilos

Hair: brown to gray

Additional: Glasses. Left-handed.

What follows are several reports of the
events between 15 August 1977 and 21 May 1978.
Special thanks to Colonel A.M., Comrade O.V.,
and Junior Lieutenant Z.G. for their reports,
and to the Committee for their review.

**Report on Events of 15 August 1977 at Moscow
International Airport by Colonel A.M.**

On 15 August 1977 I was entrusted with the
task of escorting Comrade Anna Litvak and her
two-year-old child to Moscow International
Airport, along with Junior Lieutenant Z.G.
Comrade Litvak held the small child in her
arms. I carried her suitcase while Junior
Lieutenant Z.G. held a briefcase.

Over the last three years, Comrade Litvak
has filed numerous unsubstantiated complaints
that her Jewish nationality made her the
target of racial slurs and professional preju-
dices, and thus wished to leave the Motherland.
Recently she applied to be reunited with a
distant family member and to study political
science and literature at McGill University
in Montreal, Canada. She had been awarded a
full scholarship on the basis of her academic
excellence. Upon the recommendations of the
Moscow District Party Secretary, Comrade
B.Y., her request to leave was granted on the
condition that Junior Lieutenant Z.G. join
her. Comrade Litvak was not aware of this
condition.

The plan was for Junior Lieutenant Z.G.
to accompany Comrade Litvak on the plane to
Vienna then onward to Montreal. There, they
would set up a home together. To further

their narrative, on 10 April 1977, the couple married in Moscow. In this way they would raise their child in the manner of two people who love one another. It was, so far as the Committee was concerned, a more than adequate scenario. My role was to oversee their departure.

When the Aeroflot attendant announced the commencement of boarding, I led them down the stairs and onto the tarmac. We let the other passengers pass so as not to draw attention to ourselves. The four of us then walked toward the metal steps that led to the airplane. The Junior Lieutenant told Comrade Litvak to hand him the child as she walked up the stairs. Comrade Litvak and Junior Lieutenant Z.G. were the last to board. She handed him the child, as he gave her the briefcase, then followed behind. I remained below. When Comrade Litvak crossed the threshold, Junior Lieutenant Z.G. paused and whispered to the flight attendant, who then entered the plane and sealed the door shut behind her. Junior Lieutenant Z.G. returned to the tarmac to join me, still holding the child in his hands.

I asked the Junior Lieutenant what the devil he was doing and why he hadn't boarded. Z.G. said, "It goes against my principles." I asked him what he meant by such a statement.

He said nothing. There was a look in his eyes, the meaning of which I could not ascertain. He was not himself. When I looked up at the airplane windows, I could see Comrade Litvak pressing her face and hands against the glass. The engines of the airplane were initiated. Junior Lieutenant Z.G. turned and quickly walked away. He held the child as though it were a bag of potatoes. I ran to catch him. He repeated, "It goes against my principles." This time he said it to no one in particular, as though the wind might hear his confession.

Moscow
22 August 1977

Signed,
Colonel A.M.
Committee for State Security

**Report on a Conversation with Comrade O.V., Waitress at the Restaurant Rasputin, Montreal, Canada**

On 9 November 1977, I met Comrade Anna Litvak at the Restaurant Rasputin on Boulevard Saint Laurent in Montreal, Canada, for the first time. Comrade Litvak came to the restaurant, she confessed, because she was homesick. I brought her a bowl of borscht with sour cream and three sprigs of dill. Following this I brought her a plate of vareniki, the freshness of which, I confess, was not of the first order. Comrade Litvak felt warmed by the food. I then gave her a shot of cold vodka. She ordered another. That's when she started to talk, no longer in stilted English, but in an elegant Russian. It was as though I heard her for the first time.

She explained that she is in Canada to study at the university. She confessed that she finds the studies challenging and the living difficult, that she left too much of herself behind. I put my hand on hers and said: "Life is not easy when you're alone." Comrade Litvak said her husband and child are back home in Moscow, or at least that's where she believes they are. I asked if she has friends in Montreal. She said she has some Jewish relatives, but has nothing to say to them, and that she prefers to read books and watch The Young and the Restless (Comrade Litvak confessed to a perverse fascination with The Young and the Restless). I refilled her glass and she invited me to join her. Since there were no other customers in the restaurant, I sat across from her in the booth, a bottle of vodka between us.

By the fifth drink, a story stumbled out. She mentioned a book, an American, a Chechen, a Georgian, a tarmac, a child she loves but never wanted. She spoke of Moscow, a window onto a river, a heritage she knows nothing about. Then she confessed that she misses them. So I said, "Why don't you go back?" She said she often thinks of returning but is afraid. "What do you fear?" I asked. She dodged the question, said she enjoys the freedom of not being watched but feels guilty. I said, "You have a daughter. How can you leave her behind?"

Comrade Litvak wiped tears from her eyes. I shushed her, let her cry into my palm. She said, "I don't understand. I will never understand," then wept some more. She continued to drink heavily. The bottle was finished, and she demanded I retrieve another, then stood up and tried to pull my face into focus. She commenced to vomit. I took hold of her, escorted her to the toilet, and held back her hair as she continued to expunge. When she collapsed onto the bathroom floor, I called a taxi and escorted her to the Royal Victoria Hospital. The hour was 3:15 a.m. The doctors ascertained she had alcohol poisoning. Her stomach was pumped and she was provided intravenous fluids. I waited outside the room while the doctors monitored her.

The hospital halls were quiet. I struggled to stay awake. I remember a man in a shabby coat and a blue baseball hat arriving at the room, accompanied by a nurse. He smiled at me. I tried to keep my eyes and ears open, but the doors to the room were shut. When I jolted myself awake one hour later, I looked in on Comrade Litvak but she was no longer there.

Montreal, Canada
Signed November 10, 1977
P.K., Senior Lieutenant, Committee for State Security, Reporting Officer

**Report on Observations of Comrade Litvak by
Junior Lieutenant Z.G.**

On 8 March 1978, we received valuable information that led us to a woman residing in
a small studio apartment at 12 Indian Road
Crescent in the High Park neighbourhood of
Toronto, Canada. The woman in question goes
by the name Rachel Grabinsky, has chestnut-
brown hair, and studies at the University
of Toronto, where she is undergoing a Ph.D.
in Soviet Studies and Political Science.
Following several days of careful observa-
tion, I confirmed that Rachel Grabinsky is in
fact Comrade Anna Litvak. She is no longer
herself. I will continue to refer to her by
her truthful name.

It is believed the American Gary Ruckler, who
currently works for the Central Intelligence
Agency, was responsible for ushering Comrade
Litvak from a hospital in Montreal to this
new residence five hundred and forty-eight
kilometres away. Agent Ruckler appears to be
living with Comrade Litvak. While she attends
classes, he purchases groceries and cooks
meals for her. I observed the progression of
their relationship, from a shoulder to cry
on, as the Americans say, to becoming sexual
in nature. On one occasion, I infiltrated the
house and discovered Agent Ruckler had left

an envelope containing 50 USD on the kitchen table. Comrade Litvak used these funds to purchase books, pens, and notebooks. I also discovered brown hair dye in the bathroom cabinet and a Canadian passport under the alias Rachel Grabinsky.

For several weeks, I followed Comrade Litvak and observed her patterns. Each morning, from Monday to Friday, Comrade Litvak attends classes at the downtown campus of the University of Toronto, following which she enters the Robarts Library. In a non-descript cubicle on the fifth floor, hidden amongst the stacks, she reads various articles and books, and writes in a notebook. She does this for several hours. In the early afternoon, she boards a streetcar west to Roncesvalles Avenue, where she sits at the counter of the Polish Deli, drinking black coffee and smoking Dunhill cigarettes. She always orders two pieces of Wonder bread, toasted, with butter. She is obsessed with butter and can often be observed stuffing free packets into her purse. On several occasions, I observed Comrade Litvak eating marmalade straight from a jar, knife sliding the length of her tongue. She writes with a blue Bic ballpoint pen in a red Hilroy notebook.

On the afternoon of 20 May 1978, at 14h20, Comrade Litvak was observed to enter a doctor's office where she was informed that she was six weeks pregnant. She then travelled by bus to the Polish Deli, where she ordered a Canadian chocolate known as the Cherry Blossom. She carefully removed and smelled both the packaging and contents. She placed the Cherry Blossom on a white plate and cut it in half. She ate like it was the body of Lenin Himself. Indeed, there was liquid cherry inside.

On 21 May 1978, I composed a letter to Comrade Litvak and deposited it into her mailbox. As the intent was to draw on her affections, I wrote the letter in a personal manner and requested a meeting in person. I observed Comrade Litvak reading the letter later that night. She tore it up and lit the shredded paper on fire, then wept into Agent Ruckler's chest.

Toronto, Canada
Signed 22 May 1978
Z.G., Junior Lieutenant
Committee for State Security

# 3

On the plane, Tamar manages a short, fitful sleep. She dreams
that Rachel and Anna are playing cards against each other.
But when they throw down their hands, they're the same: four
kings backed with an ace. She wakes to catch a man two rows
ahead staring at her. When he notices her watching he turns
away. The man has olive-coloured skin, a high forehead, and
deep-set eyes. He reminds her of Davit. He has the same cleft
chin and two birthmarks on his cheek and right ear, and he
dresses like him too: a blue pinstripe suit with a purple flower
in his lapel. It makes her uneasy, this uncanny visitation, and
makes her wonder: is it safe for her to go back to Tbilisi?

"Only the paranoid survive," Rachel said after Davit's
murder. The next day Tamar accepted Rachel's offer to go
to Canada. Three days later she was on a plane to Toronto.
Tamar was supposed to come for a year. She stayed for three.
Without Davit, she didn't see the point in returning.

When the plane lands in Istanbul, her paranoia keeps her on edge. As she leads her small suitcase through the airport, she looks over her shoulder several times. She believes the man from the plane is following her. She goes into the women's bathroom and washes her face. When she emerges, the man is no longer in sight, but when she checks the departures board for her connecting flight, she sees him again, loitering by a newsstand.

Her flight has been cancelled. At the customer service desk, dozens of angry travellers demand refunds. "It's not the airline's fault that the airport in Tbilisi is closed," announces the ticket agent to the jet-lagged throng. Debate ensues amongst the ticket holders. Hypotheses rife with conspiracy theories suggest why the airport is closed, who's behind it, and what God or Putin might be plotting. Tamar catches sight of the man again, his cell phone pressed to his ear. She watches him watch her. She decides to take matters into her own hands. As she pushes her way through Atatürk International, she imagines Rachel watching. When she passes through customs into Turkey, Tamar does not look back. With suitcase in tow, she opens the doors to the world and disappears into the night. Davit's doppelgänger is nowhere to be seen.

A taxi drops her off at the bazaar in Sultanahmet. Here she buys a thin black shawl and disappears into the maze of the market. She travels through rows of sugar-dusted sweets, past men playing backgammon and drinking black tea from tiny glasses, down aisles of cotton jeans and piles of nylon sweaters. Part of Tamar wants to stay here, to disappear permanently.

When she finds the dilapidated bus terminal, Tamar pays for a ticket and wraps her face in the shawl. Half an hour before her bus is due to depart to Tbilisi, a man in a black suit with a clipboard asks for identification and she hands over her passport. He looks at the picture, then at her, and she loosens the scarf from her face. *No one is who they say they are. Not even me*, she thinks. She boards the bus shortly before dawn — beginning what will be a three-day journey along the Black Sea — hoping to temper her impatience, elude whoever and whatever is chasing her, and find out who she is and where she comes from, if that even matters at all.

# 4

At his mother's kitchen table, Joseph reads through the dossiers. He's a time traveller, witness to a woman he grew up with but never really knew. Joseph is stunned by the details. His mother's secret life, laid out before him in black ink, makes him feel both sick and curious. He reads them again. The loss and suffering experienced by Rachel guts him, while her stubborn secrecy shames him. *How much of this is true?* he wonders. Should he believe in the veracity of documents that conveniently landed on his mother's doorstep the day after her body was put in the ground? And if these stories are factual, what's he to do with the truth?

Joseph does something he's never done before: he calls his boss and asks for the week off work. He's never taken so much as a sick day, not even in grad school. His boss is understanding, though concerned. After hanging up, Joseph puts the dossiers aside. His first priority is getting his mother's affairs in order. He will need to sell the house, but before that, he needs to organize her office—an arduous task. The work keeps him focused, and he is glad for the distraction. It is a ritual of coffee and cleaning. He goes through his mother's notes, folders, and correspondence. He throws out many things, reducing the accumulation of important documents into a few plastic boxes. He feels good for the purging.

That night, he reads from Rachel's books.

"She had a complicated life," Tamar once said to him.

There's a passage in his mother's first book, *Lot's Wife* where Rachel writes about watching her mother, Devorah, wash dishes. She describes the vigour with which she scrubbed a plate. In her writing, Rachel meditates on the horrors endured by Devorah as a Soviet Jew and the wife of an academic who disappeared at the hands of the KGB. Devorah took out all her frustrations on those plates, scrubbing away her anger, resentment, and fear as she tried to wash away the horrors of the twentieth century. When Joseph looks up from the book, Rachel is back at the kitchen sink, scrubbing the way her mother did. And he sees it, how history repeats itself in the hands of women.

While *Lot's Wife* is considered a political memoir, the name Anna Litvak is never mentioned in its pages. Nor are his mother's experiences in Moscow and Montreal, or anything to do with Gary. There is no talk of a man known as "Z.G.," or the fact that she had a child before Joseph—his half-sibling—who was stolen from her hands. Instead, Rachel describes the hardships of Vilnius, the neighbours and friends who disappeared, and her father's incarceration.

Joseph finds one of Tamar's cigarettes, unlit in the ashtray.

He feels the need to talk to her, but she is far, far away. Joseph tries to focus on the good, but Tamar's absence clings to him. Desire confuses things, and Joseph longs for the days when they were just friends. It was clearer then, cleaner. He can't help but worry she ran away because of him.

"There's something I need to figure out," Tamar had said. "But I can't tell you about it now, okay? I'm going home."

Was this "something" connected to the Anna Litvak papers? He lights the cigarette. What he needs is someone to talk to. But the only person he can talk to is the messenger, Daniel Daniel, whose email is included at the bottom of his odd letter. So Joseph finds himself — somewhat drunk, a little bit lovesick, and altogether bereaved — writing this strange man at this late hour.

From: <josephg@hotmail.com>
To: <daniel.daniel@recordemporium.ge>
Subject: Details
Date: 12 November 2003 at 11:08 PM


Dear Mr. Daniel,


I received your package with the documents. Is my father still alive? If so, where is he? Did Gary instruct you to send me the dossiers?


Yours truly,
Joseph Grabinsky

\* \* \*

From: <daniel.daniel@recordemporium.ge>
To: <josephg@hotmail.com>
Subject: Re: Re: Details Details Details
Date: 13 November 2003 at 12.15 AM

Dear Comrade Joseph,

Thank you sincerely for writing this brief and direct postal defibrillation. I am pleased you have emptied your dishwasher. As it is my greatest desire to be your number one record impresario, I will give you exactly what you almost need. I understand your ambivalence in all manners of fathers. We are not genetic mutants, yet we inherit parental mutations. This is frightening, especially if you are the descendant of baboons. Thank god you are not.

I am pleased you have read the dossiers, and happy you have the critical eye of your father. Incidentally, Gary very much loves my record emporium and buys all Lengthy Vinyls only from me. I can provide you with very good deals, special family price, including exclusive introductions to Thelonious Cat, resident feline genius. I have many good arrangements, including second-hand William Shatner rap album, good for Canadian like you.

Gary does not know I write you long letters, nor that I send KGB documents. I do this to help my old friend, for I am his bridge over troubled waters—sadly, Simon and Garfunkel are sold out, yet Cat Stevens purrs in one-dollar bins. Please understand: Gary is the Absent Father, full of Charlie Parker pain. He do not know you from birthday cake, though I am sure you are delicious.

Your sincere,
Daniel Daniel
Owner and Proprietor of Daniel Daniel's Record Emporium
and Eternal Coffee House
Tbilisi, Republic of Georgia

\* \* \*

From: <josephg@hotmail.com>
To: <daniel.daniel@recordemporium.ge>
Subject: Re: Re: Re: Details Details Details
Date: 13 November 2003 at 3:15 AM

Hi Daniel,

Thanks for your message. Do you know precisely where he is?

J

\* \* \*

From: <daniel.daniel@recordemporium.ge>
To: josephg@gmail.com
Subject: Re: Re: Re: Re: Details Details Details Details
Date: 13 November 2003 at 3:30 AM

Dear Comrade Joseph,

I know many things. I know Biblical Hebrew and Good
Samaritan English. I know the square root of a fountain

and the secret to all Spicy Girls. And yes, I know your father's location and desires. Indeed, he want nothing more than to meet you. This might come as a shock, but he is scared of the great intimacy between fathers and sons. So I propose the Sly and Unusual Arrangement: you come to Georgia, and I construct the tear-jerk Hallmark reunion and American movie of the week, two for one special.

Special footnote: since I am the world-established proprietor of fantastic and sublime records, I have many friends. My ex-wife Keti, by example, who hates me only a little, can take you on very authentic tours. Unfortunately, Recreation Gulag, involving supreme arrest from your hotel in darkest hours of the night, including full deluxe interrogation and cold cell latrine, is currently unavailable since the prison collapsed due to earthquake. But do not worry, we will amend all broken realities. I promise much fun while solving every family mystery. I am sure we can be best friends soon enough.

Your merchant in all resouls,
Daniel Daniel
Daniel Daniel's Record Emporium, Home of the Big Donut

\* \* \*

From: <josephg@hotmail.com>
To: <daniel.daniel@recordemporium.ge>
Subject: Re: Re: Re: Re: Details Details Details Details
Date: 13 November 2003 at 8.20 AM

Dear Daniel,

I am considering your proposal but apprehensive about the government travel warnings — is there anything I should be worried about? I could come right away.

Joseph

\* \* \*

From: <daniel.daniel@recordemporium.ge>
To: <josephg@hotmail.com>
Subject: Re: Re: Details Details Details Details Details!!
Date: 13 November 2003 at 8.33 AM

Dear Comrade Joseph,

Thank you for your email. I am glad you have made so many thoughts and cancellations — mazel tube, as your people say! (The Hebrews are my number two favourite tribe after the almighty Scythians, who bear the genetic trait of the anteater, excellent climber of mountains.) Your father will be excited to see you — I cannot imagine the surprise on his face when you two reunite like the ending of a great American movie whose name I do not know but believe must exist. I love the white picket fence; mine is too dirty.

Presently I write because I believe you are too stuffed with worry. This is typical of foreignness. Do not listen to government warnings. Stalin may be Georgian, but we are no nation of madmen. By example, my uncle Boris once drank thirteen litres of red wine from famous Racha region in one hour and thirty-six minutes. Science demonstrates he is always nice with good puke and kind hearts. To sweeten your neuroses, I therefore send you brief and original Georgian survival guide:

1) Georgia is the extreme macho country where the Man must be tough and have at least two guns;

2) In Georgia the Man must always drink unless they have serious illness;

3) In Georgia the Man must not pretend to have serious illness otherwise we shoot him for lying;

4) In Georgia it is good to carry a gun in case you really have serious illness and you are accused of lying;

5) Definitely in Georgia you must be a Christian (we are not fond of Moslems, Gypsies, Russians, Chinese, Armenians, or Indians. Hebrew is okay. We definitely like California girls, sexy French women, and Italian mobsters like Tony Soprano);

6) In Georgia all girls are beautiful and definitely virgins, so please marry at least one of them.

God Bless You Comrade Joseph, and God Bless Georgia.

Your new best friend,
Daniel Daniel
Owner of the Fantastically Delighted Record Emporium

# 5

*Istanbul, Turkey*
*November 13, 2003*

A young medical student smelling of cheap cologne helps Tamar hoist her suitcase onto the overhead rack. He can't be more than twenty-three, but he has the seriousness of a youth wanting to make his mark. He returns to his medical textbook, bespectacled and with flashlight, poring over images of the naked, the cross-sectional, and the transparent. When he turns the page, she finds herself staring at an illustrated fetus in utero, the blue cord that connects them, mother and child.

Tamar wants to call Joseph, but her cell phone doesn't work here, and besides, what would she say? She wonders what Nana will utter when she opens the door. She hasn't done a good job of keeping in touch in the three years since she moved to Toronto. The odd letter, an infrequent phone call. In part, it's guilt that has stopped her from calling. Tamar was supposed to return to Tbilisi after one year. But it was comfortable in Toronto, and every time she thought of going home, she found a reason to stay. And besides, she had Rachel. Still, Tamar knew better. Nana would've appreciated more of an effort.

Tamar feels badly for it. But Nana never has much to talk about over the phone, and besides, their conversations always end with Nana in tears. She'll be overjoyed to see Tamar again, sure to berate her for not giving advance notice of her return, all the while cooking her favorite kharcho soup, as if food and its enjoyment were the only measures of love. Yet the comfort Nana offers is vastly different from what Tamar needs. Maybe this is the real reason why she has so rarely called. She imagines sitting in Nana's kitchen, eating until it's too much, until the questions force their way out: "Who the hell is Anna Litvak? And how did I get here?" And still, Nana wouldn't say a thing.

# 6

Toronto, Canada – Tbilisi, Republic of Georgia
November 13 – November 15, 2003

Joseph closes his BlackBerry and, with it, the final mad email from Daniel Daniel. For a second, he reconsiders his plan. He unbuckles his seat belt and stands up.

"Is everything okay?" asks the flight attendant.

"Okay?"

"We're closing the gate, sir. Please take your seat."

Joseph sits down and reluctantly fastens himself in. He pops a couple of Ativan and wonders if this Daniel Daniel is some kind of practical joke, though he cannot think of anyone capable of such innovative meanness. He even wonders if, in the trajectory of mourning and loss, his mind is making this up. Yet he is sitting on a real plane next to real people. The dossiers are real—he has them in his leather satchel carry-on—and the emails are real too. His only consolation is Tamar. He needs to see her. And maybe that is all that matters.

The plane leaves the ground, and Joseph leaves behind everything familiar. He watches the city of Toronto vanish into the night, its lights diminishing with distance. Despite his reservations, he feels the necessity of this journey. After all, the two most important women in his life are connected to Georgia. As the plane levels, he feels the fatigue from the past week settle in. Somewhere over Eastern Ontario, he falls asleep.

JOSEPH DOESN'T REMEMBER changing planes, but he must have dragged himself through Heathrow, then onto another plane, where he immediately fell back into a deep, Ativan-heavy sleep. It's three in the morning, a Saturday, when he's finally jolted awake after the many hours of travel. Tires hit the tarmac and passengers begin to clap as the plane grinds to a halt. Through his window, Joseph can see the pitch-black airport. Somehow the pilot safely negotiated their landing in total darkness. Reluctantly, Joseph joins in the applause.

"When God handed out land to the nations of the world, the Georgians were too drunk to make the meeting. So He gave them His country to live in," Tamar said to Joseph one Friday night at the Vesta.

"It must be nice to come from Paradise," Joseph replied.

Tamar smirked. Now Joseph grasps the irony of her statement. As Joseph follows the rush of passengers off the plane, their faces appear menacing, augmented by the red coals of their cigarettes. Flashlights glow eerily, their flickering brightness crawling up and down the walls of the airport like enormous insects. He hadn't anticipated this world without electricity, a city absent of light.

"Passport."

Joseph slides his passport under a glass window into the hands of the customs officer. The officer looks at Joseph, then at the photograph. He does this several times. Then the customs officer writes a number on a piece of paper, which he slides under the window to Joseph.

"Fifty?" asks Joseph.

"American."

"Dollars? Seriously?"

The customs officer takes back the paper, then closes the circle at the bottom of the "5" so it reads "6." He manages a half-smile. Joseph reluctantly doles out six ten-dollar bills and slides them under the glass. The customs officer stamps his passport.

When he exits the airport doors, Joseph has the feeling someone has stolen something from him. Daniel Daniel isn't at the airport to pick him up as promised, so he turns on his phone and checks for a message, but there's no reception. He looks for a taxi to take him to the Marriott Hotel, where he has a reservation. If he gets a good night's sleep, he can use their gym in the morning. He'll be able to start fresh tomorrow.

"You come with me," a big brute of a man says as he approaches Joseph.

"Come with you where?"

"Now."

"Are you Daniel Daniel?"

The look on the man's face tells Joseph he isn't. He makes like he has a particular destination in mind, but the man is right behind him.

"Special price."

The sides of his eyes are bruised. Joseph can't tell if it's his complexion or the result of a fight.

"Twenty-five dollars. I drive you downtown."

"That's very kind, but I have a ride." Joseph looks at his watch.

"You, Captain Bullshit. Come with me."

Two men emerge from the shadows. They also have short, thick necks and wear black leather jackets. No one else is around. One of these shorter men slips his hand into his jacket pocket and points, what Joseph believes, is a gun. He has the feeling they're about to shove him into a car and throw a sack over his head. He hasn't even been in Georgia for ten minutes and already he's being kidnapped.

"We drive you," the brute says to Joseph. "Or else."

When he tries to smile, it comes across as a grimace.

"Nice car — German Mercedes. You will like."

Just then a white Lada pulls up onto the curb, nearly hitting Joseph. The driver rolls down his window and yells, "Hey man, good to see you!"

The brute looks at Joseph.

"You getting in or what?" the driver asks.

Joseph hesitates at the sight of this thick-bearded man who is wearing — in middle-of-the-night darkness — black-framed square sunglasses with bright yellow lenses. Joseph moves toward the Lada but the brute stands in his way.

The driver shouts, "Get in the car. Fuck the hairy assholes of the mafia taxi driver."

One of these short men continues to point from his leather coat, momentarily flashing a metallic gun barrel. The driver pops out of the car like a jack in the box. He wears an old

Wrangler jean jacket and a Led Zeppelin *Houses of the Holy* t-shirt that's seen better days. He's of average height, with thick sturdy legs, and his protruding belly gives him an oddly disjointed look. That is, he looks like a maniacal schlep. Despite appearances, the driver calmly assesses the situation with the air of the fastidious. He clocks Joseph, then the three men. Fearlessly, he bounds back to his car. From beneath the front seat, he pulls out a rifle, and fires three times in the air. The sound of gunfire nearly gives Joseph a heart attack.

The man goes on a long diatribe in what Joseph imagines is Georgian. Joseph believes he is both ridiculing and berating the three taxi drivers. The more he yells, the more the men turn shameful. He points his rifle and they raise their hands, slowly backing up. Finally, the three men turn on their heels and sprint toward the airport terminal. The driver returns to the Lada and tucks the rifle back under the front seat. He approaches Joseph and flips up the dark yellow lenses, revealing clear glasses.

"Comrade Joseph, welcome to my country. I am your long friend, Daniel Daniel. You must be tired from your journey. Shall we go to your hotel?"

The Lada accelerates, launching them off the sidewalk. As they leap into the air, Daniel Daniel proclaims, "Let us bear witness to the great Hollywood escape. You are Dustin Hoffman, and I am Robert Redford, your happy Sundance Kid."

Joseph reaches over his shoulder but there is no seat belt, so he locks the door instead. Daniel Daniel flicks on the stereo. Two enormous speakers, propped up in the back seat, begin to convulse.

"Charlie Parker," yells Daniel Daniel as he lights up a cigarette. "Tonight in Tunisia!"

The sax wails, the wheels screech, and Daniel Daniel flips his shades down. He drives like they're in a police chase. No concern for lanes — are there lanes? Certainly no thought for pedestrians and oncoming traffic. Joseph grabs hold of the handle by the window. It's one game of chicken after another. When he's finished his cigarette, Daniel Daniel sticks his head out the window, one hand on the steering wheel as he gulps vast quantities of air.

"What the hell are you doing?" shouts Joseph.

"It's to filter lungs!" he yells, bringing his head back inside the car. "You must try it too. Very healthy. I can see you are physically fit like me."

Joseph takes stock of where he is. Headlights blind him. He tries to glean the faces of people, landmarks, intersections, signs in a language he cannot understand. But he can't make out anything. He needs to get to his hotel and contact Tamar. He'll tell her where he's staying, and then they can meet up. He wants to show her the dossiers Daniel Daniel sent him. He wants her to help him understand.

Daniel Daniel lights another cigarette and says very seriously, "Those guys were real assholes. Good thing nobody died. This would be bad visit to Georgia. Did you bring your gun?"

"What? No, of course not."

"Problem no problem. You can borrow mine."

"Actually, I was thinking I'd get some food, then go to the hotel and sleep."

"Good idea. You must be rested for warm-hearted

reunions." Daniel Daniel pats Joseph on the thigh. "You will like Gary, I promise. But first, we take scenic routes. Everything must be seen, including ourselves."

A pair of headlights cuts through the darkness toward them.

"Why is that car driving right at us?"

"Georgian wedding party. Old tradition. You will like."

Daniel Daniel squints through his sunglasses to focus his gaze. The oncoming car isn't more than fifty feet away. Joseph tries to apprehend this strange ritual: groom gets drunk, groom drives drunk, groom challenges whoever's in their path. A trail of tin cans clangs along the pothole-laden road. Six men have their heads out the windows. Daniel Daniel guns it and Joseph's stomach lurches. Daniel Daniel honks, Joseph screams. At the last moment the wedding party swerves.

"We winning, we winning!" Daniel Daniel cackles.

"Do people ever crash?" Joseph asks, practically hyperventilating.

"All the time. This makes bride very sad."

Finally, Daniel Daniel slows down. Charlie Parker continues to wail on his sax, and Joseph settles into the ride. But the respite is brief. When they pass a police car parked on the side of the road, they're waved over by two men holding giant ping-pong racquets. Reluctantly, Daniel Daniel pulls over. When the police tap the driver's side window, Daniel Daniel starts to shake. It starts slowly in his hands then feet, travelling up his limbs, then crescendos into a full-body quiver. He waves at the cops nervously and raises his finger to indicate "just a minute." They tap again and Daniel Daniel raises his finger again.

"What are you doing? Unroll the window," says Joseph.

He continues to shake as one of the cops asks for his papers.

"Daniel Daniel don't have no papers," he whispers to Joseph, though he appears to hand the police something resembling a licence. One cop inspects it with a flashlight then holds it up to the sky. For the second time in an hour, Joseph is ready to bribe a public official.

"Here, try this," he says, handing Daniel Daniel a ten-dollar bill, hoping it's sufficient.

He hands it to the police officer, who takes the money then wanders back to his car. Daniel Daniel drums nervously on the steering wheel.

"No help."

"What do you mean?"

"Problem, major problem."

"What problem?"

"This ain't my jalopy, Chet."

"You stole this?"

"Very warm. Very red-hot. Hot stuff, hot commodity."

"Jesus Christ, Daniel."

As the cop saunters back, Daniel Daniel's shaking grows more intense. Joseph reaches into his wallet and pulls out a fifty.

"Try this."

But they never get to that. When the policeman reaches the door, Daniel Daniel turns on the ignition and floors it.

"We pay them."

The car lurches forward and the cops run back to their car to give chase. As they race past Joseph's hotel, Daniel Daniel is sure to point it out — "There it is," he says, "the Marriott! Very quality hotel" — and Joseph can see it, a jewel in the crown of Rustaveli Avenue, bright as a Christmas tree, the only lit place on the street. He gazes at it longingly. The hotel disappears as they hurtle up the road at breakneck speed. Not a single streetlight works, and while this causes both anxiety and fear in Joseph, they are able to lose the police in the darkened streets. When Daniel Daniel parks, Joseph is suddenly nauseous.

"I feel sick."

"Comrade Joseph, you are most exciting."

"I have car sickness."

"Me too, my macho male sibling. I am addicted to speed."

Joseph opens the door, leans out, and pukes onto the road. Daniel Daniel pats him on the back.

"It is good to leave your insides out, Comrade. You are far too stuffed with worry. Everything will be all right."


JOSEPH WANTS A hot shower and a clean hotel bed. He wants clean sheets and room service and a toilet he can call his own. But Daniel Daniel insists on hosting him for the night. Joseph is too ill to protest.

"Is the power always off?" he asks as he staggers toward the dark prefab building.

"Do not be absurd. We have electricity one hour a day — sometimes two. We just don't know when. Very predictable Common Socialist Diet mentality problem: no one pays their capitalist bills. Constant revolution is a permanent disorder."

From the outside the building looks like it's balanced on concrete stilts. Daniel Daniel insists on carrying Joseph's suitcase, which he is glad for. He hadn't realized that Daniel Daniel lives on the seventeenth floor of a building with no functioning elevator. When they climb the stairs, Daniel Daniel will not use a flashlight.

"You don't want to see," he says.

The stairwell smells like urine and burned rubber. Joseph feels like he's descending into a pit, even though he's going up. He wonders aloud if this is what the architects were after, some kind of test of the human soul. Daniel Daniel argues the only thing being tested was the gullibility of people's pocketbooks.

"Thanks to the Common Socialist Diet, everyone lives in the House of the Mad Thief. The only true market is the black one. Fortunately, I sell many records. You will see my store tomorrow. Tonight, let us relax amidst the opulent luxury of my late father-in-law. He is world-famous artist with excellent tastes."

Joseph harbours no illusions of luxury. Yet when they arrive at the apartment, Daniel Daniel opens the door to another world. The soft glow of kerosene lanterns, Carlos Gardel crooning on an old Victrola, and the smell of warm food. The ceilings are high and the view of the city at dawn — wide, expansive, beset by cliffs overlooking a winding, muddy river — surprises him with its beauty. Joseph still feels sick, but he also feels welcome amidst the decay of fallen buildings. In the candlelit bathroom, he scrubs his face and armpits with cold water stored in large plastic buckets, then brushes his teeth and puts on a clean shirt.

"Eat, Comrade Joseph."

It's six in the morning and Joseph feels not the least bit hungry, but the smell reminds him of Tamar's cooking. In the kerosene light, in a building on its last legs, he thinks maybe Tamar wasn't being ironic. If this isn't Paradise, then maybe he has arrived somewhere resembling home. A home he never knew he had. Daniel Daniel fills their glasses with thick red wine.

"To old and new friends," he says.

Joseph raises his glass. The nausea, for a moment, passes.

# 7

*Istanbul — Samsun, Turkey*
*November 13, 2003*

The bus leaves Istanbul and disappears into the Turkish countryside. The longer they drive, the lighter it gets. Tamar sees layers in the light, contours and dimensions she hasn't previously considered. Somewhere near the Black Sea she catches her reflection in the bus window, and it startles her. When the rising sun peers over the edge of the Black Sea, a memory appears before her, a sliver of light. It blinds her and opens a floodgate.

Tamar remembers light reflecting off metal. She remembers the blandness of concrete, the mad whirl of propellers, a hand grabbing her arm. She remembers being carried across concrete, into a car, then onto a train. She remembers sleeping in the crook of his arm, a word, many words, in languages that don't fit. Arguments ricocheting through narrow aisles. She remembers the shock of absence, tears for her mother, a story to calm her, myths that provided nourishment like milk. She remembers cotton cloth, an old woman changing her while her father looked on with a cigarette, smoke curling above his head. She remembers a woman singing, a man moaning, red velour, and seats painted paisley. She remembers yak fur and foxgloves, vodka and cigarettes, a twenty-piece brass band, circus performers, men with Kalashnikovs, and women with knitting needles. She remembers her father's panic, the mad search for cufflinks, and her trying to help, wanting to make everything better. She remembers left-alone, the tick-tock of solitude, the train's slow climb, and relief when he returned. She remembers devilled eggs and warm milk, the miracle of walking. Two impossible steps and the train swerving in its tracks. She remembers the strain, how she walked into the arms of her father. His smell, leather and sweat, what she would come to know as love. Zaza. Yet she does not understand how she got there.

She remembers daylight, mountains big, white, and blinding. She remembers Zaza's lessons in a new language, the screech of wheels, fear from beneath. She remembers him putting her in a basket, a rat in the tracks. She remembers being outside and waiting, abandoned a second time before he returned, this time in a car. She remembers the front passenger seat, crying at the light as she uttered her first word in Georgian: mama. Tamar repeats it, again and again. Mama, mama, mama. Zaza tickles and kisses her, a happiness he insists on singing: *You're my girl, you're my girl, you're mine.*

# 8

**Report on Observations of Agent Gary Ruckler
by Junior Lieutenant Z.G.**

For two weeks, I have observed Agent Ruckler
carrying out his duties on behalf of the
Central Intelligence Agency. He drafts reports,
conducts phone calls from safe houses, meets
with assets in the Toronto area, several of
whom work at the University of Toronto, the
Canadian Broadcast Corporation, and other
liberal institutions. I maintain that Agent
Ruckler is an agent of mediocre calibre. This
was confirmed when Comrade Litvak read him
my personal letter. The burning scarlet of
his face betrayed an embarrassment wrought
of carelessness. Comrade Litvak leaned into
his chest and sobbed. Agent Ruckler looked
up through the window of their apartment and
directly at me. Indeed, I was in the unit

across the street. I put down my binoculars, smiled, and waved. Agent Ruckler turned a deeper red.

Following this, Agent Ruckler left nothing suspicious in the house. If he had anything important to say to Comrade Litvak, he turned on the radio. He ducked up alleyways and into stores to elude me. Sometimes he succeeded. We became engaged in a sophisticated game of cat and mouse. When Agent Ruckler and Comrade Litvak engaged in coitus on the evening of 10 June 1978, I believed he was doing it to spite me. Indeed, he looked directly at me following completion of the act.

Having received the command to return to Moscow, I wished to inform Comrade Litvak that she was welcome to join me as per the Committee's request. I approached her at the university campus in the guise of a student. Immediately she started to scream, drawing the attention of those around her. I walked in another direction.

The last time I saw Agent Ruckler was in a record store on Yonge Street, Sam the Record Man. I followed Agent Ruckler to the third floor, where he composed various notes and observations in a brown notebook. Then I observed him speaking with an employee who handed him a list, which he then checked against his own. Later he was led to an office. I waited twenty

minutes, but he did not emerge. I never saw
Agent Ruckler again.

Moscow, U.S.S.R.
Signed 26 June 1978
Z.G., Junior Lieutenant
Committee for State Security

*Tbilisi, Republic of Georgia*
*November 15, 2003*

When Joseph awakes, he finds a new dossier on the floor next to his mattress. He reads the report then gazes out the window at tall apartment blocks with greasy windows and chipped concrete. It's a dismal view, a 1970s version of the future gone wrong. He can feel the building swaying back and forth in the wind. The other buildings in the complex are also swaying, as though the edifices are engaged in telling time. He yearns for a clean bed and a bathroom with running water, where he doesn't have to use gathered rainwater to flush the toilet.

"How do I get to my hotel?" he asks.

"Problem, no problem."

Daniel Daniel reclines shirtless on a daybed, wearing only tight black jeans. His sunglasses are flipped up. Through the clear, square lenses he reads from a well-worn book. His jutting wine belly is speckled with grey hair, and his wild beard is rife with crumbs. Holding a cigarette and a cinnamon bun in the same hand, he takes turns inhaling each.

"Who are you?" Joseph asks. "And why do you have two first names?"

Daniel Daniel appears annoyed by the question. He slams shut the Russian translation of *Moby Dick* and proceeds to tell Joseph a story.

"I am not only a great record store impresario; I am the former musician. In Soviet days, I play trumpet in touring free-jazz trio. The band is not so famous, but one night in Baku, I bring my trumpet to the opulent nightclub 'Funked Up East,' and I am invited to play with the house band during the open set. When they ask for my name, I say, 'Daniel.' Do not ask why I like this American name. Sometimes we only wish to be heroes. Like Daniel, the good and strong man from the Bible. He rocks it in the House of the Lion-Cats.

"During the set I play long, extensive solos. My new band-mates don't appreciate this gesture toward immortality. The bass tries holding me back. The sax shoots many aggressive notes. Finally, the drummer yells, 'Hey Daniel. Stop fucking playing!' But I am lost in the groove. In those days, I am not even on drugs, though I very much wish I was. The drummer yells again, 'Hey Daniel…Daniel, Daniel!' He might have said this a hundred times. Only when the drummer throws a cymbal at my head do I awake from my Charlie Parker reverie.

"When the band is introduced at the end of night, I am presented to the overjoyed audience as Daniel Daniel. Please appreciate its brevity, it is much easier than saying 'Daniel' one hundred times."

Joseph asks, "And how exactly do you know my father?"

"We meet at Moscow University. We play jazz together."

"I didn't know my father played music."

"In reality, Gary is a mediocre amateur. We drink more in those days."

"So you're drinking buddies."

"Buddy-buddies who drink."

Joseph groans. He doesn't know whether to believe these stories, or if their veracity even matters. What matters is finding the right questions. This time, he needs to be prepared.

"So how did you get a hold of these KGB files?"

"Gary gives them to me. He needs me to watch them. He cannot be trusted with anything, not even himself."

"And you decided to send them to me by regular mail?"

"Copies, Comrade, copies. I am no idiot. It's important for you to know him. You learn something, no?"

Joseph can't disagree. "So when are we seeing him?"

"Eleven."

"Like, in an hour?"

"You are not ready?"

"No, I'm ready. It's why I'm here."

But Joseph isn't prepared in the slightest. The prospect of seeing Gary in the flesh rattles him. It's a performance he's rehearsed too many times. Now that it might actually happen, he panics.

"Relax, Comrade. I understand, this is the Highly Unusual Situation. But your father has a kind, good heart. You will like him. He is only afraid."

"You mean he's a coward."

"This too."

Joseph rereads the passage about Gary's disappearance in the dossier. He thinks back to the afternoon when he was ten, when he was "kidnapped" — Rachel's term — for an afternoon of baseball. The Blue Jays got walloped by the Yankees, he drank too much sugar and ate too many hot dogs. In time, he would listen to his father's beloved jazz albums until they became his own. But the music could not compensate for what he did not know. For he didn't just forget to ask the important questions. He didn't ask anything at all.

Daniel Daniel hands him a coffee mug. Joseph takes a sip and gags. "What the hell is this?"

"Chacha, drink of the dead. My grandfather makes it."

The chacha makes Joseph feel like he's been clubbed by

a giant. He tries to hand the mug back to Daniel Daniel but he refuses. "It gets better. I promise."

Reluctantly, Joseph takes another sip. Strangely enough, this time the chacha is almost drinkable. The building sways again, and it seems to move in tandem with his thoughts. Joseph understands that he might not be totally out of control.

"There's another reason I'm here," Joseph confesses. "A woman."

"Always a woman."

"Her name is Tamar Tumanishvili."

Daniel Daniel eyes him through thick smoke. "You mean the famous and troublesome performance artist?"

"You know her?"

"Of course."

"She was staying with my mother in Toronto, and we became friends. Good friends." Joseph clears his throat. "After Rachel died, she left to come back here. I need to see her."

Daniel Daniel eyes him suspiciously. "Why don't you call her?"

"I did, but she didn't answer her phone."

"Did you leave messages?"

"Of course."

"You are mad and in love with her."

"What? No."

"You are the stupid man, Comrade Joseph."

"Can you help me find her?"

Daniel Daniel groans. "No, I will not get involved. Georgian women are dangerous, and you are here to meet my long-time friend. Only you can lift your father from his manly despair."

"I'm not here to cheer Gary up. He walked out on us when I was a kid. My mother pretended he was dead."

"I know how you sob, Comrade Joseph. All sons without fathers do. Without them, we live only with ghosts. But I promise, you will not regret your meeting. Open your heart. 'All my life, I yearn for something I cannot name.' Sounds like Whitney Houston; in reality, we are sons of André Breton. There is much to learn from those who disappear, and no one is who they say they are."

Joseph looks around the apartment. Haunted images stare back at him: Ophelia in a red dress dancing with the ghost of Winston Churchill; Richard II with a Stalin moustache smashing his fist on a table; Hamlet holding the skull of capitalism, sliced off at the top and stuffed with dollar bills.

Daniel Daniel tells him the story of his father-in-law, Zurab, the man whose apartment they are in. "He is another father who disappears. Zurab was a set designer — these paintings stand as evidence of his mad conceptions."

Zurab's old paintbrushes, jammed into tin cans, make Joseph think of dead hands waving at the living.

"Where is your father-in-law now?" he asks.

"Beside me. In Georgia, the dead are always with us. They are our very claustrophobic neighbours."

Daniel Daniel explains that Zurab used to spend his summers in Abkhazia. When the war began, he was caught in the crossfire. Zurab's neighbours — whom he'd lived alongside and known intimately for decades — came knocking on his door, carrying AKs and pitchforks. They wanted him dead.

They also wanted to burn his paintings. Zurab didn't care about his life, but he cared about his art. So Daniel Daniel organized his first heist.

"After lying, the most important thing in life is to steal. It is best to survive."

A Soviet GAZ-66 4x4, and as many paintings as he and his ex-wife, Keti, could cram in before Zurab's work disappeared in the flames of Sukhumi. Daniel Daniel figures he saved a quarter of his father-in-law's output. They drove through a landscape of murder and mines, execution and rape, following a river of refugees all the way back to Tbilisi.

"Life is not so beautiful, eh, Comrade?"

Joseph is sobered into agreement. This time, when the building begins to sway, he is prepared. All he has to do is let his mind go, left then right. Maybe he can do this. If he can learn to move with the chaos, he will learn to speak to the dead.

# 9

*Black Sea Coast, Turkey*
*November 15, 2003*

Tamar thinks of the elbow she slept in during that train ride. Landscapes that passed like scenes in a dream. She thinks of the man who held her. Zaza. But how did she get on the train? Where did she come from? And if he's still alive, why is Zaza seeking penance?

They travel East through Turkey, cliffs marked by ruins and ancient temples. Tamar has been on the bus for almost two days now. She has fallen into a rhythm of memory, cigarettes and sleep. Throughout the night the bus stops in darkened villages. During one nondescript stopover, by an anonymous building in a shadowed country, Tamar huddles into the thinness of her coat. Her fellow passengers pass around black tea and strong cigarettes. Shouting erupts from the parking lot. She sees a circle of men gathered, their silhouettes edging up a street lamp. Tamar sips her tea, a sugar cube cradled in her tongue. Sweetness oozes into her mouth, sliding warm and hot down her throat. A fire blazes in a trash bin, the night air cold and damp. If Rachel is her mother — if Rachel is indeed Anna Litvak — then how did Tamar end up with Zaza, in the house of Nana? Did Anna abandon her? What makes a mother choose not to raise her own child?

Growing up, Tamar's favourite play was *The Caucasian Chalk Circle* by Bertolt Brecht. In the Tbilisi production, Sasha played the narrator; she loved watching her adoptive father on the grand Rustaveli stage. But it was the story of Grusha the maidservant that compelled her. After the governor's wife accidentally leaves her baby behind in the chaos of a coup, Grusha takes the child into her care. She flees to the mountains where she raises him as her own. Years later, the governor's wife learns what Grusha has done and demands her son back. The question Brecht forces the audience to ask: Who is the child's real mother? Is it the one who gave birth to him, or is it the one who raised him?

Tamar leans against the concrete wall, drops a second sugar cube onto her tongue and sips her tea. She learned this from Nana: the joy of a sweet mouth full of hot tea. There's no question for Tamar — she is Nana's daughter. Nana did everything for her. Packed her lunch for swim practice; knitted her socks; taught her how to darn a sweater. Nana's love let her live. If Anna-Rachel is her birth mother, what does it matter?

Suddenly the shouting in the parking lot grows louder. Something catches fire, and people begin to gather.

"Fucking Kurds." An old matriarch grimaces from across the lot.

As Tamar watches the men burn Turkish flags, chanting for independence and nationhood, she wonders if Joseph could understand that, here, longing on a large scale makes history, and protest is as essential as breath. After all, it was here that Amirani challenged God, and Prometheus stole fire from Zeus, and Medea slayed her children. This mythical landscape, born of revolution. To live in Toronto, Tamar had to turn that part of herself off. Her life felt like it had been put on pause. And it was...nice. After the death of Davit, Tamar needed that quiet.

But now that she's returning home, she feels something shifting inside her. Tamar wonders if Joseph could see how the chants and cries of these Kurdish men and women are also her own. Stomping on the flags of their oppressors, teetering toward violence. The Kurds want their own country; Tamar wants the truth of her past. Normally, her first instinct would be to make an art piece that reflects this sentiment. But she cannot conceive the frame to hold it. For this narrative — who she is, and where she comes from — exceeds the limitations of representation and performance. Tamar misses Rachel, but she also wishes that Rachel had never come into her life. She wishes she didn't care, but she cares more than anything.

# 10

*Tbilisi, Republic of Georgia*
*November 15, 2003*

By daylight, the suburbs of Tbilisi are a melancholy hangover. Prostitutes and police officers gab by the side of the
road, dully negotiating territory. Babushkas loiter, selling vintage stamps, dried sausages, wool socks, and plastic bottles
of chacha and gasoline. An occasional pig or cow wanders
through traffic searching for grass. Daniel Daniel guides a
"borrowed" Mercedes 300 through the ramshackle streets.
(Daniel Daniel does not steal cars, he says, he only borrows
them "because they sit too sadly from being unloved.") As
they descend the cliffs, Joseph tries to take in the city. Instead,
he feels it take him. His sense of security, the ability to rely
on things familiar, is gone.

Wide avenues lead onto opera houses, gleaming empty
shopping malls, and ancient apothecaries. Slanted, ornate
roofs of blue shingle and green. There are roundabouts with
Social Realist sculptures, water fountains without water, and

bridges fallen in disrepair. The Mother of Georgia statue, an ugly silver beast of a thing, clenches a sword in one hand and a bowl of wine in the other. She looks down from her perch, clinging to the edge of the dusty, windswept cliffs. Joseph recognizes the sculpture from Gary's postcard but didn't imagine it to be so big. His unease, he understands, comes from the feeling of being watched.

Daniel Daniel jerks the car onto the sidewalk, cutting the ignition. The back end juts into the road like a beached whale.

"We are very much here. Welcome to Paradise."

On the side of an old brick building collapsing into itself, hand-stencilled letters in faded green and white: "Daniel Daniel's Record Emporium."

Joseph is led down a set of broken concrete stairs and through a shaky glass door. Expecting a tiny, claustrophobic room, he finds himself in a vast space with hardwood floors, a high ceiling, and walls painted with day-glo rocket ships and swirls of expressive colour. A cello plays Bach from old speakers, hidden from sight. Several chandeliers hang from the ceiling, holding lit candles, white and yellow wax dripping down their edges. There are orange plastic chairs in which young people sit drinking coffee, eating giant pieces of cake, and reading newspapers and magazines. A long bar stretches across one end of the room — L-shaped, panelled with faux leather and wood — on top of which sits an old cash register and a black cat with a patch of white hair on its chin. A young woman doles out coffee, cakes, and records to the patrons. Behind her, hanging on the wall in a black frame, is a *Houses of the Holy* t-shirt, much like the one Daniel Daniel wore last night, though much older, evidenced by the holes and fraying edges beneath the glass.

"This is Lali," says Daniel Daniel, indicating the young woman behind the cash, "my right-hand woman, sometimes daughter, and curator of our fantastic punk collection." Lali smiles politely at Joseph. "And this is the resident feline genius, Thelonious Cat. Behold his natural goatee bianco. Please, do not feed him donuts. He will turn into nothing." Daniel Daniel picks up the cat and affectionately kisses his forehead. "Say hello, Thelonious, to your new best friend, Comrade Joseph." The cat yawns, indifferent.

Joseph is drawn to a bin of records propped up on an old table. Flipping through dusty plastic sleeves, he discovers rare B-sides he's never listened to, concerts he's never heard of: Dizzy Gillespie in Moscow, Dave Brubeck in Szczecin, the Duke in Riga. And it's not just American jazz, but Russian and Lithuanian trios, Latvian and Armenian duos, Ukrainian and Kazakh big band — a world he didn't know existed. The richness and variety surprise him.

Daniel Daniel mutters something in Lali's ear. The music stops and a hush descends upon the shop. Customers look up from their coffees and magazines. Joseph relishes the moment before the needle is dropped on a new record. Right away he recognizes the piano's restrained melody line, a question. Then the deep tenor sax offers its response. The music is warm, beautiful, and rich. Duke Ellington and John Coltrane, their one album together, as perfect a collaboration as he can think of. Daniel Daniel hands him a cup of coffee. Joseph takes a sip and continues sifting through the records. *I don't care if my father shows up at all*, he thinks.

"This place is great," Joseph says, joining Daniel Daniel by a table.

"You like?"

"Yeah. It's cool."

Daniel Daniel bows his head in gratitude.

"'Cool' is the greatest compliment known to man. Thank you, Comrade Joseph."

Joseph eyes the young crowd smoking and drinking hot coffee beneath flickering candles. The scene is an homage to both another era and an imagined Bohemia that never existed. There are plenty of black turtlenecks. Boxcars of ashtrays and piles of Allen Ginsberg, Lawrence Ferlinghetti, and Sylvia Plath poetry stacked on tables. On the walls, he spots posters of Miles Davis, Bessie Smith, and Charlie Parker. There's even a framed photograph of a much younger and leaner Daniel Daniel with a thick, black beard and badass shades, playing trumpet.

"I didn't realize jazz was such a big deal here."

"It is the revolution without words. During the Great Common Socialist Diet, it is also essential. Before people speak, they play. Jazz makes protests without saying a thing."

For Joseph, jazz is a resting spot. Music is something he holds on to in the privacy of his most authentic self. And while his mother used to make fun of him for listening to it — "You do understand that jazz is the music of struggle, right? That you are appropriating the African-American fight to help you relax from your difficult bourgeois life?" — he's always felt there is something more to it than privilege. He needs jazz like he needs hope. It contains a beauty he can depend on.

"So what will you say to daddy-o?" asks Daniel Daniel

as he dumps teaspoons of sugar into his coffee. Once again, he's wearing his yellow-tinted sunglasses.

"I don't know," Joseph admits.

He has anticipated this moment for a long time. Even when he thought Gary was dead, he harboured fantasies of reunions. Every year on his birthday, he'd write one-line questions that he'd slip under his pillow, like prayers.

"Which do you prefer for breakfast, oatmeal or eggs?"

"Do you have trouble sleeping at night?"

"When you are dead, do you see the world from your invisible position?"

Even back then, the questions seemed ridiculous. Now it feels like there was something cruel in his mother's silence. How could she not say a thing?

Joseph looks at his watch, then the door. It's 11:15. "He's late."

"Gary is never on time. Time is his worst friend."

Joseph swills the tepid coffee. On the communal table, he notices his mother's last book, *How to Get Rid of a Dictatorship*.

"Maybe do not ask your father questions about the past," suggests Daniel Daniel. "Maybe ask, 'How are you, O Father who aren't in Heaven?'"

"I was thinking more along the lines of 'Why did you abandon us?'"

"Perhaps he has good reasons," says Daniel Daniel.

"There's always a reason."

Joseph picks up his mother's book and examines the images in black-and-white of demonstrators in various cities. He's never been one for protest. The sense of being pissed off with the world and demanding change, as though justice were owed to him, has always struck Joseph as self-indulgent. Self-important, even. And yet, when it comes to Gary, he believes some form of protest is warranted. The words "Fuck the hell off" come to mind. Did he really fly ten thousand kilometres to say that?

Daniel Daniel's cell phone rings. He picks it up and whispers. When he hangs up, he looks concerned. "Unfortunately, Gary cannot come now. He is in very big accident."

"What? Is he okay?"

"He must visit the doctor. But he is also fine. He is only mediocre hypochondriac. He asks if we can meet at your hotel this afternoon at four p.m."

"Sure."

Relieved he doesn't have to say what's really on his mind, Joseph pages through his mother's book and lands on a photo of Tamar perched on top of a tank. Thelonious Cat leaps onto Joseph's lap and nestles in, totally at home. Daniel Daniel smiles approvingly. Joseph feels the itch of something important missing, a narrative ignored. He finishes his coffee and announces to Daniel Daniel he'd like to see Tamar.

Daniel Daniel groans. "How do we do that if you do not know where she is?"

"Her brother Levan runs the Underground Theatre. Maybe he knows."

# 11

The bus rolls through the Turkish countryside, climbing hills of green clotted with sheep. Tamar tries to use her cell phone, but it still doesn't work. She watches the man in the black suit at the front of the bus. When he looks down at his clipboard, he removes his flip phone from his jacket and dials. He speaks quietly then turns around. For a moment their eyes meet.

When the bus pulls over, Tamar gets off and loses herself in a market. She takes one bend, then another, until she's teetering at the edge of the Black Sea. Afternoon now; sun reflects on each wave, and she thinks about the many forms of love. Mother love, father love, brother love, the love of hands and bodies. The love of secrets, the love of subterfuge, the love of resistance, the love of multiple identities. She thinks of Rachel's love, Zaza's love too, a love that makes her nauseous, like the sea before her that flows in two directions at once, two separate currents, east and west.

On her way back to the bus Tamar runs into a pile of cheap Nokia phones, dozens of them, a stack next to a Russian man who looks more fishmonger than merchant.

"Do these actually work?" she asks.

He picks up a red phone, slips in a sim card, and says, "Try it, darling."

She dials Lali's number, but no one answers. Then she calls Levan.

"Hey," says Tamar.

"Where are you?"

"I'm taking the scenic route."

"What does that mean?"

"The airport was shut down."

"Well, it's open again."

"I'll see you in a day or two."

She hangs up and hands the merchant several bills, then steps back onto the bus, the tiny phone in her thin hand. The medical student sleeps with his face buried in his book. She sends a text to Lali and Goran: I'm on a bus in Turkey and I'm coming home.

AFTER DAVIT'S MURDER and Tamar's escape from Georgia, Rachel turned careful.

"You need to be quiet," she said one day when Tamar came home from a protest in Toronto against rising tuition fees. "Lay low for a bit."

"And do what?"

Rachel handed her a leather-bound notebook. "Write about your experiences. You've led an interesting life."

Tamar groaned. She had no patience for sitting still and

putting pen to paper. She wanted the kind of action afforded by her art practice. But then she acquiesced, and to her surprise she found salvation in wet ink on a dry page. Putting her thoughts on paper became a kind of relief. Sometimes she wrote letters to the past: to Davit, whom she missed; to Zaza, whom she knew was still alive; to herself, a Tamar that might have existed in Berlin or New York; and to Anna, a woman she wished to know. She wrote in English because it was the language of distance, and she needed perspective.

Tamar also wrote to her friends in Tbilisi. Emails, for the most part. They wrote back in earnest. According to Goran and Lali, there had been an investigation into Davit's murder that led to the arrest of a shepherd from Svaneti, who'd supposedly been hired to do the killing. But the police never found a motive for the murder, and it was doubtful the lonely shepherd was anything more than a scapegoat — yet another victim caught up in someone else's mess. In the end, there would never be any justice for Davit's death; whatever forces wanted him erased would have it their way.

Sometimes Tamar wonders if it is a symptom of the collective trauma, this constant extinguishing of truth. Is that why Zaza was at the KGB archives that day in 1991? With the prospect of a national truth and reconciliation process, did certain truths threaten him? What horrible things had her father done? And if Zaza didn't want the public to know, why was he now seeking penance? Shouldn't he have been fighting with the protestors for honesty, culpability, and transparency?

The desire for public accountability has not completely died in the decade since the burning of the KGB archives. The facts of Davit's murder are buried — for now — but truth has a way of rising to the surface. For all the lost listlessness of her generation, Tamar feels proud of what they have endured and might still accomplish. In this way, when Tamar was in Toronto, Lali and Goran were a lifeline. She needed them to feel connected to her old self. They told her about the projects they were working on and their correspondence with pro-democracy groups in Moscow and Kyiv. They told her about the public performances they gave in city squares and parks, the media attention, and their collaboration with the Young Lawyers' Association on human rights issues. They filled her in on the university protests, graffiti actions, and the public works to help build a civic society from the ground up.

Nearly two weeks ago, they emailed her about the recent elections. The European election monitors claimed Shevardnadze had curbed results in his favour. Reports of ballot-box stuffing were rampant. Everyone knew he hadn't received 90 percent of the vote, that the young Mikheil Saakashvili had mobilized an entire generation of youth in the name of change and democracy.

"The people are gathering in the streets," wrote Lali. "They've had enough."

# 12

Daniel Daniel leads Joseph down an alleyway into a courtyard filled with trash and discarded furniture. Joseph nearly trips on an old bedframe, and his chest hurts when he breathes. He wonders what toxins reside in the air, what remnant of Chernobyl he inhales (though Chernobyl is thousands of kilometres and seventeen years distant, he imagines a curtain of radiation around him). He wonders if it's the paranoia of spy movies that makes him suspicious of the post-Soviet air, or a desire to protect Tamar. He wants to shield her from the world. Yet it's him that needs protection.

"Be careful with Levan," warns Daniel Daniel, knocking on the metal door to the Underground. "He sells many dark and mysterious things, including your soul. And do not dare tell him you are in love with his sister."

When the door opens, they're told by the leopard-print-wearing ticket seller, Vera, that Levan is visiting his mother,

Nana. She writes the address on a piece of scrap paper and hands it to them.

Daniel Daniel whizzes up one street then another. The traffic lights don't work, the city streets are a total free-for-all, and the address they've been given doesn't exist. Yet Daniel Daniel loves every moment of it, accelerating and flying around the lawless corners, asking random strangers how to find the house of Nana. Joseph closes his eyes and prays for his safety. He never considered faith intrinsic to the experience of driving.

Daniel Daniel stops the car by a cul-de-sac and draws a map on a piece of paper torn out of an old notebook. On the map is a hill with a road that snakes to the top, where a one-eyed woman named Nastia sells benzene and chacha in small plastic bottles. In his rendering, she looks like an ogre from a fairy tale.

"These details are highly important," explains Daniel Daniel, pressing up his sunglasses to examine his methodical text. "Houses do not have numbers and streets only sometimes exist. In the Georgian state, we are very much an existential problem." Then he hands Joseph the map. "I see you with Gary late this afternoon." Joseph slams the car door shut, then follows the map to the top of the hill.

The detail is precise, including markings of garbage cans and discarded syringes, though the one-eyed Nastia is no ogre but a pretty teenager with a single gold tooth, her left eye made of glass. She offers Joseph instant coffee, which he drinks while sitting on a small stool. The road is empty except for two security guards playing backgammon on a stump. The air stings his eyes, and again he has the feeling that he's breathing in bad omens. He buys a bouquet of wild irises. By the top of the dilapidated hill is a pretty pink chair. As he approaches it, he can see the back is ripped out. Foam and springs spill out like the guts of a freshly killed animal. Joseph spots a house marked by a trellis and door frame. He knocks and a woman dressed in black answers, keeping the chain locked.

"Do you speak English?" Joseph asks, holding out the irises.

She shakes her head. "Ara."

Joseph looks at the phonetic spelling as written by Daniel Daniel on the back of his map. "Is this the house of Nana Tumanishvili?" he asks in Georgian.

The woman shakes her head forcefully. "Ara, ara."

She slams the door shut. The pink chair rocks in the wind. Joseph turns on his BlackBerry, knocks on the door, and points to a photo. "Tamar. My friend. Rachel. My mother. Are you Nana?"

Through the tiny crack of door, Joseph passes the woman his phone. She squints at the photo of Tamar with Rachel, taken while drunk some Fridays ago. The woman frowns. For a moment Joseph wonders if she's going to smash his phone against the ground. Instead, she unlocks the door and gestures for him to come inside. He hands the woman the flowers and her face lights up. She says something he does not understand. A dozen yellow beeswax candles burn in the corner on a rusted silver platter. Pictures of Tamar stare at him from around the hallway. There's one of Tamar as a child wearing a yellow bathing suit with her arms around a man's waist who looks to be her adoptive father, Sasha.

In another photo, Tamar stands between her adoptive father and a younger version, who must be Levan, on the stage of a theatre. In the bottom right corner is a picture of a woman in a wedding gown next to a dark handsome man in a baby blue tuxedo, circled by friends and family. It's Tamar on her wedding day with Davit.

The front door opens and a large, burly man with a thick blond beard approaches him. "I am Levan," he says in near-perfect English. "Who are you?"

Joseph introduces himself as Rachel's son, a friend of Tamar's. He says he's looking for her.

"It's a pleasure to meet you, Joseph Grabinsky. Unfortunately, Tamar isn't in Tbilisi."

"Do you know when she's due to arrive?"

"She is on her way. Please. Come inside. Be our guest."

Levan leads Joseph into the dining room where he's told to sit down. To his surprise the woman in black has prepared an entire meal. There's cheese bread and scrambled eggs, black sausage and eggplant, and a pot of black tea. Levan opens a bottle of wine and fills two glasses.

"Do you know where Tamar is?" Joseph asks.

"No," says Levan. "But Nana is happy you're here. We're both terribly sorry about the loss of your mother."

"Thank you."

"My mother loved Rachel. They didn't always get along, but she cared about her, like a sister."

Nana enters with a cauldron of hot soup and places it on the table. She gestures to Joseph. The house is exactly how Tamar described it: the antique furniture, the framed paintings by Russian and Georgian artists, the upright piano bedecked with sheet music, and the endless books of poetry and literature. He feels like he's entered another century. Nana wears a white apron over her black dress. Joseph is taken by her warmth. He feels Nana and Levan are family, even though they've just met. And the soup smells delicious.

On the first bite, his mouth explodes with goodness. There's a fresh green herb scattered over the surface of the hot soup. Joseph doesn't know what it is, but he is convinced it is the stuff of miracles. It's like a door inside his stomach has been kicked open, and any remnants of last night's nausea are gone. Joseph moves on to the chicken and beets, the parsley and hot cheese bread. The eggplant is slathered in a walnut sauce that makes him crazy, and the garlic and dill are rich and delicious. When Levan raises his glass to make a toast, Joseph drinks heartily, one glass then another. The wine tastes like earth, and he feels his blood sprinting through his arteries. Even after he's had his fill he doesn't stop; it tastes too good. Joseph has the peculiar notion that if he continues to eat and drink, Tamar will magically appear. Nana says something to Levan.

"She would like to know if sorrow is gnawing at your heart."

Joseph is embarrassed by the emotional transparency of the question. Yet it's precise and honest. He understands that sadness can erode you. Nana clasps her hands. From behind horn-rimmed glasses, she wipes her eyes. She's crying.

"You can tell Nana I miss my mother a lot." Joseph starts to choke up. He quickly swallows another spoonful of Nana's miraculous soup.

"Grief and loss are difficult. But the loss of a mother is the ultimate tragedy," Levan says, then turns and whispers. Nana says something in return, and Levan translates. "She wants to know if this is why you're here. To be close to Rachel's spirit."

"Sort of," says Joseph. "She liked it here, right?"

"Your mother loved Georgia. She loved Tamar, she loved Nana, she loved the Kmara movement, the Underground Theatre, even me." Levan dips fresh bread into a ground spinach dip covered in pomegranate seeds. He chomps with his mouth wide open and follows it by draining his entire glass of wine in a few gulps. There is an intensity to the way he does things. Levan wipes his hands and announces: "Tonight, you will come to the Underground as my guest. There will be a big party and we will drink together. We will be friends, Joseph Grabinsky. Good friends." Levan clenches Joseph's hand so hard it hurts.

"Okay."

"Call if you need anything." Levan rises and leaves him his card. "Don't rush. Stay as long as you want. You are our guest."

Joseph is moved by Levan's hospitality. He's nothing like the brute Tamar described him to be. When he leaves, the door slams shut and the phone rings. Nana picks it up and speaks.

"Tamar," says Nana to Joseph.

"That's her?"

"Tamar." Nana passes the receiver to Joseph.

"Who is this?" The voice is husky.

"Joseph. Who is this?"

"I'm asking the questions." Joseph can't tell if the voice is male or female. "What do you want?"

"I'm a friend of Tamar's. I'd like to see her."

Silence again. The voice swallows then coughs.

"Rachel Grabinsky is my mother," Joseph adds by way of explanation.

Another pause. "Do you like cakes?" asks the voice.

"Cakes?"

"Coffee and cakes."

"Sure, I like cakes."

"There's a café off Chavchavadze. Meet me there in half an hour." The caller recites an address and Joseph hastily writes it down on Daniel Daniel's map. "Make sure you're not followed."

"How will I know you?"

The voice hangs up before Joseph can get an answer. He doesn't even know this person's name. Nana puts down the phone and points up the hall. When Joseph stands, he feels dizzy. The room shifts and the walls turn in on him; he clenches the sides of the table. Nana holds Joseph then hugs him, but the embrace only makes him feel claustrophobic. She leads him by the hand down a corridor and into her bedroom. The air is thick and there is no light. She lights a match and draws it toward a candle. Nana pulls down a book and removes a photograph from its pages. The picture is of Rachel when she was younger, like the small black-and-white photo in the Soviet passport he found in her office.

"Rachel, deda," Nana says, pointing at Joseph and then pointing at the picture.

"Yes, my mother."

Nana puts her hands against her chest and starts to cry.

"It's okay," Joseph says, trying to console her. She shows him another photograph of a large man with thick black hair and a beige wool coat, arms folded across his chest, revealing the cuffs of a shirt pierced by blue-and-gold cufflinks.

"Zaza," she says. "Mama."

*Is Nana Zaza's mother?* Joseph wonders.

Nana places another photograph on the table: Tamar dressed in combat fatigues, accompanied by an older Rachel. Joseph recognizes it from one of her performances. He saw the same picture in Rachel's book about the pro-democracy movement. The gathering of faces confuses him. Who is this Zaza?

"Tamar," says Nana, picking up the photograph and kissing her face. She makes the sign of the cross and recites a prayer. The gesture makes sense: the pictures of Tamar and Rachel feel holy. Joseph wants to pray to the two women he loves. But this mysterious Zaza hovers above them like a shadow. He wants the women in these pictures to speak, to tell him what they know.

The phone rings in the kitchen, and Nana hurries to get it. Alone in the bedroom, Joseph spots a wooden box. When he lifts the lid there's a letter written in Russian, along with a pair of blue cufflinks framed in gold. It's a haunting; the past meeting the present. Joseph doesn't understand how these objects made it to Tbilisi. Without thinking, he grabs the cufflinks and letter, and shoves them into his pocket.

# 13

*Trabzon, Turkey*
*November 15, 2003*

The medical student continues to doze, an image of a brain in cross-section displayed on the open pages of his textbook. Tamar was never any good at biology, but she liked the drawings and the Latin: cortex, cerebellum, ganglia. *Memory*, Tamar thinks, *is a lonely place with no map.* As they travel farther east and closer to Georgia, she thinks of Davit on the hospital stretcher. Who was he going to meet, and who wanted him dead? Whatever he was trying to uncover, somebody didn't want him to know the truth.

There was no shortage of enemies in Davit's line of work. Even his appearance drew raised eyebrows. Davit, in his fashionable blue silk suits, always with a purple flower in his lapel, was flamboyant, modern, and stylish. While he wasn't openly gay in a public sense, everyone around him knew the truth. Often, Tamar worried for his safety; all it took was one drunk asshole to get a crazy idea. But Davit didn't seem to worry.

He had so many enemies, Davit liked to say, they made him invincible. And besides, his employers protected him.

Tamar remembers an interview he did with Soso Abramidze, the Georgian CEO of an American electricity company. On camera, Soso told Davit he'd been threatened by the FSB: sell the company for $2 to Putin, or else. Soso had to comply, but then he went to the media. Davit told him he would reveal the facts: another Georgian enterprise sabotaged by Russia's imperial ambitions. The night before the interview was set to air, Soso was found dead, hog-tied and shot, execution-style, in his apartment. Kartli 2 pulled the plug on the show. Then, the hours of footage mysteriously disappeared. For several weeks, two armed bodyguards were hired to sit outside Davit's apartment. He insisted he wasn't afraid. But Tamar was.

"They're protecting me, Tamar. And besides," Davit insisted, "I'm too popular to be killed."

Tamar said, "Putin doesn't care how popular you are."

Davit hugged her. She didn't want to be right.

WHERE WERE THE bodyguards when Davit was murdered? Were they complicit in his death? Who else was involved? Zaza? And who was the mysterious source that Davit was supposed to meet? What did Davit never find out? There were so many questions that she never got to ask him. Tamar wanted to know about his new boyfriend in the Vera neighbourhood; about his plans for a country house; about the recipes he'd discovered in his passionate weekends of cooking. His secrets, like Rachel's, had gone with him to the grave.

THE MAN IN the black suit announces to the bus passengers they are approaching the border. Tamar's red Nokia beeps. Lali has sent a grainy picture of the protests in Tbilisi: thousands of people gathered in Freedom Square. Tamar can make out a row of tents for the protestors, garbage cans glowing like little lights in the darkness, and someone standing on the steps of parliament making a speech. The image warms her heart. There's another message from Lali.

> Lali: What time do you arrive?
> Tamar: 8 am. Central bus terminal.
> Lali: We'll pick you up.
> Tamar: Update on the protests?
> Lali: 20 000 people in the square. More coming in from the countryside.

When Tamar sees this figure, she thinks it must be a typo.

> Tamar: For real?
> Lali: Yep.

The numbers make Tamar excited but nervous. Fourteen years have passed since the April 1989 massacre when soldiers killed nineteen protestors on the parliament steps. The question in her mind now — will the army turn on them again? — worries her. And if they don't, if somehow the people do succeed in overturning the Shevardnadze government, then what? In a nation of murderers, liars, and thieves, how do you move on from the past?

Tamar dials Joseph's number. She feels badly for having left without a proper explanation. She knows he's suffering; the death of a mother can only leave the most profound absence and ache. A pain that is also hers. But when her call goes directly to his voice mail, she leaves a muddled message, betraying both confusion and longing.

The bus nears the Georgian border, and the tension ramps up. It's the anticipation of passage through the unpredictable. Up and down the aisle, a hat is passed around and money stuffed inside; the collective bribe is a ritual of passing through borders in this part of the world. Tamar knows if they do not pay off the customs officers, they will be made to wait the whole night. The medical student has no money, so Tamar puts in ten dollars for the both of them. He thanks her, embarrassed. His name is Orhan, and he explains that he sends most of his money home to his mother, who lives in a small village on the Turkish Black Sea coast. Tamar reassures him, "It's okay."

As she's putting her wallet back into her pocket, a card slips out. She picks it up from the floor. Skunk's business card with his number written in bold print. Even though she was terrified of him, Tamar kept the card as a possibility. Tracing its perimeter, she notes the hardness of its edges, like it could pierce her skin. She flicks open her Nokia and dials the number.

"Hello?" a voice says in Russian. "Hello? Who is this?"

Tamar immediately hangs up.

# 14

*Tbilisi, Republic of Georgia*
*November 15, 2003*

When Joseph finally leaves Nana's house, he's totally drunk, completely full, and definitely confused. The day is a grainy black-and-white art film. Everything seems distant and tinged with nostalgia, coded by the six glasses of wine he consumed. Joseph stumbles past the kiosk and lights up a cigarette. Nastia, the corner store girl, bends over and inspects a dead insect as though she were a biologist. With her good eye fixed on the bug, she looks like a human microscope. She stands up as Joseph passes.

"Tamar?" she says.

"Huh?"

Nastia resumes her inspection of the mutilated beetle. Its insides ooze out, black and sticky, onto the road. Joseph wonders if she really said what he thinks she said — if she said anything at all. A flame flickers at the end of his mouth. He's lit the wrong end of his cigarette. He stamps it out and continues to walk. At a bend in the road there's a large sculpture, a pink bust of a woman made in the Social Realist style. Joseph gawks at her enormous shoulders and her fearless eyes scanning the horizon. It's a posture of heroism. He believes he has something to learn from it. But what? *Everything is a clue*, he thinks, passing under a bridge where a bebia sells old Soviet stamps. Joseph is attracted to the nuclear physicists and astronauts printed in miniature. He is tempted to buy them, not for their beauty or nostalgia, but as hallmarks of another era. Like the cufflinks and watch, he is looking for a link to his past.

Joseph continues on to the address given him by the mysterious caller. To his surprise, it's Daniel Daniel's record shop. Daniel Daniel isn't there, but Lali is. The morning crowd has dwindled to a couple of students reading alone and the ever-present Thelonious Cat. Joseph orders a coffee and sets himself up in the corner, where he puts on a pair of headphones and drops the needle on Wayne Shorter's *Night Dreamer*. The fluorescent blue of the cover seems to filter into the mystery of the music. Joseph closes his eyes, lets the saxophone fill him. At the end of the first side, he decides to seek out some of Daniel Daniel's own records. He asks Lali if they have any copies.

"You want Belomorkanal or Night of the Iguana?" she asks.

"What do you recommend?"

Lali rifles through some records by the cash register. Her nails are long, her eyelashes too. She wears black eyeliner, black jeans, and a black sweater. She carries herself with the same self-confidence Joseph associates with Tamar.

"Here," she says. "It's inspired by the work of Gregor Mendel and Malcolm McLaren. It's pretty out there."

Joseph thanks her and returns to his table with *Jeans and Genes* by Belomorkanal. To his surprise the cover is in both English and Russian. It features the faded image of a hand covered in denim. Joseph places it on the turntable, drops the needle, and puts on headphones. The music is sophisticated and fast, in the avant-garde tradition. Yet he can discern the bebop influence of Charlie Parker who Daniel Daniel seems to love so much. Joseph prefers hard bop and cool jazz, but he appreciates the music of Belomorkanal the way he might Don Cherry or Ornette Coleman: it's expansive, technically perfect, and demanding. Daniel Daniel's playing is both virtuosic and eccentric, with wails and tones that remind Joseph of the way he speaks. In this way, he does something Joseph has never heard before: Daniel Daniel makes music darkly funny.

A tap on his shoulder practically knocks Joseph out of his seat. "Joseph Grabinsky? I'm Keti. Nana's cousin. We spoke on the phone."

A woman of around fifty reaches her small hand toward him. Her grip is surprisingly firm. "You weren't followed?"

Joseph forgot to look. "I don't think so." He puts down the headphones. He wants to ask: "Who would want to follow me?"

Keti removes her long trench coat and nods at Lali, who brings over several plates, each with a different piece of cake. They kiss each other on the cheek and talk in a way that feels intimate to Joseph.

"This is my daughter, Lali," Keti says.

"Nice to meet you again," says Lali, smiling coyly.

"Wait…Keti. Were you married to Daniel Daniel?" Joseph asks.

Keti turns to Lali and says something in Georgian. Lali returns to the cash. "Yes, a long time ago. But who can live with Mr. Insane?" She grimaces, picking up the LP cover and pointing to the list of players on the back. "That's me. Ketevan Marjanashvili. I play bass and contrabass." Keti explains that she grew up in a family of artists. Her father was the set designer whose paintings Joseph had spent the night with. Her Austrian mother was a sculptor. Keti has been playing music for decades and still records and tours internationally. "Which helps to explain my facility in English," she says, "unlike my ex. But don't worry, Daniel Daniel and I learned marriage wasn't our cup of tea a long time ago. We're still friends. And we have Lali."

Keti smiles proudly at her daughter, then barks out a litany of orders. Lali hurriedly brings over two coffees and sets them on the table before whisking herself back to the register.

There are four different cakes on the table, and Keti explains the origin of each one: how many generations the recipe has been handed down in her mother's family, and the precise hour they were made. Joseph tries to keep up with the colourful descriptions of liquor-infused buttercream Esterházy cake; crispy, plum beignets; double-layered chocolate sponge Sachertorte; and apple strudel. Keti is a woman who takes her cake very seriously. She spears the chocolate with her fork as if it were a wild animal bent on escaping.

"Well, what are you waiting for? Eat! It's not all for me. Though a woman my age can live on cake alone."

Joseph digs his fork into the flakey apple strudel. Suddenly, he feels warmth at his feet. Thelonious Cat purrs in the expectant way of felines. That is, he wants cake.

"I helped start the Record Emporium," Keti says. "It's like a second home for me. Daniel Daniel and Lali do the music; I do the books and curate the cakes. Any decent record store must have good coffee and cakes, don't you agree?"

Joseph nods, though he's never considered this before. The strudel, Joseph admits to himself, is incredibly good. And he likes this Keti. Not only does she excel in the art of cake making, but her English is extremely good. Joseph finds this reassuring. Thelonious Cat rubs his cheek into Joseph's calf.

"So, you're the son of Rachel Grabinsky. I'm sorry for your loss." Keti puts her hand on Joseph's. "You must be devastated. Is this why you're here? To see the country she loved?"

"It's a long story."

"I'm happy to listen."

"Actually, it has to do with your ex-husband, believe it or not."

Keti shouts at Lali, and Lali shouts back. Seemingly satisfied, Keti folds her arms and leans back, ready to listen. Feeling self-conscious, Joseph tells her, in fits and starts, how he got to Tbilisi, from his discovery of the Soviet passport in Rachel's office and the contents of the KGB dossiers, to the taxi drivers at the airport and the drunken meal with Nana several hours ago.

"I had no idea," says Joseph, "that Rachel was someone else."

"No one is who they say they are," says Keti, spearing a piece of Esterházy.

Joseph also tells her about his father, Gary Ruckler, a man he hasn't seen in almost twenty years. "According to Daniel Daniel," he says, "Gary lives in Tbilisi. For some crazy reason Daniel Daniel is trying to orchestrate some kind of reunion between us. It's all a bit weird."

"That is so Aslan," says Keti. "He's always trying to save someone."

"Who's Aslan?"

"That's Daniel Daniel's real name. He doesn't like to use it anymore, but sometimes I like to remind him of who he is."

Joseph doesn't know why he hasn't bothered asking Daniel Daniel his real name.

"Where's he from?"

"The mountains, like most of us."

"So, do you know Gary, too?"

"I don't think so."

"Daniel Daniel — Aslan — said they met at university in Moscow."

"That was before my time. Aslan studied genetics in those days. Can you imagine?"

Joseph cannot. He tells Keti that Gary also plays jazz.

"I'm sure I never met him, but that doesn't mean anything. Aslan knows everybody. And he's always on some mission to help someone out. Lord knows he can't help himself. He's a peculiar and endearing fuck-up. But I doubt I need to tell you that."

Joseph nods, his mouth full of Sachertorte, then washes it down with coffee. Though he's still quite full from Nana's, everything is incredibly delicious. The chocolate melts in his mouth. Thelonious Cat cries for a piece of it. Joseph hesitates.

"Where does Tamar fit into this?" asks Keti, turning her fork to the apple strudel, crumbs sticking to her lips.

Joseph explains that, a few days ago, she called to say she had to go home. When he realized they'd both be in the same place at the same time, he thought he'd reach out.

"We're friends," he explains. "Good friends."

"Have you called her since you arrived?"

"Yeah, of course, but her phone's disconnected."

"Email?"

"I haven't had time. But I'll write her this afternoon."

"I don't think Tamar is in Tbilisi. She would've called me. And she would've called Nana for sure."

"So where is she?"

"I have no idea. Did she say why she was coming back?"

"She said she had to figure out some things. She sounded upset."

Keti looks concerned. Joseph wants to tell her about the cufflinks he took from Nana's house, to show her the distance objects travel. Instead, he says, "If I show you something, could you help me understand what it means?"

"Of course."

Joseph hands Keti the letter written on the scrap of graph paper he found in Nana's bedroom. The Russian script — written in blue slanted lettering — appears to be from another era. While Keti reads it, Joseph touches the cufflinks in his pocket. They feel like a talisman, a compass. Anything is a clue, so everything is possible.

Keti reads out loud: "'This is not for me to give and not my story to tell. Maybe you decide to give this to her when you think the time is right.'"

"That's it?" asks Joseph.

"That's it," says Keti, passing the letter back to Joseph. "No signature, no date."

Joseph places the letter in the inside pocket of his jacket. He is confused by its contents. Did his mother send it to Nana along with the cufflinks and the watch? How else could they have reached Tbilisi? But if she did, why?

"By the way, what does the Georgian word 'mama' mean?"

"Father. Why?"

Joseph bounces his fork on the buttercream of the Esterházy cake. "Nana showed me a picture of a man named Zaza. She kept saying 'mama' and pointing to Tamar. So Zaza is Tamar's father?"

"Yep. He left Nana and Tamar when she was six. Disappeared, like smoke. Then he turned up at the riots of '91 where he tragically died. He was trampled by the crowds."

Tamar told Joseph a little about Zaza, just a few scattered memories, but never anything about a violent death.

Keti leans back in her chair. "It worries me when you say she's come back to Georgia. It's not safe for her in Tbilisi."

"Why?"

"Her husband Davit was murdered. And there were rumours about your mother."

"Like what?"

"The old Communists like Shevardnadze claim she was part of an American conspiracy to seize control of the region's oil."

"My mother?"

"They say she worked for the CIA and was trying to foment government change and usher in a Western-style democracy."

Joseph can't believe what he's hearing. "Like a coup?"

Keti shoos away his words with her fork. "Don't take it too seriously." She dismisses it as the usual paranoid nonsense, a local specialty. "The rumour—planted by the Russians, no doubt—was that Davit and Tamar were hired to work for Rachel, funded by George Soros, as American agents. As her son, they might think you're one, too."

"That's insane."

"The world is insane, Joseph. Which is why we eat cake. Go on. Have some more."

Joseph forces himself to take another bite of the strudel. It's the best of the bunch. Soft and buttery, with a texture like silk. Thelonious Cat sits patiently, waiting. Something niggles at Joseph.

"Why Georgia? Why did my mother come here of all places?"

Keti proceeds to give Joseph a lesson in history. She explains that in Georgia they've been living under one form of occupation or another for centuries; before the Russians, it was the Persians and the Ottomans. And so on and so forth for almost one thousand years. Yet the legacy of colonialism goes back even further than that, back to their ancestor Prometheus who was chained to their most sacred mountain by foreign gods.

"Georgians are resident experts in occupation. We know how to live under someone else's colonial thumb. But ruling ourselves? Taking control of our own destiny? It took someone like your mother to help us see how this might be possible. This is the real revolution your mother helped start. And she's still part of it."

Keti explains the complicated political dance of President Shevardnadze; how every time he veers toward the democratic West, he is pulled back by Russia — as well as his own interests. Ultimately, it is his constant and insatiable greed that have pissed people off.

"Do you know, Joseph, that less than a kilometre from this café, there are over twenty-five thousand people standing in front of parliament, bent on overthrowing the corrupt Shevardnadze government? They're led by people who were mentored and taught by your mother. Rachel understood that a non-violent revolution is not an easy thing to achieve in the former U.S.S.R. She'd be thrilled to see what's going on in Tbilisi right now. Your mother might be dead, but she's still an agent of change." Keti finishes the strudel and takes a final bite of the Sachertorte before placing the remains on the floor. "Well? What do you think, Thelonious? Will we overthrow Shevardnadze? Will Rachel's revolution win?"

Thelonious Cat doesn't say anything. He's too busy devouring what's in front of him.

Keti turns to Joseph: "Maybe you're right; maybe Tamar is in Tbilisi. For all we know, she could be with the demonstrators right now. Perhaps she just doesn't want anyone to know."

# 15

*Turkey-Georgia Border*
*November 15, 2003*

Tamar recalls how Nana often became quiet in the company of Rachel. Now she can't help but wonder if Nana knew that Rachel was Anna Litvak, if there was some tacit agreement between the two women. For Rachel's sudden entrance into Tamar's life must have been Nana's nightmare come true — the birth mother returned.

In Brecht's play, the decision between nature and nurture is left to a judge, Azdak, who instructs the child be put in a circle drawn with chalk. The two mothers, Grusha and the governor's wife, are instructed to pull on the boy. The true mother will be the one who pulls the child toward her. Each time they engage in this tug-of-war, Grusha loses, barely exerting effort. Exasperated, Azdak asks Grusha why she won't try harder. After all, the child's fate is in her hands. Grusha says: "I cannot tear him in two because I love him." By this statement, she is declared the child's true mother: nurture, not nature, wins out. Love stands as the final evidence.

Despite her respect for Brecht, Tamar knows the power of blood, the potency of genes. She knows that people are infected by history in ways that do not always make sense. She remembers the dark days of Abkhazia, the war that spilled onto Sukhumi's streets, neighbours killing neighbours, all in the name of heritage and inheritance. Repressed for so long by the Soviets, there emerged a storm of nationalisms, culture wars, and ethnic cleansings. And Tamar feels it now: the bloodlines that pull her, the genealogical legacies that marionette us, regardless of our beliefs.

A couple of days after Davit's murder, Tamar dropped in to see Nana. She was there to say goodbye before leaving for Toronto. Tamar had questions. Nana prepared her favourite soup, chopping onions, walnuts, and parsley.

"Tell me about Zaza," Tamar said.

Nana flinched, then resumed chopping.

"Talk to me, Nana."

"What should I say?"

"Who was Zaza? What did he do?"

Nana sighed. "We were lovers before he went to the university. Silly teenage love. And then he went to Moscow, and I didn't hear from him for years. No phone calls, no letters, nothing. Then, one day, Zaza showed up on my doorstep carrying a beautiful girl, asleep in his arms. He didn't know the first thing about raising a child. He said he needed my help. So I took you in."

"But how did we end up here? Where did we come from? Where was Anna Litvak?"

Nana stopped chopping and held her knife in the air. "I don't know."

"You never asked?"

"Of course I asked. What was I supposed to do? Make him speak?"

"Do you miss him?"

"No."

"The night before he died, Davit told me that Zaza is still alive."

Nana reached into the cupboard. Her sleeve caught on a nail and she spilled a bowl of salt onto the floor.

"Kurva."

"Did you hear me?"

Nana bent down in frustration. "Yes, I heard you." She vigorously swept salt into her hand, then tossed it out the window into the yard. "Am I surprised? No. Nothing surprises me about that man. You're better off forgetting him, Tamar. Bad things happen when Zaza is involved. He lives in a cloud of remorse and bad feeling. The only good thing he ever did was bring you into my life."

Tamar reached into her pocket and put the cufflinks and Anna's note on the kitchen table. She slid them toward Nana.

"I need you to hold on to these."

"Why? They're yours."

"I can't take them with. Please? Could you keep them? Until I come back."

Nana's eyes filled with tears.

"You're not coming back."

# 16

*Tbilisi, Republic of Georgia*
*November 15, 2003*

After Keti leaves the Record Emporium, Joseph writes in a notebook: "No one is who they say they are. Not even myself." As much as he resents his mother's secrecy, he wants to understand it. Maybe Rachel needed to let Anna Litvak die. After all, she'd had everything else taken away from her. Perhaps she believed it was her right to create a fresh persona. So who was she? Anna, or Rachel? And why was she in Georgia? Joseph doesn't believe the rumours she worked for the CIA, and while he understands Georgia was a place for her to implement her political ideas and democratic strategies, he believes there is something he is missing. A "why" he cannot see.

When Joseph looks up, it's much later than he thought, 3:45 p.m. He is supposed to meet Daniel Daniel and Gary at his hotel in fifteen minutes. He pays, then hurries to the street.

"Excuse me, I need to get to the Marriott Hotel," he says to a small elderly woman standing on the sidewalk holding an enormous bag of groceries. "Do you know how to get there?"

She hands him her grocery bag and says something in Georgian. Seconds later, a white minivan pulls up, the door opens, and the woman gestures for Joseph to get inside. The door shuts behind him, as Joseph falls into a seat and the old woman takes hold of his hand. The van is full of elderly people; everyone stares at him.

"Marriott Hotel?" he asks the old woman.

"Cho, cho."

They drive for what feels like half an hour before the van screeches to a halt and everyone piles out. The old woman nods at Joseph, takes her bag of groceries from his lap, and disappears into the crowd.

Joseph makes eye contact with the driver in the rear-view mirror and asks, "Marriott Hotel?"

"Dezerter Bazaar," the driver responds. "Get out."

IT QUICKLY BECOMES clear that Joseph is lost. "Marriott Hotel?" he says to a fruit seller who offers him a pomegranate. The fruit seller points him to a tea shop. Inside, Joseph asks for directions to his hotel. The man behind the counter offers him a small thimbleful of black tea and two sugar cubes. Joseph thanks and pays him, even though he does not want it. While he sips the hot liquid, he makes eye contact with a tall man in a grey fedora and black trench coat on the other side of the teahouse. The man quickly looks away and Joseph feels strange, not himself.

Outside again, Joseph wanders down an alley of spice. Stopping to buy some sunflower seeds, he catches sight of the man in the black trench coat, a few stalls back. Joseph makes a quick turn into an aisle of plums and walnuts and looks over his shoulder. The man is still there. Joseph keeps moving. When he stops, the man stops. Joseph ducks into another shop, his heart racing. *Keti was right*, he thinks. *Someone* is *following me*. Joseph tries to get a better look at the man in an aisle of parsley, dill, and garlic. Beneath the grey fedora, his face is hidden in shadow, an aura of black and white, like he's just walked out of a Raymond Chandler novel.

Joseph passes a wall of cheap, plastic shoes. There seem to be thousands of them, and the disembodied abundance unsettles him. When he gets to the end of the aisle, he can make out a city street ahead. There, just outside the market, a Lada sits idling with a handwritten sign that reads "Taxi." Joseph pushes forward and gets in.

"Marriott Hotel," he tells the driver.

Joseph looks over his shoulder as the taxi pulls away, and catches a glimpse of Raymond Chandler speaking animatedly into his cell phone.

# 17

There is always a sense of dread in a late-night crossing.

When the bus stops at the border and the passengers disembark, Tamar stays close to Orhan, believing she'll be safer in his company. At the Turkish customs window, they line up to have their passports stamped. The bus travels ahead with their belongings. Tamar is led through a gate into the place between countries. Here she is pierced by the cold wind coming off the indifferent sea. At an enormous steel gate, an armed soldier addresses Orhan, inspecting his documents. The soldier interrogates him with silence and threatening looks. From his canvas bag Orhan pulls out a carton of Marlboros and hands them to the soldier. He lets him through. Orhan nods to Tamar, beckoning.

"She's with me."

As they walk through the checkpoint, Orhan asks her questions: Where is she from? Where is she going? Why is

she alone on a bus? Tamar tells him she's going home to see
her mother in Tbilisi. She tells him that parts of her are missing, that the past is a burden she cannot ignore. He nods.
When Orhan talks his Georgian is stilted, but she learns
things from him: he is studying here, not because the facili-
ties are better, but because it is the only school that would
take him. He likes Georgia, but he misses home, and he visits
his mother often.

"Georgia is too violent," Orhan says. "Sometimes I am
scared. I fear for you, Tamar. Please, be careful." He says this
in the most endearing way.

They emerge from a dark tunnel; the bus sits at the centre
of an empty parking lot. Tamar notices a black van idling by
the fence. They pass a seller offering tea and bread, and she
asks Orhan if he wants anything. He shakes his head then
climbs onto the bus and waves, a puzzling gesture. While
she sips hot tea and devours fresh bread, two men approach
Tamar. One is tall and thin, the other short and stocky.

"Tamar Tumanishvili?" asks the tall man in Russian.

"Yes?"

"Would you come with us, please?"

"No thanks."

The stout man knocks the tea out of her hand, burning her.

"What the—"

The tall man tapes her mouth shut before she can get the
words out. The stocky man grabs her wrists. She tries to pull
away, but they lift her up and carry her off like a piece of
old furniture. Tamar catches Orhan's eyes inside the bus,
watching.

# 18

*Tbilisi, Republic of Georgia*
*November 15, 2003*

The taxi breaks down by an abandoned church on a hill. The driver shrugs at Joseph: "Broke."

*Right,* Joseph thinks. *Nothing in this country works.*

Outside, Joseph finds nothing but sweeping dust. The surrounding cliffs are completely barren. The driver lights up a cigarette, crouches, and waits.

"Marriott Hotel?" Joseph asks hopefully.

The driver closes his eyes, presses his palms against his temples, and begins muttering to himself. Joseph hands him a few dollars and heads toward the church. Under a collapsed roof, Joseph finds faded prayer books scattered amidst the piles of rubble. No signs of life. Behind the church, he hops a fence into a field, beyond which he can see a pillar of smoke rising into the sky.

When he reaches the source of the smoke, Joseph finds himself outside a synagogue. Someone sells wine from a metal barrel. It's warm and sweet, and after a few sips Joseph considers entering the Jewish house of prayer. But an incredible roar coming from nearby stops him in his tracks. Joseph crosses an alleyway that leads to a wide avenue, moving toward the noise. Someone grabs his shoulder from behind and pushes him into a crowd of people with placards and raised fists. Someone else hands him a piece of bread. Joseph has somehow arrived in the middle of the political demonstrations that Keti told him about earlier. He does not want to be here, caught up in this crowd with a mind of its own. He has to get to the Marriott to meet his father.

The energy of the crowd is unnerving. Joseph attempts to force his way through the throng of protestors, but a strange man pushes him against a set of glass doors. Joseph closes his eyes and yells, while people nearby laugh and take pictures. The strange man lets Joseph go, and he opens his eyes to find he's pressed against the doors of the Marriott. He stumbles into the crowded lobby but does not see Daniel Daniel anywhere. Joseph is almost two hours late.

"Can I help you?" asks the receptionist.

"Yes," Joseph says, relieved to have made it here alive. "My name is Joseph Grabinsky. Did anyone leave me a message?"

The receptionist scans the desk. "No."

"Okay, I'd like to check in then." Joseph can't wait to take a hot shower and sleep in a clean bed — the anonymous comforts of a hotel room.

The receptionist looks at his clipboard and says, "I'm sorry, but we do not have a reservation with that name on file."

Joseph shows him the email confirmation on his BlackBerry. The receptionist looks back at his clipboard.

"I am afraid there is nothing here."

"Check again. Please."

The receptionist flips through the pages of his clipboard.

"Your reservation doesn't exist, Mr. Grabinsky."

"Then I'd like a room."

"There are none."

"What do you mean?"

"We're booked solid, sir. I can call another hotel if you like."

"But what about this?" Joseph holds up his phone with the reservation again.

"I'm sorry, sir. But when you didn't show up last night, we were obliged to release your room. And now, with the protests, we're completely full. Journalists." He gestures to the lobby. "I can try to find you a room somewhere else."

Joseph groans. He steps back from the desk and looks down at his phone. He's missed a call from a number he doesn't recognize. Whoever it was left a voice message. He does not recognize the whispering voice at first, but soon realizes it's Tamar.

"Hey, Joseph. I'm sorry I rushed off like that. I spoke to my brother Levan, and he said that this guy Skunk knows something about my father. I need to find out what he knows. I'm on a bus in Turkey . . . I miss you. I hope you're okay."

Joseph stands in the lobby holding his BlackBerry. He listens to the voice mail again. The call came in a few hours ago. He has no idea how he missed it. He calls Tamar's number, and it goes directly to voice mail. He puts his phone away and looks around the lobby. It's packed with people drinking and smoking. A man in a green suit sips a fancy cocktail. *Could that be Gary?* he thinks. Why not? Everyone and no one is his father. Joseph makes his way back outside into the crowd. He does not know what to do next.

The sun begins to set as Joseph walks aimlessly through the demonstrations. He sees hundreds of faces; their foreignness and distance rattle him. He misses Tamar. The sound of her voice guts him. He wishes they could talk, go over the details of the past few days, make sense of things. Soon it is dark, and the streets are empty. He hears a loud cracking sound, and thinks it's thunder, but thunder isn't so hollow. A man darts out of an alley twenty metres ahead and disappears into shadow. Joseph sees something leaning against the side of a building. Quickly he walks across the street and finds a man lying motionless, his head slumped against his chest. A hole, the size of a quarter, sits in the middle of his forehead just above his eyes. Grey liquid seeps out, folds of skin caving in around it. It takes him a moment, but Joseph recognizes the face of the man in the black trench coat and grey fedora. Raymond Chandler.

He stares into the man's milky eyes. Joseph pats down his body, taking his wallet and cell phone. He needs to find out who was following him.

JOSEPH TAKES A taxi back to the Mother of Georgia statue. From there he makes his way to the Record Emporium, using the instructions written on the back of his homemade map. When he arrives, Joseph feels a deep uncertainty in his chest, feet, and hands. His body, the world — everything has become distant and unfamiliar.

Daniel Daniel greets him at the door. "Comrade Joseph, where have you been? I was at your hotel with Gary, yet we do not see you."

"Someone was following me," Joseph says.

"Someone always follows someone."

"He was shot dead in an alley."

"Excellent. This means he will not kill you."

"Don't we need to call the police?"

"In Georgia, the police are more corrupt than traffic lights. Come inside. We relax all tensions, inside and out."

It's past closing time. Daniel Daniel hands a warm beer to Joseph, who collapses on the couch. A cry emits from the pillows. Thelonious Cat.

"Tamar isn't in Tbilisi. She left me a message."

"Where is she?"

"On a bus in Turkey."

Daniel Daniel strokes his gnarled beard. "Why?"

"I have no idea. But I'm worried about her. What if something happens? What if she's in danger? She mentioned Levan and this guy named Skunk."

Daniel Daniel hesitates. "We go to the Underground. We speak to Levan. Maybe he doesn't tell you everything."

"Maybe."

Daniel Daniel collapses onto the couch next to Joseph. Awkwardly, he puts his hand on Joseph's shoulder.

"You are highly emotional and feel too many things, Comrade Joseph."

"I'm sorry I was late. Was Gary pissed off?"

"Your father is very tolerant and accepting. Lateness is the DNA gene you have most inherited. Everything is always too late."

Daniel Daniel is right. Everything feels out of step, out of time. Joseph is chasing the mysteries of his dead mother; a woman he loves who may or may not love him back; and a father he never knew. *I'm always somewhere other than where I need to be*, he thinks.

"Do not worry, Comrade. We will see Gary. Tomorrow, next to tomorrow, whatever you like."

"Everything feels backward and upside down."

"No 'upside down.' Everything is merely fucked up, including our souls. In a land without dogs the cats learn to bark. Famous Georgian proverb, soundtrack of our fucked-up lives."

Joseph swills the warm beer. Thelonious Cat looks up at him quizzically. "Why was my mother in Georgia?"

"Rachel hates the barking cats. So she tries to bring the dogs back. You see the protests? She prays to the god of chaotic messes. Somehow change will save us."

Thelonious Cat plunks himself on Joseph's lap, totally at ease. Joseph feels unsettled, the brimming of something beneath the surface. *No one is who they say they are and nothing is what it seems.* Joseph touches the inside of his pants pocket, Zaza's cufflinks, clues to something he cannot see. Daniel Daniel flicks on a strange red light and drops the needle on a record. He reclines into a plume of cigarette smoke, his fur cap reminding Joseph of Thelonious Monk. Then Thelonious Cat purrs, and Joseph has the strange feeling of time multiplying and repeating itself, a mirror facing a mirror.

"Do you know why I love Charlie Parker?" Daniel Daniel asks. "He sews many elegant identities into one melodic vest. I only wish I could construct this with my own art and life. Yet I cannot sing in an elegant manner. Who can do that other than Parker? Sometimes, it is better to listen."

"I'm lost, Daniel Daniel."

"No, you are only sorrowful, Comrade. In the end, we will win. But the prize is different than what we expect. No one is who they say they are; please heed the cat who goes woof. Yet everything we want will arrive: fathers, lovers, best friends, the truth of our mothers. Follow the notes to the end of the song. Like Charlie Parker, let us dance away the wicked horrors of the heart."

BRIEF INTERLUDE:
# CHARLIE PARKER'S "ORNITHOLOGY"

*

MUCH DANCING AND WICKED
PAGEANTRY FOLLOWS

# 19

*Autonomous Republic of Adjara*
*November 15, 2003*

Tamar's resistance is met with a sharp blow to the head. The parking lot spins and darkness descends as a hood is pulled over her. She's thrown into the back of a van, landing with a thud that shakes her spine. The door slides shut, and the van accelerates. Tamar tries not to panic. She hears a cigarette being lit; a radio flicked on and off. Pain shoots up her leg. She focuses on her breathing and tries to remember the lessons she learned in the hostage survival class she took at Rachel's summer retreat. She hears Goran's voice in her head: "Tense the muscles in your body and hold your knuckles together. This will make it look like you're co-operating, when in reality, you're creating space between your wrists." She tries to follow his instructions, but she isn't good with knots at the best of times. Now she's trying to do it with a sack over her head. Out of desperation Tamar bangs her head against the side of the van.

"What is she doing?" asks a voice on the driver's side. He

speaks Russian with a hint of an accent she can't quite place.

"Hitting her head," says the man seated passenger-side.

"Is she crazy?"

"Pull over."

The ignition cuts out, and a few seconds later Tamar is pulled from the vehicle.

"Are you crazy?" The tall, thin man yanks off her hood and the duct tape across her lips in one quick movement.

"I can't breathe," she gasps.

Now the two men speak in a language she cannot understand. She observes their personalities in the small details of their faces: nervous tics, scars, gold teeth. The stocky driver is agitated. The tall man from the passenger side is patient.

"No hood, no problem," he says in the same oddly accented Russian. "But we keep your hands and feet tied."

Back in the van, the driver smokes and watches Tamar through the rear-view mirror. Passenger Side carries a Kalashnikov over his left shoulder. They accelerate through the countryside. An hour passes. The driver's eyes continue to watch her. Passenger Side wears a black threadbare suit and smokes hand-rolled cigarettes. His formal character contrasts with the well-used weapon he holds.

"You're not Russian or Georgian," says Tamar. "Where are you from?"

"Would you like a cigarette?" Passenger Side asks.

She nods, and he rolls her one, deft and one-handed. She notes the small scar on his neck, a small tributary on a forgotten map. He turns around and places a lit cigarette in her mouth. Tamar lets the smoke swirl in her chest. It feels good, even when she coughs.

# 20

*Tbilisi, Republic of Georgia*
*November 15, 2003*

While Charlie Parker's "Ornithology" blares from a stack of old Soviet speakers, Daniel Daniel shakes and Joseph shimmies. Daniel Daniel has dubbed their dance "the double helix," in honour of "all genetic mutations, epigenetic retardations, and Main Street altercations." Even Thelonious Cat is no longer his normal aloof, indolent self. That is, he seems taken by the music. And while Joseph feels odd gyrating to the old jazz of a bygone era with a goateed cat and a strange man he met only a day ago, he believes there is something important about this movement. If everything is a clue, then he must learn to read the signs. He must watch and listen to everything.

Maybe Daniel Daniel is right: there is something about the way Charlie Parker slips into the multitude of notes, as though each moment, every tone, contains its own secret identity. *No one is who they say they are*, thinks Joseph, *because we are*

*too many.* "Who was Rachel Grabinsky?" isn't the question.
Instead, it's: "How many Rachels were there?" Thelonious
Cat howls in tandem with Parker's solo; Joseph closes his
eyes, praying for revelation. Instead he only sees a black-and-
white Chandler lying bleeding in an alley. And it frightens
Joseph, this dance with the dead.

IN THE HOURS since they first visited the Underground to
look for Levan, the city has changed. Gone is the ghost-town
feel of the otherworldly and the absent. The protests Joseph
witnessed that afternoon in the main square have spilled up
Rustaveli Avenue toward the theatre. Thousands of people
hang from balconies, crowd onto sidewalks and across the
wide avenue. They dance and sing and shout.

"No one is who they say they are," Daniel Daniel mutters
as he leads them through the throng up the alleyway.

And nothing stays the same. The old abandoned bedframe
from that morning has been transformed into a makeshift
bar and soup station lit by candles; Levan doles out steaming
bowls and shots of chacha to demonstrators. He greets Joseph
with an enormous hug and beckons him inside the theatre. A
big event is planned in honour of the protests.

"We will drink like pigs," Levan says, laughing and slapping Joseph on the back.

Joseph and Daniel Daniel are led into the candlelit lobby.
Vera, the ticket seller with no tickets to sell, eyes herself in a
distorted handheld mirror. Levan leads them down a steep
set of stairs that open onto a large, cavernous space. The theatre bar is deep below ground, the air thick with smoke and
anticipation. The electricity of the streets has infected the

Underground. A pink-haired cellist practises in the corner. Old men from the countryside offer roses to young actresses. A one-eyed Svanetian sings songs from a far-off land about giants and stone towers that house the dead. Middle-aged men play backgammon with incredible force and desperation, hurling their dice at the table as though gambling their fates. Teenage girls plot revolution. A general sense of restless longing and wildness pervades the room.

Joseph watches a group of pro-democracy activists scurry up and down rickety platforms. A Serb barks instructions into a megaphone; several people heave themselves at the floor and gyrate, while others remain upside down on the scaffolding, their legs clinging to metal.

"He is Goran, Lali's boyfriend," says Daniel Daniel. "He leads them in tear gas training. They need to build their strength."

Goran and his assistants spray mock tear gas and pepper spray as the activists scramble to cover their faces and eyes with bandanas, closing their eyes.

Out of the corner of his eye Joseph spots a woman wearing a brown hoodie and black jeans. She looks like Tamar, so he calls out to her, but she is quickly swallowed up by the crowd. He starts to walk in her direction, when suddenly the electricity kicks in and a group of musicians drag their gear to the centre of the floor. The guitarist strums a chord and the sheer volume from his amp shakes the entire room. Everyone starts to cheer. A girl in a khaki military outfit picks up a mic and screams:

*Hey hey hey!*
*We got lots to say!*

*Yo yo yo!*
*Kill your fascist soul!*
*Ee ee ee!*
*Who do you want to be?*

Joseph pushes his way through the agitated crowd, catching sight of the woman in the brown hoodie heading toward a door. "Tamar!" he yells, but she is already gone. The music swells, and everyone starts to dance. The raw, ear-bleeding sound of the band stretches the confines of the space.

Suddenly the singer announces something to the crowd in Georgian while the drummer builds the beat. Joseph thinks he hears the name "Tamar Tumanishvili" before the crowd begins to clap and cheer. A white beam of light is projected on the wall. Tamar stands before him in brown hoodie and black jeans, twenty feet in height.

ANTHRAX EXPLOSION:
AN EXPERIMENT IN POST-SOVIET CAPITALISM

A film by TAMAR TUMANISVILI
Subtitles by RACHEL GRABINSKY
Produced by FREEDOM INK

EXT. RUSTAVELI AVENUE — TBILISI — DAYTIME — 08:55

> TAMAR
>
> They say you can get pretty much anything in Georgia. Teenage girls, heroin, AK-47s. We've got everything, they say.

[Enter PASSERBY.]

> TAMAR
>
> Hey, is it true you can get anything in Georgia?

[PASSERBY shrugs and walks on.]

> TAMAR
>
> I wonder if it's true. I wonder how long it would take to acquire biological weapons in downtown Tbilisi.

[TAMAR shows a stopwatch to the camera and presses start. Several seconds count until —]

EXT. DIDUBE MARKET — TBILISI — DAYTIME — 09:42

[TAMAR approaches STOCKY MEN in black leather jackets and sunglasses — menacing and mean as hell. STOCKY MEN whistle and make catcalls.]·

                    TAMAR
        What are you selling?

                    STOCKY MAN #1
        What are you buying?

[TAMAR passes STOCKY MAN #1 a piece of paper. HE directs her to TURKISH TEA MAN, who directs her to AZERI FISHMONGER. AZERI FISHMONGER makes a phone call. AZERI FISHMONGER hands TAMAR a phone number.]

EXT. PHONE BOOTH — TBILISI — DAYTIME — 10:03

[TAMAR addresses the camera.]

                    TAMAR
        One hundred years after Louis Pasteur
        developed a vaccine for anthrax, we
        produce it willfully for the advancement
        of our nations. Mind you, it is illegal
        under international law. But does that
        stop anyone?

Anthrax — Easy to make — you can do it in your basement!

Anthrax — Brings the bubonic plague right into your home!

Anthrax — Peels off your skin but doesn't destroy your bones!

Anthrax — Capable of wiping out thousands!

Anthrax — Made by civilized countries like America, Great Britain, and the former Soviet Union.

I've always felt there was something beautiful about anthrax. Anarchy Anthrax. An Anthrax Orgasm. A Snowstorm of Anthrax.

[TAMAR calls the number on the piece of paper. SHE is told to wait at a certain location at a certain time.]

EXT. A BUSY STREET CORNER — TBILISI — DAYTIME — 10:30

[A BLACK CAR with unmarked plates pulls up to the corner. TAMAR hesitates. SHE walks toward the car. A door opens. TAMAR gets in.]

INT. CAR — SOMEWHERE BETWEEN TBILISI AND
RUSTAVI — DAYTIME — 10:31

[CAMERA POINTS UP AT THE SKY THROUGH WINDOW
CAPTURING RANDOM LANDSCAPE.]

TAMAR
Where are we going?

[DRIVER is silent.]

TAMAR
Hey, shit-pants. Where are you taking
me?

INT. BAR — RUSTAVI, GEORGIA — DAYTIME—14:56

[A cigarette burns in an ashtray. Enter TAMAR
in blonde wig and sunglasses. SHE sits at
a table with a man in a black suit, DR.
KOPORECKI. HE orders a cognac and coffee.
SHE does the same. DR. KOPORECKI retrieves a
briefcase, places it on the table, and clicks
open the latches. Inside are two Ziploc bags
full of coarse brown powder.]

DR. KOPORECKI
Anthrax, Vollum 14578 strain. One
hundred grams of pure spores.

TAMAR

Looks like dog food.


DR. KOPORECKI

You could kill five thousand people
with this "dog food."


TAMAR

How much?


DR. KOPORECKI

Fifteen thousand dollars.


[TAMAR puts her briefcase on the table. SHE
clicks open one of the latches. SHE hesitates,
breathes heavily, and checks HER stopwatch.]


TAMAR

(Whispering)

That took sixteen hours, thirty-two
minutes, and fifty-four seconds.


WHEN THE VIDEO cuts out, the band starts up again. The
crowd erupts into wild celebration. Joseph finds himself
standing next to Levan. Daniel Daniel is nowhere in sight.

"You see, my friend? I have brought you Tamar. Come
with me, son of Rachel."

Joseph follows Levan through a small door into a room lit
with candles. Strands of rebar erupt from the broken concrete

floor. They're in an actor's dressing room, though it makes Joseph think of an interrogation chamber. On a chair that doubles as table sit a bottle and two glasses. Levan passes one to Joseph and fills it.

"To be or not to be," he says. "There is no other question."

As soon as the chacha hits his throat, Joseph feels his mind burst into flames.

"Tonight," says Levan, "we will be."

"What exactly is chacha?" Joseph gasps.

"My grandfather's specialty. It will make you very happy — or very crazy. Now tell me, what did you think of Tamar's video?"

"I don't really get performance art."

"That's okay, nobody gets performance art!" Levan cackles insidiously.

"Did Tamar get in trouble for it?"

"Of course! Tamar likes to make trouble. So did your mother. They got along well."

Joseph thinks he sees something crawl over his shoes.

"Why are you in Tbilisi? I hope it's not just to see my sister."

"No, no." Joseph laughs nervously. Levan's energy is more aggressive and far drunker than it was at Nana's house.

He starts to tell Levan the story he told Keti in Daniel Daniel's record shop, but this time it comes out jumbled and disconnected. It's as though he doesn't trust his own voice.

"So, you came to meet your father. A grand journey!"

"I guess."

"I am glad you want to say hello to my sister. It is too bad she is not here. I am happy you are friends. You are my friend, Joseph Grabinsky. Let us drink to friendship!"

Joseph gags from the awful taste of the chacha. "I'm worried she might be in some kind of trouble," he says through gritted teeth. Levan nods, closing his eyes and swaying slightly. Joseph waits for a response, then continues. "Do you know the name Skunk?"

For a moment, Levan's entire demeanour changes. Joseph can't tell whether he's nervous, angry, or both.

"Who?"

Something tells him not to take this further. He decides not to tell Levan about Tamar's message. "Never mind, it's nothing."

"Drink, Joseph."

The third shot makes the room spin. It also unwinds Joseph's guarded tongue.

"What was Zaza like? Tamar's father."

Levan freezes. "Why do you ask these questions? I thought we were drinking. I thought we were friends."

"There's a picture of him in your house. I saw it in your mother's bedroom." Joseph slides his hand into his pocket, jangling the cufflinks like loose change. He'd forgotten they were there.

"Fuck Zaza and fuck the past. Drink."

Joseph feels the alcohol wind its way through sinew, careen off muscle, and meteor toward his cortex. The room shifts and he thinks he sees a creature lurking in the shadows.

"Why is Tamar coming back to Tbilisi?"

"You ask too many questions. None of it matters. You want to know the Georgian soul? I will teach you. Drink."

The fifth shot feels like decapitation.

"Tomorrow I take you hunting." Levan pours out two more shots. "We will kill the boar then spit-roast it, old-country-style."

"I'm not a hunter."

"You will become one, Joseph. You are Georgian. But tonight, we dance. Will you dance with me, Joseph Grabinsky?"

"Uhm, where's the bathroom?"

Levan raises an eyebrow and points a finger to the ceiling.

Joseph bursts out of the dressing room and up a staircase that ends at a door. Inside there is no light, only a deep hole, from which emanates the smell of things he does not wish to see. As he vomits into the hole, Joseph has the sensation that everything inside him is falling away. Every secret, every desire, every fear. When he's finished, he feels physically weak, yet his head is clear.

In his pockets are Zaza's cufflinks and Raymond Chandler's wallet and cell phone. Using the phone, he illuminates his surroundings. It's far bleaker than he imagined. No toilet, no sink, no window, nothing to hold on to. He pulls the blue-and-gold cufflinks from his pocket, weighs them in his palm. He's not sure why he took them from Nana's house, but he knows they're important.

"Zaza," whispers Joseph to the cufflinks. But they don't reply.

The light of the phone goes out. The darkness gives him a moment to catch his breath. It's been an insane twenty-four hours. Joseph takes stock of all that has happened since he arrived in Tbilisi. He reflects on the dossiers and the demonstrations; the murdered Chandler in the street; Daniel Daniel, Keti, Lali, Levan, and Nana. Then he moves the phone again, activating its light. He decides to look through the dead man's wallet.

Inside he finds cash, some receipts, and a piece of paper folded in four. It's a copy of a photograph, a face in black and white, taken with a telephoto lens. The man is bearded and wears a monk's robe. He bears a scar travelling from his ear to his mouth. He stands in front of a stone building on a slope. A church, perhaps. Behind the building is the blurry peak of a mountain covered in snow.

The light of the phone flickers out again. Joseph's mind travels back to the photograph in Nana's house. "Zaza," she said, pointing to a man in a beige wool coat and blue-and-gold cufflinks. "Mama." He flicks the phone on again and gazes intently at the bearded man in the photograph. It looks like it could be the same person, perhaps a few decades older, but he cannot be certain.

Just then the phone vibrates, and he decides to answer it. "Hello?"

A voice speaks to him in Georgian. Someone pounds on the bathroom door and Joseph jumps, juggles the phone, and drops it. When he reaches to pick it up, he realizes he also dropped the cufflinks. He points the cell phone at the floor. To his horror, he sees a giant rat only a few feet away. Joseph and the rat stare at each other in the near-darkness. Joseph understands: the rat has the cufflinks. It's standing on top of them.

"Shit," says Joseph.

The rat shifts on its feet.

"Come on, give them back!" Joseph kicks at the rat, but the creature holds its ground. Joseph looks around for something to hit the rat with.

"You're not looking in the right way." The voice is low-pitched and husky. It's the rat that's talking.

"What?"

"Don't be afraid of the mess. Don't be afraid of me."

Carefully, Joseph reaches toward the rat with one hand. With his other he holds the phone, using it as a flashlight.

"Don't you see? I'm the missing link."

Joseph quickly grabs the cufflinks and shoves them back in his pocket.

Then the rat says, "This is not for me to give and not my story to tell. Maybe you decide to give these to her when you think the time is right."

Suddenly Joseph understands.

"Now that wasn't so hard," says the rat, "was it?"

JOSEPH EMERGES FROM the bathroom triumphant. He needs to speak to Daniel Daniel. When he descends into the theatre bar, it's practically empty. The crowd has thinned out; everyone has moved on to the demonstrations at Freedom Square.

Standing in a circle near the back of the bar he sees a small group of men. One by one they take turns pummelling each other, shoulder to shoulder. Levan is at their centre. Next to him is Daniel Daniel wearing his yellow sunglasses and *Houses of the Holy* t-shirt. Joseph approaches the outside of the frenetic circle, his pants a mess and his shirt smeared with vomit. Sweat streams down Daniel Daniel's forehead. The music is loud, something Balkan. Suddenly a hand yanks Joseph into the circle, and he's surrounded by sweaty men in black leather coats. The music gets louder; Levan gestures for him to dance. The men lock pinkies as he steps toward them.

The clues were in front of him all along, buried in the small wooden box in Rachel's office—hidden, like her past. But now Joseph understands the cufflinks were also in the briefcase Junior Lieutenant Z.G. handed to Anna Litvak on a runway in Moscow. And the pain of it, the horrible trauma caused by the Junior Lieutenant carrying away their child. Zaza. Tamar's father.

Joseph doesn't know what to do, so he makes like Levan— lets his shoulder drop once, twice, three times, then lunges toward him. He doesn't know if this is an ancient dance or something Levan is making up on the spot. Joseph has no idea if he is using enough shoulder or if he should have his right hand in the air like Levan, as though he were twirling a gun and shooting at the night sky. Daniel Daniel grins madly. He mirrors Joseph, mirroring Levan, now a semicircle of drunk dancing men.

Why was his mother in Georgia? Why does a father kidnap his child? Why is that child, Tamar, his half-sister? And why did Rachel never tell him?

# 21

*Republic of Adjara*
*Sunday, November 16, 2003*

Passenger Side removes the cigarette from Tamar's mouth, his fingers grazing her lips. Though her head and body hurt, she can hear birds singing in the hills and feel the cool night air on her skin. Somewhere in the distance is the Black Sea. According to her rough calculations, they're just down the coast from Sukhumi, where she used to summer with Nana and Sasha as a child. For Tamar, Abkhazia meant endless summers by the Black Sea in the house of her grandfather. She remembers swimming in the sea, day and night, the sound of cicadas, and oranges so sweet her mouth salivates at the thought of them. And then it was gone, from one summer to the next. She tries to imagine who might live there now, who tends its garden, who enjoys the succulent orange and peach trees growing in the yard. As Passenger Side guides the cigarette back into Tamar's mouth, she thinks of swimming out to sea alone. She loved the freedom of surrender when she let the waves take her. To lose control, to touch a larger, mysterious power. Floating for hours until the sun set, guided home by a curtain of stars.

TAMAR WAKES SUDDENLY; she must've fallen asleep. The vehicle has stopped and the driver paces the highway, back and forth, screaming into a cell phone. Passenger Side crouches next to her, offering her another cigarette. When the ash gets too long, he pinches it from her lips, and flicks it clean.

"Do you have a name?" she asks.

"Alex."

Alex places the cigarette back in her mouth. Knowing his name makes Tamar less afraid.

"Where are you taking me, Alex?"

He shrugs. The driver continues to shout. Tamar feels a vibration in her back pocket, the cheap Nokia pressing into her. *Probably Goran and Lali wondering where I am*, she thinks.

"Can I have some water?"

Alex lifts a canteen to her mouth. The creases in his forehead tense, reminding Tamar of the lines of a river delta. When he sweeps his long hair back, she can smell his skin: jasmine oil and sweat. Suddenly light pierces the darkness of the van. A black Volga flashes its headlights and pulls over. Alex slides the door shut, and Tamar falls back against cold metal. The driver starts the engine and begins to follow the car.

Tamar closes her eyes and thinks, *I must undo this through breath. Ten in and ten out. Then ten more. Count to a hundred, a thousand, ten thousand.* Channelling Goran's instructions, she hears the voice of Rachel in her mind: "Keep breathing," she says.

# 22

*Tbilisi, Republic of Georgia*
*November 16, 2003*

Freedom Square smells like gasoline and fear. It makes Joseph
feel dizzy, though his hangover from the previous night's
debacle at the Underground doesn't help things. As they wind
their way through the crowds, Daniel Daniel delivers a brief
history lesson, explaining that it was here in 1907 that a young
Georgian poet, Iosef Djugashvili, robbed a bank and sent
the money to Lenin in the name of the Bolshevik revolution.
Iosef later adopted the name Stalin, and so it began: a different revolution for a different time.

Daniel Daniel's history lessons do not make Joseph feel
comfortable or reassured. There are more than fifty thousand
people gathered in the main square. Joseph knows that with
those numbers comes the possibility of violence. As the crowd
swells, so do the riot police and military personnel hovering
at the perimeters. Tbilisi is on the cusp of change, but it's not
a change that everyone wants.

Up ahead, Levan speaks to Goran, the Serbian activist Joseph briefly met at the Underground. They're engaged in what looks to be an intense discussion. Joseph sees Levan push Goran, but instead of pushing back, Goran simply laughs. Levan amiably slaps Goran on the back.

Joseph is here to meet Levan. Though Joseph doesn't quite remember the details — he was incredibly drunk when the conversation took place — he recalls agreeing to go on a hunting trip. And while Daniel Daniel was annoyed by yet another delay in meeting Gary, Joseph is glad for the opportunity to speak with Levan. He believes Levan knows more about Tamar than he's let on. Joseph hopes to earn his trust and press him for details, perhaps even soberly, in the quiet of the forest.

"Now you see," Daniel Daniel explains, pointing to the demonstration, "the crazy world your mother and Tamar helped to build."

Young, aspiring politicians and burgeoning activists speak from a podium on the parliament steps, their voices brimming with the hopeful and idealistic. Riot police and soldiers stand awkwardly on the perimeter, their guns pointed haphazardly at the crowd. There are tents and sleeping bags, bottles of water, and cauldrons of hot food. Teens hand out leaflets and lollipops. An old woman laughs and hands Joseph a piece of fresh bread. When he bites into it, the woman proudly holds up her hands to show him she made it herself. Joseph can feel it, the recipes and secrets passed down through generations, the tears of women mixed with dough. He's inherited it too.

Levan grabs his shoulder. "It's too bad Tamar isn't here," he says. "She would love this. Isn't it beautiful?"

Joseph reluctantly agrees.

"Are you ready to go hunting and learn the secret of the Georgian soul?"

Joseph nods. A circle of men and women begin to sing nearby. Their voices come from a place that is both foreign and familiar. The music is a cappella yet it has a rhythm, slow and sure.

"It is a Georgian song, from the mountains," Levan explains. "It says we've always been occupied by external forces and struggle to be ourselves. Isn't that what freedom is?"

The music is beautiful, yet Joseph can't help feeling duped by its message. What good is freedom if it's based on a lie? He loves Tamar deeply, but where there was once intimacy and peace, his mind now sounds alarm. Tamar and Joseph, half-siblings, truth tellers, fooled by the same mother. He does not know how to reconcile himself with this truth.

Yet their stories — strung together like beads on a string — mean little in the face of what he believes is a growing urgency: where is Tamar, and who is this Skunk? Levan pushes his way through the crowd and approaches the parliament steps. Near the podium, he greets a man in a blue suit, and whispers in his ear. Mikheil Saakashvili, the young presidential hopeful, turns toward Joseph, smiles, and gives him the thumbs-up.

# 23

*Outside Telavi, Republic of Georgia*
*November 16, 2003*

Tamar dreams of Joseph. They are in a crowd, holding hands, surrounded by people walking in the same direction. Tamar feels swept up in their passage. She believes, in the under-current of dream language, that the only thing that matters is love. And she feels it, pulsing between them.

When she awakes, Tamar is still thinking about Joseph. She is concerned by the implications of her feelings for him. She didn't know it at the time, but she slept with her half-brother. In that moment of grief, after the loss of a woman they both loved, it felt right. Like she had come home. But it can never happen again.

Tamar can see the black Volga is no longer there. The driver and Alex mutter as they pull over at a roadside res-taurant. The silhouettes of mountains, purple and blue, show light emerging from the east. She believes they're east of Tbilisi.

"Where are we?" she asks.

Alex shrugs. "Hungry?"

"Starving."

He gets out of the van, stubs out his cigarette and disappears into the restaurant. They're parked at the back of the lot, a stream rushing beneath them. Behind the creek, a forest. The driver eyes Tamar through the rear-view mirror.

"Can you open the door?" she asks. "I wouldn't mind some air."

He grunts, gets out of the van, and slides open the door.

"Got a cigarette?"

The driver grunts again and pulls out a pack of Viceroy Blues.

"My favourite," Tamar says.

He lights two cigarettes and puts one in her mouth. He doesn't need to pinch the edges the way Alex did — these are filtered. But Tamar keeps his fingers there, inviting. He's surprised by the gesture. Tamar smiles as she sucks back on the cigarette, along with his finger.

"Jesus fuck!" he yells.

Tamar bites down as hard as she can, then she pulls back her knees — feet still bound together — and kicks him in the groin. He falls back in pain. Tamar's hands slip easily out of the ropes as she jumps on top of him and reaches into his jacket. She yanks out a pistol and clubs the side of his head. She rolls off and frantically undoes the knots on her feet. The driver is unconscious, his face a mess. She hurries to the front of the van and almost runs into Alex. She points the pistol at him.

"Who sent you?"

"Please put that down. I can help you."

She aims and pulls the trigger. Boxes of food fall as blood sprays from Alex's shoulder.

"Who sent you?" she repeats.

Tamar hears movement behind her, turns to look, and then Alex is on top of her, struggling for the gun. He tries to twist her arm, but she elbows him in the chin, kicks away, and pulls the trigger a second time. Alex falls back toward the lip of the creek.

"Who sent you?" she screams.

"Skunk."

"Where were you taking me?"

"Duisi, Pankisi Gorge."

"What does Skunk want with me? And how did he know where to find me?"

Blood streams from Alex's mouth. Tamar hears the sound of the creek, water rushing. When he reaches toward her, Tamar shoots him, one last time. Tamar turns back toward the driver, still lying unconscious on the ground where she left him. She digs her hand into his leather jacket and pulls out the keys and the Viceroy Blues. Inside the van, Tamar lights a cigarette and runs her hands through her hair. The pistol on the passenger seat points northeast like a compass. When her phone rings, she jumps. She recognizes Levan's number but does not answer.

# 24

*Tbilisi, Republic of Georgia*
*November 16, 2003*

Mikheil Saakashvili is the locus of hope for fifty thousand people. The young, American-educated nemesis of President Shevardnadze demands to be declared the true victor of the people in this month's election, citing ballot tampering by the former Communist. He stands by the lectern and waits for the swelling crowds to settle.

The news, according to Daniel Daniel, and much to Joseph's surprise, is that Saakashvili wants to join Levan's hunting party. When Levan told him that Rachel Grabinsky's son would be present, Saakashvili insisted he come along. Now the plan is to travel to Saakashvili's dacha for lunch and hunt for wild boar in the surrounding forests. It is turning out to be a bigger event than Joseph expected, and he is growing more uncomfortable with each passing minute. *All I need is a moment alone with Levan*, Joseph thinks, watching him lean toward Goran and whisper something in his ear. Goran nods and produces his mobile phone. Levan turns to face Joseph. Their eyes lock and Joseph feels ill at ease. As much as Joseph wants to talk to him, Levan scares the shit out of him.

The mood is electric when Saakashvili leans into the microphone. Wearing a blue pinstripe suit and a white button-down, he looks more fraternity bro than presidential hopeful. But he's of the new generation, and herein lies the hope: only the children can transcend the sins of their fathers. More importantly, Saakashvili knows how to work a crowd. His voice gets more and more excited, and the masses are whipped into a frenzy, responding with screams and songs. When his speech ends, a roar erupts, and Saakashvili descends the parliament steps. Joseph turns to look for Daniel Daniel, but instead he's intercepted by a security guard.

"Please. Wait."

Thinking he's done something wrong, Joseph is surprised to see the ebullient, blue-suited man approach him.

"My friend, welcome to my country. Will you please take a picture with me for our national cause of democracy and freedom?"

Joseph turns around thinking Saakashvili is speaking to someone else. But microphones encircle him. Saakashvili grabs his shoulders and turns him to face the cameras.

"Ladies and gentlemen, may I present to you Joseph Grabinsky. Without his mother, Rachel, what you see here today in Freedom Square would not be possible. We are grateful that Joseph has come to Tbilisi to participate in the pro-democracy demonstrations. Thank you, Joseph. Your support means so much. This afternoon, Mr. Grabinsky and I will go on a special hunting expedition. This country has so much to offer. If I become president, I will open our doors to tourists from the West. We are a rich and beautiful nation!"

When the flashes and pictures stop, Daniel Daniel grabs Joseph's hand and leads him away through the crowd. Joseph looks back and Saakashvili gives him another thumbs-up. Joseph feels uneasy with such performances. He does not like the idea of being on TV, nor does he want to represent his mother and her notion of a freedom based on lies and omissions.

Joseph is ushered into the back of a black luxury suv with tinted windows, and the doors are slammed shut. Levan is nowhere to be seen. Mikheil Saakashvili, clean-shaven and schoolboy-excited, sits in the driver's seat. The biggest and most sinister-looking man of Saakashvili's security detail, Dato, sporting dark sunglasses, earbuds, and a black leather jacket, sits in the passenger seat. Saakashvili puts his foot on the gas and they accelerate away from the crowd toward the hinterland, in search of wild game.

# 25

Tamar steers the van onto the empty road, her hands shaking on the wheel. She can still taste the driver's flesh in her mouth, feel the burn of the ropes where it bound her wrists. When she closes her eyes, she sees Alex lying in a pool of blood. She presses her foot on the gas. She needs to come up with a plan. She tries Levan's phone, but he doesn't answer. *Why did Skunk send men to kidnap me?*

Tamar considers going back to Tbilisi. She could find Levan, ask him if he knows where Zaza is, and perhaps they could go see him together. She could ask Nana the questions that have been haunting her: Did she know that Rachel was Anna? Did she understand that Rachel had come to claim her? But deep down Tamar already knows the answers. There is an understanding between women, a knowledge without words.

Tamar knows that nothing good can come from going to Skunk. The two times she met him, he scared her. After

311

the Underground encounter, Davit uncovered information, details of Skunk as a dangerous man, a violent man, a weapons dealer with a drug and prostitution gambit. According to Davit, Skunk has deep connections in Abkhazia and Chechnya; men on the ground from Baku to Sochi; a renegade operation that stretches the breadth of the Caucasus. There's no question, the man is dangerous. And unpredictable. Yet he holds the key to what she wants. Skunk's knowledge compels her. It is difficult to turn back.

Tamar follows the long line of mountains north and east. When she leaves Akhmeta, the paved highway disappears into mud. A trio of bearded men wearing camouflage vests and black Adidas trackpants motion for her to pull over. The makeshift checkpoint is manned by Chechen boyeviks carrying machine guns, grenade launchers, and flares. With the sweep of his well-worn AK-47, a bearded man commands Tamar to open her window.

"Papers," he says flatly.

Tamar hands him her passport, as the others eye the rusted vehicle. There is no computer to check, no data to input, only their stern will and unpredictable judgement. The man hands back her passport and waves Tamar through. She revs the engine and jolts forward, passing the invisible line that marks Pankisi Gorge.

# 26

*Mtskheta – Mtianeti, Republic of Georgia*
*November 16, 2003*

Saakashvili drives speedily through narrow streets, though he
is not half as reckless as Daniel Daniel. Nor, unfortunately,
does he listen to music half as good. While the sound system
in Saakashvili's Cadillac SUV is one of the nicest Joseph has
ever seen, it's blasting out vintage Paul Anka. Saakashvili's
body convulses in his seat as he roars at the top of his lungs,
"And I did it myyyyy waaaay."

Joseph has little time for the Canadian crooner, so he sinks
into the plush leather seats, and watches a soccer match on
a mini TV. The camera focuses on a group of Turkish fans,
torsos and faces painted red. One fan smashes a lone French
fry into a bowl of ketchup and devours it.

"You are witness to the ancient rivalry," Daniel Daniel
explains. "Between the Turks and Georgians — Musselmans
and Christians. It is very exciting, like the fight between two

siblings. No one can hate each other like this. Very special rivalry of blood."

Joseph feels sick from last night's drinking. It doesn't help that Saakashvili smells like he took a bath in Drakkar Noir. The young politician swerves to avoid oncoming traffic.

"You were perfect with the press, Joseph," Saakashvili declares. Even when he's making conversation, it sounds like a political speech.

"I didn't say anything."

"And that is your genius. I loved your mother. She inspired me to enter politics. It's an honour to meet her son."

Joseph doesn't want to listen. The hubris surrounding his mother, he believes, will never end. He knows too much, which apparently isn't enough. So he focuses on the soccer match. The Georgian players goof around, passing the ball from knee to foot, while the Turks seem to be preparing for the fight of their lives. Saakashvili accelerates across a rickety bridge, beneath which flows a muddy river. They gain speed and quickly leave the city.

"Have you hunted before, Joseph?" asks Saakashvili.

"I've never held a gun in my life."

"Me neither. My father never taught me, though he talked about it constantly. This will be a first for both of us. I believe this hunting trip will be important for the future of Georgia. A turning point. If I am to become president of this young country, I must learn to shoot in the manner of the Caucasian."

"This is very true," adds Daniel Daniel. "And quite important."

"Uhm, where's Levan?"

"He had some business to take care of. Busy man. He will join us later for lunch."

Saakashvili turns onto a dirt road, switching the vehicle to four-wheel drive as they enter a forest. There is no path, only Saakashvili's will and heavy accelerator foot.

"Levan told me you're an investment banker. What do you think of international canoe racing?" asks Saakashvili.

"I've never given it much thought."

"I have a project you might want to consider."

Joseph is annoyed. But he has not forgotten the purpose of this journey: to speak to Levan about Tamar. Maybe Saakashvili is a link in that chain. Somehow, it's all connected: Gary, Tamar, the photograph of the man by the church, his mother's fabricated life.

At a clearing in the forest, the four men pile out. The sun shines through mostly leafless branches, pulverizing the forest floor. Saakashvili opens the trunk to reveal a gleaming cache of ammunition and weapons. Daniel Daniel chooses a small pistol, Saakashvili grabs a Smith & Wesson shotgun, and Joseph selects a Kalashnikov circa 1947 with bayonet. Dato stands with his arms crossed, ready to take on any foe, human or animal, with his bare hands. Saakashvili cannot contain his excitement.

"Photo op, photo op!" he exclaims as he hands Daniel Daniel a small digital camera.

With their weapons raised, Mikheil Saakashvili and Joseph Grabinsky lean toward each other in a pose that feels reminiscent of an old Hollywood Western. They're a big-time duo in the middle of nowhere. A rustling from the forest interrupts their photo session, as a wild boar emerges from the shadows and rushes past the unsuspecting men. Saakashvili immediately barrels off into the forest, chasing the woolly mammal, firing his shotgun wildly. Daniel Daniel calmly leads Joseph to a hunter's tree-stand. Hidden in the trees, Joseph looks through the gunsight. He asks Daniel Daniel where he learned how to hunt.

"In Georgia, we all know," he says. "But we don't hunt boar. Just each other. It is the second right of manhood, after stealing. Every man knows how to steal, how to shoot, and how to dance."

A plastic bottle of wine is produced and makes the rounds. Daniel Daniel explains that the bullet of the Kalashnikov can travel for an entire kilometre. "It has an arc toward the forward," he declares, which Joseph finds touchingly poetic. Daniel Daniel instructs him to be careful with the kickback, to compensate by pointing down at his target.

As Daniel Daniel continues to give instructions, Joseph's hands get excited. He feels trigger-aroused, something he has never experienced before. The forest light becomes crisper, the shadows deeper.

Saakashvili emerges from the trees deflated. "The bastard got away," he says, placing an empty plastic bottle on a bench some fifty feet ahead. As he walks to the tree-stand, he explains: "I need to practise. I want to be a true expert marksman." He puts on a black beret, as though this will help, and fires his Smith & Wesson at the flimsy plastic target. Boom! Boom! Boom!

Daniel Daniel urges Joseph to follow Saakashvili's lead. His voice is calm as he reassures Joseph, "Do not be afraid. Do not close your eyes. And do not make any jokes."

In spite of his advice, Joseph closes his eyes. He pulls the trigger of his Kalashnikov and feels the weapon shudder. When he opens his eyes, he says, "I can't feel a thing."

"Comrade Joseph?"

Joseph looks down. Blood pools around his shoe. His blood.

"Problem, radical problem," says Daniel Daniel.

Saakashvili stops shooting and looks down. His baby face changes from puzzlement to concern, concern to shock, and finally, from shock to total denial. Daniel Daniel yells at him in Georgian. Saakashvili yells back in English.

"I swear, I didn't shoot him!"

"You were the only one shooting!"

"But how is that possible? I was pointing in the other direction!"

"You are a moron, not a great president."

Blood seeps through slats of wood then drips onto the forest floor. Saakashvili panics. He throws down his shotgun and helps Daniel Daniel and Dato guide Joseph down. Daniel Daniel hands Joseph a bottle and he gulps from it while Saakashvili frantically removes Joseph's shoe and sock. Everyone watches, everything listens.

Levan emerges from a thicket of trees carrying a Kalashnikov. "What the fuck is going on?" he shouts as he runs toward them. Levan immediately goes into action mode. A strange-looking bird lands on a tree above the men, eyeing Joseph's wound. Something pulses through Joseph. *My life*, he thinks, *spilling onto the forest floor.*

"This is an emergency," declares Levan, wrapping a towel around Joseph's foot that quickly soaks through.

"He's still bleeding," says Saakashvili, stating the obvious.

Levan is agitated by Saakashvili's panic and utter inability to deal with the situation.

"The bleeding will stop. The real danger is infection. We need to disinfect the wound and cauterize it."

"How?"

Levan inspects Joseph's foot. Levan points out that there are both entrance and exit wounds; the bullet travelled clean through. Blood gushes from the two holes at once. Joseph feels like someone has lit his foot on fire.

"Gunpowder," suggests Dato, speaking for the first time.

"What are you talking about?" says Saakashvili.

"I learned it in the army. You sprinkle it on the wound then light it with a match."

"I don't think that's a great idea," says Saakashvili. "I just shot this man. Now you want to set his foot on fire?"

Levan announces: "He's right. It is our best and only option to cauterize the wound." He puts his hand on Joseph's shoulder. "What do you think?"

"Sounds better than driving two hours to a hospital."

Levan nods. Dato takes a cartridge from his pocket and removes the jacket with his knife. Daniel Daniel pours chacha over the wound and passes Joseph the bottle. Dato sprinkles a line of black powder over the entrance and exit wounds, lights a match and drops it. A flame flares up from Joseph's foot two feet in the air. The smell of burned flesh fills Joseph's nostrils and he screams.

"I can't believe this is happening," says Saakashvili, pacing nervously. "You're not going to charge me with murder, are you?"

"It was an accident," says Joseph, delirious from the pain—and the chacha. "Accidents happen."

"Do you hear this man's wisdom?" Saakashvili addresses the men. "Accidents happen! Words for the wise. Accidents *do* happen. They most certainly do." He presses the muzzle of the Smith & Wesson against his chin, pensively. The funny-looking bird continues to watch the men from its perch. Joseph feels on the verge of passing out. "If, God willing, I am ever president of this beautiful country, I will not forget this moment. I will name a street after you. No, a highway: the Joseph Grabinsky Overpass."

Levan says, "I think it's best if we end the hunting trip."

The men express their collective disappointment.

"But there is no animal yet, only American tourist!" yells Daniel Daniel, at which everyone laughs.

Saakashvili invites them to a special dinner being prepared at his family's nearby dacha. He assures them: there will be plenty to eat and drink. Joseph feels woozy from the booze and the shock. He has the strange feeling the wound isn't an accident. It's a clue to something else, an eruption of surface, an opening to the deep. Daniel Daniel heaves Joseph onto his back. Joseph curls his legs and lets himself be carried to the suv. It feels good to lie on the back of a friend.

# 27

*Duisi, Pankisi Gorge*
*November 16, 2003*

Tamar drives through a village of tar-paper shacks and stone houses. Bony oxen pull wooden carts next to a newly built mosque made of red brick, its gold minaret gleaming in the sun. She knows of Pankisi Gorge by its fearsome reputation. The gorge borders Chechnya to the north, and the Kist — exiled Chechens and devout Sufis — have lived here for over two hundred years, in peace with their Orthodox Christian neighbours. In 2000, during the carnage of the Second Chechen War, when Russian forces seized control of Chechnya, thousands of refugees fled over the mountains on foot. As Pankisi's Muslim population swelled, so did the rumours. Putin claimed Osama bin Laden was hiding in Pankisi, running terrorist training camps. Nothing was ever confirmed, of course, but all the attention created an air of mystery and fear.

Tamar slows down as she comes to a bend in the road. Reaching into her coat pocket she pulls out the pack of

Viceroys. While Western journalists write about the rumours of gang violence and terrorist camps, Tamar sees only poverty — small farms on hard land.

Tamar is reminded of a story Zaza once told her as a child: "I knew a little boy who turned into a wild animal. If you smell a skunk, you know you're too close. You'll know when you see his stripe. Remember: everyone was a child once. No one sets out to become a monster. Children inherit the work of their parents."

# 28

*Sioni Reservoir, Republic of Georgia*
*November 16, 2003*

As the SUV speeds through the hinterland, Joseph's shock begins to recede and the pain returns. His foot is on fire. He tries to meditate, to breathe the truth of suffering, but it has little effect. Through the makeshift tourniquet, he sneaks a glance at the wound. It makes him nauseous.

At a small bungalow on the edge of a lake, the vehicle stops and they all pile out. White laundry sways on a line between trees; a small creek gurgles nearby. Neatly pruned balsam and oak shade the men from the late-afternoon sun. Smoke funnels up from the cottage chimney. A door swings open and the smell of warm food wafts toward them. It's a dream out of Chekhov.

In a clearing, Levan lights a fire and Daniel Daniel mills about, smoking and talking. Mikheil Saakashvili struggles with his cell phone, seeking reception, while Levan retrieves an old wheelchair made of rugged canvas, its wheels rusted out.

Dato stands by a tree, watching and listening to everything.

"Saakashvili worships this wheelchair. His grandmother died in it," Levan announces proudly. "1937 was not a great year in the Soviet Union. But it is history."

Joseph understands he is meant to sit in it. Levan offers to wheel him through a tour of the property, which has been in the Saakashvili family for centuries. Joseph understands this is an opportunity to be alone with him, so he consents. Levan pushes the wheelchair, and they snake up a narrow path on a trail of stone. Joseph tries to adjust himself in the ancient contraption, awkwardly lifting his aching foot onto a wooden leg rest. The pain has worsened into a throbbing that makes his heart shake. He can't help but feel the wound — held together by scorched gunpowder and a tourniquet made of Saakashvili's dry-cleaned dress shirts — will be the beginning of his undoing. The strange-looking bird from the forest clearing lands on a branch above him. Joseph stares at the bird, and the bird at him.

At the top of the hill, Levan pushes him toward a building of crumbling red brick. One of its walls has collapsed inward. "From an earthquake," Levan explains. Joseph is pushed through a door frame with no door into a room with two turbine generators that stand useless and dead.

"This used to provide electricity for the village," says Levan. The brick and stone floor reveals small circles hollowed out and filled with sand. Levan kneels on the floor and sweeps one of the circles with his hand, removes a lid, then dips clay bowls into darkness.

"The Saakashvili family converted the generator room into a wine cellar," he says. "The wine is stored in clay vessels beneath the earth. Traditional method. You must try some."

When he removes the bowls from the darkness, they are filled with a liquid of a deep, earthy hue. The wine tastes rich and good. Joseph wonders how he's going to conduct his interrogation of Levan. Joseph is not a spy, nor an interrogator. But he is skilled in the art of awkwardness, and his general strategy in such situations is to ask a lot of questions.

"Did you always want to be a theatre proprietor?" he begins.

"No," says Levan, relishing the wine. "I wanted to be a criminal. Like my uncle."

He tells Joseph the story of Niko, his father Sasha's brother, who in the heydays of early '90s Georgia worked as a break-and-enter artist. Levan would often accompany his uncle on his nighttime adventures. Being both small and nimble, Levan would be hoisted through high windows, so that he could let Niko in through the door. The split was 20/80 in his uncle's favour, but Levan preferred the thrill to the money.

"Life," says Levan, "is my true art form. It's quite exhausting being a thief. Nobody understands that. Sadly, in this country, one never stops stealing. Even the theatre impresario is a plunderer of stories and souls." Levan pauses to drink more wine. "Tamar never really understood when I told her stealing is not an ethical shortcoming, but an existential necessity. She is too idealistic. It almost got her killed."

"Maybe it's about finding better incentives," Joseph suggests. "A system with fewer lies and less corruption."

"Your mother used to say the same thing."

Joseph sips his wine and leans back in the wheelchair. The wine relaxes him and helps him forget the wound.

"Why are you really in Georgia?" Levan asks.

Joseph meets his gaze. "I told you. I came to meet my father, Gary Ruckler."

"Why did you ask me about Skunk? What do you know about him?"

"Nothing."

"Then how do you know his name?"

"Tamar left me a phone message yesterday from a bus in Turkey. She said she'd spoken to you, that you'd told her Skunk knew something about her father, Zaza. Here, I can play it for you." Joseph fishes around in his pockets for his phone.

Levan paces the room. "In the last twenty-four hours, one of Skunk's men was killed, and another left unconscious on the side of the road, not far from here. Yesterday, my best friend Irakli was shot in a back alley in Tbilisi. And now Tamar has gone missing. I think you have something to do with this, Joseph Grabinsky."

"I swear, I don't. We're on the same side. We want the same thing."

"Which is what?"

"Tamar."

Levan stops in his tracks. "There's something you're not telling me. I think it has to do with your mother. Who did she work for? Do you work for them, too?"

"I don't work for anyone. I'm just worried about your sister."

"So am I."

"We can help each other."

"How?"

"Let's find her together."

The engines of the turbines rattle, brushed by the wind.

"It's the attitude of the West that I find most insulting." When Levan paces, his hands gesture to something Joseph cannot see. "You are so entitled. You call it 'help.' And it's true, you've been helping for centuries. But really, you just help yourselves. Usually, I know what people want. But I can't understand what you're after."

"I just want to see Tamar."

"You flew ten thousand kilometres to see her?"

Levan stares at him menacingly. Joseph swallows hard.

"What if I told you Saakashvili didn't shoot you?"

"What?"

"What do you want to know about my sister?"

"You shot me?"

"I like to keep an eye on people. Tell me what you know. You're not leaving here until you do. Why are you in Georgia?"

"I came to see my father. And Tamar told me she'd be here. I don't know why she's on a bus in Turkey. I haven't talked to her since she left Toronto."

Levan pulls something from his pocket. Joseph's heart sinks. "I found this during the hunting trip. It fell out of your pocket."

Raymond Chandler's wallet.

"I bought Irakli this wallet. I gave it to him for his thirtieth birthday." Levan flips through it. "Why did you kill him? Was it because of the photograph?"

"I didn't kill your friend."

"Don't lie to me. I hate liars. I kill liars."

326

Levan steps toward Joseph, fist clenched.

"There you are, Comrade," says Daniel Daniel, stumbling breathless into the room. He's carrying Saakashvili's Smith & Wesson shotgun. "What are you proud and gentle men so fortuitously drinking by the ancient turbines of this useless power station?"

Levan puts the wallet back into his jacket pocket, shifts from menacing to cordial.

"To be continued," he says to Joseph, then walks out the door. Daniel Daniel ladles himself a glass of wine. Joseph's heart continues to pound.

"We need to get the fuck out of here," he says.

"Why? What is Levan saying?"

"He shot me, not the lunatic politician."

"Then he is master buck shot. Fortunately, it is only one foot."

"I'm stuck in a fucking wheelchair and he's going to kill me."

"Do not worry, Comrade Joseph. He would not do it here. We are at the dacha of the next idiot president of Georgia. Big scandal. Now, what news of Tamar?"

"She's disappeared. Levan's best friend was murdered yesterday, and he thinks I did it. Who is this Skunk? Why does everyone freak out when they hear his name?"

"The Skunk man is never good news, bad vibes, not very relaxed. We need to get out of here."

"How?"

"Soon everyone will eat and drink too much. Ancient Georgian trick. I steal our escape. Do not worry, Comrade. I am your eternal protector."

# 29

*Duisi, Pankisi Gorge*
*November 16, 2003*

Tamar pulls over at an old schoolhouse. The windows are boarded up and a faded UNRWA flag droops from the rooftop. A red-bearded man in a dirty doctor's coat tends a fire in the courtyard, trying to keep warm.

"Excuse me, which way to Duisi?" Tamar asks in Russian.

"This is it."

He throws a book into the fire, poking the flames with a stick.

"Are you Russian?" he asks.

"No."

"Good."

The man's name is Shamil, and he welcomes Tamar to the fire. A woman steps out of the refugee centre carrying a parcel. As she approaches, Tamar realizes the parcel is a small child, its pupils darting back and forth as though it were being chased. Shamil draws a stethoscope from around his neck and listens to the child's heart. He instructs them to go back inside, then reaches into the flames and removes a pot of boiling water.

"I made a request for antibiotics, alcohol swabs, and insulin. Instead, I get instant coffee. Sixteen boxes of it. Would you like some?" He pours hot water into two cups and scoops in some Nescafé. Tamar eyes the building.

"The child has a fever," says Shamil. "TB. He got it the day the Russians bombed us." Tamar clocks the missing wall, the shattered windows. "Can you imagine? Bombing a hospital. What's crueller than that?"

He hands her coffee, hot and soothing.

Shamil says, "When our ancestors were gathered in their caves, huddled around fires, what do you think came first? Hate or fear?"

"Fear, I think."

"I think it was hate. The Russians have these camps in Chechnya..." His voice trails off. "I have plenty of fear. I'm not so good at hate. But I can learn."

Dark clouds move in from the mountains and it starts to drizzle. Tamar sees a selection of seemingly random items housed under a blue tarpaulin in the courtyard: old Soviet medical textbooks; a vhs tape titled *How to Start Your Own Small Business*; boxes of coloured pencils, "Made in China"; a green vase; and a dog-eared copy of *A Hero of Our Time* by Mikhail Lermontov. Tamar picks up the vase and holds it to the light. Taken out of context—a kitchen table, a warm home, a place for flowers—it feels alien and strange.

She turns the vase over in her hands. It's wide and curved with a hole in its centre. She feels sad for this doctor Shamil, for the baby she mistook for a parcel. She wishes she could ask the right questions, say the right things. If she did, maybe the world wouldn't be so messed up.

"That vase belonged to my wife," he says.

"It's beautiful."

"Keep it. It would make me happy."

She knows she cannot say no.

"Do you know a man named Skunk?" Tamar asks.

Shamil shifts in his seat.

"We come from the same village." Shamil pokes at the fire. "Everyone was a child once. No one sets out to become a monster. His name was Akhmad."

Then Shamil tells Tamar a story: "We were boys of eight, playing in the fields, when we heard excitement in the village: a theatre troupe had arrived. Akhmad and I ran to the square, then followed the procession to the forest. It was nearing dusk, and the whole village gathered. Torches lined the paths, the sun descended into the earth. I remember the faces of the actors, some in shadow, others in light. Some had long beards, others torn dresses. They carried a man tied to a tree. Akhmad was frightened; he held on to me for support. There was movement, a crazed dance, and the tree burst into flames. I reached out for Akhmad's hand and clenched it."

"Well?" asks Tamar. "What happened to the man on the tree?"

"He leapt out of the fire and joined the others in the dance. It was a resurrection story. And it made us gasp. Afterward, Akhmad and I followed the theatre troupe back to their caravan. Akhmad couldn't get enough of the actors. One played a game of disappearing rubles — coins produced from behind his ear and inside his nose. They were travelling on that night, and Akhmad wanted to join them.

"'You are too young,' the actor with the rubles said, 'and besides, don't you want to go home and be with your father?'

"Akhmad shook his head. 'I want you to be my father.'

"The Russian laughed and let him keep the coins, but Akhmad was devastated. The theatre troupe left the village that night," Shamil says. "And we went back to our lives. I wish Akhmad had gone with them. Maybe he wouldn't have become what he is today. Sometimes I wonder if movement is the only way to escape the evil and violence of the world. Everyone was a child once. No one sets out to become a monster."

# 30

*Sioni Reservoir, Republic of Georgia*
*November 16, 2003*

Joseph is wheeled to the fire by Daniel Daniel. His foot throbs, a sharp radiating pain that pulsates through his body. He feels sick from it. A wild boar, pierced by a metal pipe, roasts over the flames. Levan is there taking long swigs from a bottle and yelling into his phone. He winks at Joseph as they approach. Even intimidation is a game to Levan.

And yet Levan cares about his sister. Or he says he does. And if Joseph is going to believe anything Levan says — despite having every reason not to — then he has to believe that Levan wants to find Tamar. Joseph just wishes Levan hadn't felt the need to shoot him to deliver his message of intimidation. And though Daniel Daniel has parked him close to the flames, Joseph feels a chill running up his spine. He feels trapped. In this wheelchair, with these people, with his mutilated foot.

Daniel Daniel suddenly slaps the boar's flank with his hand. The skin sizzles and pops. Mikheil Saakashvili, young presidential hopeful, emerges from the dacha with two strangers and Dato trailing behind.

"This is László Hosszúlépés," Saakashvili announces, introducing a man in a white hat and white suit. "And this is Gustav-Peter Schlagzahl." Gustav wears black slacks and a blue collared shirt. "They are co-presidents of the International Canoe Racing Federation. They will join us for dinner. But first they would like to have a look at the reservoir. Gentlemen, this is the esteemed Joseph Grabinsky from Canada." Saakashvili explains to the co-presidents that Joseph is an investor from the West, and that, contrary to his dishevelled appearance — the result of a "freak hunting accident," Saakashvili says with a wink — his financial prowess and investment capabilities are without equal. The two men offer their hands to Joseph, who reluctantly agrees to shake.

Saakashvili and Levan lead the party into the forest until they arrive at a clearing. Before them, a great body of water stretches toward the horizon. Contained by sloping slabs of concrete, a flimsy bridge juts out toward an eroding observatory. The stark vastness of the scene makes Joseph think of a remote planet. He shivers in his wheelchair.

"This is the Sioni Reservoir," announces Mikheil Saakashvili, pointing to the water hemmed in by a dam. "It has incredible potential."

"The location is compelling," admits Schlagzahl, gazing at the low-lying hills.

"There are wonderful views and more than adequate sightlines," adds Hosszúlépés.

"When I'm elected president, I will construct a venue with five thousand seats to watch the fantastic canoe races,"

Saakashvili says. "Mr. Grabinsky, I would like to invite you to be a principal investor in this endeavour. Questions?"

Joseph mumbles something incoherent.

"We hadn't anticipated so many physical obstacles," says Hosszúlépés, nervously twisting his moustache.

Schlagzahl points and the men peer in the direction of his index finger.

"Is that a crucifix?" asks Joseph.

"It is the steeple of a church," says Levan.

"Why is there a church in the middle of a reservoir?"

"Because of highly intelligent Socialist Common Diet engineers," says Daniel Daniel.

"There was a village here before they flooded the area," says Levan. "Now the village is at the bottom of the reservoir. For the most part."

"For the Georgian people," announces Saakashvili, stepping onto a rock, "there are no obstacles. If I become president of this fine nation, I will bind this country together through sports like canoeing. I will remove this church and eradicate what remains of that nothing village faster than a speeding A-train." He points to his right. "And over there, we will construct the biggest waterslide in Europe. Do you like waterslides, Joseph?"

Joseph shrugs. Hosszúlépés and Schlagzahl nod impatiently. Saakashvili looks at his watch. "Gentlemen? Dinner," he says, "is served."

# 31

Shamil points beyond the hospital, to the north, away from the village and close to the mountains. "Skunk lives there. I will pray for you, Tamar. Good luck."

Tamar sets out on foot to follow the invisible line of the doctor's finger. Through unnamed streets, past unnumbered houses, northward into the cold rain. *Where does the unravelling begin? With hatred or with fear?*

As she passes a village mosque, Tamar is drawn to the sound of evening prayers. She thinks of that which is passed down and that which is changed. Generations and traditions, innovation and invention. Though she was certain when she answered Shamil, now she cannot decide. Maybe the hate did come first. If we are born from loathing, we cannot but live in fear.

She holds the green vase in her arms. Though she is too far away now, Tamar believes she can hear the fire from the hospital hiss and spit. She stumbles through overgrown gardens, past a forest trail, and attaches herself to the landmarks: This is where the path bends. This is where the creek rises. And this is where the fields end. She is trying to know the way back before she has even arrived. And when she reaches the concrete wall with an iron door welded into the corner, she does not know if she will ever return.

The tiny lens of a video camera glints from a telephone pole. On top of the wall, broken glass stuck into concrete, so no one will trespass. She bangs on the door and waits. Brushes her hand against the small of her back to remind her she is here.

# 32

*Sioni Reservoir, Republic of Georgia*
*November 16, 2003*

Saakashvili's family dacha is more hunting lodge than ski cha-
let. It's composed of several rooms, all panelled with wood.
A stove blazes in the corner of the largest room, and a lamp
from the '70s resembling an orange flying fish hangs from
the ceiling, casting a peculiar glow. A long wooden table runs
the length of the room, covered in paper plates piled high
with food. Roast chicken; boiled cabbage stuffed with walnuts; eggplant laden with fresh herbs; vegetables sprinkled
with pomegranate seeds. There are also several dozen two-
litre pop bottles filled with wine, their caps twisted off and
ready to go.

"Are we supposed to eat all this?" Joseph asks in disbelief.

"Oh yes, Comrade. And drink too. Georgian supra.
Ancient meddling feast where host says all manner of bullshit and commands you to eat and drink until you puke. Very
lethal tradition," answers Daniel Daniel.

"Khajapouri!" yells Mikheil Saakashvili. "My favourite!" He grabs a hunk of the baked bread and shoves a piece into his mouth. "Too hot! Too hot! Do not eat yet."

Dato nods solemnly with approval. Levan dims the lights with a flick of the fish as everyone sits down to eat. Glasses are filled with wine and Saakashvili stands at the head of the table to speak.

"My friends, welcome to our supra, a very ancient tradition in Georgia. A toast is a serious and important gesture in my country. Do not be shy, don't hold your tongue, and don't refuse a drink. I would like to make the first toast."

Saakashvili bows his head solemnly. "Dear friends, it is no accident that we are gathered at this magnificent table at this precise moment in time. Did you realize that just this year NASA sent a probe to Pluto, and in that probe was a time capsule containing the greatest hits of mankind, and that one of the greatest hits is a Georgian folk song?" Nobody says anything. "Of course you didn't! But before we move forward, let us pay heed to the past. Many great and famous people hail from this land. Giorgi Saakadze, for example, fought and killed the Persians in the sixteenth century. And Joseph Stalin, well, he wasn't so great, but he was famous. Mr. Grabinsky, did you know that archeologists have established the actual location of the Garden of Eden, and that it's thirteen kilometres from this door?"

"No, I didn't."

"It's all right here. A hidden jewel between Asia and Europe. If I am president of this humble and great nation, we will get back to the Garden. Paradise, baby." Saakashvili pauses for effect. "Yes, we've had trouble these last few years.

There has been great tragedy, my friends. But what is life without sadness and loss?" Saakashvili lets this sink in.

"But we're putting those days behind us. Canoe races, waterslides, wine tours, and downhill skiing. The Eden Project! We're reaching out to you, people of America and Europe, to help us. Let's join hands. Come on. Grab each other's hands." He gestures and the assembled group obeys. Saakashvili closes his eyes. "Let us pray for two tickets to Paradise. I love Georgia, and I love you. Cheers, y'all."

Daniel Daniel whispers, "That is the dumbest toast I have ever heard."

Joseph drains his glass. He tries to adjust his aching foot, but it's hard in the confining wheelchair. As his glass is refilled, he catches Levan looking at him. Levan nods and raises his glass. It seems friendly enough, but who's to say with a man who just shot him? Joseph needs to prove that he's on Levan's side, that they can find Tamar together. He wishes Levan would listen to her phone message. That would solve everything.

Daniel Daniel rises. "Usually, I make toasts to jazz and the Lengthy Vinyl Record. But tonight, I'd like to make a toast to the car thief. You see, I wasn't always the jazz virtuoso in the manner of Charlie Parker. In Moscow, I have many black market operations. I sell fake American jeans at great rip-off prices. Later, after the Common Socialist Diet ends, I become virtuosic car thief. Maybe stealing is in my DNA, or maybe I just have too much experience. We never stop stealing; it is the saddest addiction, but also quite fulfilling. I recommend this as an occupation to any of you.

"Now the car thief is sad because he is the forgotten man.

He sees the good shiny car, and he likes it. He knows it has good fuel efficiency and dynamite turbo blocks. Yet society say he cannot have it. Why is this phantom of wanting so important?" No one says anything. "I have no idea! But it's true, the car thief is malnourished in our society. Without him, there is no great police chase, no heart thump when you witness nothing in your parking spot, no special insurance requisition. Who would buy fancy illegal upgrades if not for the car thief? So, I ask you all to make a special prayer. Praised be the one who has the courage to steal." He squeezes his eyes shut.

Saakashvili says, "Thank you, Daniel Daniel. While it is true the car thief is a descendant of our national hero Prometheus — the very first car thief! — as the future president of Georgia, I'm afraid I cannot condone this toast."

Levan says, "Oh shut up, Misha. While you were eating hamburgers and listening to the Backstreet Boys in Washington, we had to survive. In Georgia, unless you are rich, you steal. And if you are rich, you steal more."

"Well, I call that breaking the law," says Saakashvili, adopting a surprisingly moral tone. "If I am president — no, *when* I am president — we will become a nation known for its good rules *and* good times. I refuse to drink to stealing. Please, everyone. Help yourselves to the boar."

Daniel Daniel sulks: "I show these assholes."

The wild animal sits in the middle of the table, its back legs splayed open. There is something about its lifeless body that frightens Joseph. The men grab at the flesh and stuff their faces, no utensils required. Levan doles out shots of chacha as though they were water. Saakashvili cheers like he's at a political rally: "You can do it! Keep going!" Every time one plate is finished, a woman comes out to replace it with another.

"Did I just say that Paradise is thirteen kilometres away?" Saakashvili asks with his mouth full. "Because I think I found it right here in your mother's wonderful chicken satsivi, Levan! Yum-o! Please, thank Nana for sending it. Do you realize how difficult it is to make this walnut paste? What's her secret? I won't tell a soul, promise." He leans toward Joseph and whispers, "My mother's is better."

"It's important to grind the walnuts properly with mortar and pestle," says Levan. "No American food processors." Levan glares at Joseph, as though he were responsible for the mechanization of cuisine.

"Joseph, let's hear your toast," says Saakashvili.

But he never gets to it. Suddenly there is a loud crash in the corner. Gustav-Peter Schlagzahl, who'd been leaning back in his chair to make room for more food, has fallen into the flying fish. The lamp smashes and the men are plunged into darkness.

"Perfect good times," Daniel Daniel whispers. "Gifts from gods."

Joseph feels himself wheeled through darkness. Chaos, clattering, a cacophony of words shouted in Georgian, German, English, Hungarian. Joseph feels giant hands on his arm, twisting. It's Levan. Daniel Daniel tugs on the wheelchair. Then, the sound of more glass shattering. This time it's close to his head, and it startles him. Levan cries out in pain. "What the fuck?"

Three women enter the room and light candles then quickly disappear again. Levan is keeled over on the floor, blood streaking down the sides of his face. He looks deranged.

"You will not kill my dumb Canadian homeboy!" Daniel Daniel yells at the top of his lungs, flinging the broken bottle against the wall. He pushes Joseph and the wheelchair toward the door. "We go now."

Levan jumps up from the floor and tackles Daniel Daniel. He climbs on top of him and pummels him with brick fists. Joseph feels the room begin to spin. Dato pulls Levan off Daniel Daniel as Gustav-Peter Schlagzahl and Laszlo Hosszúlépés make a run for the door.

"Easy, cowboy," says Saakashvili, pointing his Smith & Wesson at Levan. "This is not what we want. Let's talk this through. We're family. Right, Joseph? Daniel Daniel?"

Levan grunts.

Daniel Daniel says, "No chance, homeboys. We way too drunk. Thanks for the delicious times."

He pushes Joseph through the doorway, slams the door shut, and stacks two chairs to jam it.

"Now we run, Comrade. We run like blind men."

Daniel Daniel thrusts the wheelchair down a grass hill onto gravel. They fly a crazy, mad rush. When Joseph closes his eyes, he feels the wheelchair take flight. He is jumping over rivers, leaping across mountains, flying through the sky. Somehow, they make it to the road. Then the gunshots begin.

"What do we do now?" Joseph asks.

Daniel Daniel fishes around in his pocket and pulls out a set of keys.

"Drive like hell."

# ACT V

\*

# REVOLUTION AND RECKONING

## November 2003

\*

"An unusual beginning must have an unusual end."
—MIKHAIL LERMONTOV, *A Hero of Our Time*

# 1

*Duisi, Pankisi Gorge*
*November 16, 2003*

To her surprise, Tamar finds the metal door unlocked. She slowly pushes it open, expecting watch dogs or armed guards. Instead, an old woman, bent on her knees, does laundry by hand, scraping and pounding clothes on a boulder by a rushing creek.

From the outside, Skunk's house looks modest and unassuming. It's built in the old style, a traditional wooden farmhouse with a courtyard housing apple and pear trees. The second floor is lined with an ornamental trellis, a covered wooden balcony, clay shingles clinging to the roof. The trio of windows at the top—arranged like a lazy smile—make Tamar feel oddly welcome.

She knocks but no one answers, so Tamar opens the front door and ventures inside. Holding Shamil's vase, she feels awkward. Her previous confidence has evaporated, and she does not know how to proceed. She follows a dimly lit corridor into a claustrophobic room full of gold-framed mirrors. It's the sight of herself from multiple perspectives that scares her. Her hands, stained with Alex's blood. Her torn brown hoodie. Her blue jeans muddy. Her face bruised and tired. She's lucky to be alive.

Tamar hears a creak in the wood floors. Somewhere nearby a fire blazes. She walks toward it, passing a kitchen where five women prepare food, talking amongst themselves. Nobody seems bothered by her presence.

The house is endless. One corridor follows the next, and when Tamar makes a turn, she wonders if she's travelling in circles, if indeed she is in a house at all. Eventually she arrives at a metal hatch door, like something out of a submarine. She turns the wheel, ducks, and ventures inside.

Black and white linoleum floors sparkle, and the smell of bleach permeates the air. Tamar has entered a renovated warehouse decorated with recycled military materials. Chairs torn out of old army jeeps have been converted into a couch. Two RPG launchers hang on the wall, doubling as a coat rack. A desk lined with oil lamps, kitschy snow globes, and silver candelabras adds to the incongruity of things. The table, she realizes, is the wing of an old airplane.

"Tamar," says a voice, startling her.

She didn't see him behind the desk. But here he is: thick-bearded, camouflage-clad, crowned by an absurd mullet. Black on the sides, a streak of white shooting up the centre.

"Skunk."

"Tea?"

"Sure."

"Have a seat. Please."

346

Tamar sits down as Skunk twists in his chair, drawing from an old samovar. The tea is rich, flavourful, and strong. She pops a sugar cube in her mouth and puts the vase on the table.

"Nice of you to drop by."

"I was in the neighbourhood," she says.

Skunk laughs. "You didn't have to kill Alex."

"You didn't have to kidnap me. I was going to call you—"

"I've been waiting seven years for you to call, Tamar. When you hopped on a bus in Istanbul, I decided to do something."

"How did you know where I was?"

He shrugs. "Skunk knows."

She taps her hand nervously on the desk. "Levan said you knew something about my father. Do you know where he is?"

Skunk offers her a cigarette. "You've had a long trip. Let's get you something to eat." He takes the vase and turns it in his hands. "Thank you for the gift." Then he snaps his fingers, and the submarine hatch pops open. Three women duck through the entrance carrying trays full of hot towels, caviar, honey, bread, fresh cheese, and nuts. Tamar takes a towel and presses it to her face. The warmth feels good against her skin.

"I met a friend of yours in town. The doctor, Shamil."

Skunk snickers, as though to say, "Poor sucker."

"He said you weren't always Skunk."

"So?"

"He said you weren't always a monster." Tamar crumples up the towel and drops it on the table. "Are you a monster, Akhmad?"

Skunk smiles, revealing two gold teeth. His nose is slightly turned up to the left, a bit like a snout. It softens his face. "How's the chepalgash?"

"Good," she says, digging in. Tamar hadn't realized how hungry she was.

Skunk watches her through the smoke, studying her face. "Yes, Shamil knew me as Akhmad, but I am not Akhmad. Sometimes I forget that person ever existed. We contain many selves, Tamar, and have many names. Like your mother. No one is who they say they are."

Tamar suddenly finds it hard to swallow.

"I bet there are at least three Tamars," Skunk continues. "Tamars you aren't even aware of. Tamars you might not want to know." She pushes the plate away from her. "Keep eating."

"I'm not hungry."

"Eat. And I'll tell you a story."

As Skunk refills their glasses, Tamar feels the seed of fear growing inside her. And she has no idea what will happen next.

Skunk tells a story. "The year is 1994. Twenty-eight-year-old Akhmad Varayev, student of physics, is in his dorm room at Moscow State University. He has just received his monthly letter from his 'Uncle' Zaza. Tucked into the folded pages are the usual two hundred rubles, plus fifty extra for boots. There is also a small bag of Mishka Kosolapy, the candies he loves. Ever since Akhmad's father Aslan disappeared twenty years ago, Zaza has been a constant presence in Akhmad's life. He was his father's best friend and roommate at MSU. Now Zaza is Akhmad's godfather, mentor, and patron. He wants him to have an education.

"Akhmad is grateful for Zaza. He could not have survived this long without his help. And it isn't just the money. Zaza is a link to his home, to the past, and to Aslan, his father.

"He has other reminders of Aslan, of course. When he first moved to Moscow, his mother Amina presented him with a manuscript, a story written for him by his father. Akhmad had read it, in parts, but never had the courage to read it all. Akhmad makes himself black tea, unwraps a candy, then reads Zaza's letter by the window. The Moskva River rushes beneath him."

*Dear Akhmad,*

*I hope this finds you and your studies well. It is important you are there. The only certainty is education, and the only home, knowledge. I know you understand. We men from the Caucasus must stick together . . .*

"The words speak to him. But they're also a knife in his gut. Akhmad feels lonely in Moscow, constantly reminded of his otherness. His dark complexion doesn't help. He is a second-class Chechen in the imperial capital. Zaza understands this.

"Akhmad folds up the letter and places it in a file with the others. Then he turns on the radio. On the news he hears that war has finally broken out in Grozny; the Russians have invaded. The tension had been building for weeks. His family lived on its outskirts. In the wake of the collapse of the U.S.S.R., Akhmad's family moved from Georgia back to Chechnya. When he calls his mother, he can hear the shelling in the background.

"'Everything is fine,' says his sister Eset amidst the rumbling streets and rattling windows.

"But he knows nothing is fine during war, so he packs a bag, including his father's manuscript. He boards a train and travels home. When he sees the devastation first-hand, he is horrified. After a few days, the train lines are closed. Then the power goes down. The shelling worsens. He never makes it back to Moscow — not for some time, at least. Instead of a career in engineering or quantum physics, he drives a taxi and teaches algebra at the local high school. He cares for his mother, Amina, and his three younger sisters: Eset, Layla, and Deti. He writes to his Uncle Zaza explaining his decision. Zaza continues to send money, for which Akhmad is grateful.

"Akhmad does not join in the fighting. While he believes in an independent Chechnya, he also understands that freedom cannot be achieved through violence. Like his father, Aslan, he believes in better education; in the solidity of numbers; in music (Basie, Parker, Ellington) and literature (Tolstoy, Turgenev, Lermontov). In the early years of the first war, he becomes involved in local councils. He helps to create an association for Chechen lawyers and to build schools. He enters discussions to create an independent Chechen government. Every day there is shelling. Amina worries when Akhmad drives his taxi through city streets laden with Russian tanks and shells. Every night she is relieved when Akhmad returns.

"One evening Akhmad and Amina are home together. While his mother makes bread, Akhmad drinks tea and reads to her passages from Lermontov's *A Hero of Our Time*. It is a book his father Aslan loved; Akhmad likes to thread his fingers through the gold-embossed pages of his father's edition.

It feels like home. He pauses and asks his mother if she has ever read the manuscript written by his father.

"'Of course not,' she says. 'It was written for you.'

"Akhmad removes the bound pages from his suitcase and begins to read aloud.

"'джинсы и гены.'

"His mother chuckles.

"'Dzhinsy i geny,' she repeats. Jeans and genes.

"He continues to read. The absurdity of his father's writing — a man he remembers as quite serious — surprises him. So does the intimacy. It feels like he is reading a diary. His mother continues kneading her dough; his sisters are at their aunt's playing with their cousins. When he reads about Lysenko and his theories, Akhmad wants to laugh and cry at the absurdity and horror of that era. When he reads, 'What to do about the past?' the question chills him. His mother nods, a chorus of consent. A pause in the shelling makes them look up. The silence lasts several minutes before there's a knock at the door.

"Akhmad hides the manuscript in the folds of his chair. When he answers the door, a Russian captain barges in and yells, 'Where are they?'

"Akhmad asks, 'Where are what?'

"'Your weapons. I know you beasts strap bombs to your children. Search.'

"Five Russian soldiers tear apart closets, drawers, beds, and carpets, while Amina prepares food, an effort to appease aggression. While she brings out the food, they vandalize cupboards and shelves, root cellar and books. They stuff their bags with whatever appears valuable. When she offers them more, they grab whatever they can until there is only Amina left. A soldier, no older than nineteen, ties her to a chair.

"Another soldier ties up Akhmad, covers his mouth, and says, 'You keep your mouth shut and eyes open, boy, or she dies.'

"Akhmad watches his father's copy of Lermontov fall from chair to floor, its soft spine splayed open. Aslan's manuscript lies hidden in the folds of his seat. What he's just read, emblazoned in his mind, plays on repeat. Four of the men tear off his mother's clothes and take turns with her. It is the most unbearable thing for a son to watch. When they've had enough, the captain takes his Kalashnikov and ... Thankfully, Akhmad passes out. In his dream, his father's words collide, collapse, and create new meanings.

"'Genealogy matters. Like any good Chechen, I can recite my lineage seven generations back. I carry the history of my people. The past is a phantom limb. Our bodies do not forget.'

"It's midnight when Akhmad awakes. The soldiers are gone; his mother's body unrecognizable in a pool of blood. Another knock on the door. Kamlila, their neighbour and his mother's friend of thirty years, comes stumbling in. Horrified, sobbing, her hands shake as she frees Akhmad with a breadknife. For a long while they hold each other. Then they get to work. His wrists burn where the ropes dug into the skin. Akhmad washes his hands and face, then he and Kamlila clean Amina's body with a sponge, cold water, and soap.

"Suddenly his dead mother turns to face him and says, 'Akhmad, I'm hungry. Can you please fetch me something to eat?'

"He runs screaming into the woods. His wails join the droning bees in the apiaries of his grandfather. His weeping shoots up amongst the walnut trees and faltering electrical lines of the city. His tears descend into the earth, where rats dig their tunnels, and beyond, into loam and humus, travelling the fault lines toward magma. He falls asleep amongst the trees. In his dreams the events of the night merge with the last century. When he awakes a shock of white hair shoots up the centre of his head. The words of his father linger in Akhmad's mind: 'I was raised in a land not my own. I have felt a foreigner all my life. Even here in Moscow, I am always in exile. Yes, the past is a scar. It affects and shapes us. But like the mark on my friend Zaza's face, our scars won't determine who we are.'"

# 2

John Coltrane's *My Favorite Things* plays through Saakashvili's high-end speakers. Daniel Daniel flips down his yellow-tinted sunglasses as he guns the Cadillac SUV through the forest. "Man, behold the heavenly dispensations of angels. Hear ye old McCoy Tyner's ten fingers that sound like ten thousand." He is pleased with his "getaway acquisition."

"Are those mountains?" asks Joseph.

"Yes, Comrade. It is Chechnya."

"Are we going there?"

"I hope not."

"So where are we going then?"

"Plan one: lose Levan. If we are still alive, then we make plan two."

Joseph looks over his shoulder. In the distance, he can make out headlights, perhaps half a mile back.

"By the way, here is your wallet. I steal it from Levan,

354

along with the keys to this fine SUV." Daniel Daniel passes it to him.

"That's not mine, it's Irakli's."

"Who?"

Joseph tells Daniel Daniel about the man who followed him through a Tbilisi market, and how later, he found him dead in an alley near the demonstrations. "He's a friend of Levan's, and his name is Irakli, and now Levan thinks I'm a murderer and a foreign agent because he found this in my pocket." It sounds crazy when he recounts it aloud, but Daniel Daniel isn't fazed by the details.

"You are definitely no spy. Not even a bad one," he says, slipping an unlit cigarette into his mouth. "Why did you make this ignoble decision to steal wallets from the dead?"

"Intuition, I guess. You ever hear a voice that tells you what to do?"

"All the time, Comrade. Only, my voices make sense."

The headlights are gaining on them. Daniel Daniel revs the engine and lights his cigarette. Branches smash the car as they speed around impossible bends. The sound makes Joseph think of Levan's giant fists. His shadowy vehicle darts in and out of the trees like a raging animal.

"So, what has your intuition delivered?" asks Daniel Daniel.

Joseph rummages through the contents of the wallet. A business card; some slips of paper; a few bills in local currency. But the folded photocopy — the picture Joseph saw when he examined the wallet in the Underground bathroom — isn't there.

"There was a photograph, I'm sure of it," says Joseph, checking again. Anxiously he explains how there was a photo of a man in a monk's smock standing on the slope of a mountain. "The man had a thick black beard, and there was a scar on his left cheek that ran to his ear. I think it was Tamar's father, Zaza, only he looked older than the photo I saw of him at Nana's house."

Daniel Daniel flinches.

"Keti said you went to university together, that Zaza was your best friend growing up. What happened between you two?"

The headlights get closer.

"So, Keti tells you who I really am?"

"Yeah. Aslan."

"Better not to say his name. Better we focus on Zaza."

"Why is everyone so obsessed with this Zaza? Is this why you don't like Tamar? Did Zaza do something to you too?"

Daniel Daniel glances at the rear-view mirror, swerves right, then left, then right again. Then he floors it and the suv takes flight.

"Jesus Christ," says Joseph.

"Please, do not vomit, Comrade."

The suv lands with a thud. Joseph breathes heavily. His stomach and head are a mess.

"Was there a church in the background of the picture?" Daniel Daniel asks.

"There was a stone building."

"And you see the older Zaza on the hill?"

"Yeah, I think so."

Daniel Daniel accelerates. Joseph's stomach lurches. Just when he is sure he's going to throw up, Daniel Daniel flicks off the headlights and guides them off the forest path, through a small clearing, and into a field of tall reeds. Cutting the engine, they coast in the moonlight.

"Why are we stopping?"

"Shh, Comrade. We must be quiet as the pines during the late August breeze. Let us complete our first plan."

As they wait in the tall grass, their eyes remain glued to the forest path. Joseph understands now that Levan kept the photograph copy. But why? They follow the trajectory of the headlights, bobbing up and down, headed in the opposite direction. They wait another two minutes before Daniel Daniel starts the car, careful to keep the headlights turned off. Under the cover of darkness, he leads them across a field and onto a one-lane road.

"We have completed plan one. Congratulations, Comrade. We are alive."

"Now what?"

"Plan two: the super-duper all-star reunion. We meet your father, Gary."

# 3

*Duisi, Pankisi Gorge*
*November 16, 2003*

Tamar understands that Skunk is telling her this story to frighten her. And it's working.

He continues: "The morning after my mother's murder, with the help of my cousins, I tracked down the soldiers who raped and killed Amina. One by one we ambushed them, bound and gagged them, and drove them here, to our family farm in Pankisi Gorge. I made those five Russian soldiers dig a pit at the edge of the property. For three days and nights they worked under my supervision, living off brackish water and bowls of hard gruel. If they slept, it was outside, bound to each other, whimpering in fear.

"It's extraordinary what people will do to survive," says Skunk. "And it's equally extraordinary how quickly a man's status can change, from powerful to powerless, or vice versa. No one is who they think they are."

Tamar lights a cigarette and sinks into the leather

upholstery. She watches Skunk's face; there's a slight twitch in his right eyebrow, as though marking time.

"For three days and nights the men dug until the pit was four metres square and four metres deep. On the fourth day, I invited them into the farmhouse, where my cousins' wives had prepared a sumptuous meal. While they ate and drank to their hearts' content, I had the pit filled with rats. Dozens of the nasty creatures. When they'd finished their final supper, I ordered the men thrown in, one at a time. The screaming went on all night."

Skunk's eyebrow stops twitching. The hair on Tamar's arms stands on end.

"Have some more tea," says Skunk. He refills Tamar's glass and passes her a plate of sweets. She eyes them suspiciously. "You're wondering, 'Why is he telling me this story?' The truth is, Tamar: it's your story, too.

"The night I lost my mother — the night Akhmad became Skunk — was the night I learned that freedom and democracy mean nothing without justice."

Tamar crosses her legs.

"But what is justice?" asks Skunk. "And how do we attain it? How would you achieve justice for the senseless murder of your husband, Davit Anoshvili?"

"A legitimate investigation followed by a fair trial would be a good start."

"Come on, Tamar. We don't have fair trials in the Caucasus, and even in the best of worlds, an investigation does not bring justice. And neither can it take away the pain of what happened."

"Nothing can," Tamar agrees.

"In a land without dogs the cats learn to bark," says Skunk. "The proverb is about you and me, Tamar. We're definitely two dogs. What are we to do about all those barking cats?"

"We are not the same."

"Think about it: you tell the truth through your art, because honesty is imperative for a civil society to function. I also want the truth. The truth of justice. Because, without justice, there is no society at all. Just a bunch of barking cats. Davit deserves justice. You deserve justice." Skunk leans back in his chair. "Maybe the point is to distribute the pain more evenly, to let others know what you've endured."

"I'm sorry for what they did to your mother. But what you did to those men . . ."

"Yes?"

"It's inhumane."

"It's balancing the scales. Chacha?"

Tamar nods. Skunk opens a drawer and removes a bottle. He pours two glasses and they drink. It burns Tamar's throat.

"So, what does this eye-for-an-eye bullshit of yours have to do with my father?" she asks.

"Everything."

"I think you're just trying to scare me."

"If you're afraid now, Tamar, just wait. The truth is far more frightening than a pit of hungry rats." He smiles. Tamar lights another cigarette, and Skunk gets up to refill their glasses. "Has your brother ever told you how we met?"

Tamar shakes her head no.

"It was near the end of the first Chechen war. I was at a party held by some business associates. Levan was introduced to me, and we got to talking. I liked him straight away. So, we started doing business together. We created a trade consortium that ran between Abkhazia, Tbilisi, and Grozny — a corridor of commerce. Guns, opium, women. Everything was traded, anything was possible. We became rich, and we became friends.

"One night, Levan and I got very drunk, even by our standards. He told me about his sister, a gifted performance artist who wanted to change the world . . . through non-violent means. Levan was very proud of you, but he also laughed at your naïveté. For my part, I was captivated immediately. Optimism and art are for fools, and democracy is breadcrumbs for the powerless and weak-minded, but your story intrigued me. I began to follow your career from afar. I liked hearing about your videos and performances. I enjoyed reading Davit's undercover reportages in the papers. And I was intrigued when Rachel Grabinsky arrived on the scene and began funding your projects with money from America. Perhaps it was because I had once been such an optimist. It was like watching an alternate reality," Skunk confesses. "How far would it go? And how would it end?

"Levan confessed to me that you weren't really brother and sister. He told me that you arrived on their doorstep, a child of two in the arms of a tall man in a wool coat. The man was quick to anger and could just as quickly turn sweet. Levan reminisced about Russian chocolates that the man would give to the children when his mother, Nana, wasn't looking. Levan remembered being told great mythical stories at bedtime, tales that excited and haunted him. And then, one day, the man was gone. The man they called Zaza had disappeared as suddenly as he'd arrived.

"When I heard this story, I knew it was the same Zaza of my childhood. My father Aslan's best friend."

Tamar swallows hard. "What did Zaza do to you?"

"Not to me, Tamar. Aslan. My father." Skunk pauses to take a sip of chacha. "A riddle: Two boyhood friends return to the village of their birth. They walk up to a church on a mountain, but only one comes down. What happened in the church?"

Tamar feels her chest tighten. "Did Zaza kill Aslan?"

"You know what I'm most angry about?" Skunk says. "If my father had been home, if he'd been alive, my mother wouldn't have been raped and killed by those soldiers. He would have protected her; he would have protected us. And where was Zaza, the hero of my childhood? He wasn't there for us either; he just sent my mother money to keep his conscience clean."

Tamar feels disoriented and frightened. The chacha is going to her head.

"A few years ago, I came across this." Skunk unfolds a photocopy of a photograph and puts it on the desk between them. Tamar recognizes her father in monk's robes. He looks much older than the last time she saw him in person. Behind him, she can see the stone outline of Gergeti Trinity Church.

"Your father returned to the scene of his crime, Tamar. And so will we."

# 4

*Jvari Pass — Kazbegi, Republic of Georgia*
*November 17, 2003*

As they pass villages plunged into darkness, Joseph feels a fear unlike any other he's felt before. The darkness behind darkness. His foot throbs from the gunshot wound and he cannot trust the spiralling of his thoughts.

"I didn't kill Irakli," Joseph says, returning the wallet to his coat pocket.

"I know you didn't, Comrade. I did."

"What?"

"I kill Irakli Gonashvili, best friend and number one henchman of Levan. I put the gun against his head and pull the trigger. His brain explodes like an apple."

"Why would you do that?"

"Because he follows you."

"How do you know?"

"I follow you."

"Are you kidding me?"

Daniel Daniel leans his head back and peers at the world as if through a gun sight, revving the vehicle.

"Of course. I protect you at all costs. You are the son of Rachel Grabinsky and Gary Ruckler."

*Nothing*, thinks Joseph, *should surprise me anymore.*

"When Rachel came to Georgia in the nineties, did she spend time with you and Gary?"

"Sometimes, yes. She liked coming to the record store. Bad taste in music, but nice, smart woman. She spends much time with Tamar."

It stings Joseph to think Rachel met with Gary while maintaining the cruel fiction he was dead. And she never told Tamar she was her mother.

"Rachel wasn't who she said she was," says Joseph.

"No one is who they say they are, Comrade."

"She made up huge parts of her life."

"Everyone does."

"I don't," Joseph says angrily. "She lied to Tamar. She lied to me. How can someone hide the truth from their own children? It's beyond fucked up."

Daniel Daniel turns silent. As they hurtle through vastness, Joseph looks out at the landscape. A nearby lake reflects a sliver of moonlight, and beneath it, heaps of abandoned machinery. He feels the messiness of Rachel's life infecting him, an inheritance of something terrible. He also believes another chapter in this strange and cruel paradise is only beginning. And that the past is a shadow we cannot escape.

The road begins to climb up a mountain. They pass desolate villages, names written in chipped blue on white metal. Soon the path narrows and they follow switchbacks. Daniel

Daniel accelerates as they approach each corner, only to slow down at the last moment, spraying ice and stone.

As the sun starts to rise, they begin their descent along the Jvari Pass. Cliffs laden with ice glisten like bright steel in the dawn sky. Slick roads threaten barrier-less drop-offs that lead hundreds of metres down. When they disappear into avalanche tunnels, they reappear into blinding light. Finally, Joseph can see it: Mount Kazbek. It punctures the horizon. Legend has it that Prometheus was chained to its peak. Joseph wonders if this fate awaits all those who try to mess with the order of things. He wonders if that's what happened to Gary. He knows his life was messy, filled with mistakes. But maybe Prometheus's life was also a mess. Maybe myth is narrative's way of cleaning up the chaos. In the muck of the world and our bodies, there is no once upon a time.

IT'S LATE MORNING when they arrive in Kazbegi. The village square is besieged by beauty, an amphitheatre of breathtaking mountains. The remote peaks pierce the sky, appearing to hold it in place. Yet the village is rundown and depressing. The main square is empty except for a few dilapidated kiosks made from tin and mouldy planks of wood. Old babushkas wearing moth-eaten sweaters and faded wool dresses sell homemade sausages and wool socks. Pigs and cows gather lazily, hoping for scraps of food.

Joseph has a fever now; the pain in his foot has worsened. Daniel Daniel parks the SUV in a small alley and tells Joseph to wait.

"This not looking good, Comrade," Daniel Daniel says, inspecting Joseph's foot. "Wait here while I get medicine. You are tired from our manic depressions and wild adventures. Sleep, Comrade."

Daniel Daniel slams the car door then disappears up the alley. Joseph falls into a deep but troubled slumber. In his dreams, everyone is in danger, and death breathes through everything. When Daniel Daniel returns, Joseph does not know how much time has passed. He hands Joseph two bottles of unmarked pills. "Painkillers and antibiotics," says Daniel Daniel. Joseph takes two of each.

"We get you winter clothes. Then I call Gary and invite him to meet us," Daniel Daniel says. "After that, we find Tamar."

"Do you know where she is?" Joseph asks hopefully.

Daniel Daniel taps his head twice. "We must believe in all connections."

Daniel Daniel helps Joseph hobble through the near-empty streets. They walk through thickening snowflakes, to a small shop heated by coal and lit by kerosene lanterns. The face of the merchant is ghostly; he whispers in a way that makes Joseph feel watched. Daniel Daniel gets Joseph to try on sweaters several sizes too big before finding one that fits. Then he chooses a wool coat and hands Joseph a wooden walking stick with the head of an eagle. Daniel Daniel pays for everything, and while Joseph appreciates the gesture, he feels strangely not himself.

Outside, the village is dark and quiet. As the clouds part and a pale winter's sunlight filters through, Joseph can make out a grey speck at the top of a mountain. It's a lonely sight, and it faces a wall of ice and rocks, a massive mountain ridge across a deep valley. He cannot tell whether the grey speck is monument or edifice, but it is certainly ancient, and the breath of history and the brutal magnificence of the mountains make him feel feeble and small.

Kazbegi is divided in two by a river. On either side, small houses climb the mountains before thinning into pasture. Here, horses graze, stone dwells then disappears into snow. The frail power lines make Joseph think of mythical dental floss used to clean the teeth of impetuous gods. A bald woman lifts a wheelbarrow of old branches. Abandoned vehicles, empty workshops, walls of windows, rusted machinery. At a bend in the river they stop at a restaurant. Daniel Daniel makes a phone call, mutters something in Georgian, then hangs up.

"Gary will be here soon," he says. "Meanwhile I fix your foot and hunger."

They sit on white plastic chairs. A fire blazes in a rusty steel barrel, a wall of snow enshrouds them. In the corner, several tables of bleary-eyed men sip vodka and watch them closely.

"We are seated at the crossroads, where East meets West, Europe and Asia. Lermontov's country."

Joseph says, "I've never read him. Gary liked him, right?"

Daniel Daniel nods. "Lermontov was a soldier in the Czar's great imperial army, a reluctant occupier who only wanted to escape the boredom of his meaningless and materialistic life in Moscow. He came here to be free, in both life and literature. There" — he points to what Joseph thinks is north — "Lermontov travels the Georgian military highway. And here" — he points again — "he was challenged to grand duel. Lermontov fires into the air and is killed. Your father admires him. He dies for something he believes in."

"Which was what?"

"Nothing."

Joseph is annoyed. To him, it sounds like the reckless-ness of the privileged. He doesn't feel sympathy for this Russian Lermontov or his American father — these foreign, unwanted men who meddle in the lives of others in the name of adventure.

"So," says Daniel Daniel, checking his cell phone then putting it back into his jacket. "Soon Gary will be here. Have you decided what you will say?"

"No," Joseph grunts. A bottle of vodka and a plate of shashlik are brought to the table. Joseph dives into the vodka, then the meat.

"You have not prepared questions?"

"Look, whether he shows up or not, nothing is going to change the past. The guy was a dick. And now my foot is messed up, I feel like shit, and I don't care anymore. I need to see Tamar."

"I will help you." Daniel Daniel drags his chair beside Joseph's. He removes Joseph's bloodied shoe, then he peels off the blood-caked sock and inspects the wound. Joseph's foot is mangled, not his own. The waitress returns with a bottle of clear liquid, two clean towels, and a bucket of warm water.

"Why are we here?" Joseph asks.

Daniel Daniel nods toward the hill. "Perspective, Comrade. Everything will be clear."

Joseph turns to look. The grey speck he saw from the square has shifted into focus. It's a stone building on the flat of a small mountain, looking out at the much larger peak of Mount Kazbek. The building is a church, and there's a clear path running up to it from the village.

"That's the church from the photograph," he says. "Right?"

"Gergeti Trinity Church," says Daniel Daniel. "Where it all begins."

Daniel Daniel pours clear liquid onto the towel and wraps it around Joseph's foot. The alcohol burns, and he fights the urge to scream.

"What happened there?"

"It isn't my fault. I think it is, but it is not."

"What are you talking about?"

"Many years ago. Many things. He gives me the book."

"What book?"

"*Jeans and Genes.*"

"You mean the record?"

"First a book, then a record."

Daniel Daniel opens a small bag and removes an old leather binder tied with black string. The binder is cracked at the edges, the leather dry. He passes it to Joseph, who undoes the knots. The stack of paper is thick — at least two hundred pages, Joseph thinks. The title page reads:

**Jeans and Genes:**

**The Legend of the Midnight Wrangler**

**by Aslan Varayev**

**Translated by Gary Ruckler**

"What is this? And what does it have to do with Zaza and that church?" asks Joseph.

"Zaza hates everything it stands for," says Daniel Daniel.

"It brings the end of our man-to-man friendship and leads to terrible showdowns."

"What showdown?"

Daniel Daniel tells Joseph a story.

"The year is 1984. Keti and I have just opened the Record Emporium, home to a most excellent cruller and devastating Prügeltorte. I mind my own businesses, work the cash, listen to the great Charlie Parker, when a man-bear walks into the store. Though it has been almost ten years since I last see him, I know him right away, the enormous hands, the bulky beige coat, the smell of leather and sweat. Zaza loves the punk, no surprises; he flips through boxes, grabs Joy Division's *Unknown Pleasures* and comes to the register. He puts down the Lengthy Vinyl and opens his wallet and I freeze. I have something to say, I don't know what, but when Zaza's eyes travel to the wall and spies my most precious treasure, the framed *Houses of the Holy* t-shirt, he looks like he sees ghosts. Zaza turns on his heels and leaves."

"What makes that shirt so special?" asks Joseph.

"Because it belongs to Aslan."

"But you're Aslan. Why didn't Zaza recognize you?"

"Because the Aslan Zaza knew was dead."

"What is that supposed to mean?"

"Zaza tortured and killed Aslan at Gergeti Trinity Church. I find his body and tell his family. His son, Akhmad. It is truly horrible to tell such a story."

Joseph says, "Okay, but if Aslan is dead, then who are you?"

Daniel Daniel stares at him blankly.

"What the fuck is going on?"

Daniel Daniel slides his fingers into his mouth, removing a set of false teeth. Then he takes off his fur hat and sunglasses. For the first time, Joseph can see his grey-blue eyes.

"Jesus fucking Christ."

"Hi, Joseph."

"Hi?"

"I'm here. Well, I've been here all along, haven't I?"

Joseph gets up from his chair unsteadily. Daniel Daniel— Gary—extends his hand. Joseph swings and Gary ducks. When Joseph tries to swing again, he loses his balance. He falls to the ground and whimpers. His father reaches down to pull him back up.

# 5

*Duisi, Pankisi Gorge – Kazbegi, Republic of Georgia*
*November 17, 2003*

"Why did you come here, Tamar? What did you hope to find?"

Tamar says nothing.

"You were on a train for thirty-six hours. Two thousand kilometres, from Moscow to Tbilisi. You were two years old. Zaza took care of you. He loved you. But why does a father kidnap his own daughter?"

Tamar closes her eyes. She sees grey tarmac, and an airplane. Her mother, standing on the other side of a window, hands pressed against glass.

"If I deliver you the truth, will you promise to help me find justice?" Skunk asks.

There is no reason why she should trust Skunk, and yet he has something Tamar needs. It's there, on the desk between them.

"Where did you get that photograph? Does it have something to do with Davit's death?"

Skunk's eyes widen. "In a manner of speaking."

"Did you kill Davit?"

"No. Though nothing happens without Skunk's knowing."

"Then who killed him?"

"What does it matter?"

"I need to know."

"You want to avenge his death? An eye for an eye and all that bullshit?"

"Who killed Davit?"

"Your husband was a stubborn man who demanded the truth. It made him many powerful enemies. The photograph was taken by my associate, Irakli. He discovered where your father was hiding. When Davit learned this, he tried to buy it from Irakli. But Irakli wanted more money than Davit was willing to pay, and things got ugly. Irakli had backup, Davit didn't. But none of that matters, because Irakli is dead now, too."

TAMAR FEELS SICK to her stomach. She also feels exhausted. They've been talking, it seems, for hours, though she has no idea what time it is. Somberly, she is lead into a quiet room at the edge of the house. It overlooks a field recently harvested. In the distance, before the forest, she believes she sees a dark square in the ground. A rat scurries along the bedroom floor. She removes her bloodied clothes and climbs under the covers and into the bed. Immediately, she falls asleep.

Tamar dreams. She is back in the van, hands tied and a burlap sack over her head. She hears the sound of the engine, feels the motion of the van as it takes a tight corner. Suddenly the vehicle stops, the engine is cut, and the doors swing open.

Footsteps pound the dry earth. She feels herself picked up then heaved into darkness.

Tamar tries to wake herself from the dream. But every time she gets close to waking, Skunk is there, telling her to go back to sleep. She is no longer in the van, but lying in cold earth. She's outside, in a pit at the edge of the field. The burlap sack scratches her face. She so desperately wants to see. Her hands are still bound, she can't free herself. So, she lies back, listening to the cries of jackals, a chorus of wild howling in the night. She wakes herself, only to find herself in another dream, a matryoshka doll of nightmares.

Something nibbles at her shoe. Incisors gnaw into her leg. A small creature scurries up her body until it reaches her head and pulls off the burlap sack. A rat. Tamar can make out a patch of stars, a sliver of moon, a narrow pinhole of light. The rat points to the photograph of Zaza in monk's robes. She can see the scar that divides his face. The church on the mountain at the edge of the world. Suddenly she's inside the church. A room full of candles. A younger Zaza removes his coat. A man is tied to a chair. He wears a Led Zeppelin *Houses of the Holy* t-shirt.

When she awakes, she's in a bed in a cold, barren room. She wants to ask her mother, "How could you love him?" But she knows that isn't the right question. The door opens. Daylight frames Skunk's stocky body. He carries a tray full of tea, baked goods, cheese, and olives. He places the tray on the floor by her bed. Next to the tray are her neatly folded clothes, freshly cleaned and pressed while she slept.

"Eat and get dressed. We're going to see your father."

THEY TRAVEL UP a narrow road, passing walls of snow, gliding over sheets of ice. The higher they get, the farther Tamar feels from both herself and the world. At first the narrowness confines her, but when they reach the top of the pass, she gasps at the beauty of it. Endless peaks and a snow-capped horizon.

It's evening when they arrive in the village of Kazbegi. Kerosene lanterns glow in small, dishevelled houses. The electricity is out, and Tamar feels the failure of a dream, and its aftermath: a lone greenhouse, abandoned by its owners. Miles of silver tubing transporting gas to crumbling factories. A boarded-up Intourist hotel.

They snake through the village, climb switchbacks, enter a forest, then pass the treeline. She knows this trail. She came here once with Sasha, Nana, Davit, and Levan for a picnic. They left the car at the bottom of the mountain and spent the day hiking. It's a good memory of hot summer days, full of family and friends singing, drinking, eating.

Skunk takes them to the end of the road and cuts the engine. When she gets out, Tamar looks out at the treacherous valley, the gap between her and Mount Kazbek. It is the same feeling she had as a child—being dwarfed by a world bigger than herself. *A paradise*, thinks Tamar, *that gave birth to myth because of this immensity. We children of Prometheus and Amirani, who fight everyone and everything.* Tamar feels caught in it, and she wants it to end.

Skunk walks her toward the ancient stone church and helps her across the threshold. Doors fourteen feet high and several feet thick clang shut behind them. He leads her by flashlight through a narrow tunnel. Someone has lit candles, dozens of them, though much of the room remains in shadow. She can make out the stars and the moon through the windows of the cupola above them, a faint fresco faded into stone. Behind some candles, an icon of Mary and Jesus reflects the glow of beeswax. A modest altar, walls of thick stone. Two men in balaclavas, with Kalashnikovs hanging from their shoulders, stand behind a monk slumped in a chair. The monk is dressed in black robes and wears a large gold crucifix around his neck. She strains to see his face. Skunk invites her to sit across from the monk in a wooden chair. He approaches the monk, grabs hold of his face, and spits. Then he punches him, several times.

She cannot see him clearly in the candlelit room. But she can make out the familiar scar running from his mouth to his ear, a shadow folded into skin.

"They say every killer returns to the scene of his crime eventually. I just hadn't expected you to be living at it," says Skunk. "Tamar, say hello to your father."

Zaza grimaces as blood trickles down his face. Tamar has the urge to wipe it clean. She wants to say, "Look at the mess you've got us into, foolish Amirani."

# 6

*Kazbegi, Republic of Georgia*
*November 17, 2003*

"I understand that you're upset with me," says Gary.

"Upset?"

"I wanted to tell you sooner. But one thing led to another. We got carried away, didn't we?"

Joseph is stone-faced. "Do you lack the ability to do anything honestly?"

"Quite likely. I'm sorry I disappeared. And about all the lies."

"You're sorry?"

"Guilt," says Gary, "is the most selfish thing. But I'm sorry I wasn't there for you."

Joseph groans.

"I met Aslan at the university. We were friends, and he trusted me. I promised to get his manuscript published. I never made good on it, like so many other promises I made. It was my fault. But I didn't understand."

"What happened in the church with Aslan? What did you find?"

Gary swallows. "A rat in a cage and a pair of blue-and-gold cufflinks."

Joseph pulls them out of his pocket and puts them on the table. Gary opens his mouth to speak but says nothing.

"Why did you stay in Georgia all these years?"

"I wanted to make things right."

Gary clasps the cufflinks like a secret.

"I brought you here because I wanted to show you where everything changed. I wanted to make it right. And because Tamar and Zaza are in danger."

THEY DRIVE IN silence, focusing on the disappearing road. The sun starts to set, leaving the mountains in cold shadow. All these years, and now that Joseph finally has the opportunity to talk to Gary, he can't find anything to say.

He thinks of something Rachel once said to him: "We all lie, Joseph. All the time."

Joseph retorted, "I don't."

Rachel said, "You think you don't, but you do. You choose the story you want to tell. You leave out some parts, exaggerate others. You're part of it too, Joseph. We all are. The Big Lie."

At the top of the mountain, they find a white Niva 4x4. Gary hesitates, then parks the black Cadillac SUV down the road, several hundred metres away. Joseph leans into his cane, dragging his maimed foot through snow. When they reach the monastery, he glances over the edge of the mountain, out of breath. The height makes him gasp. A valley plummets hundreds of metres. Glaciers shimmer in the distance. A small wooden crucifix is planted in the snow. Joseph steadies himself. A belt of mist clings to the midriff of Mount Kazbek. He has no words.

It's dark now, and a curtain of stars leads the two men, father and son, along a narrow stone path toward the church. Gary points at a trail of blood. It marks a path from the Niva to the church door. Joseph feels dread and anticipation, but also relief. The vertigo has left him untethered, and the beads of blood put him on guard. Ahead, a complex of three buildings appears empty and still.

# 7

*Kazbegi, Republic of Georgia*
*November 17, 2003*

Skunk walks to the podium behind the altar. She expects a continued display of machismo and violence. But now Skunk moves with the air of the solemn and ceremonious, as though he is also succumbing to the gravity of their surroundings, the holiest of places for so many Georgians.

"Thank you for gathering here today," says Skunk, adjusting the lapels of his military coat. "It's a moment I've been looking forward to for a long time. It really means a lot to me."

Zaza's hands are tied behind a wooden chair, his feet bound to its legs. Tamar studies his face. The contours of his skin, signs of resemblance, anything that speaks to her. But it is difficult in these shadows.

"Welcome to the trial of Zaza Gogoladze," says Skunk. "You might think an ancient church an odd place for a trial, but isn't a trial a kind of theatre? And isn't a church a place for performance — before each other and before God?

"Now, I'm no Christian. But I do have a love of ritual. It connects us to the memories stored in a place. This is a house of history and hiding. In the past, during times of danger, it hid holy relics from churches under threat. And now, in recent decades, it houses a great and horrible secret. For it is here our lives were changed.

"The accused who sits before you " — Skunk points to Zaza, slumped in his chair — "made this church his home for the past decade under the guise of a monk. A fitting career choice for a former KGB lieutenant."

Zaza's head bobs up and down, his mouth drooling blood.

"But how did we get here? And why do we return to the scenes of our crimes? Zaza was not always a criminal to me. He took care of me once. As a child, I loved him and called him Uncle. Later, he shepherded me through university. But what I thought was love was guilt, and what I thought was truth was a lie."

Skunk's voice sounds oddly beautiful and resonant in the space. The high ceilings and thick walls have turned his speech into song.

"This is the trial of Zaza Gogoladze, known in the files formerly stored in the cellar of the Tenth Department of the Committee for State Security of the former Georgian S.S.R. as 'Junior Lieutenant Z.G.' I was there when the archives were stormed; I've read the files. I know the names of the people he spied on, whose lives he made miserable. But we are not here to recount every one of his sins. We're here for the particular justice of two particular families. How do we erase the sins of our fathers? How do we respond to the past and make them pay for their debts? I'd like to call upon Tamar Tumanishvili, daughter of Zaza, as a character witness. Come to the podium, Tamar."

# 8

Kazbegi, Republic of Georgia
November 17, 2003

When they reach the holy complex at the top of the mountain, Gary and Joseph do not know which door to enter. There's a stone bell tower and a round stone church with a cupola and cross, several storeys high. A stone wall encircles the buildings. Everything seems to emerge from the earth. As they get closer, Joseph can make out a monastery carved into the side of the mountain. It blends into the dark, wet stone. The church, the monastery, the bell tower—it all seems to belong here. As though God ordained this architecture.

They try the monastery first. Gary taps on a small iron door then leans against it. When the door opens, they find themselves in a small kitchen. Three propane lanterns hang from rotten beams, illuminating a stone room cluttered with dirty dishes, cast-iron pans, and recently cooked food. A propane stove sits on a small wooden table with three chairs tucked underneath. Three pairs of black military boots. It's only then Joseph realizes, in the slow reveal of light, that the boots have feet in them. Gary shines the flashlight onto the men's faces. Three monks, heads slumped over, as though at rest. Blood spills from their necks onto the floor.

"What the fuck?"

"Quiet," says Gary. He motions them out of the kitchen and into a dark tunnel. The floors are earth, the walls made of stone. When they hear a noise up ahead, Gary turns off the flashlight, and they huddle together, holding their breath. After a few minutes, they continue forward in darkness. At the end of the tunnel are stone steps, slick with moisture. They follow them up, clinging to wet stone walls. The farther Joseph ascends, the more he feels he is falling through layers of consciousness. What is up is down, and what is down is up, and no one is who they say they are. A faint light glows from a room ahead: the flickering of candles. Joseph hears someone speak in Georgian. And while he does not understand the content of her words, her voice slips into his mind with familiarity. Tamar.

# 9

*Kazbegi, Republic of Georgia*
*November 17, 2003*

As she approaches the podium, Tamar remembers small details about the man seated in front of her. Two years after he disappeared from her life, Zaza reappeared in a park without warning or explanation. She was eight years old.

"Did you miss me?" he asked.

Tamar twisted awkwardly on her feet.

"Remember when we took the train together from Moscow to Tbilisi? You missed your mother, so I told you the story of Amirani. Telling stories is easy, Tamar. It's as easy as walking. Once you learn how to do it, you never forget."

Tamar stands behind the lectern. She can't decide if the memory is real or a fabrication, if she made it up to fill the vacuum of her fatherless childhood. She counts Zaza's disappearances on her hand. When she was six, when she was eight, and then, eight years later, when demonstrators stormed the KGB archives in Tbilisi. She believed he was dead.

She told herself he might have perished in pursuit of truth, like so many others that day. Now, in this old church at the edge of the world, she knows otherwise. He'd been trying to bury his past.

Zaza was, as Rachel might say, on the wrong side of history. He tore Tamar away from her mother and ruined the lives of so many people. She is angry, not only because of the bad things he did, but because of a life that could've been. Anna, Zaza, and Tamar living in a peaceful cul-de-sac in Montreal or Toronto.

"Tamar," says Skunk. "You've travelled a long way to be here. What do you have to say to your father?"

Tied to his chair, Zaza looks pathetic. She almost feels sorry for him.

"Why did you kidnap me?" she says. "And why did you leave?"

Zaza tries to stand. But the chair buckles his knees, making him fall to the stone floor. Tamar stands still in her place, waiting for him to talk. One of Skunk's balaclava-clad men unties the ropes around Zaza's ankles. Slowly he gets to his feet. Tamar returns to her chair as Zaza is helped to the lectern. His face is bloody, his legs bent out of place. Zaza starts to speak.

"I just wanted to talk. Two old friends and a few bottles of chacha. Nothing complicated. I drove us here to the church, lit some candles, took off my jacket." He glances at his feet, then continues.

"'Let's talk,' I say.

"Aslan smokes and paces the room. I can tell he's nervous. Aslan explains, 'Look, she came to me. How could I not help? Anna's like a sister to me.'

"'But you didn't tell me,' I say.

"'I'm telling you now,' says Aslan.

"'Well, she told me last night. She says you'll help her get out.'

"'This is no place for a Jew. She's been harassed her whole life. As a little girl in Vilnius, and now at the university,' says Aslan.

"'Since when do you care about Jews?' I ask.

"Aslan says, 'If one of us can leave, why not help her?'

"I say, 'It goes against my principles.'

"Aslan says, 'What does that mean? Why don't we both help? You can go with her, too.'

"'Did you know she's pregnant with my child?'

"Aslan says, 'No . . . That's wonderful! So, then you have to go with her. It's perfect.'

"During Soviet times, this building wasn't used as a church. It was a spot for tourists to come. People would meet here and hang out. Like we were. All I wanted was to drink and talk. But Aslan had become so full of himself. With his fancy American jeans, his influential American friends, his infatuation with jazz. And he was down on me, judgemental. He'd say things like I was too conservative, too backward, too traditional. I didn't like that.

"I say, 'I just want to know, what are you telling my future wife?'

"Aslan says, 'What I just said. She came to me. We talked.'

"'How many times?'

"'I don't know. Three? Four?'

"This does not match what she told me. I understand that what is said is not necessarily what has happened. What if he already knew she was pregnant? What if it's not my child?

"'Did you touch her?' I ask.

"'Of course not,' says Aslan.

"'But you love her,' I say.

"'She's like a sister to me.'

"'So you want her to leave our Great Motherland and go to an American school? Is it not good enough for her here?'

"'What?'

"'Why do you want her to leave me?'

"'It was her idea,' he says.

"I ask, 'Were you going to meet her there?'

"Aslan says: 'Don't be crazy. You should go. I was just trying to help you both be happy.'

"'I am happy. Why do you think I'm not?'

"'Well, it's just what Anna said.'

"'What did Anna say?'

"He says nothing. But of course he's in love with her. Everybody is—even Gary, the stupid American.

"'Don't be so Georgian,' he says.

"This makes me mad. He doesn't know what I sacrificed for my future, my family, my life. I tell him, 'Anna is going to meet my family. We'll get married and we're going to have that child.'

"Aslan says, 'Great, I'm happy for you.'

"And I say, 'How could I possibly let Anna go?'

"And he says, 'Don't then. What do I care?'

"I say, 'But you do. You put ideas in her head.'

"Aslan says, 'She came to *me*.'

"I ask, 'Why you and not me?'

"'Why don't you ask your future wife?'

"'Do you work for them? Does Gary? What's your plan? What do you know about me?'

"Aslan says, 'There is no plan. I don't work for anyone.'

"At this point, we're both quite drunk. I don't remember everything but I tell Aslan to have a seat. We're sitting in those exact same chairs, right across from each other. I open my cufflinks and roll up my sleeves. The flickering candles. The wind."

Zaza pauses, and for a moment, Tamar is there, living in her father's past.

"The conversation shifts, becomes friendly. We talk about hockey, school, books. We eat a little. Calm down. But I have it in the corner. I don't know why I put it there, but I brought it. It isn't the first time. Maybe we know what we're going to do before we do it. Maybe we know everything, always. Maybe it's written in our bodies, like Aslan says. He proposes a drink to friendship. We raise our glasses.

"'I love you,' says Aslan, and that's when I hit him in the face. He falls back, and I hit him again, this time in the stomach. He falls forward. I hit him in the back, the kidneys. Again and again. He falls to the floor in pain. I go to the corner and return with the rat in the cage. Aslan sees it. He's afraid and I like it.

"'Junior Lieutenant Zaza Gogoladze,' I say. 'Committee for State Security. I have aspirations. I know you understand.' The rat runs back and forth in his cage. The cage is hot as fire. The rat is dying to get out.

"'Tell me everything,' I say.

"Aslan watches the rat. Just the threat of it is enough. He starts to confess things I don't really care about. He apologizes for a book he wrote, says it was just meant for his son, that he didn't mean to offend anyone, and he was sorry he gave it to Gary.

"I say, 'I don't know what you're talking about.' He apologizes for the black-market clothes, the records, the jazz, the hash.

"Then I say, 'What happened with you and Anna?'

"He hesitates. So I drop the hot cage on his chest. The rat wants out. It starts to dig. Aslan screams, and I like that. The rat keeps digging. Through layers of skin and flesh, into the past...

"'What happened with Anna?' I ask.

"He tries to speak but there is no answer. There is nothing left. Just the goddamned wind on this goddamned mountain. And me and a rat."

Tamar feels sick to her stomach. "Why did you take me away from my mother?"

"You have to stand up for what you believe in, Tamar. You understand. You're the same. It went against my principles. I wanted to keep you here, at home, in Georgia." He smiles sheepishly.

"Then why did you leave?"

Zaza shrugs. "When I became a monk, I thought penance and repentance was all I had left. And then Irakli showed up and took photos of me. But I was tired of running. I ambushed him and told him to send the photos to Skunk. I needed to see you again. To explain."

"Explain what?"

Zaza looks down at his hands. "I wanted a future for you. I was good."

Tamar is stunned into silence. Skunk pulls out an old revolver, opens the loading gate, and pops a bullet out of the chamber. Then he pops it back in, spins the chamber, and shuts it. He does this several times.

Skunk says, "Your father did horrible things, but what's worst of all is he had good intentions. He didn't mean to kill Aslan. He didn't mean to steal you from your mother. Yet he ruined our lives. It's the thoughtlessness that makes him awful. How do we erase the sins of your father? How do we make him pay his debts? How do we deal with the past?"

Skunk passes the revolver to Tamar.

"You want me to shoot him?"

"I want you to show him what you felt."

Tamar looks at the revolver and then at Skunk. She understands that this is a game. She just doesn't understand the rules.

Skunk says, "In Lermontov's novel, he describes a game played by the colonizing soldiers. They call it 'Russian roulette.' There's something honest about it."

"You want me to shoot myself?" asks Tamar.

"I want your father to suffer."

Zaza says, "Akhmad, this is my fault. Keep her out of this."

"Tamar will not suffer. You will. You will feel the horror and fear I felt when the Russian soldiers raped and killed my mother, and neither my father nor you were there to protect us. The horror and fear you gave to me, I'm giving back. Tamar wants it too. She promised."

The revolver has a small horse engraved on the handle. The metal feels heavy in her hand. She understands she is caught in Skunk's madness, and Zaza's.

"I promised you the truth, and I gave it to you. Now play the game, Tamar. Together, we'll make justice happen."

Tamar eyes the armed men by the altar. They point their guns at her. She has no choice.

"Death is a motherfucking injustice," Rachel used to say. *But it's also a relief*, Tamar thinks. And she can see it, a possible end. She presses the barrel against her temple. *Maybe the point isn't justice. Maybe it's nothing at all.*

"Do you have any final words for your father?" Skunk asks.

"No."

Tamar cocks the hammer and pulls the trigger. The force of the barrel pushes against her then recoils from her hand. She breathes heavily. Zaza stares at Tamar. His hands shake.

"Again," says Skunk.

Tamar slowly raises the revolver and presses it against her temple. She closes her eyes. Suddenly a flurry of shots rings out from the darkness. The two balaclava men fall. An enormous man has broken through the main doors and shouts at her to get down as Skunk turns and fires. Levan. Then a man Tamar has never seen before leaps through the air, jumping off a balcony and shooting. When she looks back at Zaza, he's bleeding from the mouth. He falls forward. Skunk cries out and falls too. Levan shoots him, again and again and again.

# 10

"I'm going," Gary whispers.

"Don't," says Joseph.

"I need to do something." Gary nods and disappears into the darkness.

Joseph waits in the stairwell. He doesn't like that Gary has gone ahead without him. When he hears Skunk's booming voice and the sound of gunfire, Joseph runs toward it. Time slows down. He sees Gary travel through air. A spinning bullet travels toward him. Joseph watches as the bullet spirals through epidermis, squamous, stratum. Gary falls to the ground. Tamar sits shaking in a chair, clenching a revolver.

"It's going to be okay, Tamar," Joseph says, though he doesn't know what he's saying. Her shaking gets worse. Levan kneels by her side, his hand on her knee.

"I'm sorry, Tamar," Levan says. "When I found out Skunk kidnapped you—"

Tamar stops him. Joseph hobbles over to Gary, lying on his back. He kneels and puts his hand on Gary's throat. His fingers come away stained with red. Joseph waits for him to say something, but his chest has stopped moving.

Joseph gets up from the floor and approaches Tamar, timidly. "Let's get out of here."

"No," she says, finally looking at him. "We need to bury them first."

IN THE REMOTE villages of Svaneti and Tusheti, far into the Caucasus Mountains, they build houses for the dead. Joseph has seen their pictures, haunted stone structures, shadows and spirits that scare him. But there are no houses for the dead here, no cemeteries at the edge of the world, and so Tamar, Joseph, and Levan drag the bodies outside. It is not easy; the men are heavy and bloated. It takes nearly an hour before they have arranged the bodies in a pyre: Zaza, Gary, Skunk, the two balaclava men, and the three monks. Joseph and Levan search the compound and discover a barrel of diesel used to power a generator. In Zaza's robe Tamar finds a sealed envelope. She slides it inside her coat. Then she pours fuel over the bodies. Levan lights a match. They watch the men disappear into flame.

Levan leaves to clean the church and monastery of all the blood and put things back in order. Tamar and Joseph stand together. The bodies burn all night, the flames rising higher. The stench of human flesh consumed by flame is nauseating. So much has happened, yet Joseph doesn't know how to put it into words.

So he says, "I love you, Tamar."

Tamar reaches for his hand. She holds it so hard he fears she's going to break him.

Joseph did not want Gary to die. He wanted to say more, to ask more questions. If they could get past the grief, then maybe they'd find a kind of living.

"What do you think came first?" Tamar asks. "When our ancestors lived in caves, was it the hate or the fear?"

"The fear, I think," Joseph says. "I think we're so damned afraid we don't know how to live."

"I'm not so sure," says Tamar. "What if it's hate?"

He pries his hand away from hers. Then he stands behind her. Tamar leans into him. Joseph cups his hands over her ears to protect her from the meanness of the world. Because she needs it. They both do.

When the bodies have burned, the ashes scatter in the cold wind blowing in from Siberia. Levan brings a shovel, and they push what remains into the valley below, between the church and Mount Kazbek, where Prometheus spent eternity before Hercules freed him from his torment.

# 11

*Tbilisi, Republic of Georgia*
*November 22, 2003*

The old yellow-and-orange Soviet bus looks like a tired ghost.
Tamar wants to hug it, to hold on to it, as if machinery longed
for affection (its sad headlights are like drooping eyes beneath
the faces of cracked glass). She's swept up in the wave of the
excitement; there are throngs of people on the roundabout by
Rustaveli Avenue. Her group makes its way across the traffic
circle toward the parliament buildings.

The day is cold and the wind presses against her. She draws
Rachel's grey shawl around her shoulders. An old babushka in
a bright-red coat shouts, "Down with Shevardnadze!" again
and again. The electricity of dissent guilds the air. Tamar
savours the feeling. She clenches Joseph's hand as they let
themselves be carried away by the crowd. They pass the architecture of her youth, the school, the library, the theatre where
she watched Sturua's productions of Shakespeare and Brecht,
enormous white columns propping up edifices of marble. The

buildings are heavy and dark, ridden with bullet holes from a civil war that ended only a decade ago.

Lali offers Tamar a bottle of water. Keti gives Joseph a hand; his foot has not healed. Goran, Nana, Levan, and Sasha straggle behind. Fresh graffiti can be seen on the walls. "Kmara," it says over and over. A cry for justice and change has spread across the former Soviet world. With the help of people like Rachel Grabinsky, the Serbians deposed Slobodan Milošević. Now Georgians hope to rid themselves of Eduard Shevardnadze — the old guard clinging to old power.

THEY WANT TO be rid of the mistakes of the past. Of government violence and lies; of gang warfare and senseless murder; of bribery and corruption, the legacy of surveillance. A prayer: *May your neighbours no longer watch over your thoughts.* They want to be rid of Stalin's ghost, Beria's sadism, Brezhnev's iron fist. For they are the children who silently watched as their parents were taken in the night. *Not justice,* thinks Tamar. *But healing.*

WHEN THEY GOT back to Nana's house in Tbilisi, Nana held Tamar in the doorway. Then Nana hugged and kissed Joseph. She was the only person alive who understood their bond and knew their full story. Now that Rachel was gone, Nana would be Joseph's mother too, she declared in Georgian. Tamar translated.

Nana prepared a meal fit for twenty. She watched as Joseph and Tamar devoured her food. They ate, drank, and talked all night. Tamar asked the questions she'd always wanted to ask. Nana explained that Zaza had never told her the story of

Anna Litvak; her name had only been mentioned once. Nana said she was devastated when Zaza left, but she accepted it because he left the best piece of himself behind: Tamar. Nana had vowed to raise her as her own. And while Zaza had never contacted Nana over the years, she felt sorry for him. He'd missed out on love; there is nothing sadder than someone sealed off from its architecture and openness.

Nana also told them about the night there was a knock on her door. It was Rachel, she had just arrived in Tbilisi for the first time, and she was drunk. She confessed everything to Nana, assuring her that she wasn't here to take Tamar away, that she was eternally grateful for what Nana had done, and that Zaza was an asshole she could never forgive. Then Rachel handed her a box. Inside were blue-and-gold cufflinks, a Rakita watch, and a brief note that Rachel had written. Rachel explained that she didn't have the courage to tell Tamar. She begged Nana to do it for her.

"But you never told me," said Tamar. "You never gave me her story."

"How could I? It wasn't mine to tell," replied Nana.

When Tamar translated all this for Joseph, he reached inside his pocket and pulled out Zaza's cufflinks. He handed them to Tamar.

ON THE STREETS of Tbilisi, amidst the crowds of demonstrators, Tamar leans into Joseph and says, "I love you." She says it without thinking. She loves him in a way she doesn't understand. But she feels it pulse through everything.

"I love you too, Tamar. We're truth tellers."

DURING THAT FIRST night back at Nana's house, Levan also dropped by. They hadn't really talked at the church or on the car ride home. When Tamar explained everything she'd been through, and about Zaza and Skunk in the church, Levan was rendered speechless. Then Joseph told the story of Anna-Rachel and Gary-Daniel Daniel. Levan began to cry, and he apologized for the bullet he'd put through Joseph's foot. By the end, Joseph was consoling Levan, while Tamar fed him and Nana wept joyously.

Then Joseph, who was more than a little drunk, stood on his chair and declared that he would quit his job in Toronto, move to Tbilisi, and take over the Record Emporium. Levan promised to help. He broke into song, trying his best to teach Joseph the intricacies of polyphonic singing. Joseph was terrible. Tamar laughed in a way she hadn't in years. And though she didn't know what was in store for any of them, it didn't matter.

"COME ON," SHE says, grabbing Joseph by the hand. "Let's make history."

A wind of change has blown away a thick layer of lead; lethargy and depression has evaporated. Tamar's city — her country — has transformed. For what is love if not a revolution?

She feels her body swell, her blood thickening. Cars blast their horns. The mood is electric and ebullient as they walk through the crowds. She wishes Davit and Rachel were here. In their own ways, they predicted this moment, when the fatigue and torpor would recede and action tipped the scales. Military personnel and riot police guard the parliamentary steps, reminding Tamar of the lessons of 1989. Yet this time things feel different.

A thickset farmer hands her a wild rose and the thorn pricks her finger. "You are beautiful," he says. "But more importantly, you are free. Even if the soldiers shoot us. Even if they kill us all. We have already won this revolution."

"HOW DO YOU mourn the past?" Tamar once asked Rachel during one of their all-night conversations.

"You don't," replied Rachel.

"There's no room for it?"

"No time. There are too many other things to worry about. We cannot fix our parents' mistakes. But if you must," Rachel said, as she inhaled heavily on her Dunhill cigarette, "then build something. Do something with the tears. For the past is and will always be too much."

Then Rachel touched Tamar's cheek. At least, that's how she remembers it. Tamar wishes she had told her. But in so many ways, she did. *Yes, Rachel, the truth is important. Mourn it, acknowledge it, celebrate it. But don't deny its existence. We cannot escape what we are born with. Our shadows follow us forever in the waning November sun.*

SOME PEOPLE HOLD signs, others hold babies. Bottles of water, loaves of bread, red roses, and white placards. Bold statements and grand gestures performed on the balconies of opera houses and old palaces. They hang Georgian flags, white with red crosses, and chant ancient songs. They laugh, dance, and embrace. They eat and they weep, tears of mourning mixed with tears of hope.

It's afternoon when they arrive at Freedom Square. Earlier that day Shevardnadze warned the media he'd be opening the parliament session, that it was his duty to do so. He said that if the current protests continued there'd be civil war. He begged the media — themselves of the new generation — to stop the protests.

"You could be my grandchildren," Shevardnadze implored. "Please, stop. These protests will tear our society apart."

Now Mikheil Saakashvili stands encircled by a group of reporters at the foot of the parliament steps. Camera lights follow his every move. He speaks into a megaphone.

"Eduard Shevardnadze is not listening to us. He has decided to open parliament without the consent of the people. This is illegal and anti-democratic. We are here to protest against those who rigged the elections. But we will not commit bloodshed. Too many have died. Enough, we say. 'In a land without dogs...' Shevardnadze, the charade is over. The dogs are at your door."

The crowd roars its approval. Davit would too. Tamar wonders if the old proverb goes beyond Georgia. Maybe nobody knows what they're doing. Maybe we're all pretending to bark, yelp, call out, be someone we're not. Maybe all our proclamations are wishful acting.

Saakashvili boldly trudges up the parliament steps. What happens next is well-documented and true. The military and riot police put down their weapons. The tanks stand motionless. The people bang on the parliament doors. Then, miraculously, the doors swing open. Not a single shot is fired. When the twelve-foot doors fall from their hinges, the river pours through unchecked. Tamar and Joseph push their way inside. Protestors bang on parliament pews. Saakashvili yells, "Resign, resign!"

Shevardnadze understands his time is up. With his shady entourage, he leaves through the back exit. Saakashvili approaches the podium and bangs his fist. Holding a single rose, he declares a new order.

*Now things begin. Now we can dream.*

And what kind of future is Tamar dreaming? Where and how will she and Joseph live, these children of Anna? What is friendship, kinship, and what are the limits of love?

Joseph takes her by the hand and says, "Come on." He leads her back into Freedom Square. A circle of people dance. The reverie and celebration could go on for days, weeks, months.

"We did it," Joseph declares. "We won."

Tamar isn't so sure. But she laughs when an old woman grabs Joseph's hand and insists he dance with her. He hobbles and manages to oblige. Levan joins them too. Tamar watches with a mixture of apprehension and remorse. From her inside coat pocket, she removes the envelope she found in Zaza's robe. Inside, she finds a carbon copy of a letter.

```
21 May 1978


Anna,


The day you left Moscow, I wept. I cried
for the sadness that is love. My tears filled
the Moskva River. They flowed east across the
```

Baltic Shield, the Altai and Ural Mountains, the Western Siberian Plain. Eleven time zones my longing travelled until it reached the Bering Sea and crossed over to you, five time zones more. I wanted to be with you. But I wanted our daughter to know where she came from.

Dear Anna, you are living in another country. You have changed your name. But none of this matters. You are still my little Anoushka. I am close, I am right here, I am beside you. How else can I say it? Come home. We are waiting for you.

Z.

# Acknowledgements

In March 2003, Christopher Morris and I entered a corner store in Kazbegi to buy a bottle of mineral water. We were greeted by a giant bear of a man named Zaza, who wore a beige wool trench coat, and had a gold tooth and a scar that extended across his face. Zaza, upon realizing we were foreigners, locked the door and plied us with vodka while citing eternal damnation to all of Canada for their defeat of Vladislav Tretiak and the Soviet team at the 1972 hockey Summit Series. Later, a Chechen named Aslan joined us. By the third bottle of vodka, we trudged through the snow to some hidden bar where we danced, drank, and were drawn into a brawl from which Chris and I narrowly escaped.

The next day I woke up, and due to a record snowfall coupled with intense corruption by the local police, was stuck in Kazbegi for eight days. It was a fascinating convergence of geographies and the unexpected. Fifty Armenians driving fifty white Ladas were stuck in the main square; journeymen from Moscow awaited their concubines; nervous Iranian carpet-sellers fretted about their shipments; Chechen, Russian, and

Georgian drinkers finished the town's supply of booze. Then there was a bread shortage, which almost caused a riot. Chris and I played a thousand games of backgammon and drank chacha to measure the time.

So began the seeds for this novel; I had entered, I believed, a land rife with mythology, beauty, and horror. And while I never saw Aslan or Zaza again, the memories of these characters loomed large in my imagination.

I am indebted to the people I met and places I saw in Georgia. First, to Paul Thompson, the legendary Canadian theatre director who brought me there in the first place — and insisted on the maddening bus ride from Istanbul in 2002. Thanks to Paul, I learned the art of the bribe, and fell in love with a country and a theatre whose spirit still infects me. A strange series of coincidences guided us into the arms of the Basement Theatre artistic director Levan Tsuladze and manager Ekaterina Mazmishvili, and many others, allowing Paul and I to return in 2003 with a company of Canadian actors including Christopher Morris, Wes Berger, John Jarvis, Bruce Beaton, and German documentary filmmaker Sven Holly Nullmeyer. The week of performances in front of a Georgian audience was an unforgettable experience. The Basement Theatre — as one of the first non-state-run theatres in Georgia — provided the inspiration for the Underground.

Over the years since, each time I returned to Georgia, I discovered many changes, and with that, new ways to love and connect with this most unusual place. In 2008, prior to the Russian invasion of South Ossetia, I connected with Human Rights Watch, including Soso Papuashvili, who was an incredible resource on the internal refugee crisis in Georgia by way of Abkhazia, and who also helped orchestrate my trip to Pankisi Gorge. In Pankisi, Ruslan was my guide and escort for the many interviews I did with Kist and Chechen refugees. As my host, he graciously let me stay with him and his family in their farmhouse in Duisi.

Caryne Chapman Clark, fellow Canadian and a resident of Georgia, and Nino Akhvlediani helped me gain insights into the Georgian arts and cultural scene. Rezo Gabriadze, the internationally renowned Georgian puppeteer, was an inspiration and a teacher even in his silence. Natasha and Ramaz Chkhikvadze, the mythical Georgian actor who played Azdak in *The Caucasian Chalk Circle*, graciously hosted Paul and me for an afternoon at their hotel. Thanks to the prodding of Natasha, we were plied with champagne and given VHS copies of their play in order to bring Robert Sturua's forty-four-person production to Broadway. Alas, nobody was interested.

I also had the good fortune to connect with members of the Kmara movement and several NGOs that helped lead to the Rose Revolution. These include Levan Ramishvili, formerly head of the Liberty Institute, and Nino Gvenetadze, head of the Georgian Young Lawyers' Association.

The Georgian artist Nino Sekhniashvili was a source of inspiration for Tamar. In the 1990s, Nino is rumoured to have robbed a bank, and the security video became a performance art piece. It was created (rumour has it) so she would not be married off. (She wanted to show she wasn't good marriage material.) While I never saw the piece, and she would neither confirm nor deny such a performance (Nino is a lover of mystery and enigma, I believe), the myth loomed large and the very idea of someone doing such an action compelled me.

Giorgi Sanaia, a journalist for Rustavi 2 who was the popular anchorman for the TV show *Night Courier*, was famous for exposing corruption in Georgian politics. Giorgi provided inspiration for the character of Davit. Giorgi was tragically murdered in his Tbilisi apartment in 2001 under mysterious circumstances, though it is suspected it was politically motivated. His murder provoked mass protests in Georgia.

The artist, anthropologist, and curator Data Chigolashvili was the inspiration for "Bring me your Tbilisi." Until 2019, Data ran Urbanare, an apartment/art space/living archive dedicated to presenting an alternative, intimate Tbilisi. Here I spent many an afternoon with moving artefacts Data had collected over the decades, including personal texts, photographs, and objects.

The other performance pieces in the book are products of my imagination, inspired by a number of other artists' works. I had the honour of spending an afternoon combing through photographs of 1990s Georgia with renowned Georgian photographer Guram Tsibakhashvili. His images capture the turbulence and despair of that time. Nini Palavandishvili introduced me to him and dragged me along to several art openings. Nino Kupatadze also engaged with me in various discussions and helped me understand the alternative music scene and where to go dancing.

The Ukrainian performance artist Oleg Kulik inspired "Man barks like dog." Originally performed in St. Petersburg in 1994, *The Mad Dog, or Last Taboo Guarded by Alone Cerebrus* featured Kulik, naked, with a dog collar around his neck and held by a chain. In the M. Guelman Gallery, Kulik barked at and bit spectators while lunging on his chain, before rushing out of the gallery into traffic. For Kulik, it was a commentary on Russian society and the art world in general.

Other art actions include Pussy Riot's *A Punk Prayer* and the work of Voina, who ingeniously graffitied a penis onto a drawbridge across from the former KGB headquarters in St. Petersburg (the bridge-penis would rise accordingly, in full view of the secret police). Warsaw-based queer artist Karol Radziszewski's bold photography projects are also an inspiration in terms of a socially engaged work and aesthetic speaking to and against an anti-queer and homophobic Polish government.

Vladimir Tarasov, Vilnius-based virtuosic jazz drummer, provided insights into the Soviet jazz scene.

Eugene Slonimerov helped me find the apartment on lonely Ritsa Street, with the best view in the city (attacks from street dogs notwithstanding). He also provided invaluable insights into Georgian politics and the Georgia-Abkhaz war. Lena Sakure journeyed with me to Tusheti and provided insights into language and tradition. Dachi Galibdze guided me through the social and economic realities of the '90s through numerous conversations.

Carl Linich, an American who fell in love with the Caucasus and stayed there to learn and perform the traditional music, as well as to collect archival recordings for the Smithsonian Institute, introduced me to Nana Gerliani, with whom I stayed for many months, eating her homemade soup, pkhali, and various homemade breads. Nana's cooking and homemade wine was an act of love.

Christopher Morris took me to Kazbegi; saved me from being killed numerous times; shared a bed, chacha, khajapouri, and eight magical days while we waited to be dug out of the Jvari Pass.

Many books were read during the research of this book. Some of the best include: *In the Mountains of Poetry* by Peter Nasmyth (in particular about the myth of Amirani and Qamari); Thomas Goltz's *Azerbaijan Diary*, *Chechen Diary*, and *Georgian Diary*; Anna Politkovskaya's books, and tragic legacy, including *A Russian Diary* and *A Small Corner from Hell: Dispatches from Chechnya* (one wonders what horrors she would uncover in Ukraine today). Mark McKinnon's *The New Cold War* provided insight into the mechanisms behind the pro-democratic revolutions in the former Soviet Union, including the Orange, Rose, and Otpor revolutions. Neil Ascherson's *Black Sea* is a marvel; Yoav Karny's *Highlanders: A Journey to the Caucasus in Quest of Memory* is a beautiful, meandering meditation on language, nationhood, and history. Gene Sharp's ubiquitous handbook, *From Dictatorship to Democracy*, is an essential guide for non-violent resistance that was used throughout the post-Soviet coloured revolutions and Arab Spring. Sharp's book was the inspiration for many of Rachel's ideas, including the notion of a dictatorship depending on its citizens for its existence. *Russian Journal* by Andrea Lee provided key insights into an American's life at MSU in the 1970s. The mythical All-You-Can-Eat-Buffet is inspired by her book.

*New Yorker* writer Wendell Steavenson, author of *Stories I Stole* — one of the best outsider takes on Georgia — provided, through several conversations, invaluable early research tips and insights into Georgia. Her *New Yorker* interviews with Saakashvili were also an inspiration.

Over the years many people read various incarnations of this book. I can't thank them enough for their time and generosity. They include: David Young, Rosemary Sullivan, John Murrell, Helen Oyeyemi, Craig Lucas, Debbie Willis, Neil Smith, Zoe Whittall, Kirby, Yaël Farber, Jules Lewis, Vern Thiessen, Frank Heibert, Bobby Theodore, Shaughnessy Bishop-Stall, Sandra Huber, Sven Holly Nullmeyer, and Paul Thompson. Andreas Stuhlmann helped me in the final stages, providing character insight, mythological imagination, and a wonderful set of eyes. He is a gift.

Shout out to Lauren Kirshner for enduring friendship and for publishing "Rachel's Funeral" in the *White Wall Review*.

There were various residencies and individuals who donated their spaces in which which I could write: Akademie Schloss Solitude; JAK residency in Budapest; the Hermitage (Sarasota, Florida); the Banff Centre for the Arts; Boris Pasternak's old room at the former Georgian Writers' Union (special thanks to Nina Lamouri and Tamta Labidze); Lisa Robertson, Rosa, James Teschner, and the muses of La Malgache; Bruce Kidd and Phyllis Berck and the former Kendal Home for the Arts; Paul Garfinkel, Barb Dorion, and the apartment in Anghiari; Julio, Letizia, and Kiki from Caffè dello Sport for the best espresso in Italy and their incomparable Negroni Spagliato. Thank you to the Toronto Arts Council, Ontario Arts Council, and Canada Council for the Arts for providing financial support. Thanks to Mikhail Iossel and Summer Literary Seminars, the Tbilisi edition, for bringing me back to Georgia in 2018.

Thanks to Sarah MacLachlan and House of Anansi Press for taking this on, and in particular to my editors Maria Golikova and Douglas Richmond, who journeyed me through the rewrites and revisions. Thank you both for pushing me and for believing in this novel; and Doug, for taking me to the finish line. John Pearce, my agent, was alongside me all the way.

While finishing the final edits for this novel, Russia invaded Ukraine under the absurd guise of "de-Nazification." Former KGB agent Vladimir Putin's unjust war has caused the largest European refugee crisis since World War II. Amongst the millions of refugees fleeing Ukraine were Georgians who had previously fled to Ukraine when Russia invaded South Ossetia in 2008. Suddenly, the world of this book felt more urgent, and the Soviet past much closer. While Putin pummels Mariupol, Kyiv, and Odesa, and Russian soldiers commit horrific war crimes against the Ukrainian people, the status of other former Soviet countries like Georgia appears more vulnerable than ever. Many Georgians fear that they could be next. Yet for Georgians and Ukrainians, the fear of Russia — of the old and brutal empire — is not new. For them, it has always been a question of when, not if, Russia would return.

Finally, I'd like to acknowledge Anastasia Aphkhazava, whom I met on a dance floor at the Basement Theatre in Tbilisi, as the other half of the inspiration for Tamar. Ana was a gifted puppeteer, actress, and beautiful wandering spirit, who died tragically at the age of thirty-three outside of Batumi. Hers was a heart and spirit that infected us all; her death is a tragedy.

I dedicate this novel to her, and to all the people of Georgia who generously shared their stories along the way, those who lived and those who died, who endured tragedy and beauty in the face of history, always with some wine and a smile.

Ana Aphkhazava 25.02.1974–2007

Courtesy of the author.

JONATHAN GARFINKEL is an award-winning author. His plays include *Cockroach* (adapted from the novel by Rawi Hage) and *House of Many Tongues*, nominated for the Governor General's Literary Award for Drama. The controversial *The Trials of John Demjanjuk: A Holocaust Cabaret* has been performed across Canada, Russia, Ukraine, and Germany. He is the author of the poetry collection *Glass Psalms* and the chapbook *Bociany*. His memoir, *Ambivalence: Crossing the Israel/Palestine Divide*, has been published in numerous countries to wide critical acclaim, and his long-form nonfiction has appeared in the *Walrus*, *Tablet*, the *Globe and Mail*, and *PEN International*, as well as *Cabin Fever: An Anthology of the Best New Canadian Non-Fiction*. Named by the *Toronto Star* as "one to watch," Garfinkel is currently pursuing a Ph.D. in the field of Medical and Health Humanities at the University of Alberta, where he is writing a memoir about living with type 1 diabetes, and the revolutionary open-source Loop artificial pancreas system. He lives in Berlin and Toronto.